The Butcher, The Baker, The Candlestick Maker

~ Returning the Favor ~

A Novel by

Bob Perez

This book is fiction the intent of which is meant for solely for the entertainment and enjoyment of the reader. Names, characters, places and episodes were created through the imagination of the author and used within the context of this story. Any resemblance to actual events, locales, organizations, persons, living or dead, is entirely coincidental.

ISBN: 978-0-615-61652-0

All correspondence can be directed to rmppbm@gmail.com

While in the process of courting literary agents for publication, this copy is self-published by the author. Any queries, comments or critiques are welcomed. As this is not officially in print by a publisher, insights from you for a better story would be appreciated and can still be incorporated. And referrals to agents and/or publicists would be very much appreciated.

Additional copies of the book are available for anyone you may feel would enjoy the read.

In Loving Memory of
Bob & Grace Perez

Preface

I got the idea for this story driving home on Powerline Rd., Deerfield Beach, FL after the requisite Saturday morning food shopping at Publix. Why this popped up in my mind at this particular time, I have no clue. I thought I'd have some fun and write a short story that I would archive in a folder on my PC with some of my other "works."

I, like most of you spending most of my time working at a job that doesn't offer much creativity other than a paycheck, have a yearning for creative outlets. We all may have a journal, some poetry or prose we jot down when inspiration strikes, or maybe we paint; some may have the chutzpah to try their hand at acting. In any case, mild in nature or extensive in detail, we'll entertain fantasies from time to time. Scrubbing out the normal sexual fantasies (and liar, liar pants on fire if you don't have any of these!), there are times when we often wish we were someone else, had done something else with our lives, or had provided something that benefited all of mankind, etc.

This is a story that started with one character and blossomed into three by the time I got home and started unpacking my bags. As I was putting away my groceries, I thought it would be kind of fun to get speech recognition software and dictate a short story that may end up being around four or five pages long.

I finally got around to it later that weekend and spent most of it just "training" the software to recognize my voice. After that was accomplished and I could now "talk" to my computer, watching the words magically appear on the screen as I spoke. Later on this allowed me to physically act out some of what a character was doing and dictate its sensation directly into script.

Not too soon after I started the beginning, this "short story" started to take on a life of its own and, before I knew it, I came out from behind the microphone and found myself deeply entrenched, realizing later that this was clearly serving cathartic purposes. Over time, the more I "spoke," the more characters seemed to surface, seemingly out of nowhere. I could be doing something innocuous, such as changing a wall switch, and a character would pop into my head, along with a situation he or she was involved in, always keeping within the texture of the original fabric of the story.

At odd times during the day, and sometimes at night with head first to pillow, a brand new aspect of each of these sub stories would occur to me; I ended up writing separate files for each just to keep track. The birth of these characters gave rise to these new avenues of the story at a pace where I began to get a nagging feeling that I'd never be able to complete this.

As each character started to "introduce" themselves, I needed names for them. Being somewhat lazy in this department, I relied on, with some minor alteration, the names of some of my dear family and friends. And a word to the wise, this is fiction; my facts will not always be right, but they will be convenient.

I took great pleasure in including some of you guys in my book. It was like you were joining me in this taking of personal inventory under the guise of "telling a story." Whether this ever makes it to the bookshelves or not is not important; what is important is that in all of our hearts, we have or want to be a hero. And in all of our souls, we have passion, love and life we share with those around us. We have dreams and hopes that continue on throughout our lives, the attainment of which only comes to fruition through our own hard work, focus, perseverance and a pinch of good luck.

CHAPTER 1

In October 1973, Bob Perry had promised his mother that if he didn't win a major championship in the six years after turning pro at twenty, he would quit boxing forever. His father's condition to this career path was that he would still continue with school, finish college and then even go to graduate school to earn his MBA. His father, Louis, was convinced that his son needed to be prepared if he should fail his quest as a boxer and live and work comfortably in the "real" world.

This put a tremendous strain on Bob, as after six or seven hours of hard work of sparring, weight training and doing roadwork, he then had to take a quick shower and go off to school for three hours of classes. After returning home, a quick dinner and then another three hours of reading and studying before he was in bed by 10:30PM. The next morning, he was up at 4AM for more running and then right back to the gym for six or seven hours of grueling, hard work.

Boxing was not a career to Bob; boxing was his passion. Evers since he watched the epic Sonny Liston and (the then) Cassius Clay fight, spellbound, seven years earlier, he knew what he wanted to do in life. He certainly had the same skills, but was severely lacking in braggadocio.

Now, on a steamy August night in 1979, staring down at his freshly taped hands, Bob was going into his pre-fight meditation, as he often did, to focus on who he was going to fight, how he was going to fight them and review over and over again in his head the fight strategy he'd been practicing endlessly the month before. The dank smell of sweat and broken dreams in the locker room no longer registered due to countless hours he'd spent in similar surroundings perfecting his dream. Consistent with his personality, not much to the liking of the promoter who was all for putting on a big show, Bob spent this pre-fight time in quiet solitude. Bob often brought his three-year-old Bassett Hound, Emma, to assume her usual position of being fast asleep most times on a pile of towels as though it was put there especially for her. She was more or less an extension of him. Emma had the same low-key personality typical of her breed. It was because of this trait that Bob subconsciously picked a Bassett Hound.

Johnny Wells, his trainer, five years older, lifelong friend and certified pain in the ass when it came to training, was also silent, entrenched in his own brand of meditation in the dimly lit locker room. Johnny wasn't exactly thrilled about the prospect of this night before the four or five more tune-up fights he felt Bob needed before meeting the light heavyweight champion of the world.

At the age of thirty-four, Gary Patton was a veteran who captured the title four years ago and held it ever since. Johnny was more concerned about the health and well-being of Bob entering the ring with Gary than he was about the remote chance he would even make it past the third round.

The state boxing commissioner entered the locker room to do the final inspection and sign off on the taped hands and the fitting of the gloves, as is customary, and went over the rules and regulations of the fight, as mindlessly routine as reading the Miranda rights.

Johnny slipped the very simple white terry cloth robe, which Bob had always worn since his first professional fight six years ago, over his gloves. He was not one of those marketable fighters who had a flamboyant costume or a theatrical entourage that came out like the second act of a Broadway musical when entering the ring. Bob didn't even have the requisite tattoos all over his body, except for the one on his right bicep, which displayed roses and thorns with a ribbon running through it. Kind of like the traditional tattoo of old, a time when tattoos were isolated statements rather than an integral part of someone's epidermal wardrobe as it is today. This was enough, Bob thought; anything more would have made him look like a bad act from a sideshow.

He took his boxing very seriously. Each fight was a special event that took long hours of training, concentration and focus. This took on special importance and concentration tonight, as Gary Patton was the top light heavyweight fighter of the world. In the sixteen years Gary was a professional fighter, he boasted a record of forty-three wins, no losses and one draw, with thirty-eight of his wins coming by way of some very vicious knockouts.

Corey "Show Me The" Green (yeah, corny, right?), the number one contender, was the fighter Gary was supposed to meet, but a torn retina during a sparring session four weeks prior to the fight put the kibosh on that. The promoters need somebody to fill in rather quickly and the two other top contenders were already booked for their own contests, so it was Bob who was picked. He was allowed only four weeks to prepare.

But this was the fight he was preparing for in his

heart these past five years and nine months. This was the last fight; if he didn't win this championship, he would have to quit boxing, as he promised his mother. And promises were like his smiles; something he was always very sincere about.

But, you know, losing wouldn't be all that bad. He'd finish his MBA and have a great career in business, and he won't have suffered broken bones in his hands, the fractured noses and the continuous swelling above and under his eyes from sparring sessions and fights. But this was not the way he wanted to end it, if he had to end it. He worked very hard and he was close, so close to winning the championship he always dreamed of.

The fight on the under-card prior to the main event ended after four rounds by knockout and it was time for Bob to start readying himself to enter the arena. Johnny was packing the kit bag with all the items that were normally needed during a fight; Vaseline, Q-tips, cold iron and a number of other items that would keep his fighter alive for the twelve rounds the fight might go, although Johnny doubted they would hear the bell bringing in the fourth round.

Most of the fights Gary Patton had fought ended in the third or fourth round. Gary Patton never went beyond five rounds of a fight and many of his knockouts were in the first or second round. This made Johnny feel even more uncomfortable, as he knew this fight would end very quickly. This meant Bob would be out of contention and put back about three notches, where he wouldn't have another chance for this championship belt for at least another five fights. But that would carry him far past the six-year mark he promised his mother, so Bob would fight no more.

Bob readied himself to begin his walk through what seemed an endless hallway into the arena. As was customary, the champion usually entered the ring last, and Gary was not a very flashy fighter himself. He was usually greeted by his proud audience with cheers from people who loved him for years and he always put on a great show for the fans. Hearing this applause, Bob thought this was going to be a hard act to follow. Bob was young, he was strong and, although at the ripe old age of twenty-five, he deserved to win. But there was nothing that replaced the many years in the ring Gary had under his belt, nineteen more times in the ring than Bob, with hard-earned knowledge gathered during those fights. The tools Bob had to counter this were his strength, endurance and an insurmountable desire to win.

It was now Bob's turn to first enter the ring. His knees felt like jelly as he took one step after another and walked into the arena. There was mild, almost polite applause from the crowd in admiration of this new young kid coming up the ranks. Gary Patton then made his way into the ring and circled several times with one arm raised to the thunderous applause of the crowd.

But they paid money, good money, to see Gary and Corey Green brutalize each other. People at ringside who could see Bob a little closer than the rest felt he looked like he might be a good contender and maybe, just maybe, put on a good show.

When Gary slipped through the ropes and caught the first glimpse of his opponent, Gary saw himself at that age as an up-and-coming cruiserweight. He remembered the thrill of reaching for that golden ring. But Gary was tired. At an age considered suitable for AARP membership in the boxing world, Gary fought hard to keep his title and he wanted to break Rocky Marciano's record of forty-nine straight wins and make it an even fifty. That would take seven more fights after he put this kid away.

He also made a promise to himself (with his wife's "condolences") that, at this point in his career, if he lost the next fight, he would hang up the gloves forever; Marciano's record would still stick, so what was the sense? He had a good run. He had a good life with boxing. He certainly made a lot of money and now, it was time to enjoy that money and see more of his kids. Either way, this was going to be a decisive night for both boxers.

Johnny took off Bob's robe. Bob took a couple of steps, bouncing back and forth, getting his legs ready, and threw a few punches in the air, getting his arms loose and ready to fight.

The ref called both fighters to the center of the ring and, with the announcer holding the microphone under his left armpit, went over the rules with both fighters. They did not stare each other down, as was the custom; this was not a grudge match. The only thing in Bob's eyes was pure determination.

He liked Gary Patton, although he met him only a few times. He seemed like a nice guy. Big and strong with a thick neck, broad shoulders and arms that looked like he could lift a truck from the backend with no problem and change a tire at the same time.

After the referee finished, the microphone traveled

up its line and disappeared into the ceiling as both fighters returned to their corners. Bob recited a silent prayer to himself, which kind of surprised him, actually. He wasn't a very religious guy, but, at this very moment, this was his only chance to become a champion and continue boxing, for that matter. Everything and anything would help at this moment, even prayer. Sure, he was almost twenty-six years old with a decent record of 24-1-1. But this was no excuse for him; not tonight, anyway.

Johnny looked at him with concern tempered with momentary second-guessing as he gave his fighter final instructions. He slicked his brow and orbital sockets with enough Vaseline to coat a driveway.

The bell rang and both fighters met each other at center ring. Bob knew that Gary had a vicious left hook. He had seen this time and time again during the long hours of film he had studied for the fight. The central part of Bob's strategy was to continually circle around to Gary's right to avoid that death blow of a left hook.

The first round was uneventful and Gary gave Bob some latitude in exploring the territory in front of him. A few jabs, a couple of combinations and some posturing just to get loosened up. For a millisecond out of nowhere, it crossed Gary's mind to let Bob win, for this to be his last fight because he was so damn tired. The years of punishment his body had taken were taking their toll; hundreds, if not thousands of hits to the head, the body, the arms, all of this adding up like bruises in a bank. He thought Bob was a great kid and deserved the chance to win, but he wasn't going to let down his guard because boxing was his life and this was all he knew. He barely made it out of high school when he began his career.

The tapping on the canvas signaled the ten seconds left in the round. The finally bell rang, sending Bob to his corner. He felt pretty proud that he actually got through the first round with Gary fairly unscathed. Johnny was giving instructions, telling him how to revise and how to recalibrate his approach, but Bob didn't hear a word. He was now over his initial nervousness and had this overwhelming excitement and thrill that he was finally in the ring with a real champion. Like being an Oscar nominee – just being nominated was testimony enough that the nominee had the talent and deserved the award.

Sure, he was fourth choice, but he survived the first round with Gary without a scratch! This was not to be any kind of walk in the park, but the impending pain may well have been worth the price of even being there tonight. But even if he did lose the fight, which he most likely would, he had a newborn feeling about himself that no one could take away. But his twenty-six birthday loomed in the back of his mind and he knew what he loved to do the most and wanted to keep on doing it.

The bell rang as both fighters rose again from their stools to begin round two. This time, Gary started to open up a little bit and started working his jab to keep Bob from circling to his right. Bob countered by circling around Gary's left, trying to fight off the shower of jabs and working the body with punches. Being a student of physiology, studying the body and the points where applied pressure could do the most damage, Bob started working the upper arms and shoulder joints of Gary, along with his lower arms and midsection.

The second round continued much like the first, except with Bob now concentrating more on pummeling Gary's arms and shoulders, slowly wearing him down. The clang of the bell ended the round.

Bob was breathing a little heavier this time from using a lot of energy to wear Gary down to a point where he felt he could start gaining control of the fight. Johnny had warned him not to expend too much gas too quickly or he wouldn't even be around for the third and fourth round or his twenty-sixth birthday if he wasn't more careful.

Round three. This time, Bob used most of his jab, but kept that in reserve and let Gary do most of the work, and most of the work Gary did. But he knew Gary would tire soon and this would be his opportunity. He continued his circling and then, in one instance where he made the fatal mistake of letting his right guard down, Gary delivered his hallmark left hook, smashing down on the right side of Bob's jaw.

His jaw was numb at first because the nerve endings were so traumatized that the pain didn't have time to travel up to his brain until a couple seconds later. The excitement and giddiness he had after the first round seemed to disappear.

My God, he thought, *this is the type of fighter who has power to send you into the next millennium.*

He was on his hands and knees now and wasn't convinced he had the power in his legs to get up and stand. He finally gained his composure and managed to get to his feet when the referee did the mandatory eight-count, looking into Bob's eyes, talking to him and asking generic questions to see if there were any telltale signs that Bob was in serious trouble and should not continue. Bob responded coherently to the questions and still couldn't get over the force and damage of this wrecking ball that just took down the first floor of his brain.

Satisfied, the ref let Bob continue. He continued working Gary's arms and shoulders, and even got in a few head shots. The ten second warning was clapped on the side of the canvas and Bob managed to stay out of anymore serious trouble by the end of the third round. Returning to his corner, Johnny could see the swelling start to form on the side of Bob's jaw and knew that for the next few weeks after this was over, most meals will be through a straw.

"You've got to settle down! Just stop wasting so much energy. This guy' s going to wear you down to a point where you'll be an inviting target and end up on your back with your eyes spinning in the back of your head!" Johnny warned him. He was becoming more than concerned about Bob losing energy and not being able to defend himself, much less winning the fight.

"I'm doing okay," Bob pleaded with Johnny in between gasps for air. "Yeah, I know I have to settle down, but I figure I'm wearing him thin with punches down to the midsection into his shoulders. Johnny, I could feel him starting to slow up. I can continue this for the next couple of rounds. I think I might take this fight."

Yeah, and bears really don't really drop a deuce in the woods, they use Sani-Lavs. "You can't be serious," Johnny warned, almost shouting. "You've lasted the first three rounds because Gary's been kind to you, not even unloading what he has in store for you. It's just a matter of time, Bob. I want to be cautious. If you get in trouble the next time and I see that you can't see straight, I'm throwing in the towel"

"I think, I think I know what I'm doing"

"I certainly hope so. Bob, the best that you can do is to try to score some points and stay out of trouble to make it to the next round."

"Got it, but you know what, Johnny? If they do take me out in a box, make sure it's a nice-looking box. I hate like hell to look cheap."

Johnny was not amused.

The bell rang in round four.

Don't be too cocky, Bob thought. *This is no picnic.*

But, at this point, he had felt the strongest of Gary's power, survived it and felt that he could go a little bit more, but not much more. Gary stood flat-footed at the center of the ring. He started to slow a little bit in his attack and was sweating a lot more than Bob. And, truth be known, Gary was starting to feel tired, realizing that this kid had a lot more than he thought, seeding a growing admiration and new found respect.

Gary started to open up a little bit more because now, his reputation was at the risk of being tarnished by not commanding the fight at this point; he was becoming more concerned that his wife might her get chance at "condolences."

Gary felt a small trickle of blood from the open cut above his left eye and continued jabbing. He knew he had to finish this kid off, and finish him soon. The fury and violence in Gary of old began to surface, reaching its zenith, determined to win and fearful of losing. A fighter had to be careful with this type of vulnerability because it became counter-productive; emotion, if left unbridled, could mean the fighter's demise.

And that was exactly what happened. Gary was starting to take swings, eager to incur immediate damage and end the fight. He became reckless, swinging wildly, leaving the left side of his face exposed.

Bob had the same opportunity right now. Pulling his arm back and gathering up all the remaining strength that he had, he hit hard on Gary's temple, twisting it as if he was twisting a cork back into a wine bottle. If enough pressure was applied, the nerves short-circuit, disabling the electronic stream the brain needed to remain conscious and alert. He heard a hoarse gasp escape from Gary's mouth and watched his body shutter, falling first on to one knee, then the other on the canvas. He was on all fours now, breathing heavily, his legs trembling violently. Bob was ordered back to his corner and did not respond immediately, still astonished at what he just accomplished. The referee warned once again for Bob to return to his corner (remember "The Long Count" from the Tunney-Dempsey rematch?).

Bob returned to his corner, feeling the whole scene was surreal. And then began the ten-count. He just brought what was considered one of the finest lightweight heavy champions of all time down to his knees with a well-placed and probably a once in a lifetime punch.

Johnny was ecstatic, rocking back and forth with his eyes bugging out of his head. "You've got to be kidding. This couldn't have just happened. The game plan worked, the goddamn game plan worked."

The ref continued his count… four, five, six. Each

second echoed in Gary's head like a deep bass church bell tolling the hour. The referee raised his hand and fingers with each count, seven, eight, but Bob thought no way in hell; he was going to get up pretty soon. You don't just knock down a guy like Gary Patton with one punch. This fight was not over yet.

The ref held up five fingers on his left hand and four on his right; Jesus Christ, this guy wasn't getting up. Gary went down from all fours now, sinking down further into the canvas, where he hit and rolled onto his right side, his left foot twitching like someone just stuck him with a live cattle prod.

The man who was considered the greatest lightweight heavy champion of all time was not going to get up!

"Ten! You're out!" cried the referee in equal disbelief.

Bob had won five years and eleven months into his career. He was now *the* lightweight champion of the world! Gary was sitting up now, regaining his wits with the realization of losing his first fight, inflicting a bit of nausea in his weary body. Gary's trainers traveled across the ring to congratulate Bob and Johnny, carrying with them the belt they so proudly brought into the arena that night and would now leave without.

Bob felt the wool on the back side of the belt as the leather waist crown was placed in his disbelieving hands. The wool lining was weathered and worn from the sweat and pain of so many fighters who had worn it over the years. The history embedded in that belt silently whispered the many years of hard work, pain, disappointment, spirit and dreams of many a man who had sacrificed a lot; even to wear it entering the ring, if only for the next fight.

Unfortunately, this, too, would turn out to be the case for Bob. His exhilaration would be soon overshadowed with a devastation that would change his life forever.

CHAPTER 2

Natalia could hardly contain her excitement as she fumbled with the buttons of the brand new dress Papa had just bought her. Today was her eighth birthday and she was a big girl! The sun shone brightly outside that Sunday afternoon, with family members gathering around the big table downstairs in their small kitchen. Natalia's house was modest, with a thatched roof, stone exterior and a small barn with a few animals. They had two chickens, a rooster, two dogs, a horse, four sheep and a cat named Ustin. Ustin was in charge of the lot, no question.

Natalia's father, Kristanf, was a proud and hard-working man employed at a government-run factory in the Lower 43. He, like many of his neighbors and residents of the Upper 14, worked for businesses and companies in the Lower 43 for half the wages paid to local residents. This, for many of the Upper 14, was the only means of a living other than those who provided local produce and meat from within their own surrounding area. Clothes, utilities and other necessities hardware in nature were purchased in the Lower 43 from what meager wages they managed to save.

Kristanf had to wait four years before his application was even looked at. They finally called him to test his skills as a mechanic and he was instantly hired. Kristanf's factory manufactured thousands of the standard twenty gallon water heaters requisite in each house in his province and other plumbing fixtures, they, too, all of the same size. Twelve hours days and weekends were not unusual and very rarely did Natalia see her father more than two or three hours a day. But she tried to make the most of it, as she loved her father very much.

Times were always hard as far back as she could remember. Meals were stretched and having chicken was a special treat. What little she had, she appreciated, provided to her by parents of steadfast love and care.

Natalia's mother, Irinia, had made her a doll out of some old fabric and wool stuffing. Wherever she went, whatever she did, the doll, Tina, was never far away; she brought it to bed with her at night to share her dreams. She was about to begin school again in the fall and was very excited about making new friends. Her brother, Luther, used to come home telling the family about all the things that he did at school, the things he did with his friends and all the different school activities he was involved in. Natalia wanted to be just like him. She was a very bright girl and by all means did very well in school. She was now entering the third grade and looked forward to her first day.

After getting her dress on and doing a final check on the long curls Mama had put in her hair, she placed a ribbon in her hair as a final touch. She ran down the stairs, greeted by her parents, some friends from the neighborhood and all her relatives, anxious to see the birthday girl. She was especially excited about the presents waiting for her, presents that were modest and mostly homemade. Luther was busy outside, cleaning the barn and sweeping the sidewalk, making sure everything was presentable for their guests. Cars started streaming up the driveway, mostly early model Toyotas and Buicks.

The people of Chevka were a proud but poor people. What little they had, they made the most of. And for this they were thankful. They believed life was a celebration and every moment should be spent in happiness and caring for each other. This was very important for people who lived under a government regime that was very class-conscious. The inhabitants of the provinces that Natalia and her family lived in were considered by the government to be of questionable breeding, less intelligent and inadequate examples of the perfect Chevkan citizen. Natalia's heritage dated back thousands of years to the peoples who first settled this region, then known as Antonia. It was subsequently dissected into fourteen provinces and appended to the latter settlement of one of Russia's satellites, Chevka.

Chevka was made up of the fifty-seven provinces, fourteen of which, not at all affectionately referred to as the "Upper 14," laid at the upper northern boundaries of the country bordering Lithuania. Ground was first broken on these fourteen provinces some 3,000 years ago, which paved the way for migration from neighboring lands over the years. The remaining forty-three provinces had been populated by a more aristocratic stock of peoples from European fiefdoms and other surrounding kingdoms. The addition of these upper fourteen provinces was by decree of the Kremlin and certainly not by choice of the reigning authorities of Chevka at that time.

It's amazing to think that prejudice as a "science" endures in every society in one shape or another. In some societies, it manifests itself as merely a rote reaction of disdain, whereas in others, it can breed such paranoia so as to lead to extinction. No one can forget the infamous genocides of Hitler and the atrocities of some of the other Eastern Bloc countries in the twentieth century.

In Chevka, this severe prejudice was still very much alive and very much in the forefront of the mind of the maniac running the country. It didn't matter that these were hard working people who raised families for generations and, in their own small private way, made a contribution to their country. It didn't matter that these people were kind and loving, born and bred into wonderful families. Because of this prejudice, they were renounced from the rest of society.

This bothered Kristanf in many ways, especially when it came to the world in which his children would need to develop coping mechanisms to live. He hoped that this might soon become a thing of the past and they, too, would be welcomed into society.

When they did venture into the city, they were clearly not welcomed. They not only were noticeable by their sparse and modest attire, but emotionally stood out from the rest of the crowd as expressions of hurt were permanently etched on their faces. So, for the time being, they were happy staying in their fourteen provinces, never wanting for much in living, except the love they freely shared among themselves. That had been their life blood for these past generations and their code for survival. But that was soon to change.

CHAPTER 3

Dimitrii Crogan sat in his office in a custom-made executive chair that was ergonomically fitted to his obese frame and sagging ass behind a desk that had probably been carved from teak wood 300 years ago by Italian artisans. Opulent fine art, beautiful sculptures and gold tinted cornices surrounded him in his palatial building befitting the president of Chevka.

Many millions of dollars that were collected in taxes each year contributed to his own working environment, militia, arms purchases, bribes and prostitutes (for himself and key contacts and connections), and some went toward government-sponsored health and other entitlement programs available only to those in the Lower 43. Anything left over would line his private silk purse. He really didn't care about too much, other than what ultimately would end up to his own benefit.

He was a true sociopath with no regard for human life. He had an iron fist that many found themselves pinned under with no escape. He, of course, grew up in one of the Lower 43 provinces to a father who was a foreign diplomat and a mother who was a physician. Dimitrii was used to fine living and wasn't about to change anything about that. He viewed the "animals" of the Upper 14 as unnecessary leeches, draining his country of what had already become dwindling resources. He made sure he denied them even the most rudimentary infrastructure; most of the "Upper 14 pigs" really did not have electricity and adequate plumbing.

As he drew a long puff from his imported Havana cigar (rolled on the sweaty thighs of young Cuban girls, he liked to think), he thought how wonderful it would be to eliminate these people and consolidate the resources they had on hand to service the pure-bred European portion of his country. This had always been a milestone in the back of his mind, but even as a certified sociopath, he never had the guts to take it any further than his own dark thoughts.

Although the Upper 14 constituted fifteen percent of the provinces per capita, the amount of land they occupied was thirty-five percent. Dimitrii thought it outrageous that there wasn't more development in this land of pigs. Chevka's main export was coal and Dimitrii was certain that with depleting coal reserves in the Lower 43, there surely were fresh, untapped reserves up in the provinces where these people lived.

His Minister of Finance had been delivering increasingly poor reports of the country's fiscal position, as diminishing coal exports were now lowering the country's coffers to alarming levels. Under the rule of Dimitrii, Chevka really had nothing else to offer the rest of the world other than this source of energy. He never really bothered to develop this country culturally or encourage any kind of scientific or industrial development. His main concern was that he was in power, a position that was attained through shrewd politics and ruthless strategy, often ending up with a bullet in the back of someone's head. It really didn't matter as long as he was driving. He was in charge and all the people, whether they feared him, loved him or hated him, respected (aka feared) him as their leader. But this was now being threatened with the ever-increasing depletion of their main export; coal.

There was a time when his country was considered

the Monaco of the Eastern Bloc. It was always looked upon as the land of wealth, genius management and ideal life: the envy of Europe. What the world hadn't really caught on to about Chevka yet was its slow walk to the poor house. But this was something Dimitrii would not stand for. Not now. Not ever. His only solution was to tap what he was certain were rich and fertile mineral veins in the Upper 14.

One thing stood in the way: *These apes, these people who don't belong in this country to begin with! They should be gotten rid of.*

Dimitrii didn't have the balls (and certainly not meant as an accolade) Hitler had, or the same level of paranoia, although it was a very close second, so the gas-and-oven atrocity was not really something that he wanted to do. Not in this modern world, not today.

He sat for hours, sometimes in the dark, into the late evening thinking of how he was going to clear that land, get the machinery he needed in there and start new quarries to extract its nation's sole exportable commodity of value. He asked his Secretary of the Interior exactly how many of these pigs lived up in the Upper 14. That number was 3,500.

3,500? That's not a lot of people get rid of! Why, we can dig a large hole, have them all jump in and cover it up with dirt. And forget them forever. Wouldn't that be nice? Dimitrii mused.

But he thought this would be a waste of land and they would surely find coal in the process of digging this hole and waste valuable time ridding them of the human waste.

3,500 people making up fifteen percent of the

provinces' populace and thirty-five percent of the landmass? It just didn't make any sense in Dimitrii's mind.

The idea of a logical genocide did cross his mind, but then, what to do with all the bodies? Surely this would ignite a media frenzy, complete with the world's press, reporters from American TV stations, helicopter aerial shots of the carnage, etc. He would be despised as the laughingstock of the international community. Somehow he had to get these people off that land, and after hours, days and even weeks, he finally had a plan.

He smiled and took an extra-long draw on his thigh-rolled Havana cigar.

CHAPTER 4

The tidal wave of media immediately surrounding him in the ring with portable TV cameras, microphones, recorders and a plethora of questions was overwhelmingly new for Bob. This was one of the many nuances he would need to get used to after becoming the new lightweight champion of the world.

To his surprise, he later found out that his mother had attended the fight with his father. Of course, his father came to every fight; he wouldn't have missed it for the world. But normally, on the night of each fight, his mother would sit at home, wringing her hands in her apron and waiting for her husband to come home with the good, or possibly bad, news. But each time when Louis came home, it was always with good news. Grace would breathe a sigh of relief but then immediately start to gather a momentum of anxiety for the next fight.

She would hold him to his promise of quitting boxing at age twenty-six if he didn't win a major championship. It wasn't that she didn't want him to do what he loved doing, but it was a short-lived, dangerous and sometimes life-threatening sport. She was glad he was at least finishing graduate school and getting his MBA so he could be prepared to enter the business world with a modicum of intelligence and, she wasn't too quick to admit, some notoriety from his boxing past that would help.

Meanwhile, for Bob, the image of Gary Patton on all fours stuck in his mind like a still frame photograph. He still couldn't believe such a powerful boxer succumbed to his own skills and couldn't quite grasp the whole concept that he was on the top now. The Big Honcho, King of the Hill, Top Banana and, in the forefront of Johnny's mind, now the most wanted man in boxing… by other boxers. Why, after returning back to the locker room, they even had police security at the door, only letting in those select people who need be there, like the press and other glad-handers of prestige.

Johnny didn't want too many people in the small locker room, as this was still a post-fight cool-down and his fighter, his friend, needed to gather his wits. And nothing could be closer to the truth, as Bob's jaw was now starting to swell, along with most of the real estate on the rest of his face from the freight train that Gary drove into his right jaw in the third round.

"Can you believe this?" Bob beamed at Johnny mouthing the words with difficulty. "I mean, can you believe this?"

"Yes, I do believe it," *that and the tooth fairy,* Johnny lamented to himself, "and you deserve it. But I have to tell you, it wasn't so much a lucky punch as it was the *right* punch that cut off the highway of nerve endings in his temple. That took the steam out of his legs. Now, to be honest with you, Bob, you wouldn't have lasted much longer if you didn't land that punch. You just happened to execute what every veteran fighter does; slowly dismantling his opponent until he could drop that one bomb and send him to the canvas for the weekend."

"Yeah, I realize that Johnny. I do realize you're concerned that now every hungry light heavyweight in creation thinks that they can do the same thing to me. They'll be gunning for me, that I'm sure of. But that only means that we have to work harder, be smarter than the next guy."

Johnny didn't have to be told that this was his major concern right now. He wasn't ready for this fight; he knew that when they first accepted it on four weeks' notice when Corey and the others couldn't make it. Johnny was always to err on the side of caution, but took the chance anyway in accepting the challenge for his fighter.

But tonight, he'd have to put that aside. His fighter, his friend, his blood brother, just won the light heavyweight championship of the world, for Christ's sake! And this meant holding all three belts of the WBO, IBF and WBF titles. This was a time to celebrate, because there'd be no other night like tonight.

There was, at minimum, a two-month waiting period until the next fight, so there would be a little time to think about a game plan. Think about the conditioning and strategy for all challengers now waiting outside the door to get a piece of his friend.

Grace Perry walked into the locker room, working her way through the photographers. The locker room smelled like old dirty socks left sitting to ferment. But, at the end of the room, sitting on a table under a light was her son, her baby. She lost her bet with him and tried to manage a collage of emotions: pride, excitement and the anxiety of knowing that this was not over yet. She loved her son and just wanted the best for him.

Why can't he just finish graduate school, work for a big company, wear nice clothes and go to lunch?, she often urged any Higher Power that would listen.

She tried her very best to pretend the right side of

her son's face wasn't really twice its normal size. "So you did it, huh, hotshot? The other man was certainly big and strong-looking. It was all I could do to even come here, much less sit in the audience and watch you stand toe to toe with him. I did a little reading before the fight, so I knew that Gary rarely goes beyond the fourth round and always finishes his fights in the fifth. And you managed to beat him in the fourth! You know how I feel about you boxing and I'm not entirely happy that your promise is now, well, not a promise anymore. So, for this moment, for this very moment, I can tell you that I love you, I'm proud of you and I will pray for your future."

"Thanks, Mom. I got to tell you, I was very nervous, especially with only a four-week notice before the 'dance,'" Grace didn't know what he meant by that. "But this is something I've always dreamed of. You know that. And you know I always try very hard with anything I do and now it's finally paid off. But not to worry, Mom, I got that one course to go to finish my Master's. I'm trying to be adult enough to understand that this is not going to last forever. And I will have my entire life to live and manage if all this were to end tomorrow."

God, she could only hope.

"I can't believe how you nailed that guy," Louis said too enthusiastically for Grace's preference. "We're very proud of you, Bob. You've worked very hard for this and now your time has come. Not only do you have an obligation to yourself, but you have an obligation to the rest of the sports world. You have to set an example. You have to be the kind of man who treats his accomplishments with dignity and good grace. Show the younger generation what hard work and perseverance does; you're going to have a lot of young boys looking up to you now."

The press finished with their questions and Johnny was attending to the contents of Bob's sports bag and medical supplies. He was happy for Bob, but the news of a young fighter literally crippling Gary Patton would spread like wildfire. Every hard-nosed boxer from gyms across the country would dream the dream that Bob realized. They would work harder and not have fire, but a furnace in their belly. They knew that this could be done. They would want their turn now.

But no sooner than the last person left the locker room, the next fight was being arranged. Promoter Steve Shelby was wasting no time. Now this would be a moneymaker. A newly minted light heavyweight champ, defending his crown, after what some felt a lucky punch, at the age of twenty-five! What greater story did that make? The only logical choice for this venue would be Corey Green, whose eye would be more than healed by fight night!

As the cleaning crew was collecting the last of the beer cups and other litter from the arena floor, Shelby was on the phone with Corey's manager, Tommy Rae. Tommy had served on the New York State Boxing Commission for twelve years before deciding to become a boxing manager. He knew the other commission members very well and on occasion had made himself and a select few, very, very rich.

Commission members secretly betting on fights were not uncommon. After Vegas came out with their odds, their first point of contact would be the referee and then one or two of the judges for the fight. This wasn't done too often, but it was done often enough to challenge the moral fabric of the commission, and the sport, for that matter.

The odds for the Gray and Brennon fight, for example, were ten to one in favor of Gray. They knew it was going to be a close fight to begin with and that it would go all twelve rounds. They were knowledgeable enough and spent enough years on the commission, watching boxing, to know this was a fight that would go the distance and be won by decision, if so mandated by their will. This gave them the perfect platform to influence the referee and judges in their calls and decisions.

During this fight, and similar fights that had bets placed by the commission, the referee, for example, would call a slip by the opposing boxer a knockdown. This, of course, awarded their fighter of choice extra points on his card. The rules regarding examining the taping of the hands were overlooked when what resembled brass (actually titanium) knuckles were placed over the knuckles of the fighter of choice and covered with tape. Unfair, but there was money to be made and Tommy was going to make sure that he got his fair share. Ensuring Brennon's victory was a piece of cake.

It wasn't to say that Tommy's premier fighter, Corey Green, couldn't hold his own without these tricks. He was young, fast and determined, and spent many hours in the gym perfecting his art. Corey was also twenty-six years old and had a record of twenty-seven wins, no losses and no ties, with twenty-two of those wins coming by way of knockout. Tommy was quite certain that Corey could probably win this fight without any of the garnishing they normally did in fixing matches. But with the kind of dinero he was putting on the table, he wanted to make absolutely certain this fight went Corey's way. And so the process began.

Corey Green was every promoter's dream. The guy was pure flash, flamboyant and loud. He was the one who showed up for pre-fight weigh-ins with a T-shirt showing his opponent flat on his back with cartoon-like stars spinning around his head. He could antagonize anybody to the point where man, woman, child, retiree, anyone would want to get up and take a swing at him. He was that good!

This can prove to be an unnerving and incredibly useful tool during a fight. Taunting the opposing fighter enough to get under their skin makes them lose sight of their game plan and they end up being reckless; a state of mind that can leave them face down on the canvas and, if at the hands of Corey Green, possibly in the hospital (which had happened twice).

But, most importantly, it makes for great marketing. This is where the coin is pressed. The whole drama and theatrics of a professional title fight, the mini-biographies of each fighter and the "fight to the death" rhetoric makes for great copy, and in turn, advertising dollars.

Corey himself felt he was invincible. He was the man, he was the chosen one and he was the rightful owner of the lightweight championship of the world. He would have put old man Patten down no later than the second round. It was almost insulting to meet up with some rookie who won with some punk-ass lucky punch. Woman!

But because of that torn cornea, he was denied his chance. This only served to fuel the fire inside of him to grab the crown that was rightfully his. He was determined to beat the living shit out of Bob and let the world know that Corey Green was on top and here to stay. The fight was less than three months from now. Corey Green was going to make Bob Perry his fool.

CHAPTER 5

It was a typical October Saturday morning in Chevka. The low overcast carpeted the sky and a cool dampness clung to people's clothes.

Dimitrii was walking the garden of his twelve bedroom estate, thinking and becoming more convinced of his plan to rid Chevka of the inhabitants from the Upper 14. His plan was so simple, it was genius! He was going to push these animals, all 3,500 of them, through the Khyber Straits back onto the islands of Svenkia, where those people first came from. It would be like funneling cattle through open gates into a pen. He would tell the world that a deadly strain of virus was found in the water tables beneath the ground that fed their faucets. Why, yes, he was protecting his people, saving them from destruction! A hero!

Thinking this through made him almost wet his pants in excitement, as this somehow provided the rationalization that would satiate any ember of decency he may have had embedded within the deep regions of an otherwise devious mind.

He already made plans with the military for their approach and attack of each of the fourteen provinces. Even at this moment, the excavation crews were gassing up and checking their machinery, tooling and man power supply in order to start breaking ground to bring up the coal that Dimitrii was certain was beneath the soil. It didn't occur to the genius to send out a geological team to confirm the suspicions of wealth beneath the ground before he forced 3,000 people and their families out into the sea. This would be the thinking of a rational man and Dimitrii was clearly not a member of that club.

If all cylinders clicked, he would have all 3,500 unnecessary human beings from the Upper 14 on their way out and their homes leveled. But what these people were going to do once they passed through the Khyber Straits back to the Svenkia Islands, their "homeland," was their business. They could live in the woods and join the other animals polluting the land with their own excrement.

Dimitrii thought this neighboring outcrop in the Arctic Ocean was a dumping ground anyway, and more garbage would go unnoticed. Nobody had lived there for centuries. He decided November 1st would be the perfect time to make this happen. Why November 1st?

Oh, it does seem like a good day for beginning the newly "cleansed" Chevka. Dimitrii estimated it would take a little under two months to erase all memory of these people making for a grand Christmas present to himself.

They would then be a country of pure Europeans, devoid of any migration from the Arctic Ocean that happened thousands of years ago. He could give a rat's ass if these were the first people to inhabit Chevka, that these were the people who first broke ground and started a civilization.

He likened this to the Indians in America, who inhabited the land as savages, only to be replaced by people of culture and intelligence. This was the way of life, this was how a civilization progressed and no one was going to stand in the way of Dimitrii Crogan in keeping this country in a bright and prosperous light. And these savages in his own country were not going to stop him from keeping his purse full and the whores flowing freely.

His home garden was his own private sanctuary. And this was where he did his darkest thinking; outside the walls of his office with his many sycophants and servants. He found this increasingly irritating, but necessary, as a staff of faithful followers was the key to his success. He needed his various ministers—civil engineering, finance, military, utilities and sewerage—foreign diplomats and a host of others who made up his cabinet.

This garden was the only place where he could disconnect himself from the stress of political theatrics. It was here among the flowers he planted himself and watched grow that he felt his only real connection and usefulness in life.

The October chill finally made him decide to walk back to the house. As was his habit when walking on the gravel path, he would occasionally kick pebbles and watch them roll forward in front of his feet. As he was doing this, he started to kick the pebbles more aggressively, with those pebbles morphing into the people he was going to force through the Khyber Straits and out of his country. They were like little pebbles, little meaningless pieces of rock that would be chased from beneath his feet as he was now chasing the pebbles away from the path into the garden beds of flowers and bushes he so loved.

He became infuriated at his clumsiness. Little pieces of dirty rock fell beneath and on top of the beautiful flowers! In what became a moment of panic after he realized what he did, he fell to his knees and feverishly started to scoop up the pebbles from around the flower beds as though they were poison. His knees grew muddy and wet and, as a fine sheen of sweat started to collect on his brow, he carefully, one by one, removed the dirty pebbles, these "pigs," away from his beautiful flowers. Making sure all the dirty little people pebbles were removed from his beautiful land, he finally knelt back up and, feeling satisfied, turned and walked toward the kitchen door.

Yeah, shrinks would have a field day with this!

CHAPTER 6

The Svenkia Islands were more or less the result of a turd laid by a glacier 25,000 years ago. As the massive glaciers of the Ice Age started to retreat, they often dug up massive amounts of land, rocks and boulders that eventually became their own islands. The Svenkia Islands were comprised of three islands, two rather small, maybe two by three square miles of mass, with the main island forty-five miles wide and 180 miles long. Although now uninhabited, the island was still host to a variety of wildlife, vegetation and other natural resources that sustained life after Natalia's ancestors finally left to explore the mainland.

Most of the island was comprised of hard granite with other mineral types layered in between with rather thin layers of soil, twenty, forty, maybe fifty feet deep in some places, with underground rivers and wells running throughout. The landscape was actually quite beautiful. It hosted maple and oak trees, a vast variety of fauna and some rolling hillsides that would have made for a very pleasant and serene mural.

Of course, being on the Arctic Sea, winters were cold and brutal as hell. But when spring finally came around, the flowers and tress blossomed and the islands came alive again, bringing new life to its silent residents. There were wild boar, deer, pheasant, fox, ground hogs and a variety of other species that completed a very well-constructed food chain equation. The islands also hosted a rare breed of lion who, through a very fortuitous and timely genetic re-engineering, managed to survive the Ice Age, before which they flourished. This surviving version had an obviously thicker coat of fur, was slightly larger and a body temperature eight degrees lower than their more southerly cousins.

In modern times, it was a biologist's dream. One would consider this the perfectly balanced environment, where nature had carte blanche to create her own mosaic in such grand fashion. It was the same now as it was 3,000 years ago when the last of its inhabitants sought more from a bigger world across the Khyber Straits, so named for Vladimir Khyber, who discovered the tidal phenomena of this passage 200 years ago.

The people knew how to hunt well and provide the primitive shelter and warmth they needed during cold and unforgiving winters. As the increasingly larger cranial size of their skulls allowed for brain development, a part of the evolutionary process promoting increased intelligence, man became more inquisitive as to what lay beyond the rolling waves of the ocean. It was some time before they learned how to use tools; once mastered, they made a floating craft and first experimented by traveling from one island to another.

And, as all things go, there were always those adventurous few who wanted to travel beyond, who wanted to see what else the world beyond their shores had to offer. They could see the mainland beyond from their shores, but the straits were still too perilous to negotiate with their primitive boats.

It wasn't until about 1,000 B.C. that the platelets beneath the narrows rubbed against each other enough to push enough gravel and earth to a height where, at low tide, enough ground was exposed that they could now walk the four miles across to the mainland. This apparently was happening over time and it wasn't until one particular day when a tribesman looked across and saw the small boulders and rock glistening in the sun with a pathway to the "forbidden land beyond."

Forbidden often translates to "dare me," and a few ventured across the "Great Gateway" one day and made it in plenty of time before the tide came back in and sealed off the connection for the next six hours. They knew of the moon, the certain powers that it had when it came to harvesting crops, but had not yet mastered the knowledge of how the moon affected the tides, the height of the water, and eventually provided the pathway to the "forbidden land beyond".

After travelling across, they were now at the northern rim of what is now modern-day Russia, undeveloped in what seemed like land that never ended in front of their eyes. The ground looked a lot more fertile, the trees were plentiful.

When they returned back to the entrance of the Great Gateway to go back home, it was covered with water and no path was visible. They panicked. Somehow they thought they were tricked and trapped forever. There was no shelter, no weapons and the only thing they had were the pelts of fur on their backs. They spent the next three to four hours gathering wood to build makeshift shelters, believing this was their destiny and they were going to die there.

As they finished placing branches and leaves across the tops of their primitive framework, one of the elders who had accompanied the tribesmen looked out toward the sea and started to see the water become brighter as the tide began to recede and eventually show the rocks and small boulders reappearing in the moonlight. They then began to realize that there was some sort of magical pattern that opened and closed the Great Gateway. They dropped what they were doing and started to run across, slipping and tumbling on the mossy rocks. They finally did reach their island and sat there on the shore, watching patiently for the next three to four hours as the tide slowly began to come back in again and cover the Great Gateway. They finally got the hint.

There was so much more to be had at the "forbidden land beyond" than they had on their island. There was more than enough room for their growing village. And they marveled at what they might find in the hills, bushes and mountains beyond. The islands they were on were still bountiful in resources, but lacked the lush diversity of this discovery. They knew their clan was getting larger by the day and as planting and hunting skills improved through the centuries, their mortality rate began to lower. More and more of the clan were living longer and longer with babies always plentiful, running around, just happy to be in the world. The head tribesmen knew that eventually their resources would run scarce. The tribal leader's instincts told him that this new land across the Great Gateway was going to be crucial for continuing their civilization. It was time to move.

And so began the migration, every six hours, mind you, across the Great Gateway to the new land. They first started in small numbers sending scouting parties to survey the land and start to map out their new village. And every other sixth hour, little by little, village members started to cross the Great Gateway to their new home. Thus began the tiny country of Chevka, from whose womb the ancestors of Natalia began to establish themselves and thrive as a community.

Life was good and resources for living plentiful. And the elder tribesman's hunch on this land proved right; crops held quickly and grew strong. For the next 2,000 years, it grew from a small number of adventurers to thousands of firmly planted citizens. In time, curious Europeans traveled east to the area, liked what they saw, settled a bit south, thereby collectively creating the 57 provinces now known as Chevka.

Multiple terms of rule by different leaders and governments eventually establish the fifty-seven provinces that now made up Chevka. In the Upper 14, they retained their ancestral customs and did not associate, much less intermarry, with the European fabric occupying the lower forty-three provinces. This prejudice would soon escalate to a point where history was soon to reverse itself. It now appeared that these people were going to be pushed back through the Great Gateway onto their island of origin. In the 3,000 years they were gone, there had been no new inhabitants, the landscape left to its trees, bushes, vegetation and animals; just as it was when the last of the clan left it 3,000 years before.

CHAPTER 7

The week before the fight was filled with its usual drama and circus atmosphere; the press busy making sure no small detail went unnoticed. Corey Green, the fighter who was supposed to fight Gary Patton for the light heavyweight championship, was postponed and along came this relatively unknown, but very skillful boxer, Bob Perry, who knocked out Gary Patton with his “wonder punch” and grabbed the title. Corey was talking it up as being an injustice, insisting the crown really belonged to him.

“I’m going to take the man and beat him down to the point where he’ll be screaming like a woman for me to stop! He won’t know what hit him! He thinks because he landed a lucky sucker punch that he can beat me? Well, let me tell you, it’s going to be pure entertainment. He won the belt in four rounds; I’m going to take him down in three.”

There was no doubt about it. Corey worked hard and even though people thought he was a lot of hot air, he always delivered on his promises and threats.

Steve Shelby and Tommy Rae were already on the phone, joking on how they were going to spend their winnings. Steve had been talking to the two members of the boxing commission who would influence the choice of referee who would fully cooperate with any plan they might have had in determining the winner of the fight. They were masterminds at this. They’d done it so many times before that it was kind of fun putting this “storyline” together. Each “fix” had its own flavor and means of accomplishment. They would have to be extra careful with this since it was such a high-profile fight.

It was no secret that fights had been fixed in the past, just like baseball, football and other major sporting events. It was a sad reality and if publically exposed, would take the excitement, not to mention the money to be made, and flush it right down the toilet. Allegations had flared in the past, but they were quickly squelched by credible statements from the commission, as well as other high regulatory authorities of enforcing tight controls in maintaining the sport, and keeping it clean. Of course, this was only known in a small circle of very powerful bookies that make up the small exchange network that positioned the "in the know" bettors. It was no secret to this underworld this fight was going to be on the fix for Corey Green with odds in favor of Bob.

Bob's manager, Clive Perkins, was aware of this, but could never put his finger on it or prove it. Clive was a manager and a businessman. He knew that if he bet against his own fighter, it would create a feeling of inner disgust he could not live with. But if he didn't, he would stand to lose a lot of money. So, he placed no wager at all; the infrastructure of corruption was too big for him to champion its exposure.

This was something he would never divulge to Bob. Here was a young kid, strong, with a fierce desire to win. He sat in his chair and stared at the ceiling, caught between owning up to the reality of what was going to happen and knowing how unfair this would be to the kid who could very well have been his own son.

The ticking of a pendulum clock on top of the credenza in the corner of the room was the only sound in the otherwise silent world of Clive grappling with his conscience. He, too, had long-term relationships with some members of the boxing commission. When he first learned of these practices of pre-determining the outcome of a fight, he was a young and impressionable manager. He still tried to hold on to his ideals, but they had slowly eroded over the years of corruption. This could be a very dirty business.

How many times did he appeal to those commission members about what was going on? In some of the higher profile fights, the legitimate members of the commission he appealed to time and time again were blind to the possibilities of what Clive was trying to warn them about, or didn't want to believe it, since, if such a thing existed, it was of such a magnitude that it was too large to surpass.

At 10:00AM on Monday, October 20th, tickets went on sale. By 10:13AM., all but a few that had been reserved, for high-ranking individuals, radio and TV contests, or family members, were sold out. The fight was also going to be broadcast on large TV screens in twenty-four cities throughout the country. This was truly standing room only, as most of the venues were large warehouses or dance clubs that could accommodate 2,000 to 3,000 people. The revenue of this night would prove to be astronomical. This was the fight people were waiting for. With all the speculation the media had propagated, the gambling circuit in Vegas was humming with activity greater than the daily hysteria of the New York Stock Exchange.

Bob knew that this fight was not going to be any type of picnic. For hours he studied films of Corey fighting and was amazed at his lightning speed, strategy and agility in the ring. He picked a high-ranking cruiserweight as a sparring partner and made a point to go twelve rounds a day with this guy. Between that, the running, the speed bag, the exchange punches with speed mitts Johnny was holding (he also wore a thickly padded vest, which always cracked Bob up), Bob's workouts lasted seven hours a day, six days a week.

The special high carb and fiber diet, along with other tasteless nutrients that were part of the prefight menu, was never a favorite part of training. He had been keeping up this pace since September 1. His work ethic was second to none in his burning desire to prevail.

It wasn't in Bob's personality to be the flashy, loud mouth, marketing machine that Corey was. He was well aware that the crowd looked for a hero, someone who lit up an arena and made headlines. Clive tried to shore up this particular part of Bob's image, but it fell on deaf ears due to Bob's innate humility and, well, shyness. He even hired a PR man to work out a strategy whereby Bob might be a little bit more noticeable, perhaps an admired icon, which could add thousands, if not millions, of dollars to his fights. The ROI on this endeavor would be less than zero. The only thing Clive could hang his hat on was the endearing story of Bob promising his mother he would quit boxing if not winning the title by the time he turned twenty-six years old. Not exactly guts and grit imagery, but he made sure this anecdotal aspect of his boxer's persona was made public in his never-ending effort to give Bob *some* kind of marketing traction.

Every time Bob walked through the gateway into the arena before a fight, he was met with applause and cheers, but it was more like he had just finished an intimate piano concerto; his greeting from the crowd usually died down by the time the ropes were separated for him to enter the ring. It wasn't the wild cries of excitement that normally followed Corey's entrance into the arena. For the most part, the roof raised with scowls and booing, but excitement is excitement and this translates to more money to be made.

Nevertheless, Bob took the mediocre crowd response a little personally and, like anybody else, he wanted to be liked, to be loved. His training, career and finishing the damn MBA left him little time to seek a romantic side in his life. This would have helped fill part of the void. Self-affirmation is an important commodity and although Bob did very well in a short period of time with his boxing record, he never felt the real electricity and excitement he so craved from the crowd.

After each win, the ref would raise his hand a victory. He would circle around once with his arm raised to polite applause and leave the ring much the same as he first entered it, quietly. He wished he could be more like Corey, somewhat like the most popular kid in school, someone everybody wanted to hang with, wanted to be seen with. Bob was always a quiet kid. He had his fair share friends and excelled in sports, his only refuge from the shyness that stood in the way of making more buddies.

Bob often fantasized about being a hero of some sort. He fantasized about people smiling and cheering him for something he had done that was revered by the rest of the world. His favorite fantasy was about saving people, one by one, from a shipwreck onto the lifeboats. He'd be the last one off the ship just before it was swallowed into the unforgiving abyss of the ocean. He would swim back to the lifeboats and everyone would be grateful and would love him. He felt these so basic of needs were unfulfilled and wished he could do something about it.

But his priorities were clear right now and his focus on training for what he believed would be the real fight of his life had to be maintained. The fight with Gary Patton seemed to open the door for him in terms of gaining more confidence in himself as a boxer and validating him as the best light heavyweight boxer of the world.

In his own quiet way, in the brutal world of boxing, he was going to teach Corey Green a valuable lesson. Or so he thought.

CHAPTER 8

On the hallway table, Mama had placed all the presents, wrapped in brown paper with a bow made of old linen. Natalia's cousin, Latvina, was barely three years old. She was running around the room and dining table excitedly, as if it were her birthday. Papa had made a fire in the fireplace to protect them from the cold November air as the evening sky filled with sparkling stars and a gloriously bright moon.

Oh, it was so safe and warm in the house. Family and friends all together were now seated around the table, eating lamb and potatoes, and tomatoes that Mama grew in her garden. Everything was so delicious. Natalia gulped down her food and wished everybody would do the same, because after that, they would be eating cake!

It took practically Papa's entire paycheck to pay for all of this, but anything for his little girl would never cost too much. They turned on the radio and, although government-controlled, they did manage to find a station with soft, cheerful music. One of Natalia's uncles owned a small butcher shop and did quite well. He could afford nice clothes. He wore a brand new shirt and shoes made from the skin of an elk. Natalia knew that his present would be among the best and was almost blind with excitement to see what it would be. Everybody was talking so loud and fast that Natalia wondered how anybody could understand each other.

Her Uncle Elizar was a local butcher who filled his tiny store with meats he hunted himself in the plentiful countryside. He was a heavyset man with a hearty laugh.

She swore that the neighbors three miles away could hear every time he exploded with his bellowing laugh. Her Aunt Dar'ya knew how to play the piano, but there was no piano in Natalia's house, so instead, she sang, and eventually everybody joined in. It was an old Chevkan song that had been passed on from generation to generation. It told of the hardships of their ancestors when they first settled in Chevka and the sacrifices they endured to survive. It reminded Natalia and her family of how grateful they really were for what little they had.

The time finally came. Everybody had finished eating the main dinner and now, finally, it was time for cake. Mama placed eight candles on a two layer cake with white icing. This was not very hard to make, with plenty of eggs from their own chickens and wheat from the neighboring fields. Cake was not a frequent thing in Natalia's house, so this certainly was a special treat. This was the second time the candles had been used; they were burned down halfway from Luther's 14th birthday four months ago. The candles on Natalia's cake were not the only thing that she had that was used and inherited from Luther; many of the clothes that he eventually outgrew were tailored by Mama to fit Natalia. But her party dress, her big girl dress, was completely her own.

"Ah, how pretty my little girl looks today," her Uncle Elizar beamed. "Why, it wasn't too long ago that I held you in one hand and a bottle of milk in the other and you fed like a hungry little bear cub. And now you're a beautiful young lady. Someday you will make one lucky man a very wonderful wife."

Natalia didn't care too much for boys, but she was

polite anyway. She smiled and thanked her Uncle Elizar. She'd much rather play with her doll than be around boys who were rough and didn't smell too good. The only exception to this rule was her brother, Luther, who she looked up to and loved very much.

One by one, the presents were placed in front of Natalia. She very carefully unwrapped each one. And with each one, her mouth opened, letting out a squeal of delight. One was a water globe that, when shaken, snowed with the flakes falling on a little cottage inside. Another was a hand-made miniature baby carriage that her doll fit into perfectly where now, she could go for a stroll and show off her baby. And still another was a strange brown box that, when the lid was opened up, played a beautiful melody that filled the room.

Luther saved the money he earned by doing odd jobs at the homes of the surrounding families for months. He finally had enough money and went into one of the larger towns of the Lower 43 and bought his sister a dollhouse. Traveling down to the Lower 43 was never a pleasant experience for him, but this was for his sister. It cost thirteen clenviks and it was well worth it to see the smile on her face. He even had enough money left to buy little pieces of furniture that she could arrange much the same as she was going to rearrange in her own home someday.

Uncle Elizar said she was going to make a good wife for a nice husband, but she didn't think that was necessary as she would have her own home where she and her dolly would be very happy. But she wasn't going to tell Uncle Elizar that. That would surely hurt his feelings. As the last present was unwrapped, Natalia carried each one up to her room and placed them in appropriate spots. Order and presentation were very important to Natalia and her tiny bedroom was testimony to that. Colorful ribbons, stuffed animals and homemade braids of material hung on a wall. One arrangement surrounded a picture of Big Bird, her most favorite character of Sesame Street.

Natalia returned downstairs where the family was still singing and the adults were now having a little bit of wine. Luther managed to get his hands on a nearly empty glass of wine in the kitchen that was intended to go into the soon-to-be washed stack of glasses and gulped it down. She thought of telling Papa, but she and Luther were secret comrades. They told each other secrets that nobody else in the whole wide world knew. They grew up together reading what few books they had about childhood adventures. There was nothing she couldn't tell Luther, her buddy, her special friend.

Kristanf heard the distant motors and at first just thought it was traffic passing by on the main road a few miles away. But then the sound became louder. It was clear that whoever was coming was coming to see them. Two Chevka Republic Guard Humvees crashed through the fence and came to a screeching halt four feet from the door. The soldiers from each of the trucks brandished M-14 rifles.

One of them broke down the door with his boot and entered screaming, "OUT! OUT!! GET OUT OF THE GOD DAMN HOUSE, YOU PIGS. YOU HAVE FIVE MINUTES TO GATHER ANY OF YOUR FILTHY BELONGINGS AND GET OUT!"

Everyone stopped and stared in shock with their mouths open, hearts beating wildly.

One of the soldiers decided that these people needed proper motivation, to show that they were not kidding around. Just for effect, one of the soldiers raised his weapon, fired and blew a hole the size of a quarter through Uncle Elizar's left thigh. The blood was starting to gush and a pool began widening on the floor. Natalia screamed and started to cry uncontrollably. Another soldier let his weapon rip through the ceiling, sending white shards of plaster to the top of Natalia's cake. They settled on top as though they were frosted ornate leaves. Another soldier shot through the walls, breaking pictures and shattering furniture. Terrified was not even a close description of the fear welling up in everyone's throats.

"I SAID GET OUT! GET OUT YOU GODDAMN ANIMALS. GRAB BLANKETS, CLOTHES, SHOES… ANYTHING!! IF YOU'RE NOT OUT OF THIS HOUSE IN FIVE MINUTES, I'LL BLAST YOUR FUCKING HEADS OFF YOUR SHOULDERS. MOVE!"

Kristanf wasn't totally surprised. It had been rumored that this madman of a president was going to actually go through with his "ethnic cleansing." Kristanf thought this was such a brutal idea that surely the president wouldn't do it.

He was wrong.

CHAPTER 9

Dimitrii was sitting at his desk, the corner of his mouth distorted into a perfect "O" blowing smoke rings from the large cigar he was enjoying. His field marshals were reporting their progress on an hourly basis. All the "animals" were being thrown out of their houses and herded through the Khyber Straits. Spread out on his huge mahogany table was a map of the upper 14 provinces, with red balled pins marking those areas that had already been excavated.

Field Marshal Julius Witkowski wore a headset connected to a communications receiver. He placed the dots with horrific frequency to personify the speed and terror in which his troops were emptying the homes of their lifelong residents. Dimitrii watched his garden of pins grow steadily as though they were a field of red roses. It was much like this garden; the land cleared, the ground made fertile for a new and beautiful life to be born.

Trucks and excavation equipment were now slowly rumbling up the North Highway, the only road that led to the center of the Upper 14. Bulldozers, backhoes and drilling equipment made up a conga line over two miles long. Most of the drivers despised the strange looking and unwelcome people of the Upper 14 and viewed them as uncivilized litter than needed to be swept away, as did most of the people of the Lower 43. It would be a great pleasure to mow down their houses and scoop up the debris to make it appear as though they were never there. President Crogan had promised them an extra bonus if they could clear the entire area by the mid-December. This made them all the more anxious to get up there and get started.

They would waste no time in beginning their work, bulldozing down the houses that were homes for the people of Antonia for hundreds of years; the land beneath for their ancestors for thousands more. In the carnage, debris would scatter the landscape like an airliner crash, with heavy-duty trucks standing and waiting to gather up precious, irreplaceable belongings.

The plan was to load and bring the lot to the harbor to be later transported twenty miles out to sea by barge and dumped. Photographs, antique clocks and figurines handed down from generation to generation, silverware, clothing, music boxes, all other keepsakes and any and all things that families accumulate over the years that held special memories now were sentenced to death: a horribly sad scene to see such unnecessary destruction from a dictator who didn't bat a conscionable eyelash, only backed up by a field marshal who got a real hard-on over the whole project.

But not everyone accepted or agreed to what they had been forced into participating in this demolition. For some reason, by coincidence, maybe demographics or something on that order, all but a few of the long-haul truckers who were to cart the contents of the home to the harbor lived at the northern fringes of the Lower 43 and knew a great many people of the Upper 14. Many of the people of Antonia worked in the same factories from which the truckers hauled goods, served food in restaurants they ate in, helped them at the counters of local department stores and fixed their cars in local garages. Exposure by a myriad of other jobs and points of contact gave way to warm and enduring friendships.

The truckers were not especially fond of their snub-nosed neighbors below them and related more to the down-to-earth people of Antonia. Strictly undercover, they were organized and had "union." Not so much to demand better conditions and higher wages from their employers, but for self-support and to discuss some of the issues of their jobs that they would resolve themselves covertly. Beyond that, if the government knew they had such a "union," all that would accomplish would be getting their asses handed to them and their licenses revoked.

The night before the excavation project was to begin, they met in a local watering hole to air out their feelings about what they were required to participate in and how badly they felt for their neighbors. They felt heartsick at what they were being forced into doing to people they had known for years. After long discussions and angst, they came up with an idea. There was not much they could do to replace their homes, nor was it probable that they would ever set foot back on the mainland, especially to retrieve many of their cherished belongings they were forced to leave behind when being exiled. But, hey, who knew for sure?

The truckers decided to take folded boxes with them in their back cabs well outside the sights of the field bosses in charge of their areas. After the bulldozer scooped up the remaining fragments of one home and dropped it in the back bay of the truck, they had moved on to flatten the next house. This gave truckers about thirty to forty-five minutes to sift through the debris in the back of their trucks to try and retrieve any valuable keepsakes.

Since they did not know the addresses of their friends, they wouldn't know whose house was being flattened at the time. So, after filling the boxes, they would write the address across the side in marker instead, then cover the boxes they accumulated with other light debris so as to be hidden from the bulldozer operators and others faithful to the cause working the fields.

On the way to the harbor, they would stop at a warehouse owned by one of the truckers to drop off the boxes before delivering the rest of the shattered homes to the waiting barge. They were clearly aware of the risks to themselves and their families. It was not so much that they expected these people to come back to gather their belongings, as it was more of an effort to maintain this precious cargo by keeping it in a dry and locked location in due respect, even if no one was to ever open the boxes again.

CHAPTER 10

Dimitrii knew that there was not going to be any international interference. Even if the world did find out about the squalor these people were living in, it was clearly an issue and concern of the nation of Chevka. Organizations such as Red Crescent, Relief International, Doctors Without Borders and other health agencies, would steer clear because it was not an emergency situation, but a decision made by the government. As Chevka was still considered an annexed satellite of Russia, there would be international repercussions in interfering with Chevka's government and its decision for the people in the Upper 14.

After being ripped from their homes, a light rain started, which made the chilly November night even more unbearable. Natalia was running with the hundreds of other people who now scoured the countryside. She recognized a friend's mother, ran next to her, grabbed her hand and they both ran through the unforgiving night. The intensity of fear drew the air from her lungs, making it even more impossible to run under the hail of crackling gunfire.

She didn't know where her father or mother was, or Luther, for that matter. And what about Uncle Elizar? He was shot into the thigh by that awful soldier and Uncle Dem'yan had taken off his belt and tied it around Uncle Elizar's upper thigh and backside to stem the flow of blood. But Natalia wondered how he could possibly run like the others. Surely he would have held things up and made the soldiers very angry.

Natalia was too close to the truth, unfortunately, and since Uncle Elizar couldn't keep up with the others, that same soldier who shot him through the leg delivered the butt of his rifle to the back of his head, making him pick up the pace, which he did painfully.

And the old people? Some of them had walkers or wheelchairs. What would happen to them? Unfortunately, most met with the same fate as those select few who were shot to death to serve as means of visual "motivation" for the rest to run. The soldiers thought these were old people, what good would they be, anyway? So most of them were also murdered and lay in what made for a horrific path to the Straits.

Natalia's pretty party dress was now soaked through, muddy and torn by the bushes. She was crying and trying to catch her breath at the same time.

Each time someone wanted to stop and rest, the soldiers would fire their rifles into the air and the people kept running. The wet and terrified people ran through the valley toward the ocean with expressions of fear, bewilderment and exhaustion lining their faces. They didn't quite know why this was happening, what it was they did wrong and why their country turned on them. They kept to themselves, as was made clear by the people of the Lower 43 who did not want them around other than for the cheap labor they offered. Could it have been that they didn't pay enough taxes? Could it have been that they didn't give enough of their crops for free to the market of the Lower 43, as they were required? What did they do to make their president so mad at them?

Kristanf was frantic. He managed to find his wife in all the chaos, but couldn't find his son and daughter. The rain pelted his face as he screamed their names, but this only proved to be in vain, as the constant firing of M-14s in the air drowned out his voice and his hopes. He had to keep running for fear of being shot.

Along with the elderly, the soldiers continued to make the point clear by sporadically killing a person here, a person there, just to make sure the throng of running people remained focused on retribution if they even stopped to catch their breaths.

While running, sometimes Kristanf would have to watch his step or else he'd trip over a body. It was three miles to the shore where they were to eventually cross the Khyber Straits. At this rate, they might make it in an hour and a half to two hours.

The rain soaked them through, sending a searing chill straight to their bones. They had managed to grab some blankets, some food, a few sweaters and some old pots to collect rainwater during the five-minute warning the soldiers granted them before leaving their homes. This only served to weigh them down as their feet sank in the marshy tundra that signaled their approach to the water's edge.

Many lost their footing in this quagmire, which was promptly remedied by the butt of a soldier's rifle between their shoulder blades. They got up, muddy and thoroughly tired, and continued to trudge through the night. Many people would end up with pneumonia and severe colds, and with medical attention practically nonexistent, end up just the same way as the elderly and the slow...

...dead.

CHAPTER 11

At the weigh-in that afternoon, it was all business for Corey. He'd been through the drill before and was dutifully followed by his entourage when he entered the press room. The fanfare, his ever present open mouth and making sure that the room came alive when he entered was his forte. He didn't really need a microphone, as his voice was loud enough for the trash talk that was coming out at lightning speed.

He was well versed in the hype that preceded a fight, which made him the darling of promoters and sports channel producers. He'd been waiting for this for a very long time. And true to form, he had a t-shirt on with a picture of Bob on the front, lying on his back with stars spinning around his head. Corey was standing above Bob, demanding he get up. The picture across his chest was in tribute to the same taunting Cassius Clay gave Sonny Liston as he was on his back during their title fight.

Cassius Clay was Corey's idol and role model. He likened himself in character and fighting style. And everyone in his entourage had the same t-shirt on. They came marching in and each took their seats at the dais. Microphones on, cameras focused and Corey took the podium first.

"What you're about to see tonight is gonna be the greatest boxing exhibition by any human being ever. But you have to make sure you keep your eyes open and don't blink, because before you know it, Bob Perry will be flat on his back, wishing he listened to his mama and quit boxing."

Tommy Rae was grinning from ear to ear. He got

out of his seat without needing a microphone and shouted, "AND, this fight will go fast as a blinking eye, as my fighter's gonna take this boy down faster than a meteor hitting earth. He's gonna want to retire at the ripe old age of twenty-six after my boy gets done with him. There's no stopping Corey Green. Not now, not ever!"

"Let this be a warning to anybody else who expects to step in the ring with me," Corey continued his shouting, even though he was using a microphone. "I'm twenty-seven years old and I've got at least ten more years of brutalizing my opponents. Look me up ten years from now and I'm still gonna be light heavyweight champion of the world with all three belts around my waist. I never had anybody who even came close to beating me, especially someone who won his last fight with some cheap-ass sucker punch."

Bob, Johnny and Clive next walked in to their places at the opposite end of the dais. But Corey wasn't quite through yet; not even close.

"I want all of you take a look at this pathetic excuse for a boxer sitting to my left. Now take a look at me! I'm a beautiful specimen of a human being." At that point, he pumped both arms in the air, flexing his biceps. "Look at me! You think for one moment that anybody can beat me, the greatest fighter of all time, the most ruthless human being ever to step into a ring? The answer is no, my friends. I have twenty-seven wins, no losses, no draws and twenty-two of my wins came from knocking the chump down through the canvas. I'm gonna do the same with Bubba the MBA here, no later than the third round, and he's gonna continue on through the canvas into the fucking basement."

Once again, the producers wanted to thank the guy that invented the seven second delay. This guy Corey had no respect for the public.

At that point, he turned toward Bob and gave him the icy stare that he had down pat. No shit, the guy had an acting coach train him, giving him all the tools for intimidation and good marketing.

Reluctantly, Corey moved down from the podium and Bob got up out of his chair and approached the microphone. Bob wished he were more fiery and flamboyant but this was just not in his makeup. He felt uncomfortable at this press conference, especially with Corey and his ranting. He'd been through this before, but Corey was the master of the mind game.

He looked around the room at the members of the press to see their faces slowly return to normal after Corey's ranting and raving. Again, this stung Bob a little bit because it looked like they were bored with him. Sure, the kid just became a champion by knocking out Gary Patton. Sure, this was exciting, but this fighter wasn't. They had respect for his skills and had covered his bouts before, but once again, that quiet and polite reception. When he started to open his mouth, he knew he was outdone by Corey's performance. There was nothing he could do to match him.

"I'm here to fight, I've trained to fight, and I'm not going to go through a lot of predictions and tell you that I'm going to flatten Corey in the third round, or the fourth, or the eighth. All I can tell you is that the man with the last word will be the last man standing."

That got the press corps revved up for sure. This

quiet, short retort to Corey's long ranting seemed to hit a chord, the right marketing chord that Corey obviously picked up on. He was enraged that something so short and sweet would trump all the theatrics that he practiced for hours (and paid for).

Corey shot up out of his seat and started to move toward Bob, with a honed appearance of wanting to get in a punch. And, almost on cue, all of the fighters' staff rose from their seats to separate the two, but the only one being separated was Corey. Bob just looked at him. He knew the knucklehead was putting on a show and refused be any part of it. Corey started flailing his arms, pulling against the grip that Tommy Rae and Steve had on him to prevent him from doing any "damage" before the fight. This, of course, was all well-rehearsed and part of the show. Bob backed up from the podium and slowly walked toward the exit with Clive and Johnny in tow.

CHAPTER 12

Bob couldn't believe the size of the locker. It was three times the size of anything he had used to prepare for fight. It had couches and mirrors and bright diamond-shaped light bulbs running around the mirror. Bob sat spinning around in his chair like a star struck adolescent.

This did not escape Johnny's attentive eye. "Come back from Disneyland Goofy and start focusing on Corey, " Johnny said snapping his fingers in front of Bob's dazed expression. "Kid's got lightning speed and he's smart. That's a dangerous combination. And remember, just as you had to circle to Gary's right to avoid his left hook, you've got the circle to Corey's right to avoid that lightning fast piston of a left jab he has. He's got three inches reach on you, so make sure you stay low and close to him, strike and continue to circle him. Don't give him a chance to wind up with a full swing; it'll hurt, all shit aside. Keep low and concentrate on the body. Slow him down like you did Gary; work on his lower shoulders and upper triceps. Wear down the ligaments in his arms so that when you do step away, he doesn't have the firepower."

Johnny was now applying and rubbing oil into Bob's knuckles while massaging the top of his hands. The oil was a mixture of seasoned herbs and fruit extracts, the secret recipe of which Johnny's grandfather, a trainer back in the days when there were *no* gloves on the fighter's hands and bare knuckle fights lasted for twenty rounds or more, had handed down to his grandson. Jesus Christ! How the hell did those guys survive beating the daylights out of each other bare fisted for over an hour?

It was kind of odd that Johnny followed in the footsteps of his grandfather, since his father was a professor of Finance and Accounting at Yale University. Go figure that one out. Where almost all boys look to emulate their fathers, Johnny was always interested in watching his grandfather train his fighters. To the little boy, his grandfather's fighters looked like giants. He would watch their sparring sessions for endless hours, and how his grandfather would yell and scream, congratulate and applaud, all at the same time. His fighters respected him and he brought in three world champions in his forty years as a trainer.

After the oil massage, Johnny started the thirty minute ritual of taping Bob's hands. This, too, was an art, with the main objective of protecting the fighter's hands from being broken. If done properly, it worked for the most part and for the time it didn't, at least it helped keep the bones within the same proximity until the tape could be removed and replaced with a cast.

The official came into the dressing room to examine them. He then observed the gloves being placed over Bob's hands and taped to his wrists and lower forearms with duct tape. This had to be initialed by the official, which meant the fighter was now cleared for a clean fight.

Bob went to his deep meditative state and began to focus from within. This was the time when he reached deep down inside and took himself to a place where nothing else existed around him; the rest of the world was shut out and he occupied the center of his own universe.

As the two fighters of the last undercard were busy beating the living crap out of each other, the NBC TV crew wanted to come into the dressing room and take some footage of Bob "warming up". That was entirely out of the question. He was not the kind of fighter who shadowboxed for the cameras with a light sheen of sweat, showing that he was ready to fight. He was ready to fight, but on his own terms.

He had asked Johnny to shut off all but one light. He prepared endless hours at great sacrifice for this fight. Now was time for him to reconcile inside himself that he was 100 percent ready and losing was *not* an option. Emma, ever present in her hallmark position of sleeping, did so in the corner of a sofa she immediately found when first entering the locker room.

Corey's dressing room was almost an entirely different story. He had every light on and brought in extra lights so the camera crews could get a clear shot of his magnificent body and form as he warmed up by shadowboxing and jabbing the air with lightning fast punches. The camera crew ate this up, along with the trash talking, and the utter arrogance that was Corey's trademark. His hands were still bare as he was hamming it up for the camera, rolling punches and grinning ear to ear.

"I'm gonna take that boy and put him into the next century. That pathetic piece of shit will finally realize that he is not light heavyweight champ of the world. Corey Green is! It takes a real man to be a champion and this Bob Perry excuse for a boxer is just not up to it. He's gonna regret the day he ever decided to put on a pair of gloves."

Corey's trainer, Bill Farlow, was giving his fighter last minute instructions. And, of course, Tommy Rae was there, just to add quality to the picture. The camera crew was asked to leave, as it was now time to prep Corey. The camera lights went off and the crew milled out of the dressing room. As had Johnny done with his fighter, Bill also did the requisite oil rubdown of fingers, knuckles and hands. But the next steps did not follow the same rules as it had with Bob. Bill applied the first layer of tape in much the same fashion as with any boxer. And when that was firmly in place, with Corey's hands tightened and strengthened, the next process was a bit different.

As there was no official in the room to witness this and to sign off on it as paid for, they were free to proceed. The knuckle wraps were set in place on each hand with one layer of tape holding them place. The second layer of tape crisscrossed and wound under the hand to ensure the apparatus did not move around. The gloves were placed on and wrapped with medical tape around his wrists and forearm, with Bill forging the initials of the official. The knuckle wrap was made of titanium, adding little weight, but Corey had prepared for this by shadowboxing with one-pound weights in his hands. No problem there. Corey "Show Me The" Green was ready to rumble.

There was not a seat in the arena unoccupied. Celebrities were scattered through the front section and camera shots were peppering the crowd, zeroing in on the best and beautiful of attending celebrities. Gary Patton, who had since retired, was also in attendance. Part of him still felt the pain of losing, but hey, this is natural. Beside him was his wife who, for the first time in years, was attending a fight. She felt better that he was not in the ring, risking the further shame of possibly losing again and doing further damage to himself and his self-esteem. But he always managed to win, except for that last fight with Bob Perry. She was glad that Gary was now in retirement.

But, as his wife of thirteen years, she felt his pain, too. It was bittersweet, but she was glad that her husband, at the ripe old age of thirty-four, was now an analyst with NBC.

He, of course, was also subject to camera shots, adding to the drama of the recently dethroned light heavyweight champion of the world who was now sitting in the crowd, watching his nemeses go against what was considered to be the number one contender in the division. The guy he was supposed to fight.

Gary was in the business long enough to understand some of the "practices" of the commission and their collaboration with boxing officials in fixing fights. Again, as crafty as they were and as politically untouchable, no one could prove what a lot of people believed.

He liked Bob Perry. The fact that he gave away his title to such a skillful and smart boxer, diffused the pain for him… a bit. But he was concerned now because he knew for sure that the winner of this fight had already been predetermined. He wished that there was some way he could uncover the truth and not watch Bob be unfairly beaten and possibly carried away with permanent damage. The only thing he could hope for was that he didn't get seriously hurt.

Let the games begin, shall we?

Now it was time for Corey to make his entrance. He did have the Vegas-type declining ramp and the neon lights surrounding it with fireworks going off, as well as two very nice looking, leggy, scantily dressed women serving as garnishment. As his name was announced, he entered into the arena from a blue sequenced declining stage. He entered with a thumping disco beat blaring as he strode down the ramp, wearing a blue satin robe with Corey "Show Me the" Green embroidered on the back and gold tassels hanging from his shoes.

Bill Farlow, Tommy Rae and Steve Shelby were following behind, wearing color-coordinated blue satin jackets. It was a great show. It lit up the crowd and they booed and screamed. It wasn't so much Corey they were standing up for (even though it was to jeer and boo), but for the image Corey represented. He was the bad guy and they wanted *someone* to knock him on his ass.

Bob watched this spectacle from the opposite entrance. Johnny and Jerry Dougan, an experienced cut man he had used for all his previous fights, positioned themselves behind him, as Bob always preferred to walk the walk himself. As always, he felt left out, alone and ignored. But he was going to do what he always did: fight smart and hard, and maintain his endurance.

He studied enough films of Corey's style and his skill of instantly switching styles, which Bob could adjust to on a dime. He had to be very careful about this. And if he was the one who was going initiate a change in style, he had to make sure he knew how Corey was going to adjust to it.

As Corey was getting close to the ring, he started to point in the direction of what would be Bob's corner making the slitting of the throat gesture.

God, this guy is arrogant, Bob thought.

Corey's people separated the ropes so he could

enter the ring, bouncing around throwing punches in the air accentuated with a moonwalk to the center of the ring with his arms raised high.

As was customary, the champion then made his appearance. Bob walked through the hallway to the arena with his ever-present good luck charm, a white terrycloth sweatshirt with the sleeves cut off. No fireworks, no laser lights, no declining stage in surrounding neon lights. Just Bob walking through, followed by Johnny, and flanked by Jerry.

The guy was good at what he did. There were times when Bob would have one of his eyelids split open and Jerry managed to stop the flow of blood into his eyes and prevent any further damage. There was another fight where Bob's right ear was almost ripped off the side of his head. His opponent that night kept on concentrating on that split ear. Jerry managed to keep the blood and swelling in check with cold iron presses.

Walking down toward the ring, Bob did have the required music that would introduce him into the arena. It was a kinda awkwardly rhythmic blues beat that did not quite fit. It didn't send a pulse through the spectators to get their adrenaline going and expectations salivating. And, as always, he was greeted with polite applause, that *irritating polite applause* as though he was entering a room to give a lecture.

The Marine Corps had their color guard holding flags and were waiting for a new, upcoming pop singer, Cheryl Adams, to sing the national anthem. The smoke and smell of the pyrotechnics that accompanied Corey's entrance still hung in the air like a cheap pool hall. The lights lowered to a spotlight when she graced the air with her beautiful voice. Bob loved her music and especially the tone of her voice. She was gifted, but also worked hard at perfecting her art. And to Bob, boxing was also an art form.

As Cheryl hit her high notes, Bob felt the reality of who he was, where he was and what was expected of him. Although he knew all the trash talk was part of the marketing machine, Corey's belittling Bob and even his family (as captured in the press from some pre-fight interviews) enraged him. Intellectually, he knew this was part of the game, but emotionally he could not reconcile this to the point of complacency. He was gonna put this guy down and confirm that he indeed was the true light heavyweight champion of the world.

Yeah, let the games begin.

CHAPTER 13

The ring was empty now except for the announcer, the referee and the two fighters. The microphone was lowered down to meet the open hand of the announcer. This was the guy with the "let's get ready to rumble" serenade. He had been using the same opening line for years, the same five words, and always got the same reaction. Bob always marveled at this. And then came the "in this corner" and "and in that corner," blah, blah, blah.

Corey wore blue satin trunks with gold trim. Whatever the hell that meant was beyond Bob's immediate comprehension. The matching gold tassels on the shoes made for a complete outfit. And he was built like a warrior, no mistake about that. As Tommy removed Corey's satin robe, Bob could see his body was cut with pronounced pectoral muscles and a six-pack that look like cobblestones. Bob thought he had enough tattoos running up and down his arm and back to map out the entire western hemisphere. Dragons and wizards and God knows what else was etched and wrapped around his torso. Bob's World War II style tattoo on his right bicep paled in comparison to Corey's epidermal roadmap.

The fine sheen of sweat on his body was testimony that he had been warming up and taking this fight very seriously. To be sure, he was not taking Bob Perry as lightly, either, even though he was prepped for success. He knew he was a good boxer, strong and smart, and knew how to do some serious damage.

Bouncing from one foot to the other, he tried to remain loose, his limbs warm and heartbeat slow and steady. One of the mobile cameras perched next to his corner zeroed in for a close-up where Corey shook his fist at the camera. If he could poke his finger out of the glove, he surely would've made the "I'm number one" sign (or just flip the bird). He made sure he had his practiced cocky grin on his face, making the world know how confident he was.

Bob, on the other hand, wore plain black trunks with a very thin silver strip on each side. His boxing shoes were regulation, no tassels, with the only decoration being the word "Adidas" on the side.

But fashion and flash are not what boxing is made of. Bob was a firm believer in the sport and not the commercial spectacle. Of course, he wanted to give the fans a good show for their money, but that was going to come by the way of boxing, strategy, endurance and, ultimately, victory.

Bob's hero, Rocky Marciano, was also a very humble guy, but one tough fighter. Watching Marciano fight was what fueled Bob's attention and interest in the sport. And back in the fifties, it was still the sport and not a spectacle. It was when two men, often wearing almost the same color trunks, met in the ring to go toe to toe, man to man, no bullshit, just a strong execution of the sport as it was intended to be.

Fighters like Rocky always had the characteristic facial structure and neck muscles of a boxer, with a primitive, almost caveman bone structure and very little contour of the neck. His strong jaw and gentle smile endeared him to the fans. And at 195 pounds, he was *heavyweight* champ, and never lost one of the forty-nine fights in his professional career. No one had yet to break that record, this coming from a soft-spoken and humble guy.

And as soft-spoken as he was, Rocky was a brutal fighter. This was what made him so popular and Bob couldn't understand why people didn't respond the same way today. He truly was Bob's hero, but in twenty years, a lot of things change. Oh, how he wished he were fighting in the fifties. But that was then, this is now.

Both fighters moved to the center of the ring. After the announcer did his thing, he placed the microphone underneath the right armpit of the referee, who gave the requisite instructions to the fighters, you know the drill; "I want a good, clean fight," and "return to your corners when I tell you," wrapping up with "obey my commands and protect yourself at all times."

Corey had an inch over Bob in height and three inches in reach. With mouth pieces in place, their upper and lower lips protruding, Corey was giving his best stare-down of his career. He knew the cameras were taking close ups and made sure he was sending glaring rockets into Bob's eyes. Bob could do nothing more than slip back into his own eyes with a calm yet fierce determination.

For a fraction of a second, a split-second, fear flickered in Corey's eyes. Even with his "advantage," he still feared the remote chance of defeat. This reaction could be a real deal-breaker and determine the outcome of the fight even before it began. They both realized this and Corey could have kicked himself for letting his arrogance slip for that fraction of a second. Once again Bob, with one single, simple act, had out trumped Corey's work at intimidation. This only served to fuel Corey's anger and, at the same time, exacerbate his fear; something that Corey would rather die than admit.

The referee's last words: "Is there anything that you'd like to say before we begin?"

Corey was quick to respond, "I'm going to kick your ass out to 35th Street and there ain't gonna be no cab waitin' to take you home, CHUMP!"

Referee admonished him for this and over the microphone told him that if he had nothing constructive to say, then he shouldn't say anything at all. The fighters returned to their corners to await the bell.

As each fighter sat on their stools, the trainers gave them the last minute gulp of water, applied Vaseline across their eyebrows and pulled open the front of their trunks to give them a moment to breathe, relax and get ready.

The bell rang and the two fighters approached each other center ring; the first round was always more or less feeling each other out, kind of breaking the ice, with a few jabs and posturing to get a feel for the other's style. It's very easy to change styles in a split second and each boxer had to gain a lot of education in a very short period of time.

So the first round was, for all intents and purposes, uneventful. Both boxers returned to their stools, a little bit more relaxed now that the hype was over, the cobwebs off and the boxing on. Johnny held the back of his hand under Bob's chin as he poured water into his mouth. Bob swished it around and spit it out into a bucket. More Vaseline was applied to his eyebrows, with Johnny giving his assessment of the first round.

"He's looking to set you up for that left jab. And

that left jab is a telegraph to a vicious right hook. You just keep on doing what we had planned, circling to his right, avoiding the left jab, and keep moving into the body when you get a chance to start working his arms and triceps."

Bob's breathing was still very even and his heart rate just right. At 183 pounds, Bob had six percent body fat. Although not as chiseled as Corey, he had a strong, broad back and well-toned arms. In addition to his boxing, one other thing that he concentrated on was endurance, and that meant staying up on his feet and moving constantly. He did a lot of roadwork and leg presses with heavy weights but his thighs and legs still needed more work. Not to worry about that now.

He did manage to catch a glancing blow off his right cheek when Corey was experimenting with his left hook. A little bit of swelling, but nothing to be concerned about. Jerry applied the cold iron press to the cheek and by the time the bell rang, it was just a memory.

It was the second round when the pace really started to pick up. Both fighters had their legs now and were delivering punches, putting the pressure on, and starting to execute their respective plans. Save for the fact that Corey's plan was without much thought due to his "extras."

Bob managed to get inside and started pummeling his stomach and his arms. He backed off, delivering two left jabs and a right hook that caught Corey on the side of the head. Stunned, but ever the arrogant asshole that he was, he smiled and shook his head to the crowd as if to say, "Nope, that was nothing; looked like a lot more than it was."

Yeah, sure, that didn't hurt, right? You bet your ass

it hurt. And Corey knew that he was in a real fight this time. Not some half assed journeymen Tommy always managed to arrange so Corey's record could maintain momentum. He managed to back Bob up against the ropes, stinging him with shots, but couldn't break through the cover-up that Bob had, surrounding his face with his forearms.

This went on for about thirteen seconds when Bob decided that Corey had spent enough gas and circled around and started his barrage. But the first part of the round when Bob was working the arms and shoulders as he and Johnny had planned, Corey's arms started feel like weights (yeah, no kidding, titanium weights!), and it was hard for him to cover up.

Bob started landing some good leather on Corey. Corey managed to break free, circle around to the center of the ring and open up with his jab to keep a healthy distance within arm's reach to be more effective. It was then that Bob let down his right guard for just a second and Corey came round and connected squarely on Bob's jaw. It felt like he was hit with a tire iron.

Bob had twenty-six professional fights under his belt and enough hours of sparring to equate to a contiguous six-month period of eight hour days. He got hit many times right on the button, but this impact was very, very different. It was a very distinct feeling of being hit with a ball peen hammer. This felt more like something was beneath the glove; hard, almost like steel. He could feel punctuated points of impact indenting his jaw. He was almost certain that it was either broken or fractured. It didn't feel right, something was terribly wrong.

The bell ended the second round and Bob returned to his corner and told Johnny of what he suspected. And although Corey's gloves had the initials of the official who was supposed to check that everything followed the rules, Bob spent enough hours boxing to know that there was something beneath the glove other than his fist.

Johnny called to the ref and explained his suspicions. He wanted the ref to do a hand press on the gloves to see if there was anything other than Corey's fists beneath them. If it were up to him, he would want the damn gloves taken off to see what was beneath.

The ref, who had been paid enough money by Tommy to buy that new boat he wanted, enough for down payment on a house, and then some, wasn't about to let any cat out of any bag. He refused to remove the gloves as Johnny wanted, but did go over to Corey's corner and asked them to hold out the gloves in front of him. He pressed on the gloves, squeezed the gloves and looked over at Johnny with an "I don't know what you're talking about" face and shrugged his shoulders. Johnny knew damn well what was going on. He most likely had titanium knuckle wraps strapped onto his hands under second and third layers of tape. Johnny had known of this before, but alas, could do nothing to prove it with so many of the governing forces on the take.

"I'm calling the fight, Bob. He's got a pair of knuckle wraps under the gloves and could end up fracturing your jaw, orbital lobes and anything else they come into contact with it. It is pretty plain to see that the authorities of the commission are not on our side. Let's end it before something regrettable happens."

"I'm pretty sure I have him worn down the way I had with Gary," Bob pleaded. "I need to stay away from his left hook, keep inside and keep working his torso. I think I could take it... the fight, I mean."

"This is insane!" Johnny exclaimed in a panic. "Bob, the fight is fixed! Can't you get that through that thick Spanish-Italian skull of yours? All it's going to take is one solid connection to your head and it's gonna fly off your shoulders. Please, there are people very high up in the commission in on this and will make a lot of money off your pain."

"I'm telling you, I can avoid being hit. I know I've got his upper shoulders and biceps worn."

There was a lot of activity in Corey's corner. Bill Farlow was serving a gulp of water, applying Vaseline to his eyebrows and then, strangely enough, Johnny observed, he reached inside behind his belt buckle with his thumb and then appeared to be rubbing something on Corey's left glove. Jesus Christ! He was putting something on Corey's glove. He was spiking the glove with something that would to end up in Bob's eyes!

Johnny was right. What Bill was applying was atropine, a chemical found in belladonna. This was an agent needed to dilate a patient's pupils before an eye examination and it dried instantly on Corey's glove. It would only be activated by the sweat off of Bob's brow and would very easily dilute and end up in Bob's eye. There was no real pain or irritation, but intensely blurred vision. The chemical instantly dried on Corey's gloves when Johnny objected and called the referee over to the corner.

"The son of a bitch rubbed something on his

gloves," shouted Johnny at the referee. "How much money does it take to do something?"

The referee gave him an angry look, called a timeout and once again went to Corey's corner to examine his gloves. The ref wouldn't ordinarily do this, but he was getting nervous and needed to make it all look legit. Corey held up both gloves in front of him and the ref ran his fingers across both gloves. He sniffed both, then looked up toward Bob's corner and shook his head at Johnny as if to say, "What is it that you think I'm supposed to find?"

Why am I wasting my breath? Johnny thought. *The fight is fixed.*

"I'm calling the fight, Bob. I'm serious. That moron just rubbed something on Corey's left glove that's going to end up in your eye and do God knows what."

"But, Johnny, the ref just checked his glove. I think you're focusing too much on the fact that this fight might be fixed. This is a championship fight and it's supposed to be clean. I know you don't think I'm ready for this, but I am, Johnny. Just give me a chance."

Before Johnny could object, the bell sounded for the opening of the third round. His mouth was still open at Bob's naivety when both fighters rose from their stools and met the center of the ring. For a split second, Bob noticed a strange look in Corey's eyes. It was rage, with the fierce determination he'd seen so many times in a boxer's eyes, but if Bob's imagination wasn't running away from him, it almost appeared as though Corey was going to spring a surprise on him, a very brutal surprise. He had that "cat that just ate the bird" smirk on his face.

With both fighters now warmed up, the action

started to pick up markedly. Bob kept on circling to Corey's right, continuing to avoid his left jab and working the body according to plan. Corey was fast and getting off jabs into Bob's right eye.

And, as predicted, the sweat poured down from his brow and interacted with the atropine coating, causing it to execute on target. Within seconds, the vision in his right eye was so blurred that all he could see where lights and shadows. As instructed, Corey started to circle to Bob's right, out of his field of vision. Now he was able to take right hooks at will.

Bob didn't really know what to do to counter the situation. He knew he was getting hit and getting hit hard. He tried to back up but that didn't do any good. Bob crouched low and tried to work the body. Corey backed off, wound up and slammed him across the left temple, the force of the knuckle rap coming into full contact with bone. All of Bob's nerve endings short-circuited and he went crashing down to the canvas.

The ref stood over him and started the ten count. He felt like he had been hit with a piece of iron, not a fist encased in a padded twelve ounce glove. His hot breath went right up into his face as his mouth was flat on the canvas. Through the haze of semi-consciousness, he could hear Johnny from the corner. The ref continued his count as Bob felt himself drift into unconsciousness.

GAME OVER!

The ref could have counted to thirty, but Bob wasn't getting up. The force of titanium steel separated by what amounted to three quarters of an inch of padding, as well as the velocity of the punch and the inertia behind the glove, rendered him immobile.

The bell chimed three times to signal the end of the fight. Corey Green was now light heavyweight champion, punctuating it by leaning over Bob, running his glove across his throat and then, shockingly, spitting on him.

Medics rushed into the ring, turning Bob on his back and giving him oxygen while putting his head in a neck brace. His body was snapping with rhythmic convulsions. The ring doctor entered the ring to examine Bob and instantly knew from the shape of the contusion on his left temple that something wasn't right. What would later be found through X-Rays and an MRI was that the left side of Bob's skull had hairline fractures in three distinct places, equidistant from each other and pulverizing the bone. At that moment, other than the medics, the doctor was the only person in the ring who was not involved in the fix. And it didn't take too long for him to realize that this was not a fair fight. But the first order of business was getting this boy out of here and into a hospital.

Johnny was livid and scared at the same time for his friend. He felt partially responsible, not stopping the fight after the second round. But, with no conclusive evidence and Bob's unchallenged determination, the third round began and ended for Bob in darkness.

CHAPTER 14

Bob slowly opened his eyes, the right side of his head feeling like somebody punched a hole in it with a nail from a pneumatic gun. He slowly began to focus, but his right eye was still blurry. He started to wiggle his feet under the tightly wrapped hospital sheets. A very worried Johnny Wells was sitting at the left side of his bed. The man was clearly upset.

"Look at this x-ray! Look at it!" Johnny was waving an 11-by-14 inch film panel in front of his face.

Bob was startled by this. "What are you talking about, Johnny?"

"What am I talking about? That dick had something under his glove! You don't get a contusion on the side of your head causing hairline fractures in concentric groups of three by a fist covered with twelve-ounce gloves. Even the doctor made the same comment. He's examined a lot of fighters who were brought to the hospital and had never seen anything like this before. He's convinced that there was something harder underneath Corey's glove that caused this damage. I filed a complaint with the commission and want a further investigation into this. The chump could have killed you, Bob. And I'll tell you what else. The doctor found a dilating agent called atropine in your right eye. Unless you decided to have an eye exam immediately before the fight, the only other way this got into your eye was from Corey's left glove! I saw his trainer slip something on. I complained, but the ref was conveniently deaf. You won't be able to see clearly out of that eye for days."

"Well, if all this is true, wouldn't this serve as hard evidence that the fight was fixed like you said?"

"How naïve can you possibly be? You know this shit goes on all the time, Bob. There are people on the commission, the referee and certainly the promoters all on the 'payroll'. The authorities that are supposed to protect the sport are the ones who stole your belt away from you. And there's not a goddamn thing we can do about it. I might as well piss in the wind rather than think my complaint is even going to reach the commission. And I bet good money Steve Shelby is behind all of this. Max Keller's trainer was right when he screamed, 'We was robbed'."

All this started to click in Bob's mind. With the half-dozen monitors blinking around his bed, it was the one registering his blood pressure that started to rise. He could feel the anger traveling from his chest right up to his head, which only exacerbated the throbbing. His face grew flush at the whole idea. He worked hard for that belt, only to have it ripped away using tactics that reduced the integrity and dignity of the sport to a joke. And he was the joke: flat on his face on the canvas after being jack-hammered like an animal into the dirt.

The morphine drip made him both nauseous and woozy. Succumbing to the latter, he involuntarily drifted into unconsciousness. In the wild collage of dreams, he felt he was being punished and chased like an animal in the woods. He was being hunted down and made to run away from something he craved and was almost willing to die for.

Johnny could see Bob's brow furrow with stress in

his unconscious state. It made him sick to his stomach. It was as though somebody died and the grieving would never end. Johnny thought about his grandfather back in the days when fights were probably also fixed, but how he trained his fighters to be clean sportsmen. He was not naïve enough to believe, especially in those days of bare knuckle fighting, that someone didn't have a roll of quarters wrapped up in their hand.

He looked down at Bob and wanted to hurt someone. He wanted to make somebody feel the pain his friend was experiencing now, to make them feel the anguish and shame of what they did to him.

An eye for an eye, my ass, Johnny thought as he walked into the hallway looking for a coffee machine.

CHAPTER 15

Of the 3,500 residents of the Upper 14, 3,000 made it across the Straits to Svenkia Islands that night. The next day the rain had stopped and the sun was shining brightly. The temperature rose a little bit and it almost felt like spring; "Indian Summer," the Americans called it. People were scattered all over the countryside with their blankets and small belongings. Babies cried in the distance, and people moaned from their broken or sprained ankles from crossing the mossy slick rocks.

With blankets spread before them to dry in the afternoon sun, it appeared almost like one huge picnic to Natalia. She missed her parents and Luther, and started to call out the names. This only added to the chorus of parents who were separated from their children, screaming hysterically trying to find them.

It reminded Natalia of a TV documentary she once saw about penguins. The mother penguins waddled or slid on their stomachs for miles to reach the sea and then brought back food to regurgitate for the young chicks. When the mothers returned, they had to find their chicks in a sea of thousands. They somehow knew by instinct how to find them. She hoped this was true of humans. Her friend's mother was also looking for her children.

Sergei was mayor of the seventh province, a born leader who often counseled mayors of the other provinces. He had good tactical skills and excellent leadership qualities. He also served as treasurer for Upper 14 provinces in the collection of the obscene taxes they had to pay the government. Since he handled the finances, he had a ledger of the names of all the families that had to pay taxes. During the visit by the soldiers to his house, amidst the barrage of gunfire running across the ceiling and shattering his wife's antique plates, he had the presence of mind to bring that ledger and a bullhorn with him.

The guy was incredible. He knew that there was going to be pandemonium once they reached wherever they were being exiled to and there would be a need to get organized. He knew that there was no turning back across the Straits to go back home. The guards had set up quite a blockade at the mouth of the Straits on the other side.

As government-sponsored cameras were rolling, several Humvees crossed over the Straits during low tide and delivered sacks of oatmeal, rice and other starch byproducts. Crogan wanted to make certain the world saw that he was taking care of his people. He was "saddened" that he had to evacuate these fine people from their "homes due to a contaminated water table." The showing up of what would be one delivery of food would be the last of the press releases and last hope for survival of these people.

Sergei found the highest hill in the immediate area and turned on his bullhorn.

"Well, it seems like our president thinks we're not worthy of occupying the land we had settled in; that we're not human beings and are to be treated like animals. We've no choice now but to survive. And survive we will. We come from an ancestry of strong-willed people with the desire to live. We're a very proud people, a very intelligent people, and we will overcome this through our own ingenuity. It's going to be hard for a while, a long while, but, as I said, we will survive."

"The Svenkia Islands had been host to our ancestors and now we return to the land where we were born. If they can do it, so can we. We need to get organized. The first step is to provide immediate shelter for ourselves, sources of water and, most importantly, find your family members. The scraps the soldiers threw us will not last us very long. Surely word will get out to the international community of this travesty and there will be some type of aid."

Sergei didn't realize the "humanitarian" act by their president would be shown to the rest of the world to prove they were now safe from contaminated water and were being cared for.

"But, in the meantime, we have to make sure we are safe and secure. We need to break up into functional groups for shelter, water, food and the general care for our children, our poor children, who will grow up the victims of a cruel and deranged dictator."

The people of the Upper 14 weren't lacking in talent. Although they weren't allowed to attend university in the Lower 43, they had, over the years, established their own university system. Some even went outside the Chevkan borders to continue their studies.

These were very hard-working and intelligent people and they knew education was a much-needed weapon in their arsenal. The people of the Upper 14 had architects, electricians, engineers, plumbers, biologists and a host of other professions that businesses and institutions of the Lower 43 would have found invaluable, especially at the pitiful going rates they earned for the non-related jobs they worked.

The geniuses of the Lower 43 didn't know the

caliber of valuable resources they had at their disposal. Nor did the people of the Upper 14 let them know of such. It was bad enough that they had to pay exorbitant taxes and give up some of their produce for free, much less give the aristocrats access to the intellectual property they had worked so hard to attain. This was their secret, something they held sacred, and the only source of pride within what amounted to an ugly caste system.

It certainly wasn't pleasant living in a country where their presence was looked upon as an unwelcomed part of the landscape. Proud or not, it hurt. And being thrust from their homes and driven like cattle and thrown onto the island was the last straw. There was no turning back, no negotiating and no chance of returning to their homes. It was a too frightening to think about.

Evstafii was an architect who studied in London and brought his ideas and dreams back to Chevka. Evstafii was very much influenced by Frank Lloyd Wright's integration of marrying a living structure into hillsides and other contours of nature. He was fascinated by the fact that a fully functional home could become part of the landscape. The designs were not homes violating the nature around them, but nature embracing the home. He designed some of the buildings and homes, albeit modest, that scattered the landscape and small semi-metropolitan areas of the Upper 14.

With what little tools some had brought with them, he started to direct the cutting down of branches, stripping bark and instructing people on how to build small triangular shaped huts, leaving holes at the top for the exhaust of fires. The sidings were draped with leaves of smaller branches. As the men attended to this, the women broke open the sacks of oatmeal and rice the soldiers left behind. It was time to stop dying and start living again.

CHAPTER 16

Water was becoming an increasingly valuable commodity than just quenching the occasional thirst. As efforts hastened and bodies heated up building shelters, there was more desire for water.

Most were looking for small puddles or troughs that accumulated some of the snow and rain water. This proved especially dangerous, as the water could have been contaminated with any number of things. There were, after all, other life forms on the islands other than themselves; there were animals of various species, all with bowel movements and no particular preference as to where they relieved themselves. As a result, snow and rain runoff into these puddles carried with it varied forms of bacteria, increasing the risk of diarrhea and other related diseases.

Hepatitis A and E are transmitted through the fecal-oral route and are primarily due to a lack of proper sanitation infiltration facilities for water purification. Hepatitis E is generally mild and self-limited, but could prove fatal to pregnant women, increasing the mortality rate to ten percent.

Given the state of what these people had just been through, running through brush, tripping over stones along and the occasional beating from rifle butts compliments of the Guard, their bodies hosted multiple lacerations and were an open invitation to disease.

Cholera and other macrobiotic and infectious organisms were literally fighting for room in the puddles into which people were now cupping their hands and scooping up water to their mouths.

People were quenching their thirst from their hard work building temporary shelters and, in a couple of days, they started to feel the effects of the-gut wrenching microbes that were now invading their bodies. More than seventy-five percent were now experiencing severe diarrhea, which only served to dehydrate them even faster. Small children were suffering the most, as their defense systems were still developing and not used to the physical and emotional hardship.

As there was no established sanitation and waste system awaiting them after being kicked off their own property onto these barren islands, their own need for relieving waste was only making the situation a festering petri dish. There was no one clean unobstructed source of water… anywhere.

Within days, the strength was being sucked out of most people and the urgency of their survival was seriously increased. Each day that was not productive was bringing them closer to the day they wouldn't be able to survive. They were still in shock from the surreal and brutal ousting just a few days before and when the shock wore off, it was replaced by panic of the gravity of their situation.

Drinking contaminated water also increased the propensity for shigellosis and typhoid fever. The pathetic outcome was that some did contract some of the above where a few, the elderly and, in some cases, infants, succumbed to some lethal strain of bacteria, marking the islands' first funerals.

What few doctors did make it over had only their hands and knowledge to try and help the infected populace. They clearly didn't have the medication to help fight this overwhelming plague that was immediately challenging their survival. It was only when some heads started to clear, one of which belong to Prokhor, a biologist, that a proactive course of action began.

Prokhor had started to instruct people to build fires and boil their water in addition to using any type of cloth to pour the water through in the guise of primitive water filtration. Also with a little ingenuity, burned firewood served as charcoal also used in the filtration of water. It was crude and didn't eliminate the presence of macrobiotic disease entirely, but it at least arrested most new occurrences of disease.

Coming from civilized suburban and rural environments, these people weren't used to having to go through an operation for something they normally just went to their sink and turned on the faucet for. This was only a few of the taken for granted conveniences they would suffer without in the weeks and months to come.

CHAPTER 17

As small stick shelters were starting to take form and scatter across the landscape, Evstafii went from camp to camp, dispensing instruction and advice, and helping put together what would be temporary shelter against the wind and rain and allow a small fire to the ventilated hollow cone of the shelter.

For some, in a strange way, it seemed natural building these primitive shelters, almost like it was some sort of embedded gene that had been tucked away in their DNA for centuries. This translated into the spirit of challenge where the pace for survival started to pick up rhythm and ripple through the crowd.

The unseasonable temperatures of this brief Indian Summer seemed as though it was God's tiny gift to give them time to position themselves for survival. The shouts, screams and cries seemed to subside; a murmur of conversation and even occasional laughter periodically pierced the oppressive veil of hopelessness hanging over them.

To some, this was still surreal and it hadn't really hit home that if they wanted a loaf of bread, they couldn't hop in the car and go to the corner supermarket. If they wanted something to cook for the evening, they couldn't go to a store like Uncle Elizar's to pick up fresh meat. Or, God forbid, they had a toothache; where was the dentist's office? Sure, there were dentists somewhere, but only a few took a collection of basic instruments; pulling teeth would replace drilling and filling a cavity.

All these small amenities they had taken for granted

were now gone. Questions like this were spinning around Sergei's mind: how to map out and triage the bare essentials, the feasibility of finding them and setting up an organization that they could function with.

Joining up with family members was the first order of business for everybody. As the soldiers ransacked their houses, people were scattered across the countryside, running for their lives. The air was filled with people shouting the names of their husband, their children, their loved ones. As these primitive shelters were now in place, the first order of business was for families to reunite and consolidate and/or share whatever belongings they had brought between them.

It was when Kristanf rounded small knoll of a hill that he heard his wife Irinia's calls for Natalia and Luther.

"Irinia!" shouted Kristanf.

"Kristanf, over here!"

"Good God, I thought I'd never find you. Are you all right?"

"Yes, I'm fine. It's the children I'm worried sick about. I've got to know if Natalia and Luther are okay. Luther is a strong boy and can take care of himself, but it's Natalia I worry about the most."

Kristanf answered immediately, "Let's go over to the shore break where we first came over and retrace her steps. We'll span out. I'll go to the left, you go to the right and we'll agree to meet at a point higher up on the hill behind those large trees. If that doesn't work, we'll try starting from another point with the same method. Don't worry, sweetheart, we'll find them."

And so they moved down to the point in which they

first came over and panned out, Kristanf calling Natalia's name, Irinia shouting out Luther's.

But Kristanf and Irinia didn't realize that they would be finding only one of their children. They were always amused by Luther's kindred spirit and outspokenness. Even at fourteen years old, he had very strong views of his community, the government and the world at large. He was of the new generation, they thought, not satisfied with the immediate world around them, but wanted to expand and see the rest of the world and bring back a treasure of experiences to possibly make a difference in their hometowns.

They were proud of him and knew he would do great things in life. But, unfortunately, it was this kindred spirit that proved to be deadly. They would later find out from a neighbor who was close by of Luther's altercation with one of the soldiers. The night before, when soldiers were bullying his friends and neighbors across the Straits, was when Luther's youthful impatience had quite enough. If they weren't brutalized by the butt of the soldier's rifle, they were killed because they weren't moving quickly enough with children's wailing screams as witness; he couldn't take anymore.

He picked up a smooth, oval-shaped stone from the now exposed pathway and threw it squarely at a soldier's head. He caught the soldier under his right cheek, rewarded with a cut followed by the splatter of blood. Luther was both exhilarated and scared shitless, while his youthful defiance made him feel proud all the same. He didn't have time to fear the consequences when the soldier raised his weapon and put a .30 caliber bullet through his breastbone and out his back. The soldier was so close and the impact so devastating, there was now a hole the size of a softball in Luther's chest where his heart used to be. The impact hurled him back, feet leaving the ground, and dead before he returned back to the tundra.

One of the running neighbors, Sof'ya, who was rather friendly with Irinia, witnessed the whole grisly encounter. She ran to his side to see if she could help, but a bullet passing three inches away from her left ear and into Luther's left temple made her back up and momentarily re-consider. The guard was not satisfied with mangling the boy with the first shot, but further memorialized the killing by putting a bullet through the dead boy's brain.

People continued to run past the kneeling Sof'ya and dead Luther, looking down and feeling utter helplessness. Having children herself, she knew she had to take some article off Luther's body to serve as a keepsake of his mere fourteen years on this earth. Knowing this warning shot would soon be followed by a crack in the back of the head, she frantically looked over his body for anything to take and then keep running. It would be hard for the time she had to undress him for some part of clothing. So she looked for the closest thing she could remove with the few precious seconds she had. She took his left shoe. It slipped off easily and she stuffed it in the breast pocket of her overcoat began to run, but she slipped and fell. She picked herself up and then looked toward running across the Straits. But before she did, she felt compelled to look back at the grinning soldier as the moonlight flashed over his silver ID tag, "5432."

Chevkan soldiers lost their identity when recruited

into the Guard. Their heads were shaved, their names replaced with silver ID tags and they became a unified unit of discipline, control and, in this case, death. This tag was easy enough to remember, as it was in sequence and, ironically, added up to Luther's age, fourteen. It had no more relevance to her than that.

Brandished in her mind nonetheless, she started a wobbly run that turned into a sprint toward the other side. Luther's body laid not thirty feet out onto the Straits where, in a couple of hours when the tide came in, his remains would float out into the Arctic sea, serving the food chain of killer whales and sharks. They would make good use of his remains. It was only with God's good grace that Kristanf and Irinia didn't have to see this.

Kristanf and Irinia's first attempt at their plan of panning out and reconvening produced no results. So they picked another point and panned out again, calling out the names of their children for what seemed like hours. It was starting to get dark and their chances of a productive search were waning with the fall of evening.

They decided to join a man and his sister in one of the homemade shelters. They had a fire going, boiling a pot of rice, and offered them what little they could spare due to miscalculated allocations. When they entered the hut, Natalia, dirty and worn, was sitting on a bed of dry grass with dirty streaks of tears staining her cheeks. The sister was the neighbor who grabbed Natalia to run across the Straits that fateful night. Nothing could have been better than for Irinia to see her daughter alive and, for the most part, well.

She still had a very sick sense about Luther. She

didn't know why, just that he wasn't part of the picture in her mind of reuniting with her children. She tried desperately to erase this image from her mind, but it just grew worse the harder she tried. Exhausted from the previous night's exile and emotionally drained, she laid down next to Natalia and fell into a disturbed and fitful sleep. Kristanf held her and felt the twitching in her body.

It's going to be a long night, he thought.

He was too worried and protective of his wife to even feel like sleeping. The night was growing dark, bringing along with it a chill in the air that would surely challenge the warmer weather hereon after. Through Evstafii's efforts and his tireless assistance with people, most had a modicum of comfort and warmth. But there were plenty others who still didn't finish their shelters and were wrapped in their blankets and sleeping close to one another to keep warm. All through the feelings of helplessness and hopelessness, and the impending hardships that would leave some ill and some dead, they didn't realize that this would turn into a better life than they ever thought possible.

CHAPTER 18

The doctor made it clear that Bob needed to get up the second day.

Got to get the old blood moving.

He urged himself from his hospital bed at NYU Medical Center. His head still throbbed, but although the X-ray showed multiple hairline fractures in his skull, he was young and quick to heal. But the doctor also made it very clear that Bob was not to even look at a boxing ring for the next four months, minimum. And Johnny would see to that.

Johnny also wanted to keep him away from the TV just in case there were highlights of the fight. He couldn't bear to watch Bob see the image of himself getting pummeled by a cheater. What really irked him was at the very authority that was supposed to protect the fairness and safety of the sport was the same authoritative body that stripped Bob unfairly of what was his. What he worked so hard for over the last six years. There was no one to cry foul. He was tossed aside like garbage, risking his life and taking a battering to line the purses of these bastards.

Bob almost felt like crying. This well-orchestrated assassination only served to rub the raw nerve of rejection he had carried around with him throughout his career, and his personal life, for that matter. They more or less plotted against him and treated him like some worthless piece of garbage. He hated himself for feeling this way. After all, they didn't play by the rules; they used lethal methods to make a mockery of him.

As far as the fans could see, Corey put on a great

performance and made Bob appear an imposter; the victim of Corey's "greatness." It was this greatness that Corey was reiterating out to the press after the fight. Usually the other fighter got a chance at the microphone, but Bob was on his way to the hospital, fading in and out of consciousness. It certainly wasn't front page news, but it was still in the sports section. They showed a picture of Bob face down on the canvas and Corey with his arms raised and grinning at the camera. At the press conference after the fight, Corey made it clear who the real champ was.

"I beat the chump so bad, he still can't speak. He told 'Mama' that if he didn't win a championship by his sixth year as a professional, baby boy will be running home to her and going back to school where he'll be safe. What kind of man lets his mother tell him what to do? He's a mama's boy and doesn't belong in the ring with a real man like me. Maybe his mama should fight me. Or better yet, maybe his mama should spend the night with me and see what a real man's like."

This was exactly what Johnny didn't want Bob to see. But it was too late. As Johnny walked into the room, he saw Bob sitting at the edge of his bed, watching a replay on NBC of the news conference Corey commandeered after the fight. He just sat there, blood rising up his neck into his head. He wanted so badly for a fair fight to see what the asshole could do with his own hands without the knuckle wrap and atropine. The thought kept on repeating in his head as to how life could be so unfair and strip him of what was rightfully his. He felt like a prisoner whose basic human rights were taken away from him. All avenues to correct this were shut down and controlled by a bunch of crooks. Who could he go to? Who could he go to who would listen to him, believe him and do something about it?

"How's that cinderblock sitting on top your shoulders you call a head feeling?" Johnny asked, trying to lighten the mood a little bit.

"I'll make it. I think I'm going to like the four months off. I'll finish my Master's and maybe look for a job. Right now, boxing is an organization that's controlled by a crooked commission and makes me sick to my stomach."

"I don't blame you," Johnny agreed. "And Bob, there's not a thing I can do about it. From what some insiders have told me, there are three members of the commission who are actively collaborating with the promoter, the managers, the referees and all the other officials on the payroll. I can understand you not wanting to have anything to do what makes boxing a disgrace. But do you really want to give it up? Don't you really want to give yourself some time to think about this? I think you do."

"Yeah, as always Johnny, filled with good sense, dispensing wise advice, you're probably right. Giving up now is letting them win. And you know me well enough to know that I'm not the kind to run from a fight. But when you fight in the dark against somebody with night vision, you'd have to fight dirty. You have to have something up your sleeve, or, in this case, in or on your glove to stand even a chance of coming out ahead. I'm not that kind of man, but in the same sense, hopefully not too naïve in believing the truth is the right thing to do, either. Right now I'm hurt, disillusioned and feeling like I've been kicked to the curb."

Bob changed out of his hospital nightgown into his jeans and sweatshirt and was already starting to feel better. They gathered the rest of his clothes in a duffel bag and waited for the doctor to sign him out.

Since this was his first title defense, coupled with the mediocre marketing on Clive's part, he drew $750,000 for his part of the fight. Corey's draw was $500,000. In 1979, this was good coin for a fighter. Corey, of course, made this clear at the press conference that this was insulting and he should have made double what Bob had been paid.

Bob returned to his apartment later that afternoon and sat down at his typewriter to edit the fourth version of his thesis. This was before the advent of a PC "in every garage" and Word Perfect "in every pot." His thesis was to be incorporated into a book, with other members of his classmates each contributing a chapter. Each time Bob submitted what he hoped was his final version, Dr. Dick Lips would find something in the news he felt was worthwhile to include (one hair away from strangling his professor, Bob eventually had his fifth draft approved… asshole).

These four months would be good for him. He could focus on his "other life." He was glad that he was talked into returning to graduate school by his parents. Even when fighting as a professional, he liked the idea of using his mind and expressing his thoughts. He did rather well in graduate school and enjoyed the challenge of building up his mind like he was building up his body.

His thesis was on product liability, the damage

caused by faulty products and the resulting award by the courts to the victim in compensating for their punitive and painful loss. He researched over 102 court cases in the university library, dating back to 1920, where injuries included anything from a small scratch on the hand to maybe losing a finger, losing a limb and, of course, the ultimate damage, death.

Professor Ashton required he write a small computer program correlating the injury to the monetary award of the lawsuit. This was kind of testing the courts to see what level of social morality prevailed when presented a lawsuit involving a person who was injured as a result of using a product. Bob got a big kick out of some of the cases that were the result of using the product and incurring injury where there was a "loss of consortium."

There was one court case about a woman who was waxing her kitchen floor, where it was later determined the viscosity rate of the wax she was using was above what the industry considered safe. She slipped, fell on her tailbone and was laid up for weeks (no pun intended; you'll see). She claimed that she could not make love to her husband for two months. She also claimed that this caused unusual stress on their marriage. As a result of not being able to get laid, she was awarded $800,000.

Although he was twenty-six, he was so involved with his career that he had limited interaction with the opposite sex. The rule that you're not to have sex two months before the fight led to several dry spells, which served to define the use of the word "testy." Given this, he couldn't quite understand why someone would be awarded $800,000 just because she couldn't point her ankles east and west and let Daddy-O bring his ship into port for only two months!

He compared this to another court case where a man operating a lathe machine got his wedding ring stuck on one of the fixtures and ended up losing his finger (and the wedding ring didn't fare too well, either). This poor sucker was only awarded $27,000! Sure, this guy could still poke his wife, but he lost an appendage he was born with! Was $27,000 going to bring back his finger?

With these kinds of statistics, the resulting correlation coefficient was thirty-two percent. This only managed to ignite Bob's anger as to how unfair the world could be.

If you have the right strength and talent behind you in the form of a lawyer, it isn't a matter how severe the injury is, it's a matter of which slick lawyer is representing you.

There is no equation of fairness in this world, Bob thought. This was clearly evident two weeks ago.

His train of thought was suddenly interrupted, "Hey, Rip Van Winkle, you think you can keep your head up long enough to finish your reading?"

"Only if you can keep your fucking mouth shut!"

"You should learn how to duck, or else you'll never get anything done."

"And you should learn some manners, and I guarantee you, you don't want me as a teacher."

Everyone knew he was a professional boxer and could not fight in public; it was against the law. This idiot knew that and thought he could taunt Bob as much he wanted and he couldn't lay a finger on him. But when somebody threatened first, sure, by all means; that was self-defense. Bob was not in a very diplomatic mood and would enjoy bouncing this idiot off the ceiling. But since this was out of question, continuing this conversation would only make him needlessly angry. So he decided to let it go and kept on reading.

"I would want a teacher who was smart, but how smart can you be if you get knocked on your ass?"

Bob continued reading with the gauges in his boiler room rising quickly. He was ridiculed once, embarrassed beyond his own comfort threshold and was not going to put himself in a position for a repeat. Losing his temper and nailing this asshole into the floor would land him in jail. What good would that do?

The other guy got up out of his chair and walked over to Bob. "I guess you didn't hear me, shithead. I want a smart teacher, not a loser like you."

Bob made a sudden movement toward him, without touching him, of course making him jump a foot in the air. The other students in the library started to giggle. The guy's face turned flush and, with that, forgetting who Bob was, did what he had done so many times in the past to others less fortunate and swatted Bob in the back of the head.

Oh, thank you, Jesus! He hit me first; got to protect myself, you know; self-defense.

Bob rose out of his chair and the other guy took a second swing at him. A classic mistake. Bob ducked the other guy's swing into the air, leaving the latter's face fully exposed. Bob cocked back his arm like a piston and, like a jackhammer, piled it right into the guy's nose, cleanly breaking it in two places. The giggling stopped abruptly, turning to gasps. The guy fell to his knees, blood gushing from his nose, holding onto the back of the chair to keep his equilibrium.

"I really, really wish you would've just stayed in your seat and minded your own business. Class dismissed."

Bob gathered up his books and turned toward the door, looking back at the poor slob, feeling a little guilty and somewhat shallow, as this episode proved nothing. He did not win a fight. He did not get his belt back. He laid some idiot out on the floor, accomplishing nothing. He got in his car and drove through the university exit, feeling even more worthless that he had to compromise his dignity and hurt someone he had no business dealing with in the first place.

Maybe he wasn't meant to be a fighter. Maybe his parents were right and this was a lifelong dream that he realized and even became champion for short while.

Maybe it was better this way.

CHAPTER 19

Bob was settling in with the New York Times when he came across the article about the people of Chevka being moved to the Svenkia Islands. It mentioned that these people had been moved from the mainland due to a contaminated water system, but the article also expressed suspicion that these people were moved against their own will to clear the way for coal extraction. He had been subconsciously following this story when he first heard a short report on the car radio on the way to class one afternoon. Then catching glimpses on the evening news by in-studio anchors (they weren't allowed anywhere near the islands) served to stoke the fire growing inside of Bob. The in depth article in the Times that morning brought all this bubbling to the surface.

The article had some of Dimitrii's quotes about his reason for moving these people and how he would "take good care of them". Being the New York Times and having access to information they did, they discovered there was only one delivery of food and the border crossing on the other Chevka side of the Straits was heavily armed with no passage back. This business about contaminated water tables was obviously a lie.

These people had been forced from their homes at gunpoint into a cold and rainy night, driven back to the Svenkia Islands, the homeland of their ancestors. Although the soldiers made it quick business to collect the bodies of the people they killed, dig a mass grave and covered them up very quickly, it did not escape making the news. These people had been robbed and ripped from the very being of their existence that they worked so hard for. There was no recourse, no authority to rely on to and have this injustice overturned.

They were suffering and denied the basic amenities of life. They were cold, they were starving and many other family members were still missing and separated from each other. It was obvious that these people were being treated like animals in the most inhumane atrocity since the mass genocide of World War II.

The reporter managed to get on the island by bribing a pilot on the mainland to cross over and land on a "runway" of an extremely firm grassy plain. Sergei had discovered this stretch of hard packed dirt; ten to fifteen feet below its surface was bedrock. It was about a mile and a half wide and almost three miles long. Sergei had traced his steps, pounding his feet into the surface and realizing it almost felt like concrete. There were some very slight inclines and declines, the degree of which made for a bit of a bumpy landing, but a reliable landing nonetheless.

The reporter from the Times had discovered this reality from a colleague who worked in the American Embassy in Russia. Though what he was being told was second and third hand information, it was still intriguing enough to pursue. Once landing in Chevka, he had been given the name of a contact who would put him in connection with a pilot who would fly into hell and back for the right price.

As this was still a very sensitive situation, the pilot practically did not stop when the door opened and the reporter jumped down, and then immediately took off again. This was a political hotbed and the pilot didn't want his registration number alongside the tail of his plane to be readily recognizable.

He couldn't believe his eyes. People were scattered about, living in the little huts, much like prehistoric times. People were cooking on open fires, with small chunks of meat skewered and turned over the fire (Uncle Elizar had formed a group of hunters, which started to forage the meat of local game from the surrounding forests). It was like a scene from *Braveheart*.

Muddy and lumpy paths had been forged by people's footsteps and the few horses that managed to get over the Straits. He began immediately going from camp to camp, speaking with the few people who know English and getting the story firsthand. This was news, big news, and something the world needed to hear about.

He took quite a few pictures, which accompanied the article that Bob was reading now. They were not pretty. People bent over fires, children crying and dark overcast skies made him shiver.

This made a direct hit on Bob's central nervous system. How cruel to take these people and throw them in the dirt with practically nothing on their backs and very little to go on surviving. Bob couldn't think of anything more heinous than a leader of a country ostracizing the very people who settled that land.

Bob studied each of the pictures, especially of one woman, and could feel her pain and hopelessness. There was nowhere to turn, no one to go to for help when the rest of the international community felt that since this was not their local government, it was none of their business.

The more he read, the more flushed with anger he

became. Bob thought putting a bullet through the head of the maniac they called a president would be too good for him. What sweeter victory would there be if these people came out victors at the expense and disgrace of this idiot?

Bob put down the paper and paced back and forth in his apartment, frustrated and angry. It was though it was done to him personally. He was surprised by his reaction and the more he thought of these people, the angrier he got and the more motivated he became to do something about it. But what could he do? What could he possibly do to help 3,000 people live again, have roofs over their heads, faucets to turn water on, warm beds and a place to be happy? Who the hell did he think he was, Houdini? It was a stupid idea, but he couldn't shake it.

He was only two weeks into his four-month hiatus from the ring and already he was getting anxious to work out. Just the fact that he knew that he wouldn't be facing an opponent and pounding somebody into submission fueled the growing anxiety inside him. He needed an outlet, no question about it. But this and the article he just read and how he reacted to it made for one very angry twenty-six-year-old professional prize fighter.

Bob called Johnny later on that evening. "Johnny, I'm taking a trip to the Svenkia Islands."

"Where?"

"The Svenkia Islands, genius. It's a little smidgen of land off the coast of Chevka. If you read the newspaper today, if you ever got past the funnies, you would have seen an article about a group of people in Chevka who were forced out of the country across a cobblestone and gravel straight to an abandoned island with practically nothing on their backs."

"So what does that have to do with you?"

"I, I don't know, Johnny. For some reason I find this almost personally offensive. I mean, I don't know these people. I even didn't know what the Svenkia Islands were until I read this article. Johnny, these people were ripped out of their homes while they were eating dinner, for God's sake! People were shot because they couldn't keep up with the other people running, scared beyond reason, for the coastline under the gunfire of their own Republic Guard regimens. There were children still running around with nothing but a blanket wrapped around them, looking for their parents. People who just managed to get across the street without being shot in the back of the head are suffering and in need of medical attention. No organization wants to become involved in the situation because this is a private matter between the government and its people. The very authority that is supposed to govern and protect them is the very one that threw them out the door into the cold."

"So, again, I ask you, what the hell does this have to do with you, Bob?"

"Johnny, I want to go there to see what I can do. For some reason I can't sit back and know that these people are being denied something that is rightfully theirs, and doesn't even remotely belong to anybody or anything else. It's just something I have to do. And since I have four months off, I guess I'll be using my time productively."

"Want to know how to use your time productively? Have your fucking head examined. You cram your ass in some puddle jumper and land on an island that has nothing and expect to create something? What is it and exactly how is it that you feel you can accomplish this?"

"I don't know, Johnny, I just don't know. But I'm going."

CHAPTER 20

As the plane was making its approach to Chevkan National Airport, Bob noticed that there weren't any really large metropolitan areas, but a collection of tiny villages dotting the landscape. He had made arrangements to meet up with the same rogue bush pilot who ferried the reporter across as he landed at the airport so he could hop over to the Svenkia Islands. He was astonished to find that some people on the plane actually recognized him and had the courtesy of congratulating him on a good fight, even though he lost to Corey.

The plane touched down with a thump and it was only a few minutes until they were taxing to the small airport terminal. He met up with Jeff Lawson, an American bush pilot, and after exchanging a few pleasantries, they were on their way to the islands.

The plane took off under heavy overcast and the entire flight lasted a little over thirty-five minutes. He still couldn't quite figure out why he was on this plane and going to an island of exiled people he didn't even know. He was still trying to figure out why he had such an obsession for something that had nothing to do with him. All he knew was that some fat, overstuffed dictator thought of these people as worthless and threw them across the water onto a pile of land that had nothing to offer but wildlife and despair.

Jeff filled him in more about what happened and what conditions these people were currently in. He also explained the prejudice they had endured from the people of the Lower 43 and progressed with an explanation of the fifty-seven provinces, and how the fourteen uppermost provinces held people who first settled Chevka and were now considered outcasts by the rest of the populace.

"What possessed this guy to be so cruel to people of his own country?" Bob asked.

"Beats the hell out of me," Jeff replied. "It's widely believed that there is a large collection of coal beneath the ground they lived on. As coal is their primary export, a major contributor to their finances, President Crogan felt it in the best interest of the country, or, should it be said, his pocketbook, that these untapped reserves of black gold be harvested. At any cost, it really doesn't matter to him."

"How could this have happened to over 3,500 people while the rest of the world stands by and does nothing?"

"This is considered a personal and internal matter to their government. Unless there was an uncontrollable crisis, organizations that would normally help stand by, not risking international repercussions."

Jeff circled the island once to give Bob a good view and then passed over the smaller two islands to the immediate west. He made his descent rather quickly and landed on the grassy patch that served as a prime landing strip. The plane touched down in two or three thumps and then taxied toward the end of the field. He could see the small rises of smoke coming from a different shelter encampments and the soft chatter of people he came to see. Before coming, Bob made a few phone calls and wrote a few large checks from his earnings from his last fight. In a few hours, he was determined to change the landscape and at least give these people the immediate help they needed.

Meanwhile, Sergei, Evstafii, Prokhor, Uncle Dem'yan and about eight other men stood at the foot of the Straits, waiting for the tide to go out. With about eight inches of water left to fully recede, they started to cross over. Every entrance back where the Chevkan Republic Guard still had an outpost strongly fortified with comfortable prefabricated barracks looked like they were there to stay to prevent the exiles from ever returning to their homes. They were heavily armed and rather jovial about having such a soft and easy duty.

The captain of the Guards was standing at the other end of the Straits with his hands on hips. He was staring at disbelief that these people had the stupidity of walking back over to the other side. He alerted his men to position rifles ready, crosshairs fixed on the target of their choice.

"We need to gain passage to pick up other essential things we need across on the islands," Sergei said. "We've only a few blankets, cooking pans, a couple of horses and the clothes on our backs. We need medical supplies, more food and fuel. We also need to try and get a few cars over there."

"You've got to be kidding!" barked the captain. "We dumped you over there because you're not wanted in this country anymore. And it's up to me to see that you never set one foot on this soil again. And I would strongly suggest that you do an about-face and return to the islands before the tide comes in."

"But we're not going to survive," pleaded Sergei. "We've got to get a few more things, people are getting sick and we need medicine and some materials to better house ourselves over there. Five minutes is not enough time to get the rest of our belongings to survive in the harsh landscape that you threw us onto."

To this the captain replied, "I will give you two minutes to talk to your other friends and make the right decision to get back on the island, NOW! Because if you don't, I'll place a bullet up each and every one of your asses, which will provide plenty of gas to get you back to where you belong, and fast!"

Back on the island, Kristanf and Irinia were still searching for Luther. Over and over again creating new search patterns and ending up at a meeting place to redraw yet a new pattern and strategy. This had gone on for hours with the growing suspicion now in Kristanf's mind that Luther did not make it. He dared not share this with Irinia because as long as there was hope, there was life. If he was correct, there would come a time when he would have to watch his beloved wife suffer the realization that they might never see their son again. But he kept this to himself as they both traversed their new pattern, calling out his name over and over again. As Irinia entered the upper right quadrant of their search grid, she came across Sof'ya.

"Sof'ya, Hello! I see that you've made it. Your husband and the children; are they here, are they alright?"

"Yes, Irinia, we managed to all make it here and Georgii built us a nice hut to stay warm and dry until we can figure something else out. Irinia, I…"

Irinia didn't even get her a chance to finish her sentence.

"Natalia is fine and back in our hut now, preoccupied with her doll and finishing a drawing she's making for us. But we can't seem to find Luther. We've been searching and screaming his name up and down, back and forth and we still can't find him. He probably found one of the neighborhood girls and decided to build their own hut," she laughed nervously, trying hard to block out the thought that already settled in Kristanf's mind. "Sof'ya, if you see that naughty boy, tell him we are looking for him. I'll show you later on where our hut is." Her voice was still teetering on a nervous giggle.

"Irinia, I did see Luther."

"You did! Where is he? Oh, wait till I get my hands on that boy," she said jokingly with a relaxed grin in earnest finally on her face.

Sof'ya's eyes grew dark, disconnected from Irinia's and looked toward the ground. Irinia's instincts were now peaking and she was trying very hard to hold back the freight train of dread about to collide inside.

"Come on, Sof'ya, where is he? Where is he? Tell me please; tell me where he is." Tears were now welling up in her eyes.

"Irinia, Luther is gone. He didn't make it across the Straits."

"No, no, he made it! Luther is strong and fast and I know, I know..." She burst into tears and let out a wail like that of a wounded animal, "Nooooooo!!!"

Sof'ya immediately ran to her and held her as she crumpled to the ground. Kristanf heard his wife's scream from not too far away and he knew the moment had come. He ran and found her and Sof'ya on the ground, Irinia crying uncontrollably.

"Irinia, sweetheart, what's wrong?" Kristanf already knowing the answer.

"Luther, my baby, Luther. They got him. They killed him! They ran him down like an animal and shot him! Those bastards killed him!!"

She was now screaming in higher pitches. From beneath her coat, Sof'ya took out Luther's left shoe and handed it to Irinia as though handing over a newborn that Irinia received and cradled gently in her arms. She brought the shoe to her chest, pressing it tightly against her breast, and rocked back and forth, letting out moans and sobbing deeply. Kristanf could do nothing except fall to his knees and hold his wife.

The reality of his thoughts now hit him full force and he, too, joined Irinia in her rocking back and forth himself sobbing, and swearing to himself that one day, somehow, someone would pay for this. He had never thought of killing another human being before, but now his primitive instincts started to surge to the top and he wanted whoever killed his son to suffer a slow and painful death. Oh yeah, somebody was going to pay for this.

He turned to Sof'ya. "I've got to know, no matter how horrible. What was the last few seconds of my son's life like? Tell me what happened. TELL ME WHAT YOU SAW!!"

CHAPTER 21

Late November and winter was in full throttle on the Svenkia Islands. Unprotected by surrounding mountains at the Svenkia “airport,” Bob was feeling the biting cold of the wind blowing against his face. Although equipped with two pairs of socks and heavily insulated boots, his feet were still freezing atop the tundra.

At about 12:13PM., Bob heard the first pulse of the powerful whine of the two Anotonov An-22 Cock cargo planes on their way. As the two slate gray behemoths became visible on the horizon, it reminded Bob of the Dumbo the elephant movies he enjoyed as a child; kind of a silly notion at such a pivotal moment for the people of the Upper 14. But, then again, Bob was still in his mid-twenties and not too far from those days.

Bob had, through a number of well-connected boxing enthusiasts, managed to deploy the use of the U.S. Government’s retired assets (now privately owned), aircraft and manpower, but as far as what it held and delivered was entirely funded by Bob and some of the scant donations of businesses anxious for the exposure they knew was sure to come. The Air Force did not want to show its presence, as this was still a political hot potato and was not classified as “emergency” relief; this was still being tagged a humanitarian necessity of the Chevkan government in relocating these people due to contaminated water supplies. Anything, even a handful of deliveries and short stays by military personnel, would be viewed as meddling and not received well in Washington, who sought to maintain diplomatic relations with Russia.

Everyone was asked to gather at the top of the bluff overlooking the landing strip, making sure their children were up front. No one was told exactly what was about to happen and they were curious as to why they were asked that their children get a front row seat. It wasn't enough that these people had to endure the hardships they had over the last few weeks; now they were asked to come out from their relatively warm huts and stand out in the cold.

After the first ration of corn and oatmeal, they hadn't eaten properly in two weeks. They were starting to feel the effects of malnutrition and, most critically, their children's health and spirits were declining fast. They were beginning to wonder whether Bob knew what he was doing. He was only in his mid-twenties and so far had shown care and interest, and he did have money from his boxing, but this was a life and death situation. What were they doing now on a hillside overlooking an empty airfield? Their curiosity had started to heighten as they, too, began to hear the low whine of the oncoming aircraft.

Bob was hoping that Sergei's estimation of the required ground needed for these flying fortresses to land was correct. They would have to come in low almost instantly over the southwestern skirt of the island and touchdown within seconds in order to have enough real estate to stop.

Bob watched anxiously as the first one started its descent. Bob was always amazed how something as small and miniscule as a human being could fly something so large, weighing in at hundreds of tons. The exhaust of the jet engines made twin downward J-shaped trails as the first cargo plane touched ground, shaking it on impact. Most children were used to seeing Piper Cub scouting planes or a twin prop airplanes at best. None had seen a jet fly before, much less one the size of their schoolhouse stacked three high and ten long. Their eyes grew wide and mouths agape in wonder.

The Antonov An-22 Cock rumbled past them at seventy-five miles per hour, making its way down to the end of the "airstrip" where it hopefully had enough room to come to a halt. Then, a second one provided the same performance and it, too, shook the ground as it roared past them.

The first one came to a stop with about 150 yards to spare (nice going, Sergei!), as did the second one. And bless those guys in the pilot's seats. Their precision and timing was impeccable as both ramps began to lower simultaneously, raising a small mist from the remaining morning dew as they hit the ground. Then there was silence.

Both adults and children were now standing there with mouths wide open in disbelief, wondering exactly what these two monstrosities were doing there after a long pause. Carnival music, cheerful and uplifting, began to blare out of the speakers from inside the cargo bays. It reminded the children of the fairs they had back home... back home, somewhere they'd never see again.

From within the cargo bays, bright white ice cream trucks started to roll down the ramps with three clowns hanging on each of the side rails, carrying balloons of every color of the rainbow. They made a thwumping sound blowing in the wind as the trucks began to slowly circle the crowd and make their way into different areas of the gathering.

In a matter of moments, the landscape was peppered with colored balloons as though some grand carnival had come to town. The children were running around with their balloons, comparing their new prized possession with their friends. As a clown was distributing the last of the balloons, the insulated refrigerator doors of the ice cream trucks opened, drawing a crowd of children carrying their new balloons behind them.

The clown started passing around the ice cream, every flavor, every shape, but all containing the same basic ingredients. Bob had worked with the manufacturer of the ice cream to make sure that they included the basic nutrients of fiber, vitamin D, vitamin C and other supplements that the children had lost in these past few weeks without proper food.

They couldn't get the ice cream down fast enough and the expressions on their faces were of children who began laughing suddenly after crying for so many weeks. Their still-developing spirits, which had sunk so low in the last couple of weeks, were now uplifted. It was fun and exciting; somebody really cared about them and was being nice to them. This was very important to their survival, emotionally, spiritually and physically. The immune system of a depressed child offers a susceptibility to illness that is much more severe and longer-lasting.

After the last ice cream trucks left, the business end of the cargo started to roll down and start the setup. These trucks were stacked to the brim with thermal tents that would serve as the temporary homes for the people of the Upper 14. The tents had been specifically provided in a variety of sizes based on the census that Tony brought with him on each family's number of children, if they had children.

The journalist who first broke the story, and one whose story Bob had read and had been inspired by, was now chronicling the entire situation and the progress that was slowly being made. This was attracting a lot of attention, both from the heart and commercially, where volunteers and donations would not be difficult to obtain.

The question was, who and how much. Bob had already been collecting small donations from corporations and created a trust fund at the Bank of America. This was a restricted fund account and Bob had to make sure that it would be subject to audit by Grant Higsby, a renowned auditing firm, should there be concern of proper use. He would be handling most of the financial distribution and tracking himself, but he wanted a third-party auditing firm to ensure that every penny collected was going in the right direction and toward the right things, and to join forces with his own advanced accounting knowledge compliments of his MBA program.

As more corporations were donating money, other businesses did not want to be left out, wanting to have their name mentioned in the cleverly constructed articles being written almost daily by the journalist at the New York Times. This soon snowballed, as the rest of the world caught on as to what Bob was trying to do.

But this was only the beginning and it was going to be very expensive. And Bob realized this was not going to be a continuous annuity as the commercial value of "sponsorship" would soon dry up budgets and the value added exposure due to the inevitable decline in drama over time as to what was now capturing the public's hearts.

Creating sustainable living for 3,000 people was demanding. What needed to be done was predicated on the desired end result. Bob hadn't thought beyond the ice cream stage and he'd have to start reaching out to the logical collection of professionals and scholars to create a livable and self-sustaining community. And he had to start acting immediately.

Tears filled the eyes of parents watching their children joyously free from the pain and anguish that had washed over them over the last couple of weeks. It was almost like a Genie popped up out of a bottle and waved a magic wand taking away all the hurt and excruciating memories that came from that horrific night they were banished to the islands. Some felt like they were back home and nothing happened at all. For those few brief moments the healing power of what Bob thought was just a good idea had far-reaching medicinal value for the tender psyches of these young children. Their parents worried about their immediate needs just as much as they did the repair of the children's emotional well-being that was so seriously damaged. While they themselves, too, while chasing after the children so they don't wander off to far started to feel like children themselves; happy and giddy without a care in the world and having, yes, fun. My God, the idea that was seemingly so far out of reach brought to bear by a 26-year-old professional boxer! The parents, as did the rest of the people gathered that afternoon at the "Svenkia Airport", cast and admiring and forever grateful toward Bob. He came to notice the thousands of eyes looking at him with hope and a "what do we do next" expression on their faces. His shyness and desire not to be too much the center of attention brought a slight blush to his face accompanied with the notion that he has started a process of trust with these people; something that he promised he would never betray and only strengthen in the months to come. Bob and Sergei were on one of the grassy knolls, overlooking the whole operation.

Sergei's father was American-born so he was also fluent in the English language. His father was a member of a geological team from the University of Wisconsin doing his graduate work on rock formations and mineral deposits of northern Russia. As this was a volatile area during and post Ice Age, his team elected to visit the westernmost edge of the Upper 14 provinces for the vast variety of geological phenomena that had affected this area due to shifting glacial movements. It was at this point the ice flow had been interrupted momentarily and created some land formations out at sea just north of these provinces (the Svenkia islands). It's there that he met Sergei's mother and the rest of course is history.

This would prove invaluable for Bob and the other members of the growing team in having an interpreter translating the Chevkan language for them until they themselves learn how to get by. The Chevkan language was not a hard tongue to learn. This sentence structures were pretty much the same as they were in English with, i.e. nouns followed by verbs, male and female conjugations easy-to-understand and incorporate, and an abundance of other similarities that one could catch him pretty quickly. The team was given a daily lesson by some of the school teachers who had ESL (English as a Second Language) under their belts during their own training.

They both stood in silence as the teams started their work placing pallets of thermal tents while weaving in and out of running children with ice cream on their faces and balloons bobbing in the wind.

"Look at their faces! Look at those smiles! Have you ever seen anything so beautiful in your life?" Bob said to Sergei and to himself at the same time, thinking out loud.

"What you've done for us will never be forgotten. Someday we will return the favor, my friend," Sergei replied.

Bob, thinking out loud again, said, "This is probably the most meaningful thing I've ever done in my life. It's hard to explain and I don't have the need to understand why or analyze why I was so driven to come here. Humanity is so precious; to throw it away in the dirt to rot is an intolerable atrocity. I'm gonna make sure these people not only have a place to live, grow, be happy and thrive, but I'm also make sure that the basic element of human beings caring for each other, no matter where they come from, no matter who they are, and no matter their color, sends a clear message to the world that human life is sacred and should be not be in the same room with meatheads like Crogan."

Then, from the inside of cargo bay number two, stepped out a woman in her mid-twenties with curly auburn hair and some carry-on bags hanging from her shoulders and hands.

Bonnie Southland was a clinical psychologist who had graduated with honors from Oxford University as a fellow in psychological studies. She had more credentials than Planter's had peanuts.

This translated into a cold and clinical personality with rare displays of emotion, very well guarded and managed. She was a beautiful woman, intelligent with a to-die-for figure that was due more to genetics than special diets and hours in the gym. She was absolutely gorgeous and caught Bob's attention immediately. He wondered who this woman was and why she was spending her time in a desolate area such as the Svenkia Islands. Taking her further out of place were her clothes, although casual, which were made of the best material and surely bought at a very expensive boutique.

Bob walked down the hill and toward the ramp to greet her, "Hello. I'm Bob Perry. Thanks so much for coming in and lending a hand."

"Well, it's nice to meet you, Bob. Your story is growing and capturing more of the world's attention. I felt compelled to offer my services to the cause. So valuable and important, it transcends anything else I might be doing in the states."

"And what is it that you do, Bonnie?"

"I'm a clinical psychologist. These people, especially the children, have been traumatized, probably some beyond repair", looking around with an increasing frown creasing her delicate features. "There are some whose souls can be reconstructed again and some not. I'm here to help both."

As a woman would do, especially when meeting a man, she instinctively did a quick scan and noticed a sincere and handsome face with an extremely well-developed body and sturdy frame. Well, after all, he was a boxer, right? Why did he drain his bank account and leave a promising career to come here and help these people? This question came to her mind as she looked around her and saw the scene of rescue and recovery going on all about her. If this guy was organizing it, especially at such a young age, kudos to him, she thought.

But she was sure he could have any woman he wanted and equally sure he did. Narcissistic sports stars do not understand social limits and grace. They are born and bred and solicited by professional teams to get exactly what they want for their performance. He might have been (and the thought appalled her) doing this as some sort of promotional stunt for his next fight.

But this was too much of an undertaking for even that kind of strategy. Whatever the reason, she was sure that all this would lead to some purpose for himself, and only for himself. What made it different than the other men she had known? Much like her father; driven for purpose, not being aware of, and probably not caring about, collateral damage.

But she was there, nonetheless, for the people who had been banished from their homes and their psyches were surely suffering as a result. Whatever this guy had in mind for himself really didn't matter. She devoted her life to helping other people overcome and work their way through the maze of unwanted emotional experiences that often left them limited in life and not taking full advantage of everything that was available to them.

"That's great, Bonnie! This is something we didn't think of, but probably is just as important as water, heat and food. These people have been through a horrible experience, and I'm mostly worried about the children."

"Well, judging by the expression now on their ice cream-smeared faces, they are enjoying the moment with smiles on their faces and some type of hope restored. It's gonna take some work, and some time on my part to understand their culture, for me to even start to be effective in reaching them."

"You're right," Bob said. "They are not too different from you and me, but they did grow up in another country under social circumstances that were very much different. As you see, some of the thermal tents are going up, and people are leaving their huts to keep a little warmer and drier. We've ordered trailers for some of the organizers of this effort, which will be here by next Tuesday. In the meantime, and I hope you're used to camping; we'll set you up in one of the tents. I assure you that it's warm and dry, and it will suit your needs until we get something more decent to stay in. And you are going to stay, aren't you?"

"Yes, I'll stay. I do have a practice in Manhattan with some other colleagues that can be maintained in my absence, but I certainly can't stay here forever."

"Well, neither can I for that matter. I'm still boxer by trade and although I'm in my mid-twenties, with each year that passes I'm closer to being put on the shelf. In addition to everything that we have to plan and do, I need to maintain regimen of readiness now," now looking around him, "so when I do return to the states, I'll be ready for my next fight."

"Well, let's get to work in the business of getting to work. And a word to the wise, Mr. Ringside. I'm not here for any type of funny business or to provide you with another notch on your boxing trunks. Now, please direct me to *my palais de la tente*."

Bob had no clue what that meant, but it did blow quite a gush of warm air all over him. Although a little bit too professional and cold, she was a knockout (sorry about the pun). He watched as she walked away with some of the women who were taking her to her tent.

Bob thought she was poetry in motion. The sight caused a stir inside him, creating a bubbling desire that he quickly had to dismiss; first, he was there for a very important reason that demanded his entire attention twenty-four-seven, and second, it didn't seem she would even know where to begin showing her emotional desires, if indeed she had any at all.

He was sure her emotional resolve was made of granite walls, the thickness of which probably resisted the most persistent intruder without even scratching the surface. But, then again, maybe it came with the territory; being overly focused on her practice and profession, obviously wanting to be the best, and shutting everything else out around her, which was the right recipe for what was needed now for these people.

By the grace of God, please allow her to help these people overcome the brutal stress they've been experiencing these past few weeks. And if the grace of God is being called upon, please also allow me to not have any more desires or entertain any thoughts of "funny business" and attend to the purpose at hand.

He was no Clark Gable and a bit concerned about his courting skills due to lack of experience. But, no matter;

although her presence was valuable, he couldn't see himself getting close to someone with a two-by-four wedged neatly up her ass. So, in short, no problema.

Next in the parade of the uninformed coming from the cargo plane was Lynne Albright. Ms. Albright was a land architect and had provided the landscape for national parks and other select upscale developments, both domestically and internationally. She, just as Bonnie, felt compelled to offer her services, no matter how premature they may have been at this point, in helping people who had been treated so horribly.

Although a downtown girl in birth, over the years she had strived to entertain uptown tastes and expectations. Marrying into wealth, *four times*, certainly helped the process. She was used to dealing with people with extraordinary tastes and equally extraordinarily thick purses. Decision making when it came to the cost of something was never a factor for her clients. This was the easy part of her job; the difficult phase was getting her very fussy clients to decide what the hell they wanted in the first place.

Both her portrait and her greatest accomplishments had been publicized over the years in many magazines. In *Architectural Digest*, they more or less devoted a separate section in every edition to just her portfolio. She was the rock star of tasteful and extraordinary landscapes.

Lynne had just crossed the delicate threshold of sixty years old and, through her own eyes of self-critique and vanity, she was thoroughly distraught over the number rather than the realization that she actually did still have a great pair of legs. But tell this to anyone who turns sixty and this is the same as you would tell somebody when they turn forty; they still look "marvelous."

She was dressed impeccably. Hanging on the inside of her elbow was a rather large straw handbag with a well groomed head of a small Shiatsu poking out timidly, eyes characteristically bulging complimented by a serious under-bite and clearly out of its element. It wasn't until one of the plane's crew followed up behind her with a hand truck holding three Luis Vuitton suitcases that Bob realized they would have to catapult the old girl across to the mainland when she had to pee. Surely there was no way in God's creation this woman was going to use the back brush of the Svenkia Islands as her commode. Shit, she was going to be a handful.

As Bob was mulling over the logistics of how to try to keep this woman remotely happy with the conditions there, he approached her. "Hello, I'm Bob Perry."

"Yes, young man, I know who you are. I've seen your picture commandeer most of the available news space recently. I've become very impressed with the care and fortitude someone your age has taken on in dealing with these poor people's plight. Your mother must be very proud."

Yeah, pleased as punch. "And to whom do I have the pleasure?" Bob asked in an overly eloquent yet awkward manner.

"Oh, you poor dear. You don't know who I am, do you?"

"No, ma'am."

"My name is Lynne Albright, at your service sir," she said with a small, yet a subtly patronizing courtesy.

"I'm in the business of making people's grounds look beautiful and flow harmoniously with their homes. I also do this for parks and the grounds of large institutional and governmental buildings."

"Well, that sounds great Ms. Albright, but look around you. This is not exactly a candidate for a botanical garden."

The dog now had its head buried in the straw handbag hoping that this was a joke and Mommy was going to take her home.

"Right now we have to provide the basic necessities for these people where aesthetics is probably last on the list, if at all."

"Ah, that's where you're wrong, my precious pugilist. There have been numerous studies on how the color and composition of the immediate environment affects people's emotions. There has been extensive research and many grants to designers who determine the colors used inside, for example, a spacecraft where weeks if not months are spent. The environment and the task at hand, along with the conditions of any environment, need to be orchestrated with proper and what can be the simplest of planning. I, along with the rest of the world, applaud your efforts, but these people have been thrust out into the naked environment and are rebuilding their lives. Other than the immediate need of shelter and warmth, their immediate surroundings are equally as important. So, please, let me help."

Thirty seconds ago, Bob thought her contribution bordered on the ridiculous, but the perspective she put it in started to make sense. He certainly wasn't savvy with design, much less good taste, but he fully understood how an environment and its orchestration could certainly influence people's emotions. And for the people of the Svenkia Islands, they needed every last drop of healing they could drink.

"I'm sure your contribution will be a major part of recovery for these people. We're so glad you can join us, Ms. Albright."

"Well, now, I won't mind roughing it for a while. Good for the soul, you know. Be a lovey and have someone bring my bags to my cabin, please."

Cabin? Lady, this is not the Catskills!

CHAPTER 22

Finally, the remainder of the cargo planes started to unload. The assets to deploy from the planes were for staging areas that needed to be assembled for the distribution of water, ice, food, sanitation and emergency medical services. This was the immediate point of attack where these staging, or triage, areas would supply the various further points of distribution (POD) around the island with, in addition to the above, food, additional materials for temporary shelter and any other immediate needs.

Each cargo plane established its own staging area, with forklifts traveling down the ramps with resources palletized, wrapped and ready to be broken down. PODs were established and scattered over the southeastern part of the island, where the masses had established their crude shelters. The new temporary shelters in the form of thermal tents were just enough to keep out the cold. Each tent had an aperture in the back "ceiling," allowing the stovepipe of a small eight cubic foot wood burning stove that came equipped with each of the tents.

Each tent had been designed to hold up to four people, the back of which could be left open to attach adjoining tents to form an elongated living space for as many people as one wanted. Roughly dividing 3,000 people by four would translate to 750 tents and stoves; but conditions are they were, and the available space on the cargo planes for immediate relief, only made room for 600 such "sets."

Also provided were sleeping bags for as many

people. These sets took up thirty-six cubic feet of cargo space, which allowed enough room for all the other resources that were of first priority.

The next installment of resources looked straight out of Noah's Ark. These were pack mules, strong and sturdy, weighing in at 1,000 pounds or more with short, stubby legs enabling enabled them to carry or haul heavy loads. And each came with its own hauling cart. Think about it. There were no roads and there was certainly not enough room on the cargo planes for trucks (other than the much-needed ice cream trucks; well worth the precious space). Mini-RVs wouldn't be on the market for another eighteen years, so donkeys were the economical mode of transport du jour (and much welcomed off the plane by the crew after spending in excess of eight hours in confined quarters with them – whew!).

Materials and cargo had to be transported far beyond the mouth of the open gateways of the planes down narrow muddied paths and up slow inclines of hillsides where people and their homemade shelters were scattered about. On some of the carts were unassembled playground sets complete with swings and slides and monkey bars. Small, yes, but something these children didn't even have at home when on the mainland.

Some of the carts carried the thermal tents, sleeping bags, parkas and other warm clothing, and small portable bathing facilities to outlying areas. And showers! These people hadn't had any type of cleansing since they were forced off the mainland. Their bodies were still dank from sweat squeezed out by the terror of running for their lives across the Straits.

These little amenities we all take for granted were now the most precious of commodities. The mules paraded past, coordinated by both the (former) clowns and Sergei, setting up and dispensing where needed. The faces of the clowns who had given out balloons that afternoon now sported a fine sheen from the Vaseline they used to wipe off their makeup.

They began setting up the showers and the play-sets as the day wore on. Very shortly, people were scrubbing down with soap in a hot outdoor shower, feeling much better, with children waiting their turn, swinging on the swings and sliding down the slides, giggling until their stomachs hurt. It was like a carnival, minus the Ferris wheel and roller coaster.

The majority of the remaining personnel on the cargo planes were volunteers, the greater majority of whom were Vietnam vets. It wasn't too long ago they were fighting for their lives in the jungles of Vietnam and returned home with a hard-earned sense of what being alive really meant (and for some, unfortunately, a well-established drug habit). It was when they heard of this travesty through their local Veterans Administration (who Bob contacted initially when putting together the rescue effort), they practically jammed the doors of the offices, eager to apply for this volunteer duty.

They had seen so much death and cruelty in their two or three tours of duty, some of which by their own hands, that a chance now to give back to life had gone beyond volunteering and was more an avenue of catharsis and healing. They knew what it meant to be in hostile territory, they knew what it meant to ration water, they knew what it meant to have their lives threatened and, most importantly, they knew how precious one more moment of life could be when you could be dead the next.

Leading the charge of this Band of Brothers was former Marine Master Sgt. Don Hayes. And a hearty crew they were. There was both passion and precision in what they were doing, a product of their endless combat training and experience. And Sgt. Hayes, the quintessential, and "you gotta love him anyway," hard-ass Marine drill sergeant, was guiding his men with intent and purpose, just as he did with his platoon in the enemy infested jungles of Vietnam.

He was Bob's age, but far older than his years, escalated by the stress and responsibilities that came with war. He had been a volunteer in his local fire department before being drafted and would later on become a NYC firefighter. In the next twenty years, he would work up the ranks to Battalion Chief. Bob watched with fascination and awe as he barked commands.

"Well, you must be Bob Perry. I'm Sgt. Hayes, the jarhead with an attitude who picked up the phone when you first called the Vet's Administration. I can't tell you how much a pleasure it is for me to meet you. Not only am I a fan, but now I'm a lifer of admiration for the balls you have in trying to help these people. I can't tell you how big a hair up my ass it is when I think of what happened to these people. I really don't believe that bullshit about the contaminated water the press keeps on insisting about, or, should I say, that Washington prefers to be printed given the temperature of our relationship with Russia."

"Yeah, the reporter who covers the story for the

New York Times has his copy edited to death before it reaches the press. He's the one who really got my juices going. And you have no idea how glad I am to see you guys. It's been a long haul for these people and this is the beginning of very long road for them; medically, socially and spiritually. As for the government cover-up in the name of international relations, I can see why that raises your blood pressure. Not that I have any type of definite information, but I would imagine that Vietnam itself is saturated with propaganda and truths that we, meaning the public, will never be privy to."

"The whole war was hell in a hand basket. I've seen men cut in half by mortar fire and cry for their mamas a good five minutes before they looked down and realized they could see daylight from their waist down and they were bleeding to death. That was war, Mr. Perry, and there ain't no fairness in war. It's unforgiving and you have no choice but to survive. Look around you, Mr. Perry. This is war, this ain't fair, but you have no choice but to survive. That's what we're here for. A bit chillier here than it was in 'Nam, though," he offered with a bit of a grin.

"Yeah, this place is unforgiving. But, unfortunately, for the sake of the eyes of the international community, this is all these people have for now. Looks like you and I will be working very closely together, so it's 'Bob', not Mr. Perry. I feel old enough as it is. Jesus, where do we start?"

Sgt. Hayes started to explain the initial concept of staging areas before fanning out to many substations serving as PODs. Each POD would have anywhere from three to seven personnel assembling tents and handing out water and MREs, with one clinician for medical needs.

Doing the math before they arrived, some of the basic calculations dictated one gallon of water per person per day, where 237 gallons fit nicely on each pallet with a month's supply for all. They also calculated two of what amounted to MREs (although the term wouldn't be coined until the 90s) per person, where 1,728 fit a pallet with, again, a month's supply.

Water for washing and portable toilets was also provided, but before a more permanent solution was implemented, this would have to do for now. The thermal tents and matching stoves would do nicely for temporary shelter, but again, there would need to be a plan for more substantial and durable housing.

Sgt. Hayes and company had brought twelve 30kw portable generators and a small tanker trailer of gas. These people couldn't run on generators the rest of their lives and it was the rest of their lives they'd be spending there unless they had the means of flight, which very few did. Power, Sgt. Hayes stressed, came next on the critical list of needs, right after food and shelter. Getting started was going to be a long, hard road, but it was a road Sgt. Hayes had been on before and he was no stranger to adversity. Bob was convinced of that.

Sgt. Hayes seemed to have his eyes riveted on every man, pallet and jug of water that passed by him and Bob to the staging areas. Bob could almost hear the wheels continually turning in his head, calculating what was needed, how much was needed and where it was needed first.

In the first few hours of knowing Sgt. Hayes, Bob quickly gained respect for the guy. He did not let the situation overwhelm him and take control of his senses, or commandeer his clear thinking and decision-making. Bob thought that Sgt. Hayes would make a great boxer, not necessarily because of his size and obvious power of his body, but because of his discipline and execution of strategy without letting any outside elements influence him.

During the war, he was in charge of maybe twenty to thirty guys in his platoon, all of whom had bull's-eyes between their eyes by the Vietcong. Sure, these people on the Svenkia Islands had been born with a bull's-eye of prejudice in the back of their heads when it came to the reception they got from the good citizens of the lower 43 provinces, but the shot had now been taken and these people were seemingly left to die.

The very life and existence they had developed over thousands of years had been, in a few short hours on a cold and rainy November night, snatched from them and thrown aside like old garbage. The comment by the sergeant about war not being fair continued to echo in Bob's mind.

The feeling of helplessness and despair that comes with a huge loss as a result of purposeful actions by someone in authority really burned Bob to the core. With Sgt. Hayes having his back, Bob felt empowered and more confident. For the first time in the last week or so, he felt he had firepower, looking at the hope etched on the faces of the people crowded around and the cargo planes, the tools for their physical and emotional rescue.

This was a definite strike back at authority and the road to defeating the injustice of taking something away from these people that was rightfully theirs. For the first time in weeks, and months for that matter, Bob felt he was standing back on his feet. His own sense of self-defeat was beginning to dwindle away and he was almost proud of himself. But this was only the first round.

CHAPTER 23

The wheels were nicely in motion now. MREs were being distributed, the first warm meal anyone had had in weeks. Sergei was helping organize Sgt. Hayes's crew in identifying the pockets of homemade huts with their respective headcounts so thermal tents could be distributed and assembled accordingly. The generators were humming in unison, providing light as darkness fell. There were spot lamps on tripods dispersed throughout the area and fires glowing, some people cooking the freeze dried meat that had been brought over by the sergeant's band of jolly vets.

Glowing embers wafting into the air created the imagery of a gypsy camp. In a sense, it was. Couldn't say that this was exactly a delightful experience, but the day had brought new hope and pumped spirit into the hearts of people who thought their end was just a few days away. The sound of conversation among families and the laughter of children made Bob feel like some semblance of civility had been restored.

The crew was wrapping up the moving blankets, straps and stacking pallets on the mule carts that would be later used for the base of each tent, elevating them above rain water. Oh, they'd be back. There was much more to do in the recovery process and establishing long-term stability. Some of the crew would stay behind and help with the first phase and the others would return to home base, only to ready for the next trip over.

The ice cream trucks were parked tightly in the base of the Antonov cargo planes silent and exhausted from a hard day's work. The bay door of the first cargo plane was starting to lift upwards to seal and make the behemoth whole again.

One of the heavy-duty forklifts was now inching its way down the edge of the ramp of the second plane with what looked like, and was, a cargo container with squares cut into the sides providing sliding windows. There was a door at the front end and steps temporarily attached to the front of the container, which would later be unfolded and laid down for entry.

"Who ordered the mobile classroom?," Bob joked.

"Classroom? Well, kinda. This trailer is for you," he replied.

"The thermal tent looks just fine to me. Why should I have a trailer when the rest are sleeping on tarpon-covered pallets?"

"This is not for your comfy convenience, Glamour Boy. This," he outstretched his hand to the trailer being set down by the forklift in a clearing, "is your war room. The boys have a wide web of friends and contacts and this was once the proud container belonging to the S.S. Everest. They pulled a few strings to get a new one 'off the dock' and outfitted it with the latest in telecommunications and computer equipment."

This, being the 70s, took up five times the room it would by today's technology.

"You're going to need a functional command post. In addition to desks, a conference table and wall maps, one of which is a topographically accurate layout of the islands, there's a cot for you. Now, if your conscience can't absorb the practicality of this one feature, sleep in a damn tent."

"Point made and duly noted. Okay, the trailer it is, for the 'practicality' of the situation."

"This ain't no walk in the park, Bob. I had thirty men under my command in the jungle where the enemy was tangible and defined: Charlie. You've got 3,000 people under your command where the enemy is the unforgiving elements, with no infrastructure to deal with it, only aggravated by the stranglehold of international politics. I think I'd take the jungle over this anytime."

"This scares the crap out of me, Sgt. Hayes, 'Don'. It's just that when I heard the news and later found out the truth, I had this overwhelming anger. And, as has always been in my life, my first instinct was to strike back. Maybe that's why I box for a living. This is different, way different. There are no three-minute rounds in a twelve-round fight. There's no person standing in front of me to hit!"

Just as Bob was finishing this thought, Sergei came traipsing down the hill, slipping and sliding every now and then on the wet rocks.

"Looks like we got the start of a brand new life here," Sergei smiled. "We've still a long way to go, but at least the people can see that the rest of the world cares, no matter how shrouded due to the weight of political pressure. But hell, we'll take it anyway. We have a lot to be thankful for and a lot to regret."

"What do you mean 'a lot to regret'?" asked Bob, furrowing his brow in confusion.

"Regret that our country had been put in the hands of an animal and that we didn't have the means or manpower to put up a fight to keep the land that has been our families' for thousands of years."

"How do you ever expect to put up with the type of militia that Dimitrii has at his disposal?"

"Hence the regret. But that's the way it is and that's the way it's going to be. But thanks to you, we have an alternative, a really viable alternative to return back to the land from whence we came and turn it into something greater than what we left," he said, meaning his newly bi-pedaled ancestors from nearly 3,000 years ago. "Bob, someday we will return the favor, my friend."

"Yes, Sergei, I know you will," Bob responded in a very polite, almost rhetorical tone.

Sergei turned and was heading back to his now new thermal tent when he turned his head back to Bob and said over his shoulder, "Someday," with a most definite intonation to his voice and not how someone would say in an open-ended way leaving that someday to chance.

He made a few steps up into the trailer door and, thanks to a humming generator hooked up to the fuse box affixed to the side, flipped on the lights. Now, remember that these were the days before laptops, notebooks, cell phones and iPads. The PCs were of the steam-driven type, with monitors the size of three-gallon containers, but state-of-the-art for the late 70s, nonetheless. Bob was thoroughly impressed. There were also satellite phones, which enabled faxing equipment to work in addition to a huge blackboard (with boxes of chalk supplied).

Just as Sgt. Hayes and his men started to nail down the situation with their precision-timed distribution of shelter, food and medical attention, an appreciable amount of weight was lifted from Bob's shoulders and he felt an additional shot of empowerment now with support equipment and connection to the outside world. He ran his fingers across the makeshift conference table and felt a surge of excitement coming from his MBA alter ego. Oh, he had it in his bones, but it just hadn't reached the surface yet. And in his later years, he would go on to a second Master's and enjoy a successful business career serving the community, in addition to an associate professorship at two universities.

He was unique, although he would instantly debate this with you, and truly a born leader. It was his passion and sincerity that fueled his actions, the type of which makes the world progress to the next level. He would find out more about himself in the next few months than he would have in years had he not been here, doing what he was doing now.

He would eventually surprise himself by the strength he possessed as an individual, something that he was not quite convinced of now and tried to compensate for in the ring. Even with a more than substantial record, this didn't seem enough to raise his self-esteem. He was approaching the plight of the people of the Svenkia Islands with the raw emotion of a warrior, and later learned in life that he did not have to use his fists to win over a situation. But hey, for now it helped him in the ring, made him a decent living and certainly pushed the situation of these people in the right direction.

Now that he had a "war room," he needed "generals." He wasn't quite sure he was going to be able to pull this off, but he certainly was going to give it his best try. He needed to surround himself with expertise for every different phase of recovery and rebuilding. This was going to turn out to be one of those situations where instead of trying to plan from A to Z, they would start with A, maybe B, but after that, it would be anyone's crap shoot. People's own sense of survival was what ultimately would dictate the path, but expert intervention was certainly going to be needed along the way.

The first point of departure had already been executed by Sgt. Hayes and his men. The people now had very dry and warm shelter. They had freeze-dried food and commodities to last at least a month or two. There was power, albeit temporary, but, if used sparingly, would do until something more permanent could be established. The publicity of outpouring of support was making worldwide news and although carefully solicited, again based on the propensity of bruising international relations, funds were coming in at a greater pace and in larger sums. So, at least for now, money was not an issue, but the careful consideration of an enduring and strategic recovery was essential, as the funds would soon dry up as this situation got old with the media.

Bob sat at the edge of one of the desks, his mind spinning in a dozen different directions.

We have to keep these people alive, healthy and strong, he thought. *We have to keep their spirits and emotions above board and not let them sink back into the depths that they've been in these recent weeks. This is going to take a lot of work. These people have been thrust from their homes and punished for the mere fact of who they are.*

Prejudice was something Bob couldn't understand, and he could only sympathize, but not empathize.

What does it feel like? What does it feel like to have someone come into your home, grab you by the scruff of the neck and throw you out into the cold? These kinds of things just don't happen in America. Or do they?

Bob sat down on his cot and let out a long sigh through his nostrils.

Well, let the games begin, let's light this candle, let's put lipstick on this pig; pick your rally cry. It's going to be a bumpy ride, everybody's invited so buckle up; We'll get this done, he convinced himself.

There was no way in hell these people were going to be subjected to ideological paranoia by some fat, piece of shit dictator. Bob brought his feet up and lay down with his hands behind his head, staring at the ceiling, which provided a platform for the imagery of his own thoughts.

People started to head back, not to their branch and leaf shelters, but to now government approved, grade-A thermal tents. He smiled contently. He could hear the adults talking and children's laughter begin to dwindle in the night air. Children would be tucked in their sleeping bags, cocooned in warmth with glowing embers from the wood burning stoves denying the invitation of a sub-zero night air.

There was hope in these voices, a steady rhythm and assured tone to their speech, and, best of all, laughter in the hearts and throats of young children. The night air started to engulf the Svenkia Islands, the stars millions in numbers, each shining bright with salvation. Bob's eyelids became soft and heavy with exhaustion.

For the first time in weeks, he felt comfort, he felt support; he had the means to make something good happen. Every now and then, for all intents and purposes, with uncontrolled minor subconscious eruptions, he would question his motives. He wasn't quite sure if he wanted to let them surface completely and entertain the reality of what he was doing and why he was doing it; pity, he would've been pleasantly surprised. But the bane of his existence had always been victory by brutality, fueled by anger which, although productive in the ring, did not have a place in everyday life.

This, however, had always been a cyclical phenomenon with Bob and served him well in his boxing career. Boxing provided plenty of fertile ground for the outward expression of anger. There was a lot of trash talk that filled the pages of the tabloids a few days before a fight, and the always theatrical weigh-ins, and in the ring, plenty of verbal abuse only topped by the pounding he was receiving.

It was always the comment about Bob's promise his mother about quitting boxing if he didn't claim the title by his twenty-sixth birthday that struck a nerve. This was often accompanied by sexual innuendos about his mother. Taken altogether turned on the switch of unbridled, check that, bridled anger that he channeled to his arms, shoulders and fists.

The one exception was when Bob, still as a super middleweight, was fighting a guy by the name of Manny Arturo, an Argentine boxer with manners, etiquette and a humble personality. No trash talk, no mother jokes, no speaking in the ring; this literally left Bob at a loss if he didn't do something to muster up the anger that was his tool in the ring. By the sixth round, Manny, a very skilled boxer in his own right, was picking apart Bob in a very concise and methodical way. It was only at the end of the seventh round when Bob returned to his corner to find Johnny Wells sitting on his stool.

"You know what? You don't want to win this fight, do you? So I'll fight for you since you can't do anything but stand up there and give this guy a punching bag and workout. Other than that, you might as well go back to the showers now and call it a night."

The crowd was going bananas over this. There were catcalls from the audience, obscenities, accusations of not being man enough and being a mama's boy, a mama who wasn't half bad looking and probably put up a better fight in bed than he did in the ring. The very fact that his lack of action was causing such disgrace and embarrassment for his mother, who was in the audience, making a rare appearance at one of his fights, was the right button to push. He knocked Manny out in the eighth round.

Whether or not Johnny had done this consciously or unconsciously, it worked. But little did he know how much more Johnny knew about him than he realized. Johnny understood anger was at the core of Bob's success. As time went on, he learned how arouse this at the right moment to give Bob an edge. Not something you'd find trainers using too often in Gleason's Gym.

The people on the island were punished and cheated out of their homes; he was punished and cheated out of his title. Was this his form of retaliation? Was he doing this for his own purposes of revenge or out of sincere concern for these people? King for a Day? Would Michael B. Anthony be knocking on his door with a check from an unknown donor for one million dollars?

The more he thought, the more disturbed he got with himself. If he was going to function for the next couple weeks, for the next couple of months, he was going to have to put this type of thinking aside and run with his emotions, unchecked and unchallenged. This always served him well.

CHAPTER 24

Natalia was sitting against a leafless tree, about thirty yards from her parent's tent. Irinia had objected to Natalia wanting to be outside in such cold weather, but Kristanf said to let her go as long as she didn't wander off too far. He realized that, even at the tender age of eight, she, too, needed to grieve in her own way.

They both kept a close eye on their now only child and allowed her as much space as possible under watchful eyes. It was quite cold outside; she was all bundled up and needed to be alone as much as one can service their own emotions at the delicate age of eight years old.

The wind whistled around her, yet the cold could not penetrate her sorrow. Losing her brother was like losing her left arm and she couldn't quite reconcile in her mind him being gone forever. Mama had said that he went to heaven and she wanted to go to heaven to be with him. That wasn't going to come for some time, Mama said, but Luther would be there waiting for her when it did.

This helped a little bit, but did nothing to lift the heavy weight off her tender little heart. Her tears would dry, only to be followed by a new set. But this was happening less and less as time went by. And so goes the nature of grieving the loss of a loved one.

Bob came walking up the side of the hill and saw the girl sitting against a tree, wondering why, in such cold weather, should she would be outside at all.

He walked up beside her and sat next to her against the tree, greeting her with a cheerful, "Hi."

She barely looked up at him with lifeless eyes and

looked down again.

Using his best Chevkan he said, "My name is Bob. What is a pretty young princess like you doing outside when it's so cold?"

Again the lifeless look, the grim face. She returned her gaze back to the ground. She knew who he was, everybody did, but she was not particularly in the mood for talking. Bob thought perhaps she had a fight with her parents and was upset. The ground was hard and cold. Bob started to feel his backside going numb and couldn't understand how this little girl was sitting outside seemingly so preoccupied with something that she didn't feel the cold.

"What's bothering you, sweetie?"

"They killed him. They shot and killed him. Mama says he is up in heaven, and I hope he isn't hurt anymore."

"Who was killed, honey?"

"My brother... my brother, Luther. They shot and killed him."

Aw, geez. Bob heard about the boy and his defiant last seconds on earth. Not far in age from him, Bob could understand the anger and the compulsion to strike back at the brutality so many people told him about. He still couldn't fathom the idea that an adult, the soldier, would shoot a boy. Sitting next to the schoolgirl whose brother was killed was the closest he'd come to feeling the horrific reality these people had gone through. Bob was at a loss for words for the pain this tender little girl was feeling. This brought his own anger to new heights and his determination to right this wrong was that much greater.

Bob stared down at the brown grass for what seemed like an eternity until he said, "You love your brother very much, don't you, sweetie?"

"Yes I do," she whispered as she hugged her doll closer to her chest. "He's my best friend."

"I just lost my best friend, too. I know how you feel," Bob returned.

"Your friend, they went to heaven?"

"Yes. It was my grandfather. He went to heaven, too. I bet he's met Luther by now."

Bob's grandfather lived in Hempstead, Long Island, was still very much alive, remarkably agile for man in his eighties. But a little white lie here doesn't hurt. Mentally, Bob made the sign of the cross, not wishing this on his grandfather, not just yet.

"What's your grandpa's name?" Natalia now started to join in the conversation.

"Mike. I miss him a lot. There are days when I feel like he's still alive and I need to tell him what I did during the day. Then I realized he's in heaven watching me and he knows what I'm doing right now, right Grandpa?" Bob said as he gazed up to the heavens, holding a conversation with an empty sky.

"Really?" Natalia asked with a little bit of excitement turning around to face Bob. "I sometimes think Luther is here and I want to tell him to come out and play with me. That's when I get very sad and cry." Her eyes started to well up.

Bob's heart started to sink lower in his chest hearing this little girl trying to cope with the pain of death. A child of eight doesn't have the faculties to recover and go through the normal processes of grief. At this point her life, this experience could travel in any one of many different directions, shaping her whole being as an adult.

Learning to cope with something like the death of a sibling at such a young age is an extremely delicate issue that needs to be handled in the right way. Bob made a mental note to make sure that Bonnie visited this family. Many families lost loved ones during that horrific night when everyone was scrambling across the Straits under gunfire. The whole vision brought out new strands of anger along Bob's neck, which ironically helped warm him a little bit.

In short, he couldn't wrap his brain around the whole concept of one human being taking another human being's life, especially in the brutal manner of punching a hole in someone's chest with a bullet. The whole idea was barbaric.

"Why'd they have to do that, Bob? Why did they have to take my brother away? Why did they have to kill him? He wasn't bad, he didn't do anything wrong. Why? WHHHYYYY?!??"

A fresh torrent of tears started and she almost gagged as her anguish couldn't come out fast enough. Bob put his arm around her and she buried her head in his chest, sobbing uncontrollably. Her sobbing turned into screams and wails as though she was falling off a cliff into a bottomless abyss. Bob felt as though the lump in his throat was going to cut off his air supply. His face flushed with feeling the pain from this child traveling through him, mixed with an ever-growing anger of what these people were put through by that bastard.

Irinia and Kristanf had been witnessing this whole exchange from their tent and they, too, were crying.

"Enough! She's been through enough." Irinia crackled out the words as she got up to go out and collect Natalia.

As Irinia rose and exited the tent, Kristanf sat in deep conviction with the numbers "5432" emblazoned across the front of his mind. It almost became a mantra the day that Sof'ya told him the horrific details of Luther's death. He picked up Luther's shoe from where Irinia kept it, looking at it, rotating it and rolling it in his hands to see if there was anything else attached to the shoe, anything that he could feel, touch and smell of his son.

His tears burned like hot lava in his eyes and his anger grew deep, focused and dedicated toward one thing… eliminating 5432 from the face of the earth and sending him to hell to suffer. Kristanf realized animals like him were not meant to roam the earth. Yes, this would be done.

Irinia was now approaching Bob and Natalia, bending down to pick Natalia up from Bob's embrace. Seeing the two most important women in his life suffering only brought more urgency for closure for them, for him… for Luther.

Back in Movania, Dimitrii was sitting in his chair made especially for fat bastards overlooking three different television sets. It seemed the journalists from the New York Times caught quite a bit of attention of the plight of the people of Antonia. TV crews and cameras were becoming commonplace, reporting live with the cargo planes serving as dramatic backdrop.

Field Marshal Julius Witkowski executed careful

planning by excavating at night and covering of all excavation machinery and mining equipment with camouflage during the day should it come within the range of satellite photographs. There was now enough growing attention to the people who were "transferred" due to contaminated water tables and their survival on the Svenkia Islands to cast attention to the land they were forced to leave behind. There were always those who questioned the political motives of leaders, especially those of foreign provinces. If there were any errors or equipment that had been failed to be concealed, Witkowski pre-prepared a statement, if need be, for the press that this was equipment to further investigate the contaminated underground water tables.

But this was not the object of worry for Dimitrii. He was more concerned with the escalating attention of these people who had been "transferred" to an environment with no amenities or immediate facilities for survival. The questionable was now becoming the obvious. Damage control was clearly needed, and in a hurry to quell the insinuations that had already been made by the press of some ulterior motive in making these people leave their homes behind.

Both Field Marshal Witkowski and Minister of the Interior Tomkin Shulvi were sitting at a large oak conference table in Dimitrii's office. All three were on a first name basis, in private, of course (they otherwise addressed each other by their titles), since they'd been colleagues their entire careers. Dimitrii only surrounded himself with appointed Cabinet members who were the longest and most trusted of friends.

"Dimitrii, we need to become more involved with our directive of pushing these slobs off their property," Tomkin wisely advised. "We have to show continued support and that what we had these people do was with their best interests at heart. We need to send troops with supplies and make sure the cameras capture this. We'll also have our own news stations filming this and distributing it to the Western media. We have to show that this is a humanitarian effort."

"Agreed," Field Marshal Witkowski said. "We have to convince the rest of the world now that this news is becoming public property that we had planned all along to continue the comfortable sustenance of these displaced people. We'll send more troops over with supplies, clothing, tarpons and even some people from the Department of Agriculture to support the education of these idiots on how to grow their own food. All of this will have to be captured on film and distributed to the media. We will show full cooperation with the Western capitalists and convince them we are taking care of our people."

"Then let's begin this immediately, Julius," Dimitrii implored. "Mobilize all the local TV stations we have and get reporters and camera crews over there immediately. Tompkin, put together a relief unit to start getting supplies over there by tomorrow morning. Make sure we give these people a little bit more than corn and oatmeal, as this is going to be viewed by the rest of the world and based on how these bleeding hearts think this should be handled. I don't want any room for criticism or judgment on their part. This won't last forever. Somewhere there's going to be an earthquake, a flood or hundreds of acres on fire, which will redirect the attention of the media away from all this. But, for the time being, we have to show concern and support as long as this is making headlines."

Dimitrii might've been delusional, but he wasn't stupid.

As the tide was slowly starting to recede, truckloads of Chevka Guard personnel and supplies were waiting at the edge of the Straits. With about inch of water left to go, the caravan started the four mile trip across to the Svenkia Islands. Bringing up the rear were two vans of camera crews and reporters, for whom this was a new experience. All of their reporting was strictly government-controlled and for those few working for the Chevkan media who had a true penchant for journalism, this was an opportunity of a lifetime to record something of human interest that would be publicized across the world. But frustration still lingered, as they were instructed repeatedly to portray this adjustment for these people as a positive experience; that they were safe from illness and even death by contaminated water and the elements, and had been given the opportunity of a new and better life.

Half the people in the vans wondered how the hell they were going to pull this off, but pull it off they better or they'd have to prepare themselves for a very long stay in prison. Sacrificing their dignity as professionals was not a new thing for the Chevkan journalists; it was just a painful load they would forever carry on their backs. The reporters were instructed not to interview anyone, and the cameramen not to film people with grim and devastated expressions on their faces. Indeed, this was going to be very tricky; one mistake by the journalists or cameramen would have them and their family locked up in a six-by-eight cell with questionable plumbing.

Dana Ruminski, very much the idealist at the age of twenty-eight, was educated in journalism abroad at Columbia University in New York City. During her four-year stay in Manhattan, along with excelling in her studies, she gained an appreciation for the Western "custom" of speaking one's mind, publicly and privately. She felt a sense of exhilaration in New York. After growing up in a government controlled state, the whole idea of free expression was not part of her DNA. She would have stayed in the States had it not been for the illness of her mother, whom she needed to care for as her beloved father had passed away three years prior. She found working in Chevka was a serious compromise to the integrity of her profession. It sickened her that even the most carefully crafted stories were subject to mutilation by government censors.

Bouncing up and down in her seat as the van traveled over the pebbles and small boulders toward the islands, she couldn't help but think that this trip and story would be the trigger point of the ultimate foundation of responsible journalism if one of them dared to show the truth. She felt the journalist had an obligation to the readers in delivering the truth of what was happening in the world, no holds barred.

Digressing from instructions would land her and her mother, who was getting worse and had to be left in the hands of an aunt, in a place where her mother would surely die from lack of proper medical care. She felt "hypocritical" was not strong enough a word as she prepared to deliver a preconceived notion of what the government wanted the rest of the world to see.

She wanted to dive directly into the hearts of the people, what they were feeling, what they experienced and how they're dealing with this "transfer." She wanted a camera crew to record the primitive shelters these people had at their disposal to endure a brutal winter. Very few Chevkan people believed the story about contaminated water and they knew about the trucks and drilling equipment searching for coal, but mouths were shut, and a few even tried to convince themselves that the government was acting in the best interests of the people. People needed faith, something to believe in and something to hold onto; but the government offered very little, if none, of this.

When the first of the Guard's caravans reached the shores of the Islands, they began to disperse and clumsily set up distribution points for people to gather bread, dried meats and canned goods. Pathetic-looking tarpons that were supposed to be tents had been passed around like blankets, seemingly useless without the proper stitching and shape needed to achieve even the most primitive of tents. It was an awkward display to say the least.

Although the soldiers were drilled to death in maintaining smiles while attempting to be cordial, it was plain to see that this was a strain for their psyche. How was it now they were serving the very dogs they had driven from their land?

Other goods and produce were also available and thrust in the hands of the people, even before they reached out or were sure what it was they were being given, and that it was critical the cameras were catching every "hospitable" moment. Field Marshal Witkowski was clear in his orders to his commanders that this was to be a jovial and seemingly standard visit in protecting the good people of the province of Antonia. More than pure bullshit; this was the golden nugget of hypocrisy.

It didn't take a rocket scientist for the rest of the media to understand what was going on, and it only served to further sicken the feeling in Dana's stomach. After the bumpy ride across the Straits, Dana couldn't decide which caused her more of a pain in the ass; the bumpy ride or the fact that she was there as a whore for the government.

As she moved about with cameras panning the crowd from a distance, closing in on her with a tight shot and with the microphone in hand for commentary, she began to extol the unchallenged care and responsibility that Dimitrii Crogan had for the people of Antonia. The cameramen were careful not to catch the scornful looks of disgust on the peoples' faces (and the occasional giving of the finger) at this insincere attempt to be jovial caregivers and make it seem as though it was one great big picnic.

This took a lot of the cameramen's attention and focus because there were very few people who didn't have that look of anger and revenge on their faces. Nonetheless, of the hours of footage and commentary that they took, they may have had around twenty to thirty minutes of acceptable tape to send back to the stringently regulated TV stations. Dana should've taken her father's advice and become a doctor.

Perched upon a small cliff overlooking this media circus, Kristanf didn't want any part of this. The sight of the green khaki wool coats of the soldiers made his blood boil and his fingers reach for an imaginary weapon. He stared down at the ragged rocks below with their cathedral like formations spiraling upwards to a sharp point with a hedgerow in front blocking them from view. He then turned his gaze back up, only to feel remorse that these people had to give up their dignity and take food and supplies from the very hands that still had fresh blood on them. These monsters who, only weeks before, were kicking, rifle butting and killing people as they were trying to escape their own mortality.

These were the real clowns of the world, whose dark psyches made a mockery of life, the human element, and who had no consciousness at all. These were the same beasts that killed his son.

Sof'ya's recollection to Kristanf of that dreadful night she witnessed Luther's killing began to flood his mind like a rushing tide. Sof'ya was so shocked by what she saw broke her will to be more tactful in explaining this to him as she was trying desperately to keep her own emotions intact. With something like this, she would normally approach it with care and caution but the anger and fear in her brought her to tears as she, in her mind, went back to that place on that rainy night when the guard punched a hole in Luther's chest. Unintentionally cathartic, her emotional outpouring of every minute detail sickened Kristanf to the point where he almost asked her to stop but in another sense he wanted to hear every last detail. He felt if he didn't know exactly what happened he would sacrifice the last memory of his son, a memory he further agonized over by not being there to possibly rescue his him. His feeling for revenge was far outside the scope of his moral sense of humanity and couldn't reach far enough for definition. His hatred was so strong it was limitless and almost delirious in nature consuming his whole being.

He forced her on detail over and over again even though Sof'ya was drained and simply wanted to stop. "Where did this happen? Did Luther say anything to you? Do you think he was in pain? Did this guard 5432 say anything to you?" She told of how the bullet ripped through the boy's breastbone making him airborne and the second humiliation of having half his skull torn off with the second shot to the head. She had to soon stop as her choking tears made it impossible for Sof'ya to enunciate any words. He too was weary of the emotional toll this was taking on him. The searing rage coursing through his body was of such volume and intensity that he quickly burned out as his mind couldn't carry the load and gravity of what he was hearing from this woman. Children simply do not die before their parents. This was a concept that was universally believed and tragic in instances such as this when death was so unnatural and so brutal.

The memory of this conversation tore to the front of Kristanf's mind and he decided to further investigate by placing himself amidst the cadre of guards putting on this pathetic charade. But first, he wanted to return to his tent for something.

Back from his tent, he then walked down the steep perimeter of the cliff to the main area where the soldiers were distributing food and mocking it up for the cameras. Kristanf played his part and put a smile on his face as he walked through the throngs of people and soldiers.

He noticed their silver badges engraved with anonymous numbers identifying each soldier as a unit of destruction of Dimitrii's Republic Guard. He took some canned meat from one soldier, a piece of bread from another, some apples and oranges from another until he finally spotted it… 5432!

He felt like his insides were going to explode. Seeing 5432 joking around, playing his role and working at the distribution point, handing out the useless tarpons painted a hideous shade of repulsion. Kristanf was gagging on his own rage, but he knew he needed to be patient. He waited until a camera crew started to work their way over to his station when he finally got his chance. He went up the soldier.

As soon as the camera started to record from a distance, he shook the hand of the soldier, out of gratitude, pointed to the tarpon's, raised eight fingers for the camera to see and pointed to the top of the cliff. The gesture was clear enough for the camera to record the communication of Kristanf asking to bring eight tarpons up to the top of the cliff, where many people were still looking for shelter.

Cameras rolling, it took a lot of energy for 5432 to force a smile and shake his head in agreement to the camera. He handed Kristanf six tarpons while he carried two. Cameras or no cameras, there was a limit to his even most disciplined behavior and he was not going to exert any type of energy for these pigs.

They were both climbing the side perimeter of the cliffs when, now well out of earshot of any microphones and cameras, the soldier offered, "You're damn lucky the media is here. Otherwise, I would rather put a bullet in your skull than lift a finger for you, you piece of shit."

"You have got to get to the top of the cliff where the eight families are waiting on the other side," Kristanf directed, ignoring his remark. The soldier, fearful of still being within camera range, resentfully obliged.

"Well, fuck you and the eight families, insect," dropping the six tarpons on the ground once reaching the top certain there were no media in sight.

To add a finishing touch, 5432 turned his back on Kristanf and began urinating on the tarpons. It was then, when the soldier was swaying side by side, glazing the tarpon with his own piss, that Kristanf got a short running start and drove his knee between the soldier's shoulder blades, knocking the wind out of him and dropping him to the ground. Kristanf immediately turned the soldier over and pinned his shoulders down with his knees. You could not say Kristanf was a very big man, but at six feet and nearly 200 pounds, he made the soldier lose all mobility. Spit and saliva was forming on the Kristanf's mouth in a froth of anger.

"What you think you're doing, asshole? Get the hell off me," 5432 demanded.

"I don't think so. Down deep in that thick skull of yours, I want you remember the night you drove us out onto these islands. Do you remember, hmm? You remember crashing into people's houses, shooting up their homes and driving helpless women and children out into the cold and unforgiving night? Do you remember?"

"Yeah, I remember. Probably the most enjoyable time I had with the Guard yet."

"You also remember a young boy who would not

put up with your brutality and threw a rock at you?"

"Oh yeah. The little dick had the balls to strike a soldier of the Chevkan Republic Guard. I put a hole in his chest, large enough for you to put your fist through."

"That little dick was my son, you bloody animal. He was just a boy. What kind of man are you, with an M-14 carbine in your hands, shooting a defenseless kid?"

"One last time, get off me or I will send you on a permanent visit to your son."

It was at this point that Kristanf reached into his coat and took out Luther's shoe. The soldier looked at him in confusion as he started to bend and shape the shoe, curling it up at its edges and further bending it into a U-shape.

As he flipped it over and put the toe of the shoe in the soldier's mouth, he said, "This is a little gift from my son, Luther. I saved it just for you."

With each word, he moved the shoe further and further down into the soldier's throat, not yet completely cutting his airway off, but making the soldier's face start to grow flush.

"This is the shoe my son was wearing when you shot him like an animal."

Kristanf started to shove the shoe down even further into the soldier's throat. This changed hue of the soldier's face from red to purple.

"This is the shoe my son was wearing when he was breathing his last breath of life that you took away from. Taste it my friend. Feel the last object of a dying boy traveling down your throat on its way to your heart."

At this point, Kristanf pushed forward and put the

palms of his hands on the back heel of the shoe, starting to put pressure on it in earnest. Further down it went with Kristanf's hand acting like a jackhammer, pushing it further and further down the soldier's throat, spreading the c-shaped cartilaginous rings of the larynx and trachea, allowing the shoe to gain further entrance down the soldier's airway.

The face of purple now transformed into a dark ashen gray color with his eyes starting to bulge out like two white marbles. The gagging and gasps for air were now coming in short bursts, with each utterance from the soldier only escalating Kristanf's already peaked anger.

He pushed the shoe down almost to the point where the heel was almost touching the soldier's top lip. His chest was heaving up and down, but there was very little air getting in. The oxygen was starting to deplete from his blood and brain damage was slowly setting in.

Kristanf pushed harder and harder until he came to what felt like the end, completely sealing off the air in the soldier's esophagus. The only remaining orifice that was in the slightest position of letting in any semblance of air in was the nose. Kristanf let this continue for a while, letting the soldier suffer by making enough available air for him to feel the pain and the horror that he had delivered to so many people on that cold and rainy November night.

"How does it feel? How does it feel to lose your life for no reason at all? This is from my son, you murderer."

Kristanf rose his head up toward the heavens and cried in a maniacal wail, "Luther, do you see what we are doing to your killer? The brave son of a bitch who took your life is not very comfortable now, is he?"

The soldier's chest kept on heaving for air, but it was not reaching its target.

"Look, Luther. Look how he struggles to hang on to life, where he took yours in a split-second. Now it is your turn, my son. Now it is your turn for revenge."

Kristanf placed his fingers on the nostrils of the soldier where bulging eyes pleaded for mercy. Kristanf strengthened his grasp on the nostrils and squeezed them almost to a point where he was starting to break the cartilage. The soldier's heaving and garbled gagging continued for almost three minutes until it finally stopped, leaving him limp and lifeless beneath Kristanf.

He held on to the nostrils for another two minutes, not only for good measure to make sure that the beast was dead, but also to reap every last second of making the prick suffer. He got off the soldier, turned him around and grabbed both of the dead man's wrists. He dragged him toward the end of the cliff until he finally had him parallel to the edge. He removed Luther's shoe from his mouth and placed it back in his coat. He brought him near enough that now it would take only the slightest touch to send him over the edge and onto the rocks below.

Kristanf looked once more skyward and whispered, "For all it is worth, Luther, so goes the killer of my boy straight down to hell. This will appear as an accident as the poor soldier obviously lost his footing and crashed to the rocks below. What a shame, eh, Luther?"

With that, Kristanf sent the soldier over the edge with one slight push of his boot, watching him fall with his midsection coming to an abrupt halt as he was impaled squarely at the tip of one of the spiraled cathedral-like rock formations.

Kristanf then sat down, legs dangling off the edge of the cliff, and wept.

CHAPTER 25

It was through her friendship with the mother of a member of the underground, who had clear knowledge of what was going on with the boxes, that Dana Rubinski's mother found out and had told Dana about this during one of her trips back home. This was right in Dana's wheelhouse: revolution, opposition and doing the right thing. How brave these truckers were to take on such a risky task in collecting, boxing and hiding the last remnants of legacy these people had left.

After hours of convincing confidentiality to the owner, she visited the warehouse and stood before the boxes with tears in her eyes. These people probably would never get a chance to see the contents again. All those memories and evidence of precious lives gathering dust, yearning to be rejoined with their families.

Well, maybe better in the warehouse of a stranger than at the bottom of the sea, she lamented.

The whole image of container loads of strewn remains of homes and years of joy being carted out for dumping at sea by a barge made her kneel down in front of the mountain of boxes, absorbing the defeat of these people. Dumped by a barge. A barge!

Suddenly, Dana stood back up with a grin on her face.

CHAPTER 26

Bob was devoted to maintain his "training" by any means possible, often abiding by the "necessity is the mother of invention" convention. Sure, road work, pushups and sit-ups required no equipment but it was agility training for which he needed props. Bobbing, weaving and ducking ranked as the more important tools the fighter needs to remain sharp with. Back in the States, the gym would have rubber ball, about the size of a small basketball tethered to the floor and ceiling by strong elastic bands. As the trainer would snap the ball in all different directions, Bob would step within range and practice his combinations while slipping through the snapping of the flailing ball perfecting hand, eye and foot movement that would keep him close yet out of shooting range of his opponent. This would present opportunities of positioning that would have his opponent leaving the front door open for a very nasty delivery of pain. He hadn't done any of this since he got to the islands and getting rusty in this department is asking for trouble, REAL trouble once back in the ring. Bob needed to keep this skillset continuously on the mark as it maintained a kind of natural rhythm essential for defense and executing the fight strategy. Some of the children grabbed their soccer balls during the "exit party", but there were no materials available to simulate the heavy duty rubber bands. One day while doing his morning road work, he came across a swamp leading to a river bed having nothing more than a muddy bottom left to its credit. Along the fringes of both were rather tall reeds, spread maybe two to three feet from each other. They would sway back and forth in the breeze in different directions and snap back into position quickly depending on the strength of their root base.

Bob thought to take a short cut back to camp through this mob of overgrown weeds and found himself moving back and forth, dodging to avoid getting popped by the rather beefy reeds, It was getting late and he picked up the pace to a slight jog, finding dodging a bit more challenging and before long taking on his boxing posture, throwing jabs and hooks while still avoiding the sting of getting batted. It suddenly occurred to him that he found his "ball tethered by rubber bands" concept and now incorporated, as it would later be referenced, "running of the reeds," to his regimen. Perfect!

Finally making it out of the clearing on the other end of the small field of reeds, he came across one of the larger enclosures that housed the children who lost both their parents on that horrific November night. Every time he visited, Bob couldn't get the image of Oliver Twist out of his head. The story and the play were sad, but it being portrayed as a musical somehow took the sting away from the lonely reality of being an orphan.

"Please, sir, I want some more." Bob had always thought this was a charming scene, but each time he came to the orphanage on the island, all the charm was hammered away by the sight of these kids' faces. Oh, these children weren't in rags or disheveled like those who clamored and sang in the streets of nineteenth century London, nor were they being trained as pickpockets, for that matter, as they were well cared for and given extra attention by the mothers and teenage girls who volunteered as caretakers. This was the way of the people of the Upper

14 provinces of Antonia. They cared for each other like they were one of their own. This was the bond and structure of a community whose culture was thousands of years in the making that even the unchallenged brutality of Dimitrii Crogan could not break.

Each time Bob visited, he'd attempt to enter with good cheer and a positive aura, but would always leave with a lump in his throat and tears in his eyes. And every time he returned for a visit, he promised himself that he would bring in the cheerful presence of a Santa Claus to help these poor little victims sort their way through the understanding that Mommy and Daddy weren't coming to get them.

With one particular visit, Bob had noticed a small boy sitting alone, cross-legged, not playing with the others and staring out the window as though waiting for two figures to miraculously appear on the horizon and take him home. This clearly broke Bob's heart, not that it didn't have enough of a trampling when he first met Natalia and understood what terrible things happened to her family.

He walked over to the small boy and he himself sat cross-legged, not too near, but close enough to join him in looking out the window. The small boy looked up at him with wide eyes; the expression alone could bring down a mountain. The weight of trauma this kid was trying to deal with was overwhelming.

"Hiya, big guy, what's your name?"

"Stefan."

"Well, hello, Stefan, I'm Bob."

"Hi, Bob."

Well, this worked a lot faster than when he first met Natalia. She took a while to come around until she could get her persona up and running to hold a conversation.

Trauma works in different ways with children of different ages; some fold deep inside themselves in search of some type of comfort. Then some, on the other hand, are a little bit more gregarious, which probably might be of more concern, as it could be the deadly signal of denial. That would be a harder nut to crack.

He continued to stare at Bob as though waiting for the next point in the conversation.

"How old are you, Stefan?"

"I'm five. How old are you?"

This sparked Bob's attention and amusement. Here was a kid whose whole world revolved around his parents. Now they were gone and he had the wherewithal to carry on a conversation as though nothing had happened. Then again, what was Bob expecting? Even though he was too young to understand the gravity of the situation, you can bet back in the deep recesses of his mind, this boy was more than just grieving.

"I'm twenty-six," *and feeling older every minute,* Bob thought.

Most of the children there had the good fortune of having relatives who eventually found them and took them, making their stay there short-lived. Unfortunately, there was a handful that had no one except their parents, probably people who recently migrated to the Upper 14 away from the hypocrisy of the Lower 43 to seek a calm, civilized and stress-free lifestyle.

Bob's guess, which was later verified, was that Stefan belonged to the latter population. Looking at this kid and the growing realization of his remaining an orphan for quite some time (eventually someone would come to his rescue, but when?) started to unnerve Bob. Then, fueled by lingering endorphins from his run, he had an idea.

Irinia had Luther's shoe wrapped in an old wool blanket tucked in the back drawer within a set of crude pine cabinets the relief party had provided. She wanted the shoe out of sight as the thought of that horrible night, and what happened to her baby, still crippled her inside. But if the enclosure was to catch fire, and the drawer stuck shut, she would go down in flames without hesitation in attempting to retrieve it. It was buried beneath wool, enshrined, and would go with her wherever she went for the rest of her life.

It was curious how the shoe was now slightly curled up and bent out of shape from the first time she saw it. Kristanf probably toppled something heavy on it, she thought, and forgot about it for a few days, then returned it back to where it belonged.

She busied herself most days with taking care of Natalia and her husband. Irinia worried most about Natalia, as she seemed to withdraw inside of herself, not making any effort to join in with the other children. This worried her to no end as she was concerned that the tragedy of Luther's death would forever hold her in its grip and never let her be a child again.

Irinia and the other women bonded that much more closely with these types of concerns and adapting their families to their new homes. The other women were very careful when extending their condolences for Luther to her, as they didn't want to spark a conflagration of tears and hysteria that could very well have been their own. The poor woman had been through enough, they empathized.

Kristanf busied himself by helping with the development efforts of the relief party, erecting enclosures serving as a point of distribution for supplies and anything else he could do to give back to humanity in replacing what had been unjustly ripped from him. He worried about Natalia and Irinia, and how his family was going to adapt.

Most of the men felt the same way. They all had the instinct of protecting their families and, in their minds, had not put out the flames of hatred and anger that still raged in each and every one of them. There had been whispers and speculation about the soldier who was found impaled on one of the spiraling rock formations. Some said was an accident, some said he was pushed, but all agreed the bastard deserved it. Only worse should happen to the rest of this band of killers that the government had "hand-picked from the very best" and trained as "soldiers." Sociopathic puppets of a psychopathic asshole is a more apt moniker.

The other men all knew about Luther's horrific end and carefully offered their condolences to Kristanf, who would force a smile, tell them (of which they would all readily agree) what a good boy he was and that he was in God's hands now. This did absolutely nothing to erase the pain that would be forever carved into his heart. But just the same, he loved his neighbors, the men around him, and would forever call them his brothers.

Bob rounded a bend past three oak trees until he finally reached Kristanf and Irinia's tent. He walked past the front doorway with little Stefan in tow. He walked slowly and looked through the doorway to see if Irinia noticed them, but she was in the back folding clothes.

He walked another ten yards to make it look casual, did an about-face and passed by the open doorway again. She still seemed pretty focused on making sure those clothes were folded properly. He repeated this ritual about six times, one of which caught the attention of eighty-six-year-old Slenka Chivonic who, perched at the mouth of her tent, thought that they were having an affair. Then again, within the glorious realm of her increasing dementia, she was certain everyone on the island was having an affair, for sure. With the last go-around Bob let out a cough that at last caught Irinia's attention.

"Hello there, Bob," Irinia greeted as cheerily as she could muster.

"Oh, hiya, Irinia. How's it going? Seems like it can't get any colder until the next day rolls around, setting a new record," which was the intention of the sentence, but he did not know the Chevkan equivalent of "record" so he made a hand raised up two times to try to act out the word.

She smiled in amusement and thought this young man was exceptional and, well, cute. "That's for sure. Thank goodness for these little wood burning stoves they supplied us. Just enough to keep the chill out of the place. Who's your young friend?"

"Oh him?" Bob said, nodding down as nonchalantly as a thief breaking open a safe in Macy's window, "This is Stefan, all five years of him. Say hello, Stefan."

"Hello," Stefan offered shyly.

"Well, he's absolutely adorable. And what a beautiful head of dark hair he has. His parents must be very proud to lay claim to such a beautiful child."

"I'm sure they would, but they're no longer with us," Bob confided gently.

Irinia's heart dropped like an elevator from the twentieth floor to the lobby in just a few short seconds. This, along with Stefan now gazing up at her with his patented big doe eyes, made her ooze with a plethora of emotions that almost made her dizzy.

She flipped forward her apron, allowing her to kneel in front of Stefan, looking back up at Bob.

"He's just a baby; a very impressionable baby, unfortunately. Does he realize what has happened?"

"Well, he's been looking out the window at the orphanage, waiting for Mommy and Daddy, yet knowing that they will never come. He's caught between a child desperately holding on to the last glimmer of hope in gaining back the ground beneath him, yet trying to come to grips like a brave little man with what happened. My guess is that he hasn't opened the floodgates of tears yet. But once this young mind reconciles this, he'll need more than a parachute to come even close to a somewhat decent landing."

Then, in an odd sort of way, Irinia considered herself fortunate, in a sense. Natalia was old enough to process what had happened to her brother, however exponentially painful it was for her at her age, but she had two parents at her side at all times to help her cope and dole out constant support.

Here was a baby, a boy of five years old, who had not yet been purged of the appropriate emotions and could be running great risk of having a buildup that might explode into thousand tiny pieces. This clearly set a platform for lifetime damage. Although Irinia only knew this child for ten minutes, she worried for him, as she was all too aware the scarring this had had on hers and all the other children.

It was about this time that the small gathering in front of her enclosure caught Natalia's attention. She was off to the right, underneath her favorite oak tree with her dolly, listlessly combing its hair in the same spot for the past hour. She got up and joined Irinia, Bob and Stefan more out of curiosity than the desire to socialize.

As Irinia knelt in front of Stefan, she greeted Natalia as she came over to join in. Increasingly curious about this new visitor, she could see the pain in his face that the adults couldn't and, in a surge of extending herself to the younger child, managed an inquisitive, "Hi."

"Hi, my name is Stefan," he shot back.

Bob also chimed in, "Hi, sweetie. How are you?"

Natalia's eyes remained riveted on Stefan. "I'm Natalia. How old are you, Stefan?"

"Gee whiz, everybody asks me the same question. I'm five. FIVE!" Holding up four fingers in front of everyone's faces, soliciting a short but much-needed laugh from Irinia, something she had not experienced since that dreadful night at the birthday party. And, to Irinia's delight, as she was studying Natalia's face, she could see a small smirk gather at the corner of her lips. This was like winning the lottery! She hadn't seen any type of reaction on Natalia's face since the news of Luther's death.

Kristanf had then returned back home, as it was getting close to dinnertime, and joined in, or one could say drank in, the innocence of the moment. He silently stood by as the conversation continued, feeling a curious warmth of emotion start to build inside him.

"Oh my, Stefan. I didn't mean to make you mad," Natalia said, now taking on a more adult tone in her voice as she was no longer the youngest, at least in this little group.

"Oh, that's okay, Natalia. I'm not mad. I'm… I can't…" Stefan said as tears started to well up in his eyes. This whole exposure to a complete family unit probably would be the final pin pulled from his resolve to start the blocks tumbling down inside.

Bob, looking to intercept this as quickly as he could, said, "Well, it's getting a little late, Stefan. We really should be heading back as everyone will be eating supper soon."

Natalia felt bad that she made this small boy sad. She knew what it was like to be hurt, when you feel like you will never stop crying. Somehow, she felt empowered that she had more "experience" with this than the vulnerable little boy in front of her. She had to, and wanted to, help him. Like the way Luther used to help her see things differently when she was sad.

"No, wait!" Natalia yelped, catching both her mother and father by surprise. "I mean, um, maybe Stefan would like to have dinner with us. Can he, Mom, please?"

Irinia and Kristanf both looked at each other, not quite getting the essence of the equation that Bob was trying to drop on them.

With tears now retreating back into his eyes, Stefan announced, “I don’t like peas. I don’t like them, I won’t eat them.”

“Why not?” Natalia asked.

“I don’t like the way they look. They’re all squishy and everything.”

Now, like gold coins showering down from heaven, Natalia let out a laugh. Irinia and Kristanf’s hearts did leap frogs.

“Well, peas are good for you and you will eat every last one of them, I’ll make sure of that.”

Like all young girls her age, Natalia took on the beginning footprints of motherhood by role playing with her dolly, developing the attributes of nurturing that she would later use in life with her own children. Now Irinia and Kristanf were looking at each other with that silent communication that only was accomplished after years of marriage of what was to come next.

“Well, okay. But I’m not going to like it,” Stefan surrendered, looking up at Bob for any last glimmer of support otherwise. No dice.

Natalia was now clearly basking in the glow of victory reserved for situations like this and commensurate of being the “big sister” – the same thought now riveting through both Irinia and Kristanf’s minds like a lightning bolt. Irinia seized the moment at full throttle.

“Honey, how would you like to stay with us? Would you like to become part of our family?”

Eureka! Correct! Light bulb moment! Scoooooooore! Bob was beginning to worry that this seed he was drilling into everyone's heads wasn't going to break ground.

"But I have a family," Stefan said stubbornly as his eyes now drifted down toward the ground in uncertainty. Bob knew this was a pivotal moment for the boy and needed to be handled ever so delicately. He knew Irinia's motherly instinct would kick in.

"I know, sweetheart, I know. Mommy and Daddy are right here," Irinia said, placing her hand gently on his chest over his heart.

Not quite there, but a softened pace toward understanding, Stefan said, "Mommy and Daddy aren't coming back, are they?" Half question, half statement. Irinia was now holding him in her arms, slowly beginning to rock him, bracing him for foul weather. She could feel the boy vibrate like a boiler ready to bust. Natalia took hold of Kristanf's hand and squeezed hard, as she, too, had tears rolling down her cheeks.

"No, baby. They went to heaven." Irinia's tears now cascaded down her wonderfully formed cheekbones. Both Kristanf and Bob, in accord with the societal expectations of stoicism in a man, turned their backs so they, too, may have their moment.

"But why? Why did they have to go?" he pleaded. Women have an instinct, part of their DNA, knowing how to say just the right things at just the right time. They smooth out the rough edges of life for you.

"Well, honey, sometimes God needs help in heaven and only asks special people to do that."

Stefan was mulling this over when he finally asked, "But why didn't he take someone else?"

This startled Irinia for a millisecond, but she let her heart do the driving.

"They must be very special people," Irinia guided the conversation.

"The very best," Stefan offered proudly.

"Do you think they would want you to be a brave boy and understand that they have to help God?"

"Yes," Stefan said, in a low whisper.

The boy's eyes then squeezed shut and his mouth opened with saliva rimming its surface, dripping to a drool down his lower lip. He buried his head in Irinia's chest and started to cry like a five-year-old should cry when he's realized he's lost his parents forever.

It was official; the floodgates were now open and the boy let out a torrent of tears that had been building up for weeks.

And Natalia now had a brand new baby brother.

CHAPTER 27

Following the 1917 revolution, Christmas had been forbidden in Russia until it was later restored with the fall of the Soviet Union in 1992. Although taboo, many villages still reveled in secrecy. This story of Christmas is very much the same as it is in America, except it is celebrated on January 7 instead of December 25.

During the times when it was okay to celebrate and the coast was clear, people would go from village to village, sharing and giving, taking in exchange what their neighbors had to offer them. It was the very festive time with a Christmas Eve fast followed by a meal commencing the celebration.

One would fast until the first star rose in the night sky in celebration of the birth of Christ, whereupon afterwards it was permitted to eat. This was part of the Old Russian Orthodox faith and meat was not allowed on the menu. The meal was referred to as "the Holy Supper" and was accentuated with one candle at the center of the table symbolizing Christ as "the Light of the World" with a round Lenten loaf of bread called pagach, Christ's " Bread of Life," set next to the lit candle.

Mothers would bless each one of their children and make the sign of the cross on their foreheads with honey, reciting the Lord's Prayer and wishing them many good things in the coming New Year. Afterwards, everyone would take a turn dipping the bread first into honey and then in a garlic mixture to symbolize the sweetness and the bitterness of life, respectively.

It was a grand and happy occasion largely free of

the heavy hand of Soviet law, since they didn't give a shit about the people of the Upper 14 provinces. The Soviet ban on Christmas translated to the replacement of St. Nicholas with Ded Moroz, or Grandfather Frost, the Russian Spirit of Winter who brought gifts on New Year's. This simply would not do, so screw the Soviet ban on Christmas.

As the first star finally rose up into the night sky and the festivities began, laughter and dance filled the top of the hill where the center of the festivities was being held. Natalia and Stefan brought along their new Christmas gifts: clothes for Natalia's dolly and a small toy truck cleverly carved from a thick tree limb. It seemed all that happened in the last two months was banished in the euphoric din of Christmas Eve.

After the meal was done, Sergei stepped atop a makeshift stage, a couple of cargo crates covered with support planks that had been used on the cargo planes. He put the bullhorn to his mouth (and Sergei really loved this bullhorn; he gave him a real big kick in hearing his voice travel across the landscape), his breath from the cold night highlighted by the light from behind the stage, and welcomed all to their first Christmas on the Svenkia Islands.

"Welcome, welcome. It is truly a blessing that we're all here together, gaining back our health, keeping warm, eating well and beginning to heal. It's been a horrible two months for us, but help is now here and we will get our lives back and continue with pride and dignity. I want to give special thanks to Bob Perry, the man who cared the most and left behind a very comfortable life in the United States to come here and help us. Someday we will return the favor, my friend."

During the time he continued his speech, the faintest sound began to emerge down below on the shoreline. Gradually the rumbling began to get louder and pick up momentum. It was the sound of hooves click clacking on a stone and mud path leading up from the beach. It sounded like an army of horses accompanied by the sound of clapboards squeaking.

The mules first appeared at the top of the rise led by handlers with squeaky carts in tow, continued past the crowd and started to line up around the top hill were Sergei was standing on the stage (Sergei was privy to what this parade was all about). In the carts stacked five high and four across were boxes of the same dimensions with writing on the side. The mules were guided to line up facing a crowd of people of full bellies and good cheer (some of which was provided by wine the adults had the pleasure of having thanks to Sgt. Hayes and his team's second return trip to the islands).

After the surprise and delight of the ice cream trucks rolling down the ramp of the C- 27 cargo planes, they had expected this show to somehow bring more delight to their children. No one knew what could possibly be in the boxes, but all being of equal dimensions, it had to be some more standard supply issues of survival; maybe blankets, pillows, toilet tissue or something like that.

Sergei got down off the platform, picked up the first box and announced, "1225 Harvest Lane." People looked at each other in bewilderment not yet making the connection of what this shouting out of addresses was all about.

"Hey, that's our address," a man named Losif

shouted out.

"Well, come up and get your box," Sergei bellowed through his bullhorn.

As Losif made his way through the crowd to retrieve the box, it was anybody's guess what this was all about. Sergei continued to call out the addresses and people would raise their hands, go on up and grab their box.

Losif was the first to open the box. Inside, he found his favorite books, some of his children's toys, an old clock that to use to belong to his grandfather, some jewelry and photographs. He and his wife Holga were choking back tears as they were unloading each item in the box one by one as though they were defusing a bomb.

"Look, Holga, our wedding picture!"

She felt overwhelming joy holding the family pictures close to her breast, never wanting to let them go. As the others were opening up their boxes, there was the murmur of their voices, squeals of surprise and tears of emotion. However small and insignificant, each item gave them back a piece of their homes that they were forced to leave behind. This was something they could now introduce into their new homes, continuing their legacy and heritage.

Dana knew the captain of the tugboat, also an Antonia sympathizer from the northern fringe of the Lower 43, who was hauling the barge holding the precious cargo, again, underneath a light coating of debris as camouflage. Before heading out to sea, he took a hard right for the Svenkia Islands' southwestern portion of the beach. The timing had to be just right for low tide to allow the barge to be pushed forward with his flat bottom resting perilously less than two feet above the sea floor, allowing the mules with their carts to line up and gather their precious cargo.

The whole operation took a little over an hour and had to be hurried as the tide started to rise, signaling to the barge a window of time to make an exit. The cartons from the warehouse had to be hurriedly smuggled under the cloak of darkness to the waiting trucks heading toward the piers. What turned out to be a good idea of the truckers was made into a great idea by Dana and her ingenuity.

Merry Christmas to all and to all a good night.

CHAPTER 28

He must've done it at least a dozen or more times, mostly in the dark when getting up in the middle of the night to pee. Sometimes he did it in broad daylight by simply not paying attention. The familiar curled-up furry back of a sleeping Emma served as a good trip point at ankle height on many an occasion. This was much the same sensation as he was running the reeds this one particular day, except feeling and tripping over a furry back well above the shin and almost knee high.

Normally tripping over, landing gracefully and regaining his balance, this time he went head over heels, crashing into the wavering reeds ahead. He thought he might've tripped over a sleeping cow or steer, but after rolling back on his side and looking over his left shoulder, he was about six yards away from and face-to-face with a lioness. She sat up instantly in a crouched position and roared menacingly, snarling and baring her well-stocked shelf of front fangs and additional rear dental work designed for some serious damage.

At this point, Bob was waiting to be mauled, his only wish being that it would be quick and he wouldn't have to suffer the pain of sharp claws piercing his body and strong jaw muscles crunching his bones. He knew he was a dead man when an eerie calm took over in resignation, accepting death.

She continued to snarl when Bob noticed her back right leg was quivering as though hooked up to an electrical outlet and was convulsing out of control. She laid down in a crouched position when it became apparent she had a deep gash in her right hindquarter. By the looks of the coagulation and the growing scabs, Bob surmised that this may have occurred five or six days ago. He surely wasn't any kind of expert, but he had watched enough of Mutual of Omaha's Wild Kingdom to realize that here was probably a deposed matriarch of her pride who had been ousted in what looked like a very ugly battle for position.

No longer in control, not leading the pride in overnight hunting parties; she was now not very useful. She probably was of an age where she wasn't even considered attractive enough to get a rise by the one or two males in the pride for breeding, no matter how much musk and other lioness perfume she spayed about pathetically.

Clearly an outcast with a debilitating wound, she probably hadn't eaten in a week or two. And coming across a lion that is very hungry and in pain is just as good as putting the barrel of a gun squarely in your ear and pulling the trigger. This was one bitch you didn't want to piss off.

It was quite evident that she couldn't move quickly enough to do any damage to this moron who just tripped over her. Her paws were the size of a catcher's mitt, which surely housed razor-sharp claws, each one of which she was probably itching to rip across this idiot of a human. Oh, the pain in her thigh ripped through the side of her torso all the way across her back. She could barely walk and was losing weight, as evidenced by the row of ribs clearly visible.

She snarled and roared again in defiance as Bob started to edge backwards, only to be held back by the reeds. As it was evident that she wasn't able to kill, although surely that was on her mind, Bob stood up and edged his way to the left to get out of the field of reeds. As he was doing so, he could hear her roar in an attempt to hold on to any remaining dignity she might have had, any pride in herself as a once powerful and dynamic leader of a hunting pack and mother to dozens of cubs. She was practically crippled, unable to stalk and kill again, and her animal instincts of impending death made her seek a place within the reeds to invite death to come and quietly take her.

It was only after Bob got into a clearing that he started to shake uncontrollably from the suppressed fear of what he thought was his inevitable death. So much so that he almost fell to his knees as he felt all the blood drain from head down to his arms and legs. He realized he was no immediate threat to her and also understood that if she didn't get something to eat soon, she would die.

He walked back to one of the portable meat lockers and pulled out a section of quartered pig (this was how it was delivered on dry ice; it was up to you to slice it into the right sizes for cooking). He brought it to the edge of the reed field and inched his way back to the spot he thought would be his final resting place. The lioness could smell the pork even before Bob entered the reed field and it only served to heighten her agony of hunger.

Once he got within fifteen feet, he threw the quartered pig near enough so she could probably carefully and painfully crawl to greet it. It was the most precious thing for her right then and she tore into it, devouring large chunks in one ripping thrust of her powerful jaws. Bob could hear the bones crunch as she made sure her she made good use of everything the clumsy human threw to her. Ah, but now she needed something to wash it down.

Bob went back to the supply shed, got a five gallon basin and filled it three quarters to the top. As he was returning to the reed field, he realized that this would be a good object to incorporate into his work out for forearm presses. Note to file. But the basin clearly couldn't be thrown from ten feet; he'd have to get closer to her so she could negotiate the one or two feet to drink.

As he was progressing toward her, he could feel the weight in both his forearms and chest, and decided that this definitely was to be added to his "gym equipment." But he had to focus on the subject, the approach and definitely a plan B in case the flank of pig she just inhaled renewed her strength and energy. And clearly plan B was simply to drop the basin and run like a bastard.

As he carefully walked toward her, she was still working the last remaining bone marrow, crunching it under her powerful jaws as though she was chewing gum, which made the hair on the back of Bob's neck stand up. Ever sympathetic to those in pain and trouble, he knew that she needed to drink. What a prince, huh?

As hc got within a foot or two, she did nothing but begin a low resonance of a snarl. Bob placed the basin carefully within two feet of her, taking in what he thought might be his last moment on this green earth, but she made no attempt to engage him. Her basic instinct for survival was to attack first and never be on the defensive. It was how she survived and how she warded off potential enemies in the past. But that was then and this was now.

But Bob wasn't done yet. He was really pushing the envelope with the next task. He went back to the supply shack, got a very large Slurpee-type cup and filled it half with warm water and half with some peroxide he found on one of the medical supply shelves.

He once again traced his steps back to the lioness and this time approached from behind, which really was stupid, since to her this meant he was planning on attacking her, at least in wild kingdom terms. She strained her neck around, twisting her torso, only to aggravate the wound, sending rockets of pain through her lower right side.

This time he decided that he could execute at a distance because the results would be excruciating stinging and wound aggravation. And having been in fights in which getting beaten up pretty well enraged him, the pumping adrenaline helped him manage the damage he accumulated to find the strength to summarily pulverize his opponent. He wondered if this would be the same with his lioness.

But, nonetheless positioned behind and slightly to her right side with a clear shot at her, he threw the cocktail of watered peroxide directly on the wound, soliciting almost what sounded like a human scream of pain (very spooky) as the peroxide began its work dissipating all the dirt and germs from the wound where a ring of foam around the gash in her leg came bubbling up high and white. He didn't especially enjoy hurting the animal, but this was necessary. And seeing as she wasn't going anywhere or attacking anything, which oftentimes meant the animal rolling in the dirt while clamped down on a water buffalo's nose, she was at least in a position to keep the wound clean and let it heal.

He decided his luck was just about spent and to leave well enough alone. It was getting dark when he returned to his trailer and got back to the business at hand of reviewing the day's notes and financials on the progress of the Svenkian Islands' new habitants. Having filled her tummy, at least temporarily, and quenching the thirst that left her mouth and throat dry for the last week, she slowly curled up, laid head down her head on those massive paws and fell blissfully asleep.

Bob repeated this ritual of feeding and providing water for his lioness every day for two weeks. As each day passed, each visit became less and less tense. He now walked up to her with a flank of meat and returned with the basin of water (which he was now using to do arm presses during the delivery), with no snarling, but now a look of curiosity on her face. She was starting to believe that this other animal who walked upright was a caregiver, making her feel good, hunting for her (not really) and providing her with what she needed so badly.

The wound on her back leg started to grow pink around the edges with the healing flesh starting to close the hole a very powerful female competitor had inflicted. On one particular visit, she was standing upright, which made Bob hesitate before delivering the meat. Instinctively, he did not sense danger and, just as animals can sense/smell the body language of their opponents or other colleagues of the pride, can humans also gather that sense.

He placed the meat before her. She sniffed at it and looked up at him complacently.

For some reason, he wanted to touch her. He wanted to feel her fur; he wanted to feel the life beneath such a strong and powerful animal. Now he realized why Johnny would call him a dumb ass sometimes. Go figure.

He lifted up his right hand and drew closer to her, ready to step back and run at the slightest indication that she was faking it and was going to rip his bowels out from under him. She did nothing when he raised his hand and moved it toward her snout. Bob gently placed his hand on her and let it rest ever so gradually. She received his hand and tilted her head upwards, nudging Bob's hand as if to say, "Come on, lover boy. Give Mama some stroking."

He withdrew his hand after what seemed an eternity and decided that was enough for today and that a long and dangerous bridge had now been crossed. He felt as good about what he did for this animal as he did for what he was doing for the people on the island. She then went into a crouch in front of the meat and started to get down to business. Bob returned about five minutes later with the basin of water. It was a good day.

Now she has to have a proper name, Bob thought.

What should he call her? Shena, Queen of the Jungle? Betty, Beast of the Wild? Louise? Yeah, Louise. Louise the Lion. Pretty corny, but he liked it. Now he realized why Johnny also called him, "knucklehead." Some people just do not have a good imagination. By this time, she was up and nimble, walking and even trotting after small game. Sometimes she would try to keep up with him when he ran the reeds, but still wasn't quite up to it… someday, someday soon.

Then, one day, as he exited the field of reeds, she tagged along with him. Hell, there was no one around. Why not? He continued walking and got lost in thought about the next phases for the Islands and didn't realize he was walking through the main encampments with her tagging along behind him. Immediate reactions of some of the people were open mouths and slowly backing away, breaking into a run when sufficient distance was met, too frightened and speechless to even sound out a warning. Bonnie was coming out of her trailer when she witnessed this; her expression also gaped.

"Bob. BOB!" *He never listens goddamn it.*

"Hey, hot stuff."

Hot stuff?...asshole. "Bob, be still. Bc *very* still."

"Why?" he asked innocently, savoring the moment.

"There is a very large lion stalking you," she whispered, close to tears. She was incredibly frightened and didn't want to make any sudden motion or noise that would agitate the beast into a killing frenzy. Emma, now always in force with her new BFF, let out a menacing, albeit easily retractable (if necessary) growl between the safe confines of Bonnie's ankles.

"Oh, you mean Louise."

"Louise?"

"Oh, where are my manners? Louise, meet one of the brightest and hottest psychologists on the island. Bonnie, my sweet mistress of the brain, meet Louise."

Bonnie's jaw dropped almost touching the top of her chest. Since this was confusing Louise, she decided it was a good time to crouch down on all fours. She could sense that this was another female who also had two legs like the leader of her new pride (she was still looking for Bob's tail).

It's one of those wonderful phenomena of nature that animals of any kind can sense one another of the same sex. Must be the smell of feral hormones or some other uneducated guess like that.

Louise was curious about the bitch who looked angry at her leader and thought that she would probably have to share him with her. In her last pride, she was one of eight lionesses who mated with the same male. But this was only one more and she was hoping that would be it. "Bob, it's a fucking lion. It could tear you to shreds in minutes, seconds!" Bonnie urged.

With that, Bob turned around and walked toward Louise and knelt down beside her. He started to stroke her back. "Can I keep her? Can I? Can I please?"

Both astounded and horrified, she said, "Bob, there are children around here. Very tasty morsels that I'm sure she, I'm sorry, Louise, would enjoy very much as an appetizer before she took a big chunk out of *your* ass."

Louise could sense tension in the other female. *Same to you, too, sister,* Louise thought, or however that would be translated in lionese. Whatever may be, Louise would have to get used to sharing the way she did with those seven other females that were really her loving 'sisters.' But this bitch may take some getting used to.

"Instead of you wetting your panties, why don't you come over here and say hello?"

"No way, Buster Brown. I'm no animal biologist, but relying on a woman's instinct, my guess is she's not too happy with another female being near 'her man'." She couldn't resist giggling, which made a rattling sound since it was still peppered with fear.

"Come on, Bonnie. Come meet and greet, she won't bite."

Still wincing over the wetting her panties remark, which, by the way, she actually did, she slowly took one step off her trailer, very slowly tiptoeing toward Tarzan and his ever faithful Queen of Mauling. Halfway between the distance of her trailer and the lion, she stopped and hesitated for a moment, deciding whether she was crazy or just really curious to be close to something so powerfully beautiful and yet so seemingly gentle at the same time.

She closed the distance and carefully knelt quietly down beside Louise. Louise turned her massive head and looked at Bonnie. Again, the wonderful throngs of nature switched on a silent female communication where Bonnie could feel the sense that Louise would tolerate her, but wasn't exactly glad she was joining them. Bonnie very carefully placed her hand on top of Louise's head and stroked her fur, increasing the rhythm as her pleasure and desire to get to know this docile beast increased.

Louise liked the stroking, thinking that Bonnie wasn't so bad after all, confirming this by treating her to a serenade of purring that sounded more like an idling power lawn mower. Bonnie's eyes were wide open and she couldn't believe what she was doing. In a very short period of time, this 400-pound beast would be forever endeared to her.

Louise the Lion. How corny is that? But you gotta love it anyway.

CHAPTER 29

He knew he had to stay in shape. Not necessarily the grueling pre-fight regimen that usually preceded the two months before a bout, but a level of physicality and metabolic condition that would allow him to easily slip into that pre-fight training mode. So how did he accomplish this with no gym, no punching bag, no Johnny, or any other type of weight training and conditioning equipment? Again he needed to be creative.

One of the first things that caught Bob's attention, even before running the reeds (which he continued in order to maintain his bobbing and weaving skills) and finding dear old Louise, was a sand dune. Berm would probably be a better description. It was further inland and to the southwest, rising above the shrubs as if almost calling out to him. It was about seventy meters long, thirty meters wide and about ten meters high.

His objective would be to run the dune down, from bottom to top, top to bottom, back and forth each side, zigzagging while digging his feet in and kicking back the sand until such a time the berm was no more.

He looked over the sand dune one afternoon and decided that this was his silent beast to conquer. With dogged persistence and focus, he would wear down the sandy hill until it was perfectly flat and contiguous with the rest of the landscape. He was good at setting goals for himself when it came to training and could enter the zone of discipline and remain there for many hours until he reached whatever benchmark he set.

He tried it out one afternoon and, being the time of

year when the temperatures were so low, the granules of sand were contracted, leaving very little air in between, making it hard to for Bob to drill down into it. He would need some extra weight, maybe fifty or sixty pounds, to make any kind of dent.

What he decided to do was to carry one of the children on his back when traversing the dune. This would certainly give them the poundage he needed to grind away the sand. He would line up a child every ten meters, scooping one up, zigzagging up and down both sides of the sand dune a number of times until he reached the second child. He would then scoop up the second child, who, by this time, was giggling and laughing like a little maniac, riding piggyback on Bob's back up and down the hill. Crazy Americans!

Naturally, he was never at a loss for volunteers and as time wore on, he had to start scheduling the many children who wanted in and making sure everybody had an equal amount of time in joining this deranged boxer in his training.

What Bob found was that on the way down the dune, he would be working his front thighs and calf muscles. On the way up, stress was on the back of his legs and buttocks. After a while, when the province people would hear the laughter and screams of the children, they knew that Bob was "running the dunes." Eyes rolled and grins appeared. All this seemed strange to them (not to say the least his "running the reeds" as well), but they admired him nonetheless, as they knew he had a life back in the States that he was still accountable for.

Oh, there were, of course, those exercises that he

did with very little or no equipment. Bringing the basin half full of water when nursing Louise was a good source for lifting, depending on how he held the handles, developing the forearms, biceps and, when laying prone on a table and lifting it up and down beneath him, strengthening his back.

This was steadily supervised by his "interim personal trainer," Emma. She would lay curled up in any spot that cut off the chilling wind and other than an occasional lift of the right leg in the name of good hygiene, would just "be" there for motivational purposes. She was a good and faithful dog. Just maintaining connection with Bob made her feel safe. Peppering her with treats sporadically during the day also served as an incentive to keep him under her keen eye. By this time, she had resigned herself to the fact that Bob also gave attention to the overgrown cat (she never saw one so big; the largest was Mrs. Flattenholtz's Maine Coon next door at home).

For a punching bag, one of the guys had filled a double insulated burlap bag with sand and hung it from a makeshift rafter. Unfortunately, Bob made short work of this and within ten minutes of the first workout, put his fist through the double lining of burlap, spilling sand like an hourglass.

It was only thereafter that some people realized the opportunity to "return the favor" by stitching together a number of leather jackets that some managed to bring with them and filling that with sand. Although it leaked a little bit, like a dripping faucet, it held together enough to give Bob an imaginary opponent to pummel.

For most of the routine to work the chest and lateral muscles, he used two good sized lava stones lying on a bench and crossing them over above his head and to either side simulating "flys." Now, given that these two stones weren't of equal weight, he kept careful count in his head out of his repetitions so he could switch them over to the other hands, equally distributing the intention.

He did endless sit-ups, push-ups and arm presses using two food crates and dipping in between the two to build the shoulder and pectoral muscles. Naturally, all of this translated into working up a good sweat, although he needed to be careful given the time of year and its bone chilling temperature. The sweat gushing from his open pores underneath his clothes could quickly freeze if he didn't wind down his workout slowly and retreat back into his trailer.

He also had a routine that he had recruited Louise to help him with. It deployed the use of ducks. And, believe it or not, in this frigid part of the world, there was a species of duck that inhabited the Arctic coastal plains of northern Europe, Russia and Alaska, which served as their breeding ground. The Eiders duck was not the most attractive of ducks, but had its own color distinctions that set it apart from the Mallard duck that usually flies colorfully in the skies of North America.

As with any species of duck, the male was more colorful, but both sexes displayed a proud iridescent blue edge to their wings. The Steller's Eider was the smallest species of duck. They would breed this time of year, with the whole idea of having their clutches hatch under the gradual warmth of the early spring months. It was now that the males were proudly displaying their colors to attract females to do what most animals do and that's procreate.

The males would circle the females, wagging their tails with the occasional head bobbing and quacking accompanied by a wing span spread. As a male duck, you're going to great lengths to bust your best moves to get noticed. Proud wing spreads were a must in this highly competitive environment. As the males outnumbered the females, there was the occasional skirmish as to who got screwing rights. As what can be described as the most equitable aspects of nature, most of the males did do the wild thing with a female duck, even though it meant sloppy seconds, thirds, and even fourths. No one was counting amidst this love fest on the cold windswept beaches of the Svenkia Islands (it was debatable, though, who gave out the cigars when the clutches hatched!).

For Louise, this was too good to pass up, like taking candy from baby. She would crouch down in the prone, pre-attack position, moving her position in secrecy for the impending charge using the undergrowth that edged the beach for stealth. She would get close enough with her instincts telling her to stay down wind so as not to give herself away.

The last two months of being fed well and keeping up with Bob on his daily runs left her very fit and feeling good, almost back to her old self. She was still a ruthless, fearful hunter, and queen of the Svenkia Islands (or least part of it, in her own mind, as there were plenty of healthy, truly deadly prides miles north). And her carefully executed strategy of positioning that took anywhere from thirty minutes to an hour was not done out of hunger (she was conditioned by now that there was a reliable and really tasty source of chow in abundance), but just to screw around with the birds.

At the right moment, she sprinted out onto the beach toward the center of the flock pawing as many of the ducks as she could tag without really bringing any of them down (which, at this point, she probably could have). She would dart back and forth, dispersing the flock in all different directions. She really got a kick out of this.

Lynne Albright witnessed this one day when surveying the grounds. She was mentally leveling, graveling and placing the "correct" trees and shrubbery. Supposedly tame or not, she still kept her distance from Louise, as she feared the lion may pick up the scent of the cat that barked she called a dog and ultimately lead the lion to making it an hors d'oeuvres.

But Bob told her the story of how he first found Louise and what kind of condition she was in. This intrigued Ms. Albright as she watched the new and rejuvenated Louise now stalking, well, ducks. So what? Queen of the jungle, right?

She seriously doubted that the old girl could bring down a water buffalo like on National Geographic; ducks would do and she did not seem to want to hurt them (there were wild boar on the island, which she did hunt in earnest, sometimes dragging the carcass in her mouth and between her legs back to Bob; he always passed on the dinner invite but not without praising Louise for such a fine catch). Ms. Albright told Bob about how "cute" this was and that he should take a look someday when Louise was back on the prowl.

And he did just that. And as older folk do, Louise would establish a schedule, always picking the same time of day to engage and reliable enough to set a watch by. And as for the ducks, you would think that they would pick another venue, but the instinct for breeding is far greater than the expected onslaught of Louise.

First instinct identified her as a predator, but after fleeing, all were accounted for and none killed. So, after a while, who was fooling who? Didn't really matter, all in good fun, right?

What really caught Bob's attention was the pattern of the scattering ducks. When Louise burst into motion, scaring the living shit out of them, he noticed that the ducks needed a little bit of a runway to gain motion for lift off. Since Louise was swinging her paws in every direction, the ducks would scatter, crisscrossing each other and sometimes, pathetically, bumping into each other to escape.

Although this may have been comical in practice, Bob couldn't help but empathize with the male ducks. If he were one, decked out in his Sunday best, strutting his stuff, executing every move in the book to attract a female when here comes some frustrated mountain of fur flailing her meaty mitts breaking up the party. Not only would this cramp his style, but it would ruin any type of "mood" the females might have possessed before fleeing for their lives.

But what he also noticed was the direct reverse correlation of the movement and direction of the flight of the ducks to Louise's frantic swinging in the air. Much like a boxer swinging from every different direction, the ducks would follow the lead of Louise's paws away and in the exact opposite direction of her motion, looking to avoid her swings.

What Bob realized would be an invaluable training

tool would be to run head on into the panicked ducks, using their escape routes as simulated punches with him bobbing and weaving through the frantic cloud of fowl.

As the incline of their ascent was fairly low to the ground for a good ten to fifteen meters, he would have plenty of dodging ducks he could parlay by running straight into them. When running into the field of ducks, he would use the heel of his hand to bump up a duck in a simulated jab or counterpunch.

At the end of this encounter, which lasted about fifteen seconds, he would meet Louise in the middle of the now barren beach. She would sit up resting on her back legs, flailing both paws, much the same way a kitten does when surprised. She just thought this was great fun and then would roll on her back, paws folded across her chest, legs spread like a whore, wanting her tummy stroked (to which Bob gladly obliged).

Nutty lion.

CHAPTER 30

The crowd at Madison Square Garden grew restless at the conclusion of the two undercard bouts. They were really waiting for the welterweight championship fight between Toby Grant, the reigning champ, and Felix Rivera. Felix just so happened to be managed by Tommy Rae (Tommy managed seven fighters, three of whom were rogue boxers and well trained and adequately equipped in the fine art of crooked boxing; next to Corey, Felix was a key player in his stable), with none other than Steve Shelby as sponsoring promoter. You can guess the rest.

Toby was the favorite with the "legit" bookies in Vegas and all the other underground gambling networks had Toby as a five-to-one favorite, so the stakes that both Tommy and Steve had wagered were well into six figures.

With the three members of the boxing commission sufficiently oiled, along with the official who overlooked the titanium knuckle wraps taped to Felix's hand, and the referee handsomely paid to ignore any objections or insinuations, the setup exactly mimicked the Perry-Green fight.

Felix had his gloves coated with the same dilating medication, the contact and mixture of sweat of which would render Toby's eyes practically useless. When the damage was ultimately inflicted and the suspicions were flaring from Toby's corner, the referee would ignore any contentions and let the fight continue. It was in the bag, baby!

But the fly in the ointment occurred twenty minutes before Toby and Felix were to meet. It seemed the referee who was scheduled to officiate the fight was suddenly bombarded with a killer virus that left him heaving his guts, white as a ghost and unable to stand. He was so bitten by this bug that he was both delirious and dizzy, having a real hard time remembering his own name. John Thompson, the referee from the previous fight, and a tough one at that, with an honorable and highly ethical twenty-two years under his belt, was elected to step in as his replacement.

It was ten minutes before the fight when both Steve and Tommy found out about this. Almost blind with panic, they knew that if anything suspicious came up during the bout, this referee would follow normal protocol. This definitely put a gun to their heads and they needed to do something fast, real fast.

They rambled down a stairway to the office that served as the entranceway to the referee's locker to try to intercept and convince John within a matter of minutes to drop twenty years of integrity as the fair, professional and underpaid referee to make some quick money. The only trouble was that the office door was locked and it was when John finished showering and putting on his street clothes that he was called upon to referee the main event.

There was another doorway opposite the entrance from the office that let out to another tunnel leading to the arena. John stepped out, headed into the arena, took his position at the corner of the ring, grasping the two ropes on either side, and waited for his second wind; for him, this would be a long night. He would've much rather been heading to Maggie's bar where many of the refs, managers and even some of the fighters hung out. Sure, he could use the extra cash, but he was irritated with having to stay on, especially with title fights. These could usually last all twelve rounds, leaving very little time for a drink or two before his wife's curfew for him would force a quick exit.

This could prove to be very dangerous to Steve and Tommy's plans, as John would take out his usual pissed-off mood by overbearing scrutiny of the boxers. And the real icing on the cake was that one of the three judges had also been replaced at the last moment, leaving the other two suddenly suffering a loss of memory about having been given quite a sum of money to fix the scores in Felix's favor.

There was no room for collusion now, something Steve and Tommy did not know and, for the sake of Steve's seventy-three-year-old bladder, which had been on the fritz lately, it was better off left that way.

Introductions of the boxers were accentuated with the requisite pyrotechnics and, what was in vogue at that time, disco music and bubbly-boobed showgirls complementing the entourage for each of the fighters. As the last-minute replacement, John didn't have the requisite conversation in the dressing rooms of each of the fighters, but nonetheless, recited the mantra as the two boxers came together at center ring for their final instructions.

"... and, as we discussed, obey my commands at all times, move to your respective corners at my direction, protect yourself at all times and have a good, clean fight."

After the textbook stare down by each of the fighters and touching of the gloves, they returned to their respective corners. Each of the fighters received their final opening instructions from their trainers. Vaseline was applied to the cheeks and over the top of their brows and for Felix, a discreetly applied swath of atropine on his left glove. As it had served Corey so well, the liquid dried very quickly, but left the chemical embedded on the leather, which would ultimately reactivate.

Felix was still amazed how the custom-fitted titanium knuckle wraps fit so nicely, like a natural extension of his knuckles. For the few fighters that used these, a mold would first be made of their clenched fists, whereupon liquid titanium would be poured over, creating a customized piece of hardware that perfectly gripped their lightly padded knuckles.

He was instructed not to deliver any haymaker punches too soon into the fight and to allow the knuckle wraps to deliver the most damage after the eighth round. Prior to that, he was to continue with the left jab that would slowly work the stinging liquid into Toby's eyes.

These people came for a show, some paid $125 for ringside (a premium price back then), and a first, or even third, round knockout would not make for good business (although Mike Tyson broke this rule in the 80s with savage flair for his first twenty professional bouts. Knocking out Michael Spinks in a little over ninety seconds makes for bad cable TV revenue). And, in this particular case, only Felix's right hand had the knuckle wraps. He had a vicious right hook that would deliver the final package so he would continue with his fight plan, which also included covering up, holding and just staying out of Toby's way in general.

The first few rounds proved to be uneventful, as per plan, with Felix backing up against Toby, throwing a few jabs to keep him off-balance and, for the most part, covering up every time Toby started to move in. Every boxer has their strengths and weaknesses, but one of Felix's better attributes was his ability to keep the fight moving in his direction. But this strategy only lasted a very short period of time before the other boxers adjusted to it, rendering it ineffective.

This was the case by the third round, when the crowd was booing at this lackluster performance by Felix, only further frustrating Toby. It was then that Toby altered his approach and started to cut off the ring for Felix. The plan was for Felix to go at least eight rounds before he looked to use his right in great measure and by that time the sweat would be pouring enough to activate the atropine on his glove and into Toby's eye. It was Toby's frustration that turned to aggression and put a wrinkle in Felix's plan.

By the fourth round, Toby was coming out in full force and all bets were off that Felix would even see the seventh round. Even Felix started to realize he was a dead man. The fight picked up momentum in the fourth round with the fighters now exchanging leather at a greater pace and with beaucoup ferocity. A cut opened up over Felix's left brow had started to drip into his eye.

It was time to use the left jab in greater measure, twisting it against Toby's right eye, pushing the sweat into the glove to activate the medication, and this he did with skillful repetition. The atropine was now starting to take effect, blurring Toby's vision.

Toby's trainer had been doing this long enough to understand the body language throughout a boxing match. The squinting and excessive watering of Toby's left eye caused him some suspicion and he asked the ref to check

Felix's gloves. Since the atropine was dry and odorless, John's inspection of the front of Felix his gloves did not immediately reveal anything that would cause further examination, much less disqualification.

Hence, the fight went on, but not without John's lingering suspicion that he could not prove right now, right there, in the ring. He made a mental note to have the gloves immediately sequestered after the fight and subjected to a lab test. The outcome of a bout had been known to be overturned due to a post-fight examination by the commission with forensic evidence of inappropriate material on the glove.

Felix made Toby swing with blurred vision with the idea of wearing down his arms so he could deliver that crashing right haymaker that brought him up through the ranks to be the number three welterweight in the world.

It was during round six that Toby's arms started to get weighed down from the missed punches due to his blurred vision. After a missed right hook exposed the right side of his face, Felix wound up and delivered a powerful right hook to his left temple, putting all his weight behind it.

Sergei hit the canvas like a bag of cement. He was out cold with his right leg twisted behind his left, almost in the same disjointed limpness you see in the positions of people who fall to the ground after being killed while standing. His nervous system and muscle control were in shutdown mode.

John had never before seen a power punch like this leave a boxer so completely devastated, with their lights shut out at lightning speed. He started to think that this

Felix character was some type of anomaly. John knew it was out of character for a welterweight who weighed 140 some odd pounds to deliver such tonnage of force to render someone so clearly damaged.

John stood over Toby and did the mandatory ten count, but it was almost a fallacy that he had to even go through the motions. The poor kid was breathing unevenly and John knew that he was not going to leave the ring on his own two feet. He called for the ring doctor and an ambulance crew to come and gather Toby.

In the meantime, Felix was raising his hands in victory with his gloves still on. It was customary for them to be taken off, exposing the wrapped hands and fingers for handshakes, etc., and more times than not, this also included cutting off the tape holding the boxer's hands intact. John's attention was on Toby, so he didn't see this, as it would surely have raised a red flag.

As they were loading Toby onto the gurney, John looked at the left side of Toby's face and noticed three raised bruises, thick, identical in circumference and equally spaced apart. Toby's trainer also noticed this, raised his head to meet John's eyes and then looked over at Felix parading around the ring with his gloves still on.

"His gloves are loaded!" Toby's trainer shot at John with a mixture of surprise and anger. "I want those gloves checked, NOW!'

He hadn't even finished his sentence when John called Felix and his trainer to center ring and motioned to Tommy Rae in the front row to join them. He also asked two other boxing officials from the commission (one of which was the one who cast a blind eye when Felix was getting his hands wrapped and signed off on the wrist tape on the gloves), the judges in addition to the referee of the first undercard bout of the evening (who decided to stay on and watch the fight) to also come up.

Surrounded by police and the arena security team, John also motioned for Steve to come up, but he grabbed his crotch and made motions of having to go to the men's room and that he'd be right back. It just so happened that this was the truth and the sequence of events went straight to his bladder where now he had to piss like a racehorse. He was waddling up the aisle with the commotion of the ring behind him, thinking of just keeping on going right out of the place when, at that point, the facility of the men's room became pointless.

"Take off his gloves," John commanded Felix's corner man.

"Go on, take off his gloves," Tommy proudly proclaimed. "If you're looking for something, and I don't know what that something is, you're not going to find anything."

The gloves came off and the hand wraps looked identical. This was because they were made to look identical with extra tape on the left hand mimicking the slim knuckle wraps hidden beneath the tape of the right hand. The two officials, the first referee and John inspected the taped hands. It was hard to tell anything as John held Felix's hands in his own and ran his thumbs across the taped hands.

"Cut off the tape," demanded John.

"And what is it that you're looking for?" demanded Tommy, putting his hands in front of the pair of scissors the trainer had ready to cut up the front sides of the bandaged hands.

At this point they had Toby securely strapped into the gurney under a blanket. His head was in a neck brace and John could still see the three rising welt marks on his left temple like UFOs you'd see on the late night news caught by an amateur photographer in the Midwest somewhere. The officials and the one legitimate judge now also saw the rising welt marks, realizing the predictable series of events that were to unfold in the next few minutes.

"Please remove the tape," John repeated. Tommy looked from John to the officials and only glanced at the two collusive judges realizing the top was about to blown off and was targeted for a crash landing down on their heads.

The trainer cut off the tape on the left hand, unraveling the gauze revealing a swollen but naked hand. Tommy looked up at John with an excruciatingly executed look of confidence.

"Satisfied? This is the most ridiculous and publicly insulting experience I've had in my thirty years of managing boxers. I've got some pretty hard-earned connections with the commission and I'm going to try with all my power to get your license revoked. Now can we leave the ring and celebrate?"

"Now the other hand," John directed.

"This has gone far enough and…"

"CUT OFF THE FUCKING TAPE!" John almost screamed out of disgust and contempt for Tommy Rae, who he knew was crooked, but always escaped undetected through clever maneuvering and graft. This was an opportunity John had dreamed of for years and he was about to nail the prick. The trainer cut and opened up the taped right hand as if performing an autopsy and began unraveling the tape and gauze.

Eventually the knuckle wraps appeared and Tommy, with all the acting that he could muster, and he had conned his way through dozens of tight spots before, exclaimed in surprise, "What is this? This is cheating!" looking at the officials.

It was time now for dirty pool and Tommy was just the man to shoot. Looking at the officials he shouted, "You supposedly checked his gloves and knew he had these knuckle wraps underneath? You're going to pay a heavy price for this; not only a job, but criminal charges as well," he said with authority looking at John, the other official (the honest one) and judges.

He was counting on the fact that the penalty the paid-off official would incur would be smoothed out by those members of the commission who were still part of this equation. And he also felt that this "accused" official realized that he would be paid handsomely; maybe not keep his job, but certainly be well taken care of with an early and very comfortable retirement.

Tommy pushed his luck a little too far when he looked to seal up the issue by reprimanding the official, "You should be ashamed of yourself dishonoring a revered sports such as boxing."

What Tommy didn't realize was that the official was not going to be embarrassed, have his name spread across all the papers in the morning with his wife and children also reaping ridicule from family and friends. It was Tommy's unfortunate selection of this official, as the latter felt family and honor rose above the dollar.

"I intend to get to the bottom of this," Tommy furthered. "We'll find out who else is responsible for this travesty," Tommy said confidently, thinking that the direction was going his way when the official finally spoke up.

"It was you, Tommy. It was you, the referees you hired to turn the other way and some members of the boxing commission and well paid judges who are responsible. I have the bank records of the transfers you made to my account. I've saved all the memos you were stupid enough to send that would seal any doubt who was behind this. You're not going to push this on me, I promise you that." All of this was captured by a NBC reporter who was taping the exchange the whole time.

In addition to full public disclosure, late night talk show hosts and the likes of Saturday Night Live were going to have a freakin' field day with this!

A full-scale investigation ensued, including chemical swab tests on Felix's gloves that later revealed generous doses of atropine covering the left glove. The scandal made front page news on all major newspapers the next day. It was one of the biggest busts in organized sport gambling since the infamous "Black Sox" scandal, when the Chicago White Sox threw the World Series in 1919. The police had a court order to sequester the crooked official's PC almost as soon as NBC fed the tape for broadcasting.

Johnny Wells was up at the commission's office the

next day, waving X-rays and MRIs of Bob's noggin. As the X-rays showed scattered hairline fractures, and since it had been just two years since the inception of the MRI, the images were less than clear. Although the remaining members of the commission were convinced, there wasn't enough definitive evidence to re-open the decision of the fight that cost Bob his belt. But being no dope, and looking to make the public his jury, he gladly handed the images to the press, which proceeded to have multiple orgasms over the explosive revelation.

With a mouth full of whole grain cereal, Corey Green read the headlines the next day in his kitchen and ran straight to the bathroom, "giving penance" on his knees in front of an open toilet.

CHAPTER 31

Bonnie kept on tossing and turning and couldn't quite find the avenue to the deep sleep that she so sorely needed. Some of the experiences she had treating the people of the Svenkia Islands, especially the children, deeply disturbed her. She treated so many patients in the past, but in completely different circumstances. These were people who lived in suburbia, had homes with plumbing and electricity, the usual workday and slept securely at night.

These people were thrown from their homes out onto the dirt across the water and onto a relatively uninhabitable island. She'd been trying her best with the children who had been suffering from recurring nightmares. And no wonder. They watched their families get torn apart, their people killed and brutalized by the Chevkan Republic Guard.

"It's just not right" was not enough of an explanation or justification for what she had seen over the past few weeks. No one had the right to treat human beings like dogs, regardless of the economic benefit. Unfortunately, this was not something new and had been going on for centuries. Her job was that of a healer, that was what she came here for. And that was what she intended to do. She tried to piece together the broken lives of people and their children so they might have some hope of putting their lives back together someday. Having had her fair share of emotional obstacles during her younger years due to the absence of love from overachieving and successful parents, she decided to devote her life to helping people like herself to overcome involuntarily planted scars to lead more productive lives and have access to happiness.

Much like Bob, she didn't have time for romance, as she was becoming more adept at her profession and opening a small clinic in Manhattan. This was not all by choice; she shied away from the whole prospect of a relationship with a man due to the disappointment she experienced by not having access to her father when she was a little girl. This left her a little defiant and under the notion that men were more than selfish and only looked for what they wanted in a relationship with absolutely no regard for the woman. It rendered her more than jaded when it came to having an honest relationship with a man. Her professional posterior had provided just the shield she needed and often was on the cusp of outright despising men. In her growing friendship with Lynne Albright, she would talk about this as Lynne proved to be a very good listener. The two women often exchanged their polar viewpoints on men and found this co-miserating mutually comforting.

It was about 2AM when she stepped out into the bitter cold of the arctic night. She needed time to collect her thoughts and breathe in fresh air, a rare thing back in the States. The stars shone so brightly out here, as though straight from a textbook or one of those glossy paper foldouts in National Geographic.

Her gaze turned toward Bob's trailer and she saw that his light was still on. What was the palooka doing up at this time of night? Shadowboxing, writing his memoirs, or taking in the gravity of what he was trying to do at the age of twenty-six? It was a large, daunting task he put on his shoulders. She couldn't help but admire him for that.

As a matter of fact, he was having a strong influence on her changing her way of thinking of sports stars, and men for that matter, and how they viewed themselves. Bob was very different. Humble would be a too strong a word, but he was not one to toot his horn and probably did not have a narcissistic bone in his body. Something unusual for somebody of his stature.

In her profession, she was so used to the inflated egos of the movers and shakers. She would tire of it so fast that she would almost forget why she studied so hard and worked her way through Oxford. Her world was one of overachievers and strong-willed individuals. Bob was different, very different. He had enough ammo to shoot around to make a big stink about himself, but he was not the type, something she was sure that his manager and promoter wished he could transcend. With the rest of the world asleep around her, she felt a little lonely and decided to see what we he was up to.

She knocked softly on the trailer door. "Bob, Bob? Are you awake?" No answer. She tried again. "Hey, Bob, we are you doing in there? Isn't it a bit late to be playing with yourself? Instead you should be resting for a full day tomorrow." She smirked to herself. Still no answer.

She turned the knob on the door, which was unlocked, opened it slowly and walked in. She found Bob in front of the desk, PC in front of him, spreadsheets and financials scattered about the desk. He was slumped back in his chair; head tilted back and to the right with his mouth wide open in what looked like a very deep sleep. She thought that this looked like an uncomfortable position to be asleep in and thought it best that she drag his superstar ass into bed.

She walked slowly up behind him. “Bob! Come on, big boy, time for bed.” Still no reaction. “Bob, I’m serious. Let’s go! Bedtime,” she said with her hand gently on his shoulder.

“Bonnie?!” he mouthed, still very much asleep.

“Yeah, Bonnie! Let’s go; it’s 2AM and the bus to La-La Land is about to pull out of the station without you.”

“Bonnie?!” His brow was now starting to furrow still very much asleep.

She knew that he was beginning to enter into a distress state while still deep in the recesses of his mind, fast asleep. She knew, as a clinician, to disturb somebody so deeply asleep and in a distressed state would not be a good thing.

So with that she said softly, “Bob? Come on, honey, it’s time for bed.”

Honey? HONEY?! Where the hell did that come from? It slipped off her tongue so easily. She was both amazed and frightened at the same time. She, the Queen of Distance, and the Purveyor of Nonchalance, calling some rock star of the ring honey! She quickly checked herself while at the same time, and still very deep in sleep, Bob reacted to her call.

“Bonnie? Bonnie, I can’t see you. Bonnie, where are you? I can hear you, but can’t see you!”

She was a little bewildered. She knew that he was floating around in his subconscious and reacting to an audible from the real world. But why was he reacting this way about her?

"Bonnie, please! I can't see you. I can hear you. But I can't get to you." His voice started that slight hiccup sound just before someone is about to cry, but not quite there yet.

"Bob, I'm right here. I'm right in front of you."

She could see tears starting to collect underneath his lower eyelashes and one trickle made its way down his cheek. Her heart started a slow melt.

"Bonnie, I can hear you, but I can't see you. Please. I need to find you. I need to see you!" He was frantic now.

Now she was really torn. The subconscious is the window to the soul, and he clearly had her pegged in his heart and in his mind. She didn't quite know what to make of it. She felt her heart slip through, down between her ribs and into her stomach. It was a warm feeling, something she hadn't ever experienced before with anyone, not even her father (clearly another story, a very sad story, one for the books).

"Bob, come on, sweetheart. I'm right here. Come toward me. Follow my voice, I'm right here."

"I can't… can't see you. Please, Bonnie, I need to find you."

Both eyes watered now and the distress in his voice now very visible on his face. She was touched and also angry that she was allowing herself to feel this way.

He slowly started to lift up his right hand as though to reach out to something and cried, "Bonnie, please, I can hear you. You must be very close to me. Please, show me where you are."

"Bob, I…"

"Bonnie! Bonnie, please! No!! Don't go! Please

don't go!!"

Now, even she started to panic. She had seen this a dozen times in her practice, but why should she feel as deeply as she did now? She slipped the top of her hand underneath the bottom of his raised right palm and gently made contact. His heavy and labored breathing started to slow down, and she could see the tension start to leave his body. The distress disappeared from his face and he fell back into a very peaceful sleep. She was trying very hard to convince herself that it was her imagination, but she could swear there was a very, very slight smile on his face. She, too, now had tears in her eyes and looked down at this wonderful human being. This was a moment that she'd wear like a necklace around her heart for the rest of her life.

Bob started to make that smacking noise with his lips and shifting position as though to get more comfortable. His eyes fluttered open and, like the rain stopping, the last drops of his subconscious were starting to trickle away along with the memory of his dream. Part of Bonnie was hoping he didn't hear or will remember the "Honey" and "Sweetheart" business; part of her did.

He looked up at Bonnie. "I... I," he stumbled as he felt the wetness of tears on his cheeks that were still fresh. As his dream was quickly retreating for cover, he had a vague sense of disappearing distress and, as when he was a child, having everything being all right after being very upset. He was both happy and relieved to see Bonnie standing over him. He couldn't quite make the connection, because, well, he saw her every day, for Pete's sake, and what a pain in the ass she was!

Ah, now wouldn't it be a great segue to say that

they both went back to one of the other's bedroom and consummated this epiphany by shooting off a rocket? That would be the ideal path in such a situation, yes? But, truth be known, Bob went back to his room, emotionally exhausted and yet with the strange feeling of relief, put head to pillow and just caught the last bus to La-La Land with no time to spare.

Bonnie's night ended on a slightly different note. She wandered back into her trailer and sat at the edge of her bed, still very surprised at herself and feeling very vulnerable, but increasingly not caring. She, too, rested head to pillow and thoughts still spun around in her mind at a pace and it was not too long until she, too, bought a ticket and caught the bus. As sleep gently overtook her, she realized she finally found something she never realized she was looking for.

Sweet dreams to all.

CHAPTER 32

It was unseasonably warm for that late Sunday afternoon when Bob and Louise made their way up atop the hillside, the highest point in their area of the islands. Although it was January, the sun managed to push its way through the cold air, causing an extra bustle of activity during the day where people were enjoying being outside without having their lips quickly chap or their ears feeling like they would fall off.

The late afternoon sun, now signaling the coming of nightfall when the temperature plunged, prompted a hasty return to their tents, blanketing the community in peace and quiet. It was usually this time of day that Bob did most of his thinking and climbing to the top of the hill with Louise in tow was just a quiet time he seemed to need.

Once on top of the hill, he sat down as Louise parked her bulk right beside him. He looked down upon the tents with smoke wafting through the air from the makeshift stovepipes, the storage sheds and the dirt tracks that the mules had been steadily deepening, and paused for deep reflection over the last couple of months. A lot of progress had been made from what seemed like a hopeless situation to one that seemed like it was going to succeed, but with much more work ahead.

He still couldn't quite figure out what was driving him so he promised himself to keep the self-analysis to people like Bonnie. His thoughts would oscillate from feeling he was doing some good for these people back to thinking maybe he shouldn't have been there at all.

The air was so quiet around him and all he could

hear was Louise's heavy breathing. Poor old girl. Even though she made great strides in her recovery, she still had the years stacked up against her and the trip up the hill took a little wind out of her sails.

He rose to his feet and took off his jacket. Ah, the sun felt so good on him that he proceeded to take off his shirt, bearing his chest to the west, bathing himself in the warm afternoon glow. In keeping with his promise to say in shape for whenever he returned back to the States for a bout that would surely be waiting for him, his body testified to that promise. He literally did not have any body fat, other than what could be measured by the most sensitive of equipment.

Everything he did during the resurrection of the people of Antonia, he tried to make it as physical as possible to keep his body moving. Hauling water, lifting timber, removing rocks and making paths, and the other creative work-out regimens he invented. His arms swelled with pure muscle, his forearms thick with steel, legs like iron and an unmatched will and determination to someday take back the title he was unfairly stripped of. This was what fired his motivation for perfection both in his mind and his body – failure was not an option.

He arched his back and tilted his head backwards, closing his eyes and allowing his eyeballs to slightly roll up into his head in a gesture similar to that of sleeping standing up. His hair was long and flowed down his back and his beard was now full and robust. He surely had the Sampson thing going on.

He went into almost a meditative state, letting his body relax, as his veins pushed up against the surface of his skin like taught ropes with a slight green hue that visibly made their route across his shoulders, through his arms and into his hands. He had the requisite six pack abdomen with an eight pack slowly making progress above his groin; flat as a board and as resilient as concrete. He truly was a magnificent figure and, accentuated with a large and healthy lioness beside him, made for a portrait of a Greek god in the sunlight.

Bonnie and Lynne Albright were in Kristanf and Irinia's tent with photographs from Irinia's Christmas box spread across the floor. She was showing Bonnie and Lynne each and every photograph with its own story and loving biography. The photos were more precious than gold for Irinia.

When the truckers were organizing the rummage, they focused on finding photographs, as these were the most sacred keepsakes for the families. Sitting cross-legged on the pallet floor for over an hour, Bonnie's legs began to get stiff and she decided to get up and step outside to stretch them. She only had to put on a sweater to walk out into the semi-chilly afternoon air, as it was delightfully warm for this time of year.

As she was taking a few steps to get the blood circulating better, she veered to the left and that was when she saw Bob sunning himself atop a hill. She stopped in her tracks and was completely spellbound. It appeared that he was opening himself up to the heavens and letting the heavens come raining down onto him. As this was such a striking image that washed over her, she suddenly became overwhelmed and could feel the support of her legs beginning to challenge her ability to remain standing.

She stood transfixed when suddenly from behind her she heard, “That’s some side of beef up on the hill there, my dear.”

A little surprised, Bonnie folded her arms to her chest and turned halfway around. “I just can’t figure this guy out. I mean, a big sports star and all of that, presumably narcissistic and self-absorbed, but he’s none of that, at all.”

“Yes, he does seem a bit different, doesn’t he?” Lynne said with a growing smirk that Bonnie couldn’t see.

“I mean, not that I care or anything—” by this time she had stopped struggling with the “honey” business in Bob’s trailer that night and began to let her feelings lean hard against the barriers that she constructed over the years “—but I did a little reading on him—” newspapers were now being brought over on the cargo planes with each new delivery “—and this guy won twenty-six fights, twenty-one by knockout, if that means anything to you, except for his last fight. He was knocked to the ground and suffered some damage. They said the fight was fixed, but they could never prove it.”

“It seems like you’re quite a fan.”

“Oh, I think boxing is a crude form of entertainment. The whole notion of two guys standing toe to toe, beating the crap out of each other just doesn’t make sense to me,” Bonnie said as she stood with her eyes locked on Bob on top of the hill. This didn’t go unnoticed by Lynne Albright.

“Then why don’t you go up there and join him, Bonnie?”

"I can't. I meant to say… I'm scared, Lynne. I mean I'm really… very… frightened." The bubbling cauldron of emotions that Bonnie fought to hide away for so many years like a sleeping volcano suddenly gushed up, pushing against the back of her throat. The last word of her sentence was barely an audible squeak. She was visibly shaken and on very thin ice.

"What is it that scares you so much, honey?" Ms. Albright asked in a surprisingly motherly tone (she didn't have any children of her own, just jewelry, the result of some very tasty divorce settlements).

"My father. My goddamn father! Every time I tried to breathe my emotions with him as a child, he would cut off my air. I was suffocated into submission by his constant criticism, ridicule and, worst of all, pure neglect." Her voice was cracking now with tears quickly pooling in her eyes.

She continued, "He would say things like, 'That dress you're wearing makes you look like a pinwheel, especially with those two sticks you call legs,' or, 'Why is it that you get a B in math; do you know how to count the fingers on your hands, I doubt it,' or even better yet, 'With all those freckles on your face, you look like Howdy Doody, except he had more brains in his wooden head then you have in your entire body.' This set him off on a string of laughter as he was so pleased with his own wit. The death blow would come with the periodic, 'You were a mistake. We weren't planning on having another child. Be thankful I didn't put you up for adoption before your first bowel movement.' Pretty, huh?"

Ms. Albright was clearly feeling the pain this must have caused, not to say the deep emotional scarring. Her father sounded like a top notch jerk.

"He doesn't sound like a very nice man," Ms. Albright offered. "As a matter of fact, he clearly had his own issues and unfortunately he beat you over the head with them."

Bonnie was now choking back the tears, trying her very best to not have this sleeping volcano blow its top and spew forth its contents all over the ground for everyone to see. She had all the instincts and yearnings of a woman and had been very successful in cementing over this and keeping her feelings airtight in a vault. The men she dated fit her father's profile almost to the last follicle. She knew why she was doing this and following this pattern.

She dated somebody like her father in order to have the perfect excuse to keep her feelings in check. It was really easy not getting involved. There was another side to this, which was more or less a dichotomy in that she dated these men to seek their approval, to gain their attention and acceptance. She was fully aware of this and was more comfortable this way than she would be in being forced to crack open this oh so well sealed vault. Someone was now breaking into her vault and it scared the living daylights out of her.

Lynn Albright moved closer and placed her hands on the back of Bonnie's shoulders. "And just how long do you think you can keep on doing this without strangling yourself emotionally? You have to get over this, baby. You have to open up the door and let this man in and God be damned you if you don't keep your hand of the doorknob."

"I can't, Lynne," Bonnie was now sobbing uncontrollably. "It's just too much for me. I don't think I have the strength and resolve. Oh, just look at me," she said, patting herself on the chest, mocking herself while still shrouded in tears, "the bright young psychologist who can put together the disjointed pieces of a person's life and supply those pieces they can't find anymore. I mean, the irony makes me want to puke." She was starting to wipe away the tears with the heel of her hand. "No, no. I just can't do this. I just… ca…"

Lynn Albright now spun Bonnie around and squared her off by the shoulders and looked her straight in the eye. "You're going to have to stop this bullshit, Bonnie. Women dream of moments like this; that their knight in shining armor comes galloping up on a white stallion, scoops her up and takes her into a life of enduring happiness. For Christ's sake, Bonnie…" Lynne's voice was now starting to also crack, her lower lip and chin quivering, fighting to hold back angry tears.

"Don't be like me, Bonnie. Don't wake up someday and find out that you're completely alone and it's too late. Too late to do anything!"

Ms. Albright was now agonized at the very thought of how her life could have been different if she were standing where Bonnie was standing now, at her age, and came across a man like Bob. She wasn't so lucky in this department; financially, yes. Emotionally, she had neglected herself in exchange for a lavish lifestyle, plenty of money, plenty of places to go and pursuing her one true passion without having to worry about making a living at the same time.

"Let him in, Bonnie," she was now starting to calm down and her tone was more reasoning. "It's gonna hurt, it's gonna be confusing, but if you can get past this, you will have all the fresh emotional air you want to breathe. Fill your lungs!'

Bonnie could only nod in quick jerks of her head with lips pursed and hands folded against her chest in a tensed posture. She felt sorry for Ms. Albright, but in the same instance, admired her for being so candid about a part of her she was sure she shared with no one else.

Bonnie's mother, as was customary during the time in the early fifties, was the wife who would mimic her child-rearing from the husband. This kind of acquiescence that was taught to her as a little girl by her mother was duplicated when it came to marriage. Although Bonnie's mother felt for her daughter, there was very little intimate interaction, only until the latter years when Bonnie was a grown woman but then it was too little, too late.

Her mother was a dutiful wife and in a well-honed state of denial about her husband's affairs where Ms. Albright was the antithesis of her mother. Ms. Albright seized the moment, pushed Bonnie into an emotional corner and didn't let her go until she was sure that she absorbed everything she was telling her.

Ms. Albright lifted Bonnie's lowered chin her voice still cracking with emotion. "Promise me you will do this. Promise me you will not let Bonnie's own security force prevent her entrance to something really beautiful. Promise me!"

"I promise," Bonnie whispered.

The two women then embraced each other, both hanging on for dear life.

CHAPTER 33

Sustainable Development was one of those phenomena that had existed since the beginning of man, but only became academically defined and publicly discussed during the 1970s. Basically, the concept talked about the addressing of the immediate needs of people while laying a foundation for future generations.

It seemed evident that at least for the immediate future, the Svenkia Islands was the new home for the people of Antonia. Under this concept, a society needs three forms of capital: economic, social and natural. The situation here was doubly problematic in that there was an urgent need to hang onto life while not creating an overly primitive structure for immediate relief the undoing of which for a more permanent solution would be equally if not impossibly complex. Among the many questions, the answers of which would determine the course of action for sustainable development included what was the state of the environment now, where was it that the environment needed to go and how did you get there?

The Svenkia islands had all the markings of a primitive ecosystem with trees, soil and a small variety of animal habitat. The forest maintained biodiversity, the regulation of water flow and the absorption of CO2. The immediate needs of hygiene these people needed were water and waste management, both human and garbage. For example, if waste is not properly disposed and treated, it emits nitric oxide and methane gas that creates a health hazard, something these people did not need in addition to what they'd had already been thorough.

In the War Room, were Bob, Sergei, Petr, an electrical engineer named Luk'yan, Sgt. Hayes and a small visiting cadre consisting of a geologist, civil engineer and a technician from Greenfield Waste Management, the largest such facility in Europe that also was instrumental in containing and developing waste management in Malaysia, India and Bangladesh.

Bob knew that the islands' development would happen in phases, with the most immediate needs to be met first; hence "water and waste" occupied their initial focus. They knew the "what" in the conceptual equation of the environment, they had a rough idea where it was to go and believed they now had the means to get there.

The Antonov cargo planes were averaging two trips a week and continued the flow of resources in a rational order: servicing first the front end needs and then later on the tools for a more permanent and comfortable sustenance. The most recent arrival of the planes brought backhoes, tractors, well drilling equipment and hundreds of feet of PCV pipe.

The temporary Sani-Lavs were serving the purpose for now, but changing the waste containers meant the contents had to go somewhere. As far as some of the water issues emanating from the discharge of the animals, well, that would continue as nature would have it. As long as a source of uninterrupted water and purification could be established, this was not an issue.

Bob and Sergei were looking at the map plans the civil engineer had drawn in tackling this first phase.

"This is really a three-pronged approach. First, our geologist steers us to a source which will serve as the water supply. Second, thanks to Sgt. Hayes and his band of outlaws," he said with a smirk on his face, "we have all the proper equipment we need to finish up this first phase rather quickly. I do say quickly as the people are in dire need of infrastructure NOW." Sergei was trying furiously to translate for Petr and Luk'yan and eventually asked the civil engineer to slow down.

Unfortunately, Sgt. Hayes didn't share in this brief moment of levity as there was a lot of work to do and he didn't take a shine to this guy to begin with.

"We need to find water on this godforsaken place and, once we do, drill a well, of which we'll need the means to bring the water to the surface and distribute it accordingly. We brought seventeen windmills, much the same you see on Ma and Pa Parker's Farm, but more of the industrial size and grade; each windmill provides 100kW of power. We need to situate them in the path of the strongest wind and being located off the Arctic Ocean, you're lucky in this department."

"We'll need to position these windmills for optimal wind exposure. Normally a windmill needs to be thirty feet higher than all objects 300 feet from it. Looking at the map, if we were to position these windmills here," he pointed to the southwestern tip of the second island, "this would not be an issue, as they will have full frontal access to the Arctic blast of air. We calculate that winds are normally gusting between forty and sixty miles an hour at that particular point, but windmills come equipped with an over speed governing system to keep the rotor from spinning off its turret in excessively high winds."

It had been decided from day one that they would

live on the southernmost part of the main island, protected by mountains and hills from the northerly blast of arctic air coming off the ocean. The civil engineer calculated approximately fourteen miles of cable, some of which would travel underwater, would be needed to link to the main power hub to be positioned on the southeasterly portion of the main island. From there, smaller cables would be running to substations scattered within the developing community. Electrical current loses power the farther it has to travel and given the extremely tight budget that they were working with, this seemed to be the best option in terms of the hardware."

Luk'yan had already started the algorithms in his head. He wasn't an expert on windmills, but he certainly was an accomplished electrical engineer when it came to any type of mechanism providing current through conduits. From casual reading, he knew that a 1.5kW wind turbine would provide the basic power needs of a home that required 300 kW per month facing a wind at an average of fourteen miles an hour. No problem with the wind part of the equation here. The power that turns the turbine is also based on the size of the rotors, its sweep area and air density.

For this part of the infrastructure, Sergei and Luk'yan had begun a dialogue almost immediately after arriving on the island. Given the approximate 3,000 people that made it over, and further verified by Sergei's census that he had taken the weeks following, there would be approximately 600 to 700 dwellings. These would vary in size and shape from a husband and wife with children to an elderly couple where it was only the two of them.

Since they were still very much in survival mode, Sergei and Luk'yan were able to discuss what they believed would be a very rough schematic of structures on the island that would require power; this would include not only homes, but water pumps, storage areas, stores or simply points of distribution of goods, common area lighting and the like.

This was really the first time they were putting pencil to paper and starting to draw up and execute a plan. Rough estimates by Luk'yan put power usage by each home at an approximate 400kW per month. The amount of other power that would be needed was determined on a prorated basis at 200kW per household. With 600 homes, there would be a power requirement of 1.5MW. The 17,100kW wind turbines would provide 1.7MW, providing more than enough horsepower with some reserve. Sounds like a plan.

The geologist added to this final piece of the equation with (Sgt. Hayes thought *this* guy was okay; thank God, right?), "Although this might seem a rather quiet and disconnected parcel of land, there's quite a lot going on beneath the ground. There are characteristics of the terrain that are very similar to that of South Africa where there are caverns that had been formed by water percolating underground for millions of years. Eventually, surface springs are formed and provide a source of water for animals and other inhabitants of the area. So, as far as the presence of water, geologically it is in more abundant than you think, you just can't see it.

"The downside of this is that during the dry season, the springs submerge back into the underground caverns where animals seeking water fall in and die, and their decomposing bodies and any diseases that they may be carrying also find their way into the water systems. What you folks are doing now by boiling water and siphoning it through cloth is about the best you can do under these conditions. But once a purification system is up and running, you should have clean drinking water."

The civil engineer continued, "You would need to assign some qualified and trained people to run and service the main power station on the southeast portion of the main island. We can provide the training and most certainly would serve as backup if anything were to go wrong."

Bob was scratching his growing beard and asked, "How long do you think this might take? Right now, we have water purification crudely under control, but not only for drinking; we need a sanitation and waste disposal distribution system yesterday, that's going to require power to run."

Sgt. Hayes interjected, "We've managed to get a barge with all the main cabling to the first power station on deck and on its way as we speak."

Bob was still amazed by how Sgt. Hayes managed to get his hands on all these resources and didn't want to know. Pretty industrious guy alright.

The civil engineer, not wanting to be bested, added, "The fuse housings and other components of the main power station should be coming on Sgt. Hayes's next flight over due when, Sgt. Hayes, this Tuesday?"

"Yep, that along with most of the secondary cabling that will run from the main power station to the substations. The second aircraft is carrying well drilling and dredging equipment, plus hundreds of feet of PCV piping along with eleven commercial water pumps. I think if everybody could hang on for a couple weeks we'll be able to deliver water, clean water, to most of the area."

The civil engineer continued, "And along with that, those flying beasts are also carrying four huge septic tanks that will be placed in the ground and routed to the water system from each and every toilet you guys can install. There is enough ground area for adequate septic fields for the waste to be broken down and dispersed without affecting the water tables."

Bob felt as though a huge lifesaver had been thrown on the island, finally showing some concrete progress. A clean running water system and sources of power provided a very powerful foundation in the first few steps of rebuilding these people's lives and bringing them back to some semblance of normalcy.

Bob was now focusing his thoughts on the next few steps in the process. They would have the basic tools for sustenance and now they had to learn how to use them without any help from the outside.

Bob walked outside of the trailer into the cold night air and looked around at the fires that were glowing outside of the tents. It was still fairly early, so children were still running about, chasing each other with plumes of frosty breath trailing behind them as they laughed and giggled their way back to their respective tents.

For the first time in many weeks, things started to seem to gel. But with everything seeming to be so right, why did he feel a nagging notion pushing up in the back of his mind? He couldn't quite put his finger on it, but there was something wrong with this picture and he wasn't quite sure what. He tried to dismiss the whole thought from his mind and focus his attention on the 'here and now" and worry about the "later" when it came.

Or should he?

CHAPTER 34

This particular time a year, with its permafrost on the ground, was not being very cooperative in giving the backhoes a fighting chance to dig up the earth to lay down the septic tanks. The first six feet or so weren't that bad, but further down, the ground grew more solid. This wouldn't pose a problem for the drainage tubes that led out to the septic drain field, but the tanks were one story tall and had to be buried at least thirty or forty feet beneath the ground to ensure there would be no adverse effects if a crack or split in the tanks were to occur.

It had been decided for sake of expediency that the best approach would be to drill bore holes, plant dynamite and blow the whole nine yards to smithereens. Although these tanks were going to be an appreciable distance from the settlement area, the blasts would still be loud and certainly play upon the nerves of people who just a few months ago were forced from their homes by gunfire. The real concern was for the children, as they were the ones who were especially traumatized.

Sergei held a few group meetings and got the schedule from the geologist and civil engineer for the blasting times. The objective was to do as much of this as possible in the shortest amount of time. It had been concluded that the best time to accommodate the temperature and for people to be wide awake and alert, were the hours between 2PM and 4PM and for the next few days would be accentuated with the pounding sound of blasting dynamite.

Although this was good news to all and a huge step

in the right direction, this posed a particular concern to Irinia. Keeping a close eye on Stefan in the last few weeks after he joined the family, what she witnessed was a rather reserved and protected personality start to blossom and take on the versatility of that of a typical little boy. She worried that whatever defense mechanisms his tender young mind had constructed to suppress what had happened to his parents would eventually fade away, and the reality would start to surface and harden. But this would happen in its own time, taking as long as his individual resolve needed.

People she had talked to who had been Stefan's neighbors did not witness any account of his parent's disappearance. She desperately wanted to know what happened to them so when the time did come that this monstrous memory came to greet him square in the face, she would be prepared. She wasn't quite sure if it would be now, a few years from now, or maybe never. Who knows? But whatever the case, she was now his mother and it was her innate duty to protect him emotionally.

What had started to unnerve her was some of his recent comments of, "Mama made biscuits before we left," or, "The soldiers drove over the wood pile that that Papa just made." She knew the time was coming soon and the pieces would start to fall together; she feared he simply would not be able to handle it.

She expressed her concerns to Kristanf who had his own sensitivity to the boy the son who replaced the one she lost. Irinia also knew that Natalia needed to be in on this and tried to explain very carefully to an eight-year-old about trauma and how this may be creeping up behind Stefan.

With budding maternal instincts and her big sister mode in high gear, she surprised her mother by understanding that Stefan probably saw things he shouldn't have, bad things, and that he still might be in kind of like a dream and when he woke up, he would be terrified. Irinia almost fell back on her keister at her little girl, ahem, her young lady, and how well she understood Irinia's concerns.

On Wednesday at 1:45PM, Irinia put down the clothes she was folding and brought Stefan to her and began to tell him a story, like the stories she used to tell Luther when he was about Stefan's age. She could feel his breathing slow down as he settled into the soft and sweet smelling nest she made for him in her lap. His eyes turned upward and glazed over as children's eyes do when they're starting to be carried off in a story providing their own imagery in their minds. The further she went on with the story, the more tightly she held on to him.

Then, almost to the minute, at 2PM., the first blast reverberated into the open air against the mountains, bouncing off hills and shaking the small settlement like a small earthquake.

"Nooooooooooo, ah, ah, ah, noooooooooooo!"

Okay, it's started, Irinia thought. She now had him completely enveloped in her arms and started rocking back and forth, "Shhh, shh, I'm here, honey. No one is going to hurt you, I promise. It's going to be okay sweetheart."

Stefan's mind left the room. "Run Mama, run! Don't let the bad man get you. Run!"

A second blast followed moments later.

"Argggggghhh, ah, ah nooooooooooo. Run.

Mama!"

"Shh, shh, baby. It's okay, I got you." Irinia was now rocking back and forth at a feverish pace, trying to soothe herself as much she was trying to comfort Stefan.

What really happened that day was Stefan's mother tried to open the door to the closet he had run and hid in when the soldiers burst into their small home. When she finally did open the door, she went to grab Stefan to run. He had been so frightened by the two soldiers standing behind her that he was afraid she wouldn't be able to get away because he couldn't run so fast. That was as much as his consciousness allowed him to remember. What happened next was too horrific and, thanks to the laws of human nature, he was well protected by his own emotional defense mechanisms blocking out the events that followed.

As she went to grab Stefan, an impatient soldier who shouted at her to get out after using up the five minutes they were allowed, drew his weapon and blew a hole in her back, killing her instantly and toppling her on top of Stefan. This gave way to full view of his father lying dead in his own pool of blood. The soldier grabbed Stefan by the scruff of the neck and dragged him out the front porch and threw him like unwanted garbage out into the front yard. It was only when one of the neighbors, unfortunately one Irinia didn't have the opportunity to talk with, saw him topple down the stairs, grabbed him by the hand and ran with the others to the Straits.

A third blast shook the ground beneath him and Stefan's wailing frightened Natalia and she now started to sob. Kristanf had her in his arms as he knew this was going to be dramatic for the both of them. And, unfortunately, theirs was not the only tent that had crying and sobbing coming from it.

The geologist, having learned of this reaction, stepped up the schedule. Blasting for the first day didn't last the planned two hours. The rest of the day was devoted to boring all the other holes that would be needed and on the second day they could blast rest of the ground and be done with it.

The children didn't stop crying for days after that.

CHAPTER 35

As it had happened, the blast had fractured enough of the surrounding area that the backhoes were now able to dig out areas for landfill. The accumulating garbage was beginning to pose a real problem. The plan was to have landfill manually managed to safe levels until the time the soil would cooperate in the spring and summer, providing enough soft soil to cover it up.

The mules and carts proved to be far more versatile than originally intended. Transport proved to be an essential ingredient in the progressive development of the blooming settlement. They now served as garbage trucks scheduled to visit different areas and have the people there load the back of the carts with their refuge to be brought out to the landfill site for dumping. The mules especially enjoyed this duty as with every stop they were given treats of carrots or corn meal.

The landfill was filling up quickly where piping was inserted in the ground, pointing skyward to eventually release the methane gas that would be admitted as the garbage decomposed under the soil. Eventually there will be a recycling program, but that was a long way off.

The heart of this effort came next: housing. Bob had arranged this via satellite radio with a company in Arkansas that manufactured what had been termed “interim housing.” Basically, these were structures of galvanized steel panels that were bolted together. Since they were pieced together and the interiors easily partitioned, it was not hard to comfortably accommodate all.

Sergei was a very meticulous man, a CPA, and, as

mayor of one of the larger provinces, had been involved with urban development. He kept very meticulous records and he knew what the family compositions were of the 3,500 inhabitants. With that information, he then determined what type of housing the remaining 3,000 would minimally need to be comfortable.

Much in line with Bob's concerns all along, the drama of the people of the Svenkia Islands was starting to lose steam where other newsworthy catastrophes were occurring and corporate sponsors that had been funding the islands were now looking toward their corporate and publically emphasized American responsibility to these other unfortunate episodes.

In short, the flow of funds was starting to dwindle as were the reserves; the tight fist on finances would have to get even tighter. Most the materials that had been provided so far were donated, or provided at cost, but shipping and freight had to be paid, as these businesses could simply not afford the expense themselves. You'd be amazed, or maybe you already have firsthand knowledge, of how expensive logistics can really be.

A little Star Trek-ish, but whenever teleportation is invented, there's going to be a lot of people out of work and the cost of transportation a fraction of what it is today. But hey, our old friends, supply and demand, would surely put the lid on that thought.

Footprints for the new housing had been sketched out by the civil engineer based on Sergei's statistics. The generic sidings were flown in earlier that week and were now starting to be stacked at the new home sites, awaiting assembly. The windows were made of double paned gas filled glass, which would retain heat in the winter; one of many measures and designs that would keep power usage at a minimum.

Each unit could be transitioned into a permanent home with the addition of a second layer of heavily insulated siding and other structural improvements the interim homes availed themselves to.

Plumbing would be very primitive, but an effective sewer system was in progress, linking each home to central pipelines that were being laid down. The whole settlement area was starting to look like one huge construction site as a real community was starting to take shape.

Bob and Sergei were surveying this dazzling regeneration of life. "So what do you think, Sergei? We got a growing town going on here?" Bob asked very coyly.

"This is beyond magnificent, Bob. Just a few months ago we were scrounging for clean water, burying some of the dead who didn't make it and now," Sergei's voice started to crack with emotion, "now we have our lives back. Someday we will return the favor, my friend."

Although this promise of returning the favor was getting old, what Bob was looking at now was his reward.

"Luk'yan tells me that the power station will be tested next week. The windmills went up rather quickly and are cranking out the kilowatts thanks to that 'delightful' Arctic 'breeze' bombarding the eastern shores of the second island."

"You know, it's ironic, Bob. Our people will have a better life than what they had when they were forced to leave and what they felt was a great loss. But you know, in a very odd way, it is like coming home. I mean, this is where our ancestors first establish themselves. Who would have thought we would return back to where it all began?"

"Yeah, this is gonna give Dimitrii Crogan a lifetime wedgie."

"Wedgie? What is this wedgie?"

Bob smirked and patted Sergei on the shoulder as he stepped forward to make his way to the storage sheds. "Something that can ruin your whole day and make you use an extra heavy dose of bleach in your next wash."

This was so far beyond Sergei's cultural base that he just filed it away as American slang.

By this time, the lid was beginning to pry loose off of Dimitrii's ulterior motive and, to put icing on the cake, some of his closest advisers had gone public about Dimitrii's genocidal intentions toward the people of the upper fourteen provinces. This was also backed up by personal journals and memorandums sent by Dimitrii to his field officers and ministers. These testimonies were under the guise of patriotism, but were really an effort to save their own asses as Dimitrii was going down in flames. Some believed it just the venting of disgruntled staff, some just didn't want to believe it while at the same time the rest of the world's suspicions were all but confirmed.

CHAPTER 36

Dimitrii was still reeling from the news. He couldn't believe it! He just heard that the Kremlin had granted the people of Antonia, these insects, the Svenkia Islands as their own. This more or less would become another one of Russia's satellites and they were free to govern themselves as they wished and live their lives as they saw fit.

The governing body of Russia still embraced the public notion that they were extradited due to poor and irreversibly water supplies. Although most in the Kremlin knew this not to be true, admitting anything else would demonstrate negligent governing of a rogue territory. As long as the Chevkan government played a major role in a seamless transition for these people, all was well enough left alone.

But Dimitrii's plan was now gathering momentum in becoming one of history's greatest backfires given the high degree of suspicion of his real reason for expelling these people. If the world were to witness what one of Russia's satellite territories had done to its own people, the Kremlin would have a replacement waiting in the bullpen. They were well aware that they would have no choice but to put Dimitrii on trial for his atrocities if it came to that, which would surely send him to prison to join some of the people he put there himself.

The guards would manage the other inmates intensely to ensure no real harm came to Dimitrii, but just enough to degrade him in much the same way he degraded the people of the upper fourteen provinces. They would purposely keep him in general population instead of solitary confinement. Dimitrii would become someone's bitch in under a week.

He was flush with anger and weakened with embarrassment in view of his inner circle, and once the real news was confirmed and spread, the rest of the world would have nothing but contempt for the fat bastard.

He had to show the rest of the world (and, of course, the Kremlin) that not only did he care for his people (the thought of which only exacerbated his hatred), but was at the heart of their survival.

After careful and rather rapid fire thought, he decided the remedy was to come in two forms: One, he would need more in depth press coverage showing his support of the survival of the people he banished from their homes, and two, that this American's objective was to gain attention to make his boxing more marketable and profitable in addition to the questionable distribution of sizable funds being donated to this "cause." Dimitrii, being the mastermind of unscrupulous execution, gathered his forces and laid out a plan.

He decided to first hold a press conference and invited the American media to attend. He also asked Interior Minister Shulvi to have his finance team work up some numbers; real and imaginary, but both made to appear believable. Dimitrii would first applaud the efforts of Bob Perry and then raise an eyebrow as to the motivation behind his supposed heroic efforts.

Both local and foreign press corps gathered quickly in the reception area of the palace in the Movania. Some time ago, Dimitrii had learned English, primarily for diplomatic reasons. Today it was proving invaluable.

"Good afternoon ladies and gentlemen, thank you for attending our announcements on rather short notice. The Russian government, as you probably heard, has bestowed the three islands of Svenkia to the people of Antonia for their development, sustenance and, most of all, their happiness. It was with a heavy heart that I had to ask them to leave their homes, but as you all know, there had been significant levels of contamination found in their water tables. And we of Chevka, a humble and simple nation of peoples, did not have the infrastructure or the equipment to provide pipelined water to the area. That is why I had to suggest they move to the Svenkia Islands, which is right across the Khyber Straits so they would be near the motherland where the water is pure (Lie# 3,467).

"On my first visit over there, we supplied them with the basic needs of food and shelter. Now we are ready for the next step of providing them permanent homes, running water, sanitation systems, sources of energy and other means to survive on their own. But they can always count on the nation of Chevka to be fully supportive and to fill in any of the voids they may experience so there'll be no interruption in their lives.

"I'm very pleased to announce that these efforts will begin this weekend and will be carried through until I'm convinced that the people of Antonia are safe and have all the tools for living and a fruitful future."

Dimitrii was carefully scrutinizing the expression on each person's face in the room. He was warming up and had captured their attention, but had a ways to go.

He continued, "I applaud the efforts of Bob Perry,

who has been instrumental in helping us with the recovery and development of the new home for the Antonian people. He has managed to raise significant amounts of money from corporate sponsors and individuals worldwide. I'm not quite sure of the figure, but from what I understand of the magnitude of these collections, he would've had enough to build new homes and to give them all they need by now.

"I can understand that it's a difficult task for a twenty-six-year-old, but they need to have someone at the helm who has had far more business experience and can manage the funds and be held accountable for every penny. And who knows where every penny is going right now? There are no records or public disclosure of what is being spent on what. We need to know that the funds that are being offered generously are being put to good use and not finding—" one eyebrow raised "— 'other' directions." He pronounced this in his best thespian baritone.

"I will now be more than happy to answer any of your questions."

A sea of hands was raised quickly and Dimitrii, being the accomplished adulterer that he was, quickly chose the hand that belonged to one of the prettiest journalists in the room. What he wasn't aware of was the hand Dimitrii unknowingly called upon was that of Dana Ruminski. She took a deep breath and rose from her seat with all cameras now pointing toward her and hand-held recorders and boom mics surrounding her every word.

Dana had obtained a working visa to join the staff at NBC in New York City. The eyes of the world were now on the Svenkia Islands, with many twists and angles providing fodder and fair game for reporting. A few of the many stories were about the relationship and involvement of the nation of Chevka and the contiguous support of the people they had relocated from their lands due to "contaminated water." Since they were under the most powerful of microscopes, they had relaxed a lot of their restrictions for their peoples.

In the past, travel out of the country was highly discouraged, with strict and intrusive customs practices with transfer fees so high that most people couldn't afford it. To obtain a working visa to another country would be near impossible, much less for working for a political lightning rod the likes of NBC reporting. You'd have better odds trying to get a highly claustrophobic person to accompany you in a diving bell down to the bottom of the Mariana Trench.

Dimitrii was now forced to show that they were a friendly nation and their people were under no requirements that would jeopardize their freedom, especially movement within and outside of the country. Dana seized this sudden change in venue, taking full advantage of fulfilling her dream of being a true investigative reporter with the most liberal of press and had to read the letter of offer three times before it sunk in.

Hiring Dana was a no-brainer for the news organization. As the charm and drama of the blooming new country of the Svenkia Islands was capturing attention and hearts all over the world, hiring a native of the mainland dedicated to the reporting of their progress made a world of sense. What really sealed the deal were samples of copy Dana had written about the true plight of the Antonia people that she never dared to submit to the Chevkan news media, much less have it published anywhere. She was convinced she would look horrific in prison "grays."

Her goal, as the cover was coming off Pandora's Box, and sure as shit tootin' it was, was to apply for permanent citizenship. NBC was thoroughly impressed with her ability to create imagery in the minds of the readers, making for some extremely interesting copy and powerful exposure of one of the world's worst treatment of people since the Holocaust.

She had made no mention to them of her donkey cart trick, but she was saving that and dozens of other episodes to be compiled in a book once the Svenkia islands had developed enough, were protected and recognized as their own sovereign nation.

As the instinct and passion of a journalist was in her blood, her greatest triumph would be the thorough and accurate documentation of the real reasons behind the journey of the people of the Upper 14 Provinces.

She knew she could never return to Chevka, nor did she have any desire to do so. She would gain modest public spotlight for journalism and would send for her mother to join her. Any suppression of an elderly woman to leave would only serve as reinforcement to some of the stinging revelations Dana's reporting would surface.

"Mr. President, is it not true that there is no water contamination in the upper fourteen provinces, and recently some of your geologists have suggested that there are several veins of coal that may be extracted and stall the growing deficit of the Chevkan economy?"

Dimitrii instantly recognized the accent and felt his

bowels do a slow and agonizing tango. He summoned up all of the diplomacy and posturing that he could, "What a pleasant surprise to see one of our own people working for such a prestigious news agency as NBC."

Dana wanted to throw up, preferably all over the crisp white shirt Dimitrii managed to grab from the back of his closet for such an auspicious occasion.

"Well, to answer your question Ms., ah…"

"Ruminski, Dana Ruminski. Is it true, sir?" *Remember the name, asshole*, she thought, *you'll be hearing it a lot.*

Three different methods of torture and slow death entered Dimitrii's mind immediately. How much he wanted to see this bitch suffer; after her last breath, he would take great pleasure in raping her corpse. He would have her whole family brought in for questioning and then have them summarily tortured.

"Yes, Ms. Ruminski, it's true our government has been experiencing financial difficulties and again, yes, it would be fortuitous for us to find new thick veins of coal to mine, as this is our main export and would fill up quickly emptying coffers. But my people come first; they always have."

A second wave of nausea hit Dana and thought a second barfing on his shoes would be a nice complement to his already soiled shirt.

"Then why is the landscape of the upper fourteen provinces dotted with heavy drill holes and widened craters making it look like Normandy after the invasion and not a house in sight?"

He decided he would stretch her limbs, tying down

her wrists and ankles to pegs dug into an open hotbed of dirt under a blazing midday sun (naked of course), pouring honey over her, heavily on her face and privates, and then unload two full buckets of fire ants on her to feast.

"Those drill holes are in search of the contaminated water beds, as our geologists are seeking samples so we may possibly come up with a solution and bring our people home. The houses needed to be removed as the threat of radium had come under serious concern."

A brand new "development," but Dimitrii had to think quickly. This would come and bite him square in the ass later on. He had not thought of high flying reconnaissance flights taking pictures.

With this new revelation, a new wave of hands shot up into the air and Dimitrii attempted to call on somebody else in an attempt to short-circuit the fuse on this time bomb Dana had put on the table before him.

"I have one more question, sir," she said sternly enough that it piqued the curiosity of the other journalists and they immediately put down their hands and wanted to hear what this native Chevkan journalist had to say.

"Then why is it, sir, that one of the reconnaissance aircraft operated by NATO had photographed what appears to be an open mine tunnel in the northwestern corner of the twelfth province?"

It was true. The geniuses in Dimitrii's Ministry of the Interior had thought they found a modest strain of coal and began digging an interim mine to begin the process of harvesting.

Dimitrii thought just slitting her throat, being done with it and being home by dinner time would do just as well.

He was becoming visibly agitated when he replied, "Your NATO plane did not take very good pictures, Ms. Ruminski. That was not a mine, but a, ah, storage tunnel to keep delicate instrumentation cool and without humidity." He knew he was losing ground and losing it fast and once again attempted a diversion. "Next question please."

The press corps stayed silent. There was not a hand raised in response to the question. They knew where this was going and didn't want to stop Dana now that she had momentum. She remained standing.

"Well, if there aren't any other questions, I like to thank you all for coming today."

Dana wasn't quite through. Having done her homework thoroughly (she relished this new spin about radium where this would also be researched and easy game for a second round of ball breaking), and in speaking to the proper experts asked, "Mr. President, the area of the upper fourteen provinces occupies 15,750 square miles. Underground water tables stretch for miles in both length and width, unlike veins of coal with a maximum length of only hundreds of feet and only a few feet in width and depth. NBC had gotten the opinion of geologists from four different institutions, all with high credentials, where they, with the utmost certainty, would estimate in order to find and research water tables, there should have been no more than 280 holes drilled sporadically no closer than thirty miles apart in that given area. How do you explain the 976 holes and the craters the NATO plane had spotted in one province alone?"

This brought a little undercurrent of murmuring

from the other journalists. Christ, this woman should have been a frigging lawyer; she'd win every case and have a seat on the Supreme Court before her first gray hair.

Dimitrii's nuts were now creeping up into his lower intestine and he sought no other alternative but to announce, "Thank you all for coming today and stay tuned," he said in a jovial and comical sort away, "to the continual progress as Chevka makes way for their people of the Svenkia Islands."

He then made a hasty retreat for the door.

Dammit, Dana thought. She had him by the throat and was about to squeeze when her pager went off. The press conference came to an abrupt end as she rushed to the phone in one of the other offices. She didn't have access to Reuters press machines in Movania and felt a little cut off from the rest of the world. Getting information back to her office for somebody to write copy and make the evening news was just as difficult. Chevka was truly constructed to have the rest of the world mind their own business.

After the international operator finally connected her to the NBC newsroom, a colleague of hers answered the phone and immediately gave her the news. It was a short phone call and she put the receiver back in the cradle with her hand resting on the handset, not knowing to jump for joy or cry.

Bob Perry had been nominated for the Nobel Peace Prize.

CHAPTER 37

That weekend, trucks and other armored vehicles were lined up at the edges of the Khyber Straits, waiting for the tide to go out for them to gain entrance to the Svenkia islands. Field Marshal Julias Witkowski was dressed in full regalia in the lead vehicle; an early model Mercedes convertible, much like the one you used to see Hitler standing in during motorcades passing his frightened public.

The news crews were poised around the outer periphery ready to film and comment on Dimitrii's second elaborate show of support for the people who, unknown to them, he initially branded as pigs and thrust from their homes. Dana was with the NBC crew trying to get the taste of hypocrisy of her mouth so she could focus on her job. This was a huge task in that this "support" was only symbolic and didn't offer any substance in regard to the very complex strategy of reinventing Antonian civilization.

There must have been thirty or forty trucks carrying everything from the inescapable oatmeal and corn to primitive and lightly sheathed house parts they intended to snap together like something from a cheap Lego set. The slightest gust of wind would either whistle through or flatten these structures.

There were even a few trucks with goats and pigs with the brilliant idea that they would propagate and become a source of meat for these people. Witkowski's officers were more than pleased to offer the press this disingenuous idea behind helping the people of the upper fourteen provinces help themselves. The whole display was a sick gesture coming from a man who would not think twice about plucking out your guts and using it as fertilizer for his own beloved garden.

Dana's cheeks grew flush at the sight of some of the smirking soldiers who took great pride participating in this cover-up, pulling the wool over the eyes of the rest the world.

As the tide slowly ebbed out, the rocky and pebbled path of the Straits began to come into view. Trucks and other vehicles then started their engines, cameras began to film and media crews once again clambered back in their vehicles for the ride across. If you'd had an aerial view of this procession, it would've appeared as many tiny ants crawling along this scraggly path on the way to a small group of islands four miles away.

As Dana had gone through this drill before, she had brought along a supple pad to put on the seat in the back of the van, as she knew her buns couldn't take another trip bouncing up and down on the metal seats. The surface of the path, rough and irregular as it was, allowed a top speed of ten miles an hour, translating to about a half-hour ride.

On the other end of the Straits and across the edge leading to the island entrance were thirty men. They had lined up ten yards apart stretching almost a quarter mile of the width of the Straits, clearly intent on blocking the oncoming entourage. In addition to Bob and Sergei, there was Luk'yan the engineer, Kirstan the electrician, Evstafii the architect, Makarii the plumber, Uncle Dem'yan, Prokhor the biologist, Uncle Elizar and a series of others. They had assembled and stood vigil once they heard the distant sound of the trucks starting their engines.

As Dimitrii's men started to come into sight, their resolve became even greater and they started to move slightly closer together, forming a human shield to the entrance of the main island. Their faces were taut and their feet were planted firmly in the rocks and pebbles at the shoreline. If a freight train were coming up, there be no question in their minds that they would collectively block it from gaining entrance to the place they now call their home… the operative word being "their." There was no chance in hell they were going to let Dimitrii get away with this debacle. This was going to be their victory and their victory alone.

As the trucks finally came within twenty yards of this line of men, Field Marshal Witkowski jumped out of his lead vehicle and started walking toward the group. The news crews, smelling the obvious, jumped out of their vans, cameras and microphones turned up and ready to record what was turning out to appear as a confrontation. Bob left the line and walked forward to meet (but certainly not greet) Witkowski.

"Mr. Perry, so nice to see you. I am Field Marshal Julius Witkowski and today we bring you food, we bring you supplies and we bring you new homes! The motherland has come here to help its children in a time of dire need and distress," he said, turning his head slightly over his shoulder and to the right so his profile (the good side) and voice would be picked up by the sea of journalists.

This idiot looked like something out of the March of the Wooden Soldiers. Overly dressed with a gross display of gold braids adorning each shoulder and a collage of medals, most of which meant nothing and the rest of which meant carrying out the tyrannical orders of Dimitrii. Bob was also convinced that his mustache was dyed. A small spasm created in his throat to keep from laughing when he returned Witkowski's greeting.

"I'm afraid your gesture is too little, too late Field Marshal. I'm going to ask that you and your men do an about-face and return to the mainland before the tide comes in."

The other men in the line now started to converge closer, forming a U-shaped crowd around Bob and Field Marshal Witkowski.

"Why, why I don't understand," Witkowski returned innocently. "We have an obligation to our people to help them during times of hardship and need. Why do you turn us away while we're trying to help our own people?"

Witkowski became noticeably nervous and angry at the same time. This insolent, muscle-bound piece of trash was purposely embarrassing him in front of the world! He absolutely was not going to turn around in defeat.

"You're dealing with people's lives here, Mr. Perry. We applaud you for your efforts so far, but now it's time that an experienced organization takes over and help these people. It is not without responsibility that our trucks will move forward and save the people you've tried to use for your own purposes."

Out of anger, Witkowski went out on a far, far limb and there was no turning back now. The men in the crowd started to become visibly agitated with such a horrendous accusation.

"If it wasn't for Mr. Perry, *Field Marshal*

Witkowski, there would be no people for you to 'save'," shouted Sergei.

This was further emphasized by a chorus of rage and retaliation from the other men; all captured on camera and audio, thank you very much. The producers of the news media didn't give a rat's ass at this point if profanity was used or not. They clearly were on the same page as this group of men defending their islands.

"And what purposes are those, Field Marshal Witkowski?" Bob asked with the address of title characterized by a sarcastic tone in his voice.

The media was lapping this up, moving in for close up shots of Bob's and Witkowski's faces. The expressions were clearly growing with anger; this would be gold on the evening news and in the papers.

Witkowski was now grasping for straws. "Well, ah. Your fighting match! Yes, the fighting match. It would reap greater rewards for your purse by all the publicity that you're squeezing out of these poor people."

A fresh torrid of shouts blew up from the men, drowning out anything further that Witkowski was trying to allege along these lines.

Bob put his hands in his pockets without flinching and addressed the shouting men, "He's right. Something of this magnitude would bring greater attention to me and fan the flames in marketing my 'fighting match'," he said mockingly. "But, then again, I could've saved myself a lot of time and trouble by just getting caught drunk driving, or beating my wife—" if he had one "—or stealing money or peeing purple in a cup for drug testing. But why would I drain my bank account, come here, try my best to stay in shape for my next fight without proper equipment and have my heart broken by the tears and fear on the face of these children just to promote a 'fighting match'?"

This was like pouring gas on an open flame for his comrades standing behind him. The uproar was reaching riot proportions and some of the soldiers started to ready their weapons, with some of the commanding officers in charge motioning them furiously to put them down. Too late. All captured on camera. Good job, boys!

"And what about the money, Mr. Perry? Generous contributions coming to you from corporations and wealthy individuals? Hmm? What about that? By our estimates, from the funds that you probably have received, these good people should be sleeping in warm homes by now with all the amenities of a small city."

Bob was gritting his teeth and summoning all his will to not blow the lid off of Pandora's Box by publicly announcing to the world what Chevka had really done to their own people. He wanted to shout out that these people were ripped from their homes on the greedy and narcissistic whims of a deranged and ruthless leader. He wanted to look the camera straight in the lens and tell the world in a few short sentences what really happened. But it was too much on the line in terms of diplomatic relations and the ripple effect internationally would be irreversibly damaging. But then again, this would not be news to the rest of the world.

"I'm not sure what figures you're working with, Field Marshal Witkowski. Every dime has been documented, records kept and audited by one of the most prestigious auditing firms in the United States. There are clear, concise and accurate ledgers for review by anyone at any time. But we do not feel compelled, nor obligated, to hand these records over to you. If anyone, the benefactors of these funds, or anything else for that matter, have clear and ready access to this information. Since you, your men and the government of Chevka have done nothing other than publicly offer a pathetic token without substance, these records remain under the auspices of the people of the Svenkia Islands."

Okay, that really did it. Witkowski's face was now purple with rage. Oh, how he wished he could give the command with one sweep of his hand and have his men mow these insolents down in a barrage of gunfire. Field Marshal Witkowski was not used to losing. As a matter of fact, he'd never lost a fight before. This seemed to be turning into an agonizing first.

He decided to draw one more card rather recklessly and shouted to his entourage, "Proceed. Move forward. Our people await us!"

Trucks revved their engines and started to move forward. The media was almost skinning their knuckles trying to unload and reload new film in their cameras. They couldn't do it fast enough, as the sequence of events were turning quickly.

Dana was now becoming nervous in earnest, as she knew the short boundaries Witkowski and his men had with civility and their propensity for brutality. Witkowski returned to his lead car and ordered his driver to proceed. Bob and the men moved closer together and waited, blocking the path to the islands.

Witkowski's car started to pick up speed until members of the media themselves started screaming, "Stop!

Stop! You're going to kill these people. Have you gone mad?"

The fascination of the story now left the media and the reality of an impending catastrophe took hold. Witkowski, being no fool, knew the situation was turning clearly against him and could see Dimitrii signing the orders for him to be placed in prison for the rest of life. He ordered his driver to stop immediately.

The driver slammed on the brakes, but the car continued as it traversed atop the wet rocks and pebbles before coming to a stop, mowing down three men, one of whom was pinned underneath the vehicle. Two of the men were rewarded with broken legs, a fractured kneecap and a dislocated hip. The man underneath the car wasn't so lucky. He was dead.

"See what you made me do?" Witkowski screamed like a frightened little girl at Bob. "You killed one of our people. If it wasn't for you, that man would still be alive."

Witkowski's driver, not exactly a candidate for taking post-graduate courses at Harvard, backed up the car, only causing further damage to the corpse.

"Get out of here," Bob seethed in a growling baritone. "Take your men, your guns, your worthless supplies and go back. Now! Get out of here while you still have a chance before the tide comes in. You've done enough damage discrediting yourself, your country and anything that the government of Chevka seemingly stands for"

Witkowski didn't know whether to shit or go blind. He had clearly made a huge mistake in trying to take over the situation. This would be all over the news for the world to see and Dimitrii would have his prison cell, and a rather large "associate" for a "talk," ready for him before he even got back.

Witkowski ordered a hasty retreat. The vehicles almost collided with each other trying to make U-turns, some of which ending up in the water as the incoming tide picked up momentum. The truck caravan started zigzagging back across the increasingly narrow Straits before becoming submerged.

Bob and the men were furious, with some choking back tears and others close to rushing the soldiers at all costs. The men took their two injured comrades and placed them on makeshift gurneys to be brought back for medical attention. The body that had been so gruesomely mangled by Witkowski's car was carefully wrapped in blankets and ceremoniously brought back up the embankment by the men.

The man in the blankets was Natalia's Uncle Elizar.

CHAPTER 38

Bob, Sergei, Petr, Luk'yan, Lynne and Bonnie were sitting in the War Room with ground plans and mechanical drawings now taped all along the walls, leaving only the windows clear. It was 8PM after a long day and exhaustion was etched on everyone's faces. On the table was paperwork of all kinds; financial reports, bank statements, bills of lading, punch lists of every sort and letters from very influential people that needed to be read and responded to (the cargo planes were now delivering mail simply addressed to whomever, Svenkia Islands; no type of zip code, just the province. That would eventually change).

Bob's hair was well below his shoulders and the bottom of his beard to the middle of his chest. Bonnie was paying special attention to this, as it was starting to get weird enough to be kind of a Howard Hughes thing (fingernails clipped though). He would certainly make a good fit to audition for ZZ Top, but the man couldn't even toot his own horn much less play an instrument. Still, for all he'd done at an age where most men were drinking beer, driving fast and chasing skirt, he was becoming increasingly endearing to her. This guy would win awards as mercenary of the year, that's for sure. News of the Nobel Peace Prize had not yet reached them.

The conversation was going in all different types of directions; the windmills were up and running, spinning their little hearts out, kicking back enough juice to the power station, resulting in the rapid installation of water pumps along with purification systems, running water and waste careening through miles of pipe. The housing was almost completed with only the plumbing to be linked to the water systems running along the edges of designated areas.

Sgt. Hayes and his men did remarkable work and Bob would never ceased to be amazed by how they got their hands on all the heavy equipment and barges, much less the twin Anotonov An-22 Cock cargo planes. All that mattered was the recovery of people who were treated like animals.

Funds were slowing down and Bob wanted to have a healthy reserve for contingencies that God knows would rear their ugly heads. The people now had everything they needed and now had to enter a maintenance mode. The nagging thought that was sitting in Bob's head, unidentified for the past few weeks, was now starting to come to fruition.

You got the engine running, he realized, *but now how do we keep it idling smoothly? How are the people going to fend for themselves now? What if they need food, what if they need clothing, what if they need repairs, what if they need containers to put their food in, what if they need batteries, what if they need... anything?*

With all the distractions of the past few months, no one really thought out what was to happen after all was done for immediate recovery. And for all intents and purposes, they had just created a new country. A country with no money for imports and no means of production for exports, much less servicing only their primal needs. The thought terrified Bob.

His stress caught the attention of the others and as he stroked his beard (which annoyed Bonnie to no end), he said, "What happens next, guys? These people have everything they need, but there is actually no organization in how they can provide for each other in a balanced environment of exchange. Funds are about drawn down to the point where the rest is going to be held in reserve for any emergencies that might come up. I mean, who's going to maintain the electrical systems for this island?"

Sergei was a little surprised at the question, "Why, Luk'yan, of course."

"Okay, what if Luk'yan needs to have an overcoat when working the power station, which is a whole lot colder?"

"Nikifor, one of the finest tailors, would make him a coat. He can make all the clothing for the people here. He would have to have, well, employees." Sergei was starting to pick up on the rhythm of the conversation.

"And what if Nikifor needs meat to feed his wife and kids?"

"Oleg, although he was a warehouse supervisor on the mainland, is a superior hunter and had the heads of many animals covering the walls of his home as testimony, although it pissed his wife off."

"All right, fine. Now what if Oleg, after a long day of hunting, wants to come home, take off his shoes, sit by the fire and enjoy a cold beer?" Bob thought this exchange was going to come to a screeching halt right here.

Sergei was starting to look like a little boy waiting to get on the Ferris wheel. "One of the finest brewmaster's in Europe happens to be our Parkhom. He'd put your finest American beer, domestic or imported, to shame."

Bonnie could start to feel fluttering in her chest

witnessing what she was sure was going to be the biggest victory for these people, but needing an incredible amount of strategy, development and maintenance. She rested her chin on both hands with elbows propped on the table waiting to hear the next step in this conversation.

Bob was starting to feel the same excitement. "And what would happen if the machines curing the hops and barley in those huge tanks brewing the beer come to a screeching halt because of some type of mechanical failure?"

"Why, Luk'yan, the engineer would fix it, of course."

This struck directly into the circuitry of Bonnie's memory of one of many rhymes her grandmother would read to her when they would go visit her.

The Butcher, The Baker, The Candlestick Maker.

CHAPTER 39

Professor Emeritus Lord Parisellan buttoned the top of his overcoat and pushed his scarf further up beneath his ears as he and two colleagues exited the cargo plane.

Cold. Damn cold, he thought as the sudden drop in temperature from the aircraft tore into his face.

Even though the dead of winter had begrudgingly begun to say farewell to the islands and a hint of spring was in the air, it was still cold by an Englishman's standards. Lord Parisellan was a striking man of sixty-three years old and a full shock of silver hair, his six-foot two-inch frame as erect now as it was thirty years ago.

John Parisellan II was a graduate of Cambridge University, served on the economic boards of many local governments, contributed as an advisor for numerous international economic councils, forgot the number of books he had written and had settled down in the autumn of his career into one of the most highly prestigious positions at the London School of Economics. He was revered worldwide for his contributions to the economic development of some Third World countries, some of those countries being ravaged by internal civil war and unimaginable sectarian violence. A few weeks ago the phone rang with the call he had been expecting for quite some time.

"May I speak with Lord Parisellan please?" Bob was stretching his luck in trying to reach out to Lord Parisellan, as he was a very busy and sought after individual. His influence had stimulated international stock markets just by the mere few spoken words during a public interview. His involvement and effect were unmatched in lifesaving and salvaging life under severe economic distress. But, nonetheless, Bob had nothing to lose in trying.

"This is John Parisellan. And whom do I have the pleasure of speaking with?"

"It's, um, Bob. Bob Perry. I…"

"Ah, yes. I was expecting your call. What took you so long, young man?"

"Sir?"

"Well, for heaven sakes, the world is watching what you and the others have been doing for those poor people. As an economist, I paid especial attention to the inflow of funds, how it was used and now wonder how you're going to figure out where to go from here."

"Well, that's just it, Professor. We have all the tools, equipment and manpower, but how do we make it work on an ongoing basis? I mean, it's a communal concept at this point where one produces goods for services for another and that other for someone else; so on and so forth, but… "

John Parisellan was especially excited with his inclusion, especially with this young man, in rebuilding the socioeconomic infrastructure of the Antonian people. He had been involved in similar projects in the past in an advisory capacity, but there had been a government in place from which to execute recovery measures. In this particular case, there was no government, there was no parliamentary procedure, and there was no pecking order or useless politics… nothing!

At least at its inception, it had traces of the origins

of communism and socialism. Right now, there were no bourgeoisie or moneyed class; everyone was on the same plane, but with a diversity of skills that could symbiotically serve each other.

"You were smart enough to use your contributions wisely, my boy. Investment in the 'means' instead of the 'end' was a very good start. But now the real work begins. This will have to be constructed as an airtight and closed economy; at least for now. Resource planning, rationing and fixed pricing will be our starting point. We can build a system that makes sense from there."

CHAPTER 40

It seemed the epiphany that was gleaned from Sergei and Bob's dialogue that one evening in the War Room was a firm, albeit initial, basis of a self-sustaining economy. Bringing Lord Parisellan and his two graduate students onto the team encouraged hope, much like a doctor pronouncing the correct diagnosis and performing a successful treatment.

Bob, Sergei, Petr, Luk'yan, Lynne and Bonnie sat around the conference table with Lord Parisellan at the head. He folded his hands, cleared his voice and class began.

"During ancient times, a shepherd would bring one of his sheep to the open market with the hope he would find someone offering, say, grain, who would be in search of a sheep for its wool or its meat. These markets needed to be wide and diverse to increase the chances of a one-for-one exchange; hence the barter system. The market may have had several farmers with grains and other produce, but only one who had been in need of a sheep. If the shepherd was lucky enough to find him, negotiations begun. How much grain is worth one sheep? How many kilos of grain were appropriate to exchange for sixty-five pounds of sheep? There was no clearly defined pricelist and it was entirely up to how much grain was available in the market and how desperately the particular merchant was looking for sheep.

"On the other side of the negotiating equation was how much the shepherd really needed grain to make bread for his family. This causes an imbalance, since each exchange is unique and inconsistent. Why, look how much was paid for your Manhattan Island; twenty-four dollars' worth of relatively worthless trinkets! Hence, the classic intersection of supply and demand curves that govern practically everything in the world around us today. As you can imagine, these markets were highly inefficient and people often returned home with not exactly what they needed. The shepherd may not have found someone offering grain who wanted a sheep, but found a merchant offering firewood who was in need of a sheep for its wool. So the shepherd returned home with firewood, although he had sufficient supply for the short-term and, needless to say, suffered the wrath of his wife for not returning home with the ingredients to make bread for the family."

This brought a slight chuckle from the group, with Lynne Albright rolling her eyes as she mused of her second husband coming home from the supermarket, with explicit instructions, mind you, with something completely different than what she wanted. This often served to jumpstart heated arguments on topics completely unrelated to his bringing home a white onion instead of a red one.

"Now, what if that shepherd had in his possession something that could he exchange with *anyone* in the market? He could go to the first farmer offering grain and give him that something in exchange for the grain. The object of exchange would need to be something that was in scarcity, in high demand and universally accepted in its intrinsic value. During the evolution of money as a medium of exchange, spices from faraway lands, gold and other precious metals served as objects of practically universal value.

"The real strength of the value of an object of

exchange came from the confirmed designation of value of something by a king or other people in authority. This eventually gave way to standardize coins of less precious metal, but of authorized value. This made it easier for someone to get what they needed, but negotiation for the exchange of value always took place, succumbing to the supply and demand phenomena of the day, continues in almost every transaction today and will continue as such for as long as human beings have different perspectives of value."

"Are you saying that the Svenkia Islands need their own currency?" Sergei asked.

The rest looked around at each other, befuddled, as this was an escalation toward a civilized society that was far ahead of their current mindset. In the few seconds this part of the conversation took up, the Svenkia Peronka, using the first three letters of Bob's last name, immediately flashed across Sergei's mind. It would end up sticking, but including the image of Bob's profile would immediately be vetoed by him.

Lord Parisellan continued. "The example of the full cycle exchange of goods and services among the people here, as you had explained to me based on the conversation Bob and Sergei had the other evening, makes perfect sense. There are approximately 3,000 people here, all of diverse backgrounds in terms of their skill sets, thank goodness, where each can contribute to the next and the next can contribute to another, all coming full circle to the first person in the chain of exchange. This works well in theory if the timing is right, the need is there and the supply is proportionate to that need. But I'm afraid it's far more complicated than just printing paper bills with a configured denotation of unity and value in different denominations."

"Just how will this work, Lord Parisellan?" asked Bonnie. "I mean, would this be some sort of massive Monopoly game where everyone is given a certain amount of cash before the game begins?"

Lord Parisellan chuckled with the others and said, "That's precisely it, Bonnie. People will be given an allotted starting sum of cash, but I assure you there will be no Park Avenue. To determine this amount of cash, we need to work backwards in the Supply and Demand chain. Based on Sergei's census of the people on this island, we need to understand what each person needs, how much and how often. We then determine the relative cost based on the labor and materials used. There will be no overhead introduced into this equation, but I'll explain that later. Ms. Albright, I hear you've done some fantastic work and I've given seminars in some of the buildings that are graced by your landscaping designs. I would suggest that you be in charge of designing the bills and notes to serve as money."

Lynn Albright perked up and savored the opportunity, with designs and colors already swimming around in her head. Prior to that, the academia was starting to bore her. But she did take an earnest interest in the good professor and by this time, she had already picked out the morning suit he would wear at their wedding and was starting to mentally work out the floral centerpieces for the reception.

Bob now picked up the ball with the next series of questions. "But what happens when people start, you know, as you mentioned before, to negotiate and change pricing?

Would that start to make the equation lopsided and a bit out of control?"

Lord Parisellan smiled at the intuitiveness of this young man. He was still from the school of thought that, although an avid boxing fan, propagated the impression of boxers being a little punch-drunk and not too savvy educationally. This Bob Perry seemed to defy those odds and was one intelligent young man.

"Very good. Very good indeed! You just introduce my next point, Mr. Perry. Prices must be fixed. There should be no deviation or finagling with the prices of any goods or services. I suggest you form a counsel, Ministry of Finance if you will, that would manage pricing. I'm sure there are quite a few CPAs and your own finance people you can choose from to either join your counsel or act in an advisory capacity."

This touched upon a tangent thought that Sergei had been mulling over since the reality of being there permanently set in. They would need a governing structure body; this Ministry of Finance would be an excellent starting point from which to build upon that thought.

Lord Parisellan's gaze now narrowed as he was clearly entrenched in the academic stream of the economy he was helping to build. He felt exhilarated.

With the persona of a commander, he decreed, "And there will be absolutely no imports or exports, whatsoever! For the time being, this must be an airtight and closed economy. Only a certain amount of money will be created and distributed, as this money needs to stay in circulation as does the blood of one individual man. Anything else would upset the balance at this point, but eventually, someday, after the social and monetary system has settled down and is running smoothly, you can start to think of dealing with the rest of the world. But right now you're going to be a little bubble in your own world, which will also help the healing process. We must make this work if we are to restore the confidence of your people."

Petr now joined the conversation. "I realize that this is a necessary approach, but I can't help but shudder at the feeling of this being turned into some type of dictatorship, the same thing that kicked us out of our houses and put us on this rock in the first place."

"Yes, Petr. This is a dictatorship, at least for now. It will be a benevolent dictatorship and will not have all the other nuances of restricting freedoms and that sort. And it does have a pinch of communism and socialism, as there will be no lower or higher income groups as many have existed in the Upper 14 provinces. Everyone will be on a level plane economically; those who are considered wealthy back on the mainland will receive proportionately the same money to start as that of a neighbor who may have been of a middle or lower income status. Kind of like when you join the military and everyone's a private, all on equal ground."

The last forty-five minutes was starting to untangle the concern Bob had been harboring, although he still wasn't able to articulate it in its entirety in his own mind. But the more Lord Parisellan spoke, the more his thoughts and concerns started to coalesce. The feeling of confidence of the others from their conclusions the other evening segued with a supporting and credible explanation with an approach, as Lord Parisellan explained, of dealing with the intricacies of their economics, even at the simplest of levels.

John Parisellan looked around the room and let this sink in for a while before he continued. “From what I understand, the rest of the world is under the impression that the Chevkan government is providing for your people here when we all know that’s not true. But in keeping international face, this is the image the Kremlin looks to maintain to escape accusations that they do not have a handle on one of their satellites.”

“Well, the international community can all shit in their hats, including the Kremlin. We have everything we want right here,” Sgt. Hayes offered.

John sniffed at this little slice of vulgarity as though somebody just put a plate of dog poop under his nose. “I’m afraid you don’t, Sergeant. For all intents and purposes, you are isolated from the rest of the world with no money. You’re going to have to produce your own goods and services in sufficient quantity at the correct time and have a balanced means of exchange.

“For example, eventually you’re going to need drinking glasses, bottles, windowpanes, baking dishes, storage jars, test tubes and the like. For that, you’re going to need to make glass. To make glass, you’re going to need quartz sand or silica, along with magnesium, aluminum and calcium oxides; materials or adequate substitutes of which your geologists tell me can be mined from within these islands. These raw materials will need to be melted down in furnaces and further processed by glass blowing or insertion into steel molds.”

Lord Parisellan was only warming up. “Eventually

you're going to need weather stripping, wheels or tires, shoe soles, hoses, boots, raincoats, waterproof gloves, electrical housings and insulation and, least to say, toys, rubber bands and any other common household item you can think of made of rubber. To produce rubber, you'll need to have rubber trees that are seven years or older, as this is the time in their maturity that they will reap rubber latex.

"To have rubber trees on this godforsaken island, you'll need greenhouses, for which, as I just mentioned, you'll need glass. You'll need the equipment to process the rubber latex into a usable compound and then by means of introduction the injection mold machines and steel blanks, the final products. Those blank steel molds will need to be shaped into usable product cavities using air turbine spindles."

During all of this, Sergei had been rolling a pen between his fingers and begun to think about all the raw materials and machinery that went into making this simple pen; the plastic, the ink, the spring inside the plastic cavity. He suddenly stopped twirling the pen between his fingers and put it down with as much reverence as one would when delicately placing the Hope diamond on a display pod.

Lynne Albright, traveling along the same plane of thought, looked down at her watch, put her hand over it and didn't even want to go there.

The pace of the lecture quickened and everyone was now taking notes.

"Of course, you will need steel and concrete for obvious reasons. Carbon is the primary ingredient for iron where other alloying elements are used, such as magnesium, chromium, vanadium and tungsten. Once again, you're lucky on this hiccup of an island that most of these ingredients are present and would take minimal mining. As for the concrete, I'm almost certain that the basic elements also are available here: clay, shell, sand, iron ore, bauxite, fly ash and slag."

Lynn Albright was waving her hand furiously and Lord Parisellan responded, "Ms. Albright."

"So, basically, what you're saying, John, is that we have all the ingredients here and are calculating and budgeting for the means in which to process these materials, making us completely independent and self-sustaining." At the same time, she had decided against the morning suit for the wedding and thought John Parisellan would look better in a tux. But alas, this would turn into an effort in futility. He still had a heavy heart as his wife of forty years had passed away the year before. They had a wonderful marriage and he didn't think he could ever love someone more than his Beatrice until the birth of their daughter, Marie. Due to complications that eventually lead to her death thirty-three years later, she could bear only one child. The two women were the loves of his life.

Marie grew up to be a beautiful young woman so much like her mother it often left John speechless. She had met and married a German naval officer and now lived in a small village near the naval base of Wilhelmshaven; the same base that the British Royal Air Force had bombed in 1939.

John was a twenty-three-year-old navigation officer on one of the bombers that delivered the goods one particular Saturday morning. In addition to the irony, he wasn't exactly thrilled when, forty years later, his daughter invited young Stuart Gustloff to their home in Sussex. Although the world had changed considerably since the time he tried to negotiate the best route to Germany on a paper map bouncing around on a converted cargo plane traversing the English Channel, he still harbored a slight disdain for the "Gerry's."

After another one of Beatrice's superb dinners, Stuart asked if he could have a word with John in the den. It was there that he asked for his daughter's hand in marriage, which, for the one of very few times in his life, caught John off guard and he didn't know quite what to say. His daughter had just turned twenty-seven and he and her mother were beginning to reach a point of concern that their one prized child would have difficulty in finding a nice Englishman and settling down.

Never one to assume a Romeo and Juliet perspective with their daughter's infatuations, this pushed the envelope a little too close, but he saw in his daughter's eyes… love. So married they were and they produced the most beautiful grandson he could ever want. And as sad as it was, the timing couldn't have been better, for at least Beatrice enjoyed one year with her grandson before she passed on. Lord Parisellan was to visit his daughter and grandson, but had not yet purchased his ticket. He had been waiting for Bob's call first.

Returning back to Lynne's poignant observation, Lord Parisellan nodded in agreement. He continued by picking up a piece of paper from the table and holding it up. "So this is simply a piece of paper, something that often clutters our desks, and we find ourselves fumbling through layers trying to find something. Everyone knows that paper comes from pulp and pulp from trees, a raw material that is in abundance on these islands. The process of producing paper from pulp gives way to other products, such as toweling, napkins and other absorbent materials."

Luk'yan picked up the rhythm. "So in order to produce pulp, we need to harvest trees. We'll need chainsaws, a means to transport the logs to a wood mill, which we don't have, and then from there, the proper equipment to further process it."

With intonation of amusement in his voice, but in all seriousness, Lord Parisellan confirmed this by saying, "By George, I think you got it."

He went on to explain the raw materials needed, along with the processes and equipment required for clothing and other innocuous basic commodities, such as plastic, textiles along with food processing and storage.

The group now sat in silence and was a bit dumbfounded as to how seriously complicated simple things could be. Just how in the hell they were supposed to do this? A mass exodus from the island was entirely out of the question. Where would they go with no money? And what about the ones who were left behind? Who would care for them? It was clear that this would have to be a massive group effort, carefully planned and managed.

After absorbing everything, Sergei joined the conversation. "Lord Parisellan, everything that you described and the type of manpower needed, we have it in one degree or another. There are people who know how to do most of the things in the chain of processes needed, but need to learn to do it on a more grand scale. Then we have people who don't have the skill sets and need to be trained. I have nothing but faith in the determination of our people. We can do this."

Lord Parisellan admired the spirit of this group, and the rest of the people on the island, for that matter. That was the premier reason he was sitting at the head of a flimsy conference room table off the coast of Russia in the biting cold.

"You'll need an immediate infrastructure to get things started. Luk'yan, you mentioned a wood mill, which would need to be built immediately. There's no time to gather and process the resources in its construction. Along the same vein, you'll need at least two hospitals, a pharmacy, churches, schools, greenhouses, manufacturing facilities, such as a steel forging mill complete with crucible and furnace, a wood and pulp mill and mold injection machines, including the blank steel molds I mentioned before. I'm certain from there, you'll have enough of the equation to start providing for yourselves. Having this pre-assembled overhead, prices for goods and services mentioned before would be minimal since it would not include this portion, as it was provided for free."

It was at this point that Bob's concerns surfaced, something that he had been worrying about all along...Money. "The international community has been very generous so far, Lord Parisellan. We were able to provide food and permanent shelter, a source of power and water and a considerable stockade of food and supplies. This, of course, will run out and yes, we will need to provide for ourselves. I'm almost afraid to ask, but ballpark, how much do you think this 'immediate infrastructure' will cost?"

One of Lord Parisellan's doctoral students, Nigel, now took center stage. "We've done some rough estimations, Mr. Perry. Each of the structures Lord Parisellan mentioned would be a mini version with only minimal requirements, meaning the absence of any needless amenities. The schools will be constructed from much the same material as the pre-fabricated homes you've built. There'll be running water, heat and lighting with chairs equipped with armrests for all the students. The hospitals would be constructed the same way, each equipped with just the most minimal diagnostic equipment; an x-ray machine, blood testing equipment, one MRI machine, etc. The manufacturing facilities will be equipped with some of the machinery Lord Parisellan has mentioned."

Gloria, Lord Parisellan's other doctoral student, took the baton. "Given the population and the denomination of the people here, three small churches should be a good starting point for them to keep their faith and, most importantly, their spirits intact. Providing a minimal stock for the pharmacies of medicines is something you can't produce here. We've managed to appeal to several well-funded, low-profile international agencies who have agreed to provide the basics for as long as you need it."

Bob let out a sign of relief, as that this particular aspect was crucial for survival. "Very well planned out, thank you guys. But funds are dwindling and there is the need to keep a reserve in the bank in case of contingencies. So, how much is this going to cost us?"

“In the neighborhood of $5 million,” Nigel said.

There currently was $4 million left in the account and estimated that at least $2 million would be needed as an emergency reserve. Quick math told him that they would need $3 million, and fast.

CHAPTER 41

Bob's flight(s) back to the states took almost an entire day. The drama of a fighter, after a one-year plus hiatus, returning to the states to challenge the champion and take back the belt he lost over a year ago was glamorized by the press, which squeezed every last drop of melodrama. The sports channels were running the usual biographies and interviews when available, building up the momentum for next Saturday's night at Madison Square Garden.

The papers had been chronicling Bob's mission in the Svenkia Islands for the past eight months as the story began to unfold with substance and its own momentum that seemed to never end allowing reporters to fill pages of the newspapers with the constant new developments.

The news had crafted a very clever and enticing stage for the fight whereby the marketing had strength and a full capacity, SRO crowd was almost a given. Promoters had been scrambling to make sure that this fight had more than its fair share of coverage and would be filmed and later marketed to the media, reaping a nice purse and chunk of change for the networks.

Bob's manager, Clive Perkins, was equally excited as the bigger the spectacle in the public eye, the more money there was to be made. He did feel a slight sliver of guilt that a lot of this hype was at the expense of the plight of the people of the Svenkia Islands. It was almost kind like taking advantage of the pain and suffering, albeit indirectly, of these people in adding quality fodder for this particular sports "product."

This is how it's been viewed by the boxing world,

that each fight with its own story, especially this one, behind it makes for invaluable publicity. An important part of the process had been unavoidably delayed due to the non-stop work on the islands. Bob needed to be in NYC to sign the fight contract today in his manager's office before heading to Oslo (he finally got word of the Peace Prize and, after nearly fainting, made his travel arrangements).

Bob was running late and he had to go for a second fitting of the tuxedo he was buying for his trip. He still couldn't get his head around the fact that he had been awarded the highest accolades anyone could be recognized for by doing what he felt came naturally and was part of his being. The whole idea this made him feel uncomfortable; almost like he didn't deserve it.

At first, he thought the phone call from the Norwegian committee was a joke. You know, some ploy by Green try to get under his skin even more. But it was the real deal and had been verified by Clive. There was a downside though: the reception and ceremony was just two days before his contracted fight with Green.

He had asked that the fight be moved back, at least for a couple of weeks, so he may be in good spirits and well rested after the inevitable jet lag after appearing before the most heroic agents of world change and delivering the obligatory acceptance speech (something he dreaded), was something he didn't particularly care for especially in front of a group of people on such a formal basis. But the issue at hand right now was getting properly outfitted. Coming to this particular establishment had been Lynne Albright's suggestion. She certainly knew how to dress a man, especially since she had practice on so many husbands. But dressing this guy was going to be a real challenge. Bob had a twenty-nine inch waist with disproportionately larger thigh muscles, complements of the sand dune that he finally flattened after months of carrying giggling children on his back up and down the small mountain. In addition to the aerobic value he gained by flattening that mound, his legs now were built for stamina.

Oh, the jacket fit just fine and had been taken from a tuxedo set for heavier men, discarding the pants in favor of what now would turn out to be custom-made trousers. He hadn't really bought any new pants in the past year, of course, since he was on the islands. His standard choice of clothing was primarily very loose thermal outerwear that made him look like a crew member from Perry's Antarctica adventure, but offered the much needed space for Bob's expanding muscle structure.

He really didn't notice any of this and the progress he made in maintaining his training regimen until he saw himself in the mirror in just his underwear with two tailors measuring and scribbling down dimensions so they could get it right. This type of customer service was not a daily occurrence for these guys and it presented a once in a lifetime testimony of their skills.

The next stop was Marcelo's Hair Emporium. This was Bonnie's part of the "gentrification of Bob" project (the biggest mistake was to introduce her to Lynne Albright; between the two of them, he wasn't quite sure if his skull could endure all the "attention to detail" crap). Bob had not cut his hair nor shaved for the entire year plus he had been over on the Svenkia Islands. Corey Green was taking full advantage of this anomaly, calling him all types of names, only fueling the fire that Bob had growing in his chest during the plane ride over.

Even the press poked polite fun at Bob's appearance. He indeed looked like he had been living under a rock. He intended to get his hair and beard trimmed, but not cut entirely. To him, it was living testimony and tribute to those brave and wonderful people back on the Islands. He was going to carry it with him during the biggest fight of his life. Sitting beside him in the cab, Johnny was still pleading that he just shave off the whole goddamn thing, including the beard.

"Don't you understand asshole? The hair and beard will retain heat and bring on exhaustion a lot quicker if you won't just shave your head bald and lose the fucking beard."

"I kind of like the way I look, Johnny," Bob said with a smirk on his face that Johnny would've loved to have ripped off with duct tape. Johnny knew since they were boys, there was no contest as to how stubborn Bob could be and dig his feet in firmly when he wanted to. The cab took some bounces through a couple of potholes, lifting them out of their seats, and nearly hitting their heads on the underside of the roof. They sat in silence as the cabbie made a left on 34th St. and headed toward Murray Hill where the House of Marcelo, or whatever, or even if there was a Marcelo for that matter, was now just a few minutes away. She didn't suggest, she *insisted* Bob get his hair trimmed there as it "was the finest place ever to have your hair coiffured in the most precise and proper manner. Presentation is everything, you know," Bonnie lectured.

"Yeah, presentation my ass," Bob grumbled to

himself. All the presentation he needed was in his right hand. He remembered the conversation before he left the islands.

"Bob, if you insist on looking like a goddamn refugee from Woodstock, at least get your hair and beard trimmed so you exude a modicum of civility."

"Bonnie, what the hell does it matter? I'll be in ring with a guy looking to take my head off; who cares what I look like?"

"I do. We'll be together in Oslo three days before the fight and then back to NYC for your date with "Show Me My Left Nut" Green before coming back home—" the word suddenly sketched out the thought that the Islands would be her home for a while "—besides, the moment you get on the plane back to the states, the press is gonna be all over your ass. The work you've done here, sweetheart, has been extraordinary and the world is very, very interested in you; not only as a human being, but as someone who is coming back for some kind of retribution and proving who the real champion is.

This, under circumstances of not having this moron strap on knuckle wraps! You're going to be under the microscope where every burp and fart is going to make headlines. If you won't cut it all off like Johnny wants you to, at least have an artist sculpt your hair and beard so you can provide an orderly presentation to what, for the most part, is hair gone out of control."

The cab pulled up in front of Marcelo's house and the two got out. It was a corner brownstone with a well-manicured yard and Neo-Georgian exterior. Bob wondered how much they charged for a haircut there, as the upkeep for this place must have cost some serious scratch. They entered through the double doors into a large hallway with marble tile (probably from an exclusive and well-guarded quarry in Italy or something), up to a curved, meticulously carved mahogany desk toward in the center of the hallway. Behind the desk was a young lady who looked like she was home on leave from some high-profile boarding school (which, in fact, she was).

With an air of confidence for all of her twenty years on earth, she asked, "And we are…?"

"I'm Bob Perry and this is my trainer, Johnny Wells."

"Ah yes, the boxing person. Which of you gentlemen is here to be attended, or may I make a conjecture that it might be you sir?" she said, directing her inquiry (with a premature and clumsy air of sophistication) with a smirk toward Bob.

Little smart-ass bitch. "Yes, I'm the one getting my hair cut." Bob thought "attended" meant he might've been there for kidney dialysis for Christ's sake.

"Phillip will be attending you, Mr. Perry. Take the staircase up to the second floor, make a right and through the first entranceway on your left." She returned her attention to a Coach leather bound date book and, using a Montblanc fountain pen, "received" Bob's appointment (compliments of Bonnie). After that, she probably didn't have a thing to do except trying to look like Greta Garbo.

Feeling like he was going to the principal's office, he and Johnny climbed the steps, followed the instructions explicitly and entered the first entranceway on the left into an empty room. There was the low leatherback chair in front of a mirror that had what looked like (and probably was) a Louis XIV frame. The walls were covered with textured wallpaper, complimented by expensive wainscot and very tasteful crown molding with a finale of incredibly plush yet subtle carpet. This obviously was a room where only one individual was "attended."

There were end tables and lamps and original paintings lining the walls (no bogus prints allowed).

This is gonna cost a pretty bob and schilling, Bob thought. *I should've just gone to a barbershop and lied through my teeth to Bonnie*, he lamented.

He sat in the leather chair, watching through the reflection of the mirror as Johnny sat down, or, better yet, sank down, into the soft plush leather of a sofa, trying to find something to read other than Architectural Digest or some high-end interior design magazines where bathrooms cost twice as much as the car he drove.

Why the hell don't they have a Sports Illustrated or a car racing magazine? Johnny pouted to himself.

"You sure this is where you get your hair cut?" Johnny teased Bob. "Looks more like a place to get laid; then again, you wouldn't know the difference." This, of course, was a boyhood tease in that Bob had not had the volume of sexual exploits most men his age had.

"I wouldn't throw mud my way, big boy. With your looks, I wouldn't be getting dressed up to accept any awards for setting any records of infidelity. Look, Bonnie recommended this place, I'm going to get the hair and beard trimmed and we'll be on our way. Think you can keep yourself occupied for the next forty-five minutes or so?"

Just as Johnny was mumbling something about having a woman tell you what to do beneath his breath, in came Phillip, or, more aptly put, in floated Phillip. Bob could see him in the reflection of the mirror and couldn't believe his eyes. Where most people have a slight gate to their walk, you know, that bobbing up and down, Phillip came in behind Bob and seemed to glide across the floor as if wearing silent roller skates. Complete with scarf and a satin blouse, Bob's immediate impression was that this guy was a little light in the loafers.

"I'm Phillip and I'm here to…"

"Yeah, yeah, I know 'attend' me."

Half in boredom and three quarters in disgust, Phillip replied, "Attend wouldn't even minutely address the challenge. Your hair is atrocious," he almost squealed. Under his arm, he carried a thick leather portfolio binder with the initials "PHL" engraved in gold leaf across the front. He place it on the marble vestibule below the mirror and untied it (yeah, no zipper; it had leather strapping holding it closed), revealing gold plated tools of the trade. He looked as though he was preparing to set a fine dining table instead of getting ready to cut someone's hair.

"Look, Phil…"

"Phillip. My name is Phillip."

"Okay, Phillip. I'm here just for trim at the suggestion of a friend, Bonnie Southland."

"Oh, Dr. Southland. A wonderful woman. I attend one of her clinics."

Yeah, I'll bet, Bob thought as he spied Johnny through the mirror with a smirk on his face, burying his face deeper into probably was the latest issue of *Vanity*

Fair looking for the pictures of women with big tits.

Phillip began to run his fingers through Bob's hair, airing it out across his shoulders so he may spread his work out before him. This began to make Bob a little nervous. As Phillip was starting to comb and groom Bob's hair in different directions, he could see the intense look on Phillip's face in the mirror. He floated around, picking up different type of combs and a special pair of scissors, and constantly re-positioning himself around Bob with what felt like a gust of air encircling him.

"We're going to have to do some work to restore the grain and continuity of your hair, then we'll have to take a close look at restoring any semblance of humanity while, and God knows why, keeping your beard."

"Look Cinderella, just trim his hair and pull back the beard a bit so I can empty my bank account to pay for this and get out of here," offered Johnny from the couch. "That's what you get having your hair cut by a fairy," he mumbled to himself, but not low enough to pass under Phillip's acute radar.

"Fairy?" Phillip directed his attention toward Johnny. With that he took a pair of gold plated scissors, left his station, went over to the couch and, with the backend, tapped Johnny sharply on the head. "Poof, you're a bucket of shit!"

"Oh, come on Phil. We haven't all day and I'm due at my manager's office to sign my life away and then need to catch a flight, of which I'm sure to be late already," Bob pleaded.

"I stress one more time, Mr. Perry. My name is Phillip and please address me as such if you have to address me at all," Phillip commanded with sincere indignation.

"Look, Phillip, I didn't mean…"

"Let's just continue so you may 'get out of here'," Phillip said, his voice resonating hurt anger.

The next twenty minutes was spent in silence with Phillip working his magic and making Bob's long hair an actual work of art. He finessed the flow of hair sculpting his face and shoulders in a way that really pleased Bob. He really could have strangled Johnny for some of his remarks.

The consummate professional, Phillip chose to break the silence. "You're that boxer who helped all those people in the northeastern block of Europe," he offered without breaking stride in the rapid layer cutting he was so used to executing.

"Those people really helped themselves, Phillip. All I did was facilitate a hunger to survive by providing some upfront resources and they've been doing all the rest."

"Soooo, now you've come back to regain your crown by fighting that awful man Corey Grant."

Bob was sure that he was confusing him with Cary Grant (no doubt) and he corrected him, "Corey Green. You know, Corey 'Show Me the' Green."

Disgusting, Phillip thought.

"Are you scared?" Phillip asked in earnest.

Momentarily taken aback by the question, he answered, "I'm not scared of getting hurt Phillip if that's what you mean. I've had plenty of that and know what that feels like." thinking of how he lost count of how many stitches he owned and finished by saying, "I am scared of losing."

Phillip frowned as he was working on the continuity from Bob's newly trimmed and layered hair to the growth on his face that was clearly like a field of underbrush gone wild.

"This Corey Green has been saying a lot of nasty things about you in the papers. A lot of hurtful things. He seems like a real jerk. I mean, after all that you've done, saving people's lives and all, anything bad someone would say about you would be just plain mean."

"Why, Phillip, I didn't know that you read the boxing news," Bob offered in jest.

Phillip placed his hands on Bob shoulders and lowered his head next to his and, speaking through the reflection of the mirror, said, "It's huge news, Mr. Perry. It's all over the papers and TV. Why, there are even articles in the Gay section of the New York Times," he offered tongue in cheek.

"Look, Phillip, I'm the one who feels like a jerk about some of the cracks I made before."

"Forget it," said Phillip shooting a diametric gaze back at Johnny as he was putting the final touches with a very slim electronic razor in sculpting Bob's beard beautifully, much like that of the Czar of Russia, leaving a majestic full handlebar moustache.

"Do you hate this Corey Green?" Phillip asked.

"I have my reasons," Bob replied in a low and menacing growl vehemently accentuated with the expression of an animal about to kill, sending a fresh surge of blood up his neck.

Phillip also had a surge of blood, but in a more southerly direction.

Phillip was clearly done, removing the apron and tissue around Bob's neck, finishing up with a dusting of scented calcium powder (which was probably imported from Tibet and made by Buddhist priests using secret ingredients). He did incredible work. Bonnie was right. And even if it this day cost a bundle, it was worth it. Phillip was clearly an artist.

"This looks great, Phillip!" Bob said, almost squealing himself. Johnny now had his head out of the book and was listening in on this conversation with a look of surprise instead of the condescending smirking that had prevailed just thirty minutes ago.

"Well, this is gonna cost a lot of money, but I got to tell you, Phillip, worth every penny."

"Oh, they didn't tell you at the front desk?"

"Tell me what?" Bob's memory went back to Little Miss Perky Tits at the front desk.

"There'll be no charge for our services today, Mr. Perry. It is our honor and privilege to have you as a client, but there is one condition."

I knew it, Bob thought, waiting for the punch-line, "And what is this one condition?"

"Kick his ass, Bob."

CHAPTER 42

The Nobel Foundation in Stockholm had been honoring people of exceptional distinction for as long as Bob's grandfather had been alive (Grandpa Mike was born a year before the Wright brothers caught some sweet air at Kitty Hawk). In addition to physics, chemistry, physiology, medicine and literature, the real prize of distinction goes to that of the winner of the Nobel Peace Prize. In Oslo, the Nobel Peace Prize Laureates receive award from the Chairman of the Norwegian Nobel Committee in the presence of King Harald V of Norway. An important part of the tradition is the presentation of the Nobel Lectures by the Nobel Laureates except for the recipient of the Peace Prize. In Stockholm, these lectures are presented days before the award ceremony, and then in Oslo, the recipient of the Nobel Peace prize delivers their lecture during the ceremony itself.

Due to his date with Corey, when training was crucial, Bob couldn't make his appearance in Stockholm, but he readily prepared for his Oslo lecture, although with his fair share of nerves. Clive had offered to write his lecture for him but cut no dice and dropped the effort quickly. He knew Bob will enough to know that this was very personal and any interference was as good as no interference at all. He just wanted to be helpful, as he had been around the block a few times, more than a typical 27-year-old. But over the last year or so, Bob had surpassed a level of maturity far greater than the years calculated from his birth certificate. He had assumed responsibility for the health and well-being of over 3,000 people, something that you don't just wake up one day and decide you want to do. He had a lot of respect for Bob as did the thousands if not millions of people who had watched the plight and then rebirth of the people of the Svenkia Islands.

As skilled a job as the tailors did in custom-fitting Bob to his tuxedo, he still fidgeted, especially with the white tie around his neck. He did look dapper, if he didn't say so himself, and relished admiring himself in the mirror, since he had only worn a tux a few times before for friends' weddings. He was not vain by any means but just enjoyed his sophisticated appearance, even by his own standards. Bonnie was wearing a long, black slinky evening gown that hugged her waist, hips and ass in such perfection that Bob should have instructed the tailors to account for his appreciation of her in the crotch of his trousers. She was impressed and in awe of the event and the people surrounding her. As a professional, she admired the work of many in her field, some of whom were in the room this evening. She couldn't quite decide which she was more excited for: Bob, or being in the presence of some of the greatest scientists in the world. She decided her heart was for Bob and her intellect for the latter. She was nervous for Bob because she knew of his humility and how this must be very uncomfortable for him. She wanted to hear his lecture beforehand but he had refused, joking that she would find out how literate he was on the evening of the awards. This made her doubly nervous as she understood his humbleness and reticence, as well as how unpredictable and forceful he could be. Bonnie knew he was going to deliver a roundhouse punch but just how was up for grabs. She would soon find discover how well-developed her woman's intuition really was.

The auditorium in the Oslo City Hall was at full capacity. Bonnie, now sitting in the audience, swore she would tear a neck muscle looking all around at the wonderfully splendid people. The very atmosphere of aristocracy clung to her making her feel a little bit out of place. Oh, she had a very nice lifestyle and a modestly self-perceived notion of good taste and culture but knew that she was far, far out of her league compared to her companions in the audience. The men were all dressed elegantly in white tie (no fidgeting). And being a woman, she paid especially close attention to what other women were wearing both on their bodies and around their necks and wrists. She never saw so many diamonds in one place; it must have equaled a full week's draw from the mines of de Beers. The whole concept of her being here for Bob was mind-boggling. One day they were slushing around in mud carting food and supplies, feeling like crap from the cold, and the next they were sitting in plush velvet chairs dressed to the nines and surrounded by royalty. The dichotomy made the whole evening seemed surreal. Part of her mission in life was to impress her father by emulating him in his profession and possibly outdoing him, in retaliation for the neglect and love lost to his servicing his ego. She just began to realize now, sitting with these people and sharing part of the reason why they were there, that she achieved something without ever having her father in mind. This epiphany, combined with everything else, left her both confused and satisfied at once. She made a note to file that when she had the opportunity she would sit down and analyze this or, just not give a shit and enjoy the moment.

After a brief bio and slideshow (yeah, slideshow: usage of large multiscreen HDTV monitors were being worked on in a lab somewhere) of the succession of progress on the Svenkia Islands, Bob was introduced to the waiting audience.

"Your Majesty, members of the Nobel Committee, ladies and gentlemen: it is indeed with great honor and humility (*Yeah, you got that right, bro*, Bonnie thought) that I stand before you this evening and accept the Nobel Peace Prize. It's not every day that a guy who beats up people for a living gets a 'peace' prize."

This brought a modest but healthy chuckle from the audience. Standup comedy wasn't Bob's forte and though he had thought of cutting this part out of his speech, he was glad he left it in; a little reinforcement never hurt a guy like him. With his confidence up two notches, he continued, "This prize is a true testament to the will and strength of the human spirit over the tyranny and selfish prerogatives of despots the likes of Dimitrii Crogan (mild applause). The people of the Svenkia Islands have a resolve and prevailing spirit of love for family and friends that serve as the ultimate defense to anyone who dares try to take that away from them. And one man did try to take this away from them in a very harsh and brutal manner… and lost."

The second and more robust round of applause.

He could feel that familiar warmth in his neck pushing up and creating pressure under his jaw the more he spoke and the more he related his experience to these people. They never had to experience humiliation, cruelty and prolonged denial of the basic necessities of life. Any traces of nerves that he might've had before stepping up to the podium were dissipating quickly as he got more involved with the subject and less involved with standing in front of such a prestigious audience.

"I'm a boxer, ladies and gentlemen. I wear gloves to work, but they need to be laced up like a pair of shoes. I can report to work without a cleanly ironed shirt and only have to stick around for 48 minutes." The audience responded a bit more warmly, joining in on the joke.

"Given that, I've been asked why, why did I became so deeply involved with this particular situation? 'How can you leave now when you're at the top of your game and making real money?' people asked, or, 'Why not hold a boxing exhibition and donate the proceeds to help these people?' Some people think about what they're going to do before they do it, and then some just react. I belong to the club of the latter. The best way I can explain my reasons is through example."

The hundreds of pairs of eyes that had Bob squirming moments ago were now under his command. He was now riding on a river of his own passion, putting aside his humility and public caution to the wind. Bonnie's back was arched, having her sitting close to the edge of her seat as she knew something was coming; just what she didn't know. Bob was an endearingly complex man, one of the characteristics that made her feel the way she did for him. But he was full of surprises and she got the feeling that this was going to be a Lu Lu.

"I'd like everyone to close their eyes please. No worry, I won't sucker punch you." More laughter as Bob was now gathering momentum, "Go on, close them. I'm watching you," Bob teased. These were not the kind of people who were into audience participation, much less during a coveted event like the Nobel Peace Prize ceremony. But they had great curiosity, not to say at least admiration, for this young man, and obliged him.

"Breathe, breathe in slowly and hold it…, and exhale. Do it again for me, won't you?" The auditorium reflected the sounds of hundreds of mouths breathing, like wind blowing in an open field.

"Rest your hands in your laps, palms down, between the inside of your upper thighs without using the armrests of your seats. Make them go limp as though they've just left your wrists. Breathe."

"Let the weight leave your shoulders and arms as though they were no longer part of your body."

"Breathe."

"Lie back in your seat and as though lying in bed. Breathe." Bob could now hear the slow rhythmic breathing of the audience. Bonnie, too, was under this spell, but with one foot on the ground waiting for the next shoe to drop.

"Now relax, no one is watching. Break away from the tether of today and let yourself float effortlessly back to the time when you were 7 or 10 years old . . . Breathe."

He continued. "Are you there yet? It's okay, I'll wait. I have nothing but time," he soothed. "Think in your mind where you were living, what was your favorite toy was and what things you most liked to do. Gee, it looks like fun! There's sunshine and smiles on faces. Your brothers or sisters are playing with you and you have friends over. School let out for the summer and you feel free forever. It's getting dark now and mother calls you in for supper." For most of these people, it would be the nanny calling them in and as far as the mother/father combo, some would have experienced childhood with either a single-parent or step parent. But for the most part these subtle replacements were easily integrated into the imagery Bob was cultivating in their minds.

"The kitchen is bustling and you and your brothers or sisters are running about through your bedroom and other bedrooms in a game of chase. You can smell the roast cooking in the oven and after playing outside all day, can't wait for dinner. Oh, you're starving, you tell mother. When are we going to eat?" Smiles started to form at the corners of mouths; eyes remained closed.

"After simmering down a little bit mother calls you down to join the family around the table. Father of course sits at the head and mother at the other end of the table. There are all sorts of food on the table in a room full of laughter and talking. It feels good, doesn't it?"

"Breathe."

As chests were rising rhythmically up and down with eyes closed, their smiles broadened as they traveled back to a time of innocence and carefree joy. They can see the table, the food and the pictures on the wall. They can visualize the rug, the high-backed chairs they always thought were uncomfortable, and the teasing back and forth with their brothers and sisters. Their breathing and heart rate slowed down considerably as they journeyed back to sweet, distant memories.

"And what's for dessert? Could it be ice cream? Mother always had strawberries and raspberries that she put over the ice cream that you would eat, slowly savoring every mouthful. It tastes good, doesn't it?"

A man in the audience was "sitting at the table" and enjoying orange sherbet with whipped cream on the top.

"Breathe."

"You begin to hear rain lightly sprinkle on the windowpanes overlooking the backyard from the dining room. The momentum of the raindrops picks up until it's a steady stream soaking everything outside. Can you hear it? You press your nose to the window and see it raining 'cats and dogs' outside and you're inside where it's warm and all your family is around you. You feel secure with strong windows in a sturdy house with your parents there to protect you."

"Breathe."

A woman in the audience remembers the pit-pattering of rain on the windows of her bedroom at night as a young girl when she was lying in bed. Such a warm, safe feeling under the covers, staying dry and gazing out the window at the wet streets reflecting the lamppost light on the corner.

"After finishing dessert, it's time to play with your dollhouse, the secret fort that you made out of blankets in your room, or perhaps Monopoly with your brother. It's summertime. You know after going to bed and waking up tomorrow you'll be outside playing with your friends."

"Breathe."

Many people in the audience were back in a safe place, their eyelids at rest and their bodies in a free float, while their minds drifted effortlessly wrapping around the imagery resurrected by their memory.

"After dinner, Father is downstairs in his den reading, and there to protect you from just about anything; even that monster in your closet that you swear you can hear at night. He looked in the closet with you watching and every time tells you that there's nothing there. But you know if there is, he'll be there in a second to take care of it. Mother is in the kitchen (actually the maid) cleaning the dishes and making sure that everything is right in her house and for her children. There really is no one like your mother, is there?"

For some, especially those from wealthy, traditional families, the dysfunction that typically affects blue-blooded families made this vision a bit of a reach, so for these folks, they imagined more what they had wanted rather than what they had. It didn't really matter, the effect was still the same. Tears started to well up beneath the closed eyes of those who had already lost one or both parents. The memory and imagery were bittersweet as they traveled deep down to the depth of their souls.

Bob let the moment soak in for a while. The great hall was enveloped in complete silence save for the soft blanket of breathing from the 800 in attendance. Bonnie was going through this exercise but cheating with one eye open to see the effect of Bob's hypnotic trance on these people. It was a little frightening, the strength he wielded on the world's most disciplined and intelligent people. Her respect for Bob picked up another couple yet another couple of levels as she anticipated a conclusion she knew would be dramatic

Bob slipped from his jacket pocket the new Sony Walkman that just came out the previous year. It was truly revolutionary that you can play a cassette while, well, walking. You didn't lug around those big and bulky tape players but could put this thing in your pocket and enjoy your favorite songs anywhere. He placed the headset upside down with the earpieces fitting snugly around the microphone and hidden by the lamp fixture on the podium. He pushed the play button and the sounds of gunfire, bursting plates and shattering furniture filled the auditorium. People's eyes snapped open as did their mouths!

"GET OUT! GET OUT NOW YOU FILTHY PIGS!! YOU HAVE FIVE MINUTES TO GRAB YOUR SHIT AND GET OUT OF THE HOUSE (more sounds of gunfire with the volume turned up a notch). YOU GOD DAMN ANIMALS, MOVE OR WE'LL FUCKING KILL YOU ALL!" Bob screamed into the microphone.

Returning back to earth but to a still very stunned audience, "Everyone is running in all different directions bumping into furniture and tripping over chairs that were thrown to the ground, destroyed by the soldiers. Everything around you is shattering and bursting to pieces from the gunfire. Shards of glass and plaster bursting from the walls threaten to cut you in the face and the thick waft of gun smoke is beginning to make you cough violently."

Going back into character, "I'M GOING TO SLIT YOUR MOTHER'S THROAT IF YOU DON'T MOVE… NOW!!"

"The rain gets louder outside. The doors are open and some of the windows have been shattered by gunfire. Family members disappear into different rooms and the fear of separation begins to set in. The soldiers grab your father by the back of the shirt and shove him out the door. Then one of the soldiers knocks your mother down, drags her in the other room and rapes her. You and your siblings can hear her screams and are crying, scared to death like you've never been before. You don't know what to grab but you know that you were ordered to get something or else you would be killed. You might grab a coat, a loaf of bread, maybe some of your toys. You don't know because your mind has been violated with an surreal brutality. Eventually, everybody is shoved out the door, where you see your neighbors also running in the streets, fleeing in different directions. You lose sight of your father and your mother and discover you're running in the rain with some of your neighbors past armored tanks, some of which are shooting in the air to keep you moving. How does it feel, hm? How does it feel to have your very existence at a tender young age ripped from you like someone pulling your guts out through your mouth?' He knew he was getting unnecessarily graphic, but he couldn't help himself.

The audience was in shock. Some started hyperventilating; others were frozen and pushing back into their seats while others started crying, men and women alike. They felt their hearts sink through their chest into their stomachs with a queasy feeling in their intestines. People were startled, speechless. No one spoke as they remained back in the recesses of their mind and found themselves struggling to get back to the here-and-now, to escape the horror that they just "experienced" with their family. Bob's dramatization was a precarious one. Many in the audience were elderly and had heart issues. As a matter of fact, a few people felt their hearts palpitating to the point of pain. Bob expected a reaction, but nothing like what he was witnessing now. He was almost, but not quite, at the point of regretting his words. Bonnie's concern escalated as she looked around at disoriented, confused and terrified people. She thought that Bob pushed the envelope a little too much. *Nice going sport!*

Slowly, a chorus of murmurs emerged as the shock started to wear off. It was kind of like after people emerging from a near-fatal car accident, escaping serious injury and then talking aimlessly until reality checks back in and they feel as though their legs are going to give out from beneath them. For most of the audience, the exercise brought home just exactly what the people of the Svenkia Islands experienced. Being people of public stature and Philanthropic sensibility, most felt almost guilty they hadn't taken a more active role in contributing cash. Some felt a sincere anger firsthand at how horribly intrusive something like this really was. Both reactions prompted scheduling appointments with their accountants and lawyers in the coming days to contribute large sums of money for a reserve that was badly needed, as the funds donated had dried up. Bob had by no means intended this to be a fundraiser, it was just that the whole subject of the people of the 14th province drove a stake through his heart down to the deepest recesses of his being that he reacted in the way that he did. It was with personal conviction for this heinous act by this fat bastard that made it imperative that the whole world, especially tonight's guests, realized the tragedy and outrage of this act.

Mission accomplished.

CHAPTER 43

Within four days, $3.75 million was deposited into the Svenkia Island working capital account. After Bob's lecture, he was crowded with dignitaries and other people of international power, giving them instructions and account numbers in which to send the donations they were so adamant about giving. Bob was completely amazed at the strength of the reaction of what amounted to just him pouring out his heart over events from the past year.

He had planned to approach Steve Shelby for an advance on the upcoming fight with Corey; Bob was to receive $7.5 million and Corey, as reigning champ, $10 million. This was a negotiation that would have gone far beyond any negotiating skills he may or may not have had. This clearly would've been handled by Clive Perkins. But this wasn't going to be necessary now, as they now had the funds to complete the plan as outlined by Lord Parisellan. He and Sergei wasted no time in getting in contact with vendors and suppliers, ready to execute once the funds were available.

For expediency's sake, much of the material was purchased in Europe and trucked to the shores of Norway to an awaiting air strip that Sgt. Hayes used as his base and fueling depot.

As the Euro would not be introduced until the early 90s, Bonnie managed the exchange of whatever currencies were needed for each of the countries for their respective contributions: French francs were needed for the purchase of the preassembled framing and side panels for the buildings and other structures as planned; German marks for the crucible furnace and other equipment needed to forge steel; Norwegian krone for the cement mixers; Swedish krona for tree cutting equipment; Italian lira for steel molds and die casts, etc.

As much as the vendors sympathized with the cause, they would not be able to release anything until paid. At the gathering menagerie of equipment and building materials, lines formed at the phones with vendors calling into their banks and confirming the multiple wire transfers Bonnie had set up.

The labor came in a little bit over budget, but thanks to Lord Parisellan's negotiating skills and the extra three quarters of a million dollars collected, this absorbed any deficit due to the calculations.

The cargo planes were making roundtrips almost around the clock. No sooner did they deliver their payload, there were closing their hatches and taxing down the airfield to go back to Norway to pick up the next load.

Sergei and a civil engineer had been plotting out scaled footprints for the structures and the assembly went fast, as most had arrived preassembled and just needed to be put together. The plumbing and electrical connections were done rather quickly and soon enough, they had one hospital, two auditoriums (for town meetings), two churches, four schools, two pharmacies (where medicines were beyond the immediate reach of self-sufficiency and were being provided free of charge by the international Red Cross indefinitely until such a time that they could be either manufactured on their own or global exporting and importing would enable their procurement), a wood processing mill, a steel mill, two manufacturing facilities and one helluva greenhouse.

Things were really starting to take shape and form very quickly. Once again, during the course of this rather quick deployment of resources establishing permanency, Sergei spoke with Bob via satellite phone, and yes, once again, “Someday we will return the favor my friend.”

Yeah, yeah, favor, Bob cascaded over in his mind, but once again the gracious smile, the gratuitous “thank you” and on to other business.

CHAPTER 44

After a long flight back to New York, followed by a hurried cab ride, deposited Bob arrived at the Lincoln Hotel, where he would soon take on a pre-fight press conference. Bob was still jet weary and had only two days before the fight to gain back his internal clock and get back in gear.

The press conference was due to start 2PM Bob and Johnny tore out of the cab at 2:15PM, and hustled up to the fourth floor to a throng of waiting reporters and an already warmed up Corey Green. He was there with his normal entourage, which consisted of five bodyguards, three of whom were missing necks. It wasn't so much that he needed five bodyguards; one "able-bodied" assistant would've done very nicely. But, as the reigning champ and fight purses for winners starting to skyrocket, he was flush with cash and enjoying being able to have people on the payroll that he could flaunt. He really let his success go to his head making a U-turn through his mouth.

In the last year, he had three fights, none of which lasted more than four rounds. He was determined to firmly cement his title with this fight. There had been so much talk about the erosion of boxing as a clean sport due to recent exposures. Corey Green's name came up during these inquisitions, but nothing concrete ever made it onto the table. This still burned Corey's ass, as it implied that he could not beat Bob fair and square. This fight was very important to him to prove to the world that he was a true champion. He knew that he could have put Bob down without all the hardware they put in his right glove, not to say the least all the medication they smeared on his left glove.

"I stand before you now and I'll be standing up in the ring looking down at Perry after I finally prove to you guys that our last fight was legitimate. All this nonsense about the fight being fixed is pure nonsense. This Saturday night, the world is going to see what I did the first time was because of my own power as a boxer. I don't need no knuckle wraps or any other type of crap. I'm going to cut this chump down piece by piece and after I'm done, my gloves will be tested on site by some lab technician not on anyone's payroll and nobody's bitch. I'll have the tape cut around my hands and when I raise my arms in victory, you and the rest of the press who have been accusing me will see I am bare knuckled, great and... well, realize y'all been full of shit for a year."

Cameras and microphones were picking up every word and expression of Green's. The staff back at the TV stations cringed every time they had interviewed Corey because the editing of his vulgar language took a lot of time and technology was not as sophisticated as it would be in later years. It was the usual podium that had about eleven microphones and recorders from the different stations capturing every word of the King of Grandstanding. Bob came in with Johnny and Clive sans bodyguards, since his humble nature and sensitivity to attention clearly dictated a subtle and unassuming posture. This irked Clive to no end, as he knew he had the better fighter and this wasn't just out of pride or wishful thinking. He'd been in the business for over thirty years and he knew Bob's capability and, seeing his further developed body, knew that this was gonna be a demolition. He wished Bob would take advantage of the moment and be more animated and vocal. But, alas, the subtle entrance it was as he made his way to the podium and took his seat opposite Corey's army of genetically challenged goons.

"And this mama's boy is going to take a real whooping. This guy spent the last year on the island in the middle of nowhere and comes back looking like a caveman. Looking like a goddamn hippie who should be out putting flowers in gun barrels and screwing chicks in ponds," he said, obviously making reference to the Woodstock Festival. "I mean, this guy doesn't look like fighter, he looks like a prehistoric bum. I'm going to cremate this caveman/hippie and send him back in time where he belongs."

Now it was Bob's turn to take the podium. He rose out of his seat, pulled down the sweater he still had on from the airport and ran his fingers through his long hair to clear his face as he took to the podium. It was only a few days since Phil, sorry, Phillip, worked his wonders and it still maintained. He did look like a caveman, a very well coiffured caveman and, well yeah, a hippie. You could say that.

Corey returned to his side of the dais, but did not sit down to make sure that the cameras caught his every expression and of course the rude interruptions he would dig into Bob when he spoke.

"First, I want everyone to know how great it is to be back. We did a lot of work on the Svenkia Islands and its payback is really starting to show. They give the world a quick lesson of the human spirit in the face of adversity of a despot who clearly lost. Ironically, he ended up giving these people he ostracized in the name of ethnic cleansing a new opportunity at an even better life than the one they left behind. It was, and probably always will be, the proudest moment of my life working with an able bodied crew to get these people on their feet and thriving in a stronger community."

"Well, I think I'm going to just drop down and start bawling like a baby. That is so sweet, isn't it, y'all? As a matter of fact, I'm so emotional right now I think I need a case of tissues."

This solicited a nervous teeter from the press corps, only turning up the momentum of the photo op with their flashes popping off like firecrackers. The press made sure they had pictures of Corey pointing his finger at Bob during this outburst. Even with Corey far to the left of the podium, they were close enough to fit he and Bob into one frame for a great picture of the antagonism and hatred between these two boxers.

Corey took full advantage of the intensifying theater of the moment. Again, Clive wished that Bob would catch some sort of aggression and maybe even jump across the table and take a shot at Corey. Bob's devotion and public promise of quitting boxing was a sensitive hot button inside him. Negative and crude references of any kind about this usually set him off. An explosion of this sort is what was needed here, now. Jesus, wouldn't that make great press. It would make revenue from the replay telecasts of the fight rise exponentially.

"I hear you collected a lot of money, didn't you, Bubba? How much of that went into your own pocket, huh?

And how much of it went to that whore of a mother of yours? I heard there's a lot to be made by taking advantage and tugging at the heartstrings of corporate America and the public. You should just quit boxing to make all your money skimming off the top from the donations you're taking away from those poor people on the islands."

Marketing or no marketing, this set Bob off like an erupting volcano. The only saving grace was that Bob's legs were underneath a very low table and getting up fast enough to get Corey did not happen. When he rose, the table lurched forward and Johnny quickly responded by pulling Bob back.

"I'm going to kill this guy," Bob whispered vehemently to Johnny.

"Take it easy and save it for the ring," Johnny replied with the classic cliché.

Some of the press sitting close to the front pushed the table back onto the dais with their left hands while snapping pictures and holding up recorders with their right. This was exactly what they came here for and yes, this was going to make for great marketing. Bob's eyes showed that deeply focused hatred and intense anger that won him most of his fights.

Clive Perkins was sitting in the third row and thought, *Finally! Finally, goddamn it. This moron punched Bob's hot button squarely on target.*

Corey finally opened his mouth wide enough to get Bob's anger to practically burst a pulmonary artery. This was going to be one hell of a fight; brutal. He knew Bob and these types of emotions were going to translate into Corey thinking about heavy-duty armor in the ring. This type of adrenaline was going to push Bob far enough that they'd have to drag him out of the ring during the ten count to prevent him from inflicting more damage after he put Corey through the canvas.

A small corridor opened up in Clive's subconscious leaking fear. Part of him began to get nervous at the thought. Unfortunately, there were boxers who lost their lives in the ring. As much as he hated Corey Green, he still didn't want to watch Humpty Dumpty here beaten to death. But, as quick as that thought surfaced, it was suppressed. The footage of this press conference televised on the evening news now sealed it, making this fight the battle of the century. Ca-ching, baby!

Bob finally gained back his composure and looked to wrap up the press conference before he lost control completely. "I had planned to cut my hair for this fight, short, and completely shave off my beard. Well, that's not going to happen. You keep on about fighting a caveman, a hippie. Well, here's your chance. And we wanted to reschedule the fight a few weeks after my trip back from Oslo to get back in the groove, but you rejected having the contract revised. You see Corey, we gave in to all your demands. We gave you all that you wanted."

Bob looked around the now silent room and turned his gaze toward Corey. He got out of his seat and finished by saying, "Now I'm going to make you pay for it."

CHAPTER 45

At Madison Square Garden, tickets for the Corey-Perry fight sold out in a matter of hours. Crafty scalpers outside the Garden entrance were getting three times face value and were gone with pockets full of cash in about half an hour and in some bar celebrating by the time the cops showed up.

With all the hype and drama over the last couple weeks, this was billed as the fight of the century. Bob Perry was coming back for revenge for the belt he felt was rightfully his. After the scandal of the Grant-Rivera fix broke, it was no secret and widely held that there had been a fix on the last Perry-Corey fight. As a result of the investigation that followed the Grant-Rivera discovery, there were now two officials inspecting the hand taping before a fight. The gloves that were to be used were lab tested a week before, held in lockup in sealed air tight plastic bags up to an hour before the fight and then escorted by two officials, one delivering each boxer their gloves.

The most telling part of the investigation was the uncovering of the three dirty members of the commission. Charges of racketeering were cleverly sculpted by the prosecution. This held up in court with the judge rendering a no-brainer decision, sentencing each of these members to a considerable vacation in the state penitentiary.

Now being billed as the Green-Perry fight, as Corey was now champion, the crowd was seething with anticipation with what should have been a contest without any unfair advantage. Electricity permeated through Garden; if anybody lit a match, the place would have blown up. There was a thick fog of cigarette and cigar smoke already circling around the spotlights hanging above the ring.

As is customary in a championship bout, the champion comes out second and is presented to the crowd with the challenger entering the ring first. But Corey wanted to change the rules which had been no objection from the boxing commission, as they were now purged of their rogue members and in great anticipation of the fight.

Corey wanted to enter the arena first, with Bob following in second. He knew and attended enough of his fights to know Bob had a dreary entrance and felt that by having him come in after a spectacular introduction would be that much more demeaning. So who cared if the idiot wanted to tweak a bit of protocol? The boxing commission allowed it.

Corey realized that this bit of theatrics would only exacerbate and move the general hatred of him by the public up a few notches. He thrived on this and in his mind translated this into some form of attention, recognition, and didn't care what the equation was in the process. This was his house, his arena and his time for putting to rest any doubt that he was the greatest light heavyweight boxer in the world. He'd call the shots, make the rules and have complete power over this night.

Somewhere back in the recesses of his mind, he felt belittled that he had won his fight with Bob by fix. Didn't his trainer and manager think he could do it without all the shit they jacked him up with?

Well, I'm going to put this pussy on his back so bad, the only way he's gonna leave the arena is on a gurney, he promised himself.

This more or less became a mental mantra when he was warming up. And he made sure that there were all the requisite cameras and reporters in his dressing room recording all he had to say and all he promised to prove.

"You're going to see the first light heavyweight boxer embarrass himself by having the balls step in the ring with me. I'll tell you this, and I'll tell you this now… fourth round, baby! I'm gonna play around him for three rounds and punish him, so by the time he gets off his stool for round four, he will not know which way is up, down, left or right. It'll be a chore to find his way to the center ring, but when he does, I'm going to nail him and I guarantee you, that clown ain't getting up!"

Cameras and audio picked up every word along with Corey's animated gestures. Once again, the censors back at the station editing room would be clocking in overtime in massaging the audio for this tirade. And for those lip readers out there, the video also was edited to erase any mouthing of foul language.

A few weeks ago, Bob finally got the phone number from Clive Perkins.

"I should be making this call, Bob. I'm the manager and making arrangements for you is part of my job. So let me do my job and stay out of it."

"I'm making the call myself," Bob countered stubbornly. Most professionals at his level would have "their people" on the payroll to do practically everything; even wipe their ass. Oh, but not Bob. He didn't put himself on the podium and waste his money on something he didn't need. He really never had a clue of public image and that extravagance that was part of "product presentation." It was this type of humble attitude that drove Clive crazy.

"This is my fight. I want this done my way, which means I do some of the legwork. End of discussion, okay?"

"You can end up botching this whole thing up. Do you realize this?"

"No, I don't and I won't."

What Bob didn't realize was that Clive took matters in hand already, giving the publicist and manager the heads up that his boy would be calling. At least Clive had some control and arranged for the time of Bob's call. It was to be later on that afternoon at 2PM but what Clive didn't realize was that Bob was not going to ask for the publicist.

The phone rang three times before somebody answered.

"Hello?"

"Um, yeah. I'd like to speak to Derek Brown please," Bob said with a mixture of humbleness and nervous teeter to his voice.

"You're speaking to him."

"Come on, really, I'm sure he usually has some of 'his people' field these type of phone calls," Bob answered back. "This won't take long and it's pretty important."

"Pretty important, huh?" The voice on the other side of the line questioned sheepishly. "And who should I say is calling?"

"Bob Perry. I'm a professional boxer and…"

"Yeah, yeah. I know who you are." The voice now sounded more familiar Bob. "You're the guy who risked it all to drop a high-paying career and help those poor people. The whole world knows who you are, my friend."

"Mr. Brown?"

"Drop the 'Mr.' bullshit. I'm just four years older than you. I watch tapes of your fight when we're on the road. You've got some great hands, man. I can see you doing some serious damage to a brick wall. I would really like to see you shut Green's mouth permanently. With all the trash talk he's been spitting about you, he needs to be taught a permanent lesson…moron. Hey, how does it feel to be back in the states after so much time on an island freezing your ass off?"

"Oh, there's still a hell of a lot of work to be done. I feel kind of guilty being here, serving my own needs. I plan on returning straight from the Garden after Saturday's fight."

"So, you got my curiosity. What's behind this phone call?"

"I need a favor."

CHAPTER 46

After the prelims and all the other dogma network bios on each of the fighters, the lights grew dim and the crowd completed a circuit around the arena of deep, powerful excitement (Truth be known, though, of the hour long bio of each fighter's lives, also shown on the huge arena screens, and what brought them to this point, forty five of those minutes were on Bob and what he's done for the people of the Svenkia Islands. If Corey were aware of this, his trunks would've caught fire!). Promoters purposely let ten minutes pass after the last fighter of the preliminary bouts left for their locker room. They were experts at letting the anticipation fester like a pot of boiling oil until it was ready to bubble over and ignite into a conflagration of flames – it made for good TV and made people return to the Garden for more.

The staff of Corey Green, with Garden officials' permission, borrowed some of the techniques used in concerts by groups like Kiss and Iron Maiden in the deployment of pyrotechnics. This, too, was in its infancy as far as creating excitement and visual bombardment during major events. But Corey made sure he had at his disposal the latest and the greatest facility for the introduction and admiration of the greatest… him.

The lights grew dimmer until it was pitch black when suddenly, over the garden surround speakers came blaring Michael Jackson's recording of "Off the Wall" with flares and spitting fire in unison with the beat. Up from behind a pale blue lit backdrop, Corey walked slowly up an incline with only his shadow silhouetted.

Whether you like him or not, the man put on a great show and the crowd affirmed this. There was cheering, shouting and booing across a spectrum ranging from admiration to downright disgust. He liked the attention no matter what flavor it came in and was so narcissistic that he truly believed he was wowing the audience with such a gnarly (remember, early eighties) entrance.

He walked up to the top and then down to the bottom of the incline where six spotlights highlighted his him from different angles as he proceeded toward the ring. He made pumping motions in the air and was outfitted in his trademark green satin robe with gold trim. And as was true to form, his entourage was coordinated with modest short-sleeved satin shirts adorned with the same concept in gold trim.

He entered the ring, then side stepped full circle from corner to corner, continually pumping his fists up, accentuated with an occasional lightning fast piston of punches into the air. The guy was good, if not the best. He reinforced this with his appearance of owning the ring; this was his house and nobody leaves alive.

One of the members of his posse paraded around the ring behind him, holding his belt above his head as though providing a mobile throne for the King. Corey had a smirk on his face, as he knew this first lap would be in Bob's face to match, which he wouldn't. He knew he would come in with his usual lackluster entrance and the crowd would give him their polite applause as they always did.

The magnitude and depth of the world's kudos of what Bob had accomplished with 3,000 human lives was suppressed behind closed doors in his mind, since Corey's ego would not allow someone to outdo him in any venue. He tried to convince himself that this was some kind of self-serving and moneymaking deal, the exposure of which would be the final nail in his coffin. He faced the entranceway where Bob was to make his appearance and waited eagerly for this lame duck to begin his waddle.

A full five minutes passed and by this time, the Marine Color Guard and rising country music star Jenny Walkins (who was to sing the national anthem) were now waiting impatiently in the ring for Bob. With animated sports spectacles such as this, where the anticipation grew every second, every minute, Bob's absence seemed like another hour passing by.

Bob's delay wasn't by design, it was due more to the last minute instructions/argument he was giving to Johnny Wells and his cut man Jerry Dougan that set them both back like chasing a wild curve ball. He wanted them to walk out to the ring first and he would follow a few moments right after them. They thought this was ridiculous and were getting really impatient with Bob's increasing eccentricity, especially during such a tense moment as this. But they didn't have time to deal with this or try to reason with him, they decided to do whatever the hell he wanted so as long as they got the show on the road.

When they both appeared from the tunnel the crowd responded wildly, but then toned down just as quickly as they realized it was only Bob's trainer and cut man. Steve Shelby, who was promoting this fight, had been licking his chops since last Tuesday. He thought this out of the box protocol strange, but whatever excited the crowd was just fine by him. Corey's switching of the order of entrance and now this delayed walk through the tunnel was having the crowd biting at the bit. Double ca-ching, baby!

Bob was standing at the back of the tunnel with his mind going in a dozen different directions; obviously from the fight, to the Islands, his trip two days ago to Oslo and the crowd outside eagerly awaiting his entrance. He was wearing his traditional white terry cloth robe with the hood over his head concealing his long hair with nothing but his brow and beard visible. He looked like some sort of Messiah coming to greet his people with hope and promise.

He was still covered with a fine sheen of sweat from his warm-up, only further perpetuated by strain of nerves from the strong beacon of attention he was creating. Being back in the States, the reality of the last year or so started to creep in and cement a permanent place in his mind that would accompany him the rest of his life. He hated like hell to disappoint people and now had a whole new group that he had to please in the next forty-eight minutes, although there were serious doubts, no matter which way the count went, that this fight would last a full twelve rounds. It was time.

He very slowly took one step after the other and started to pick up the pace as soon and as he entered the arena. The sound system delivered with a crushing blow straight to the heart and up to the brain the first few chords of "Villains Left Behind" with Larry Wentworth providing the soulful guts through his rapid and smoky drum intro accompanied by the rhythmic pounding of Derek Brown and Jamie Farrell's guitars. This was framed by adding the glockenspiel as icing on the cake delivering the melodic overtones to this volcanic beat. The only difference here was that this was live! At the beginning explosion of their set, spotlights revealed the band lined across the top perimeter of the Garden all connected by miles of cable to the central sound system. This *was* surround-sound, baby. This could have easily replaced the defibrillator.

Bob started his walk to the ring and the crowds were on their feet and toes.

"Coursing through the veins of some human being
"There lies the heart of a brutal fiend"

Bob walked a straight line down the narrow aisle, with people reaching out just wanting to touch him. Men, women and teenagers were flocking and crowding twenty plus people deep to the center aisle to catch a closer glimpse and, for the lucky few, a quick brushing touch to either his robe or his gloves. It was kind of like the Blarney Stone of boxing.

"Villains commanded by thoughts of driven evil
"Wanting only to lay prey to their own desires"

The rhythm of this was ripping through the audience like steroids. This only served to compound the spirit of the event of seeing their hero come back after being victorious in saving the people of thc Svenkia Islands.

"Knocking down walls and people's dreams,
"Power and greed only fuels the fire
"I gotta know where I can run and hide"

He wanted to come back carrying the spirit and fire he had experienced being a driving force against tyranny and the authoritarian body that ostracized their own people. He claimed a sort of "the pen is mightier than the sword" type of victory over Dimitrii in that there was no retaliation in the form of violence, but instead, a very huge and clear insult to his position of power in bettering the lives of the people he threw off his country's mainland.

"Run and hide baby, Run and hide

"No one knows where to run and hide!"

The entire song lasted three minutes and thirty seconds and good thing; what Bob didn't count on was the crowd's reaction to him, trying to touch him, which made his progress toward the ring that much slower. The New York City Police Department was on hand and stepped in and tried to disperse the crowd to give Bob some room. The shouting and cheering was so loud that you couldn't hear yourself think and although of sturdy construction, the Garden actually shook from the ground floor to the highest rafters. Bob finally made it to the ring and stepped between the ropes with the commotion increasing by at least twenty decibels.

"Stand up now and gather 'round, there's no need to hide

"Plant your feet hard to the ground with hearts of pride

"Push hard, push fast, then look around and you will find"

"All the Villains Left Behind"

At that moment, Johnny took off Bob's robe, revealing his extremely cut, tan torso with tree trunks for legs, arm pistons flaring with thick sinewy muscle bulging with rope like veins of a blue/green hue connected to a well chiseled and two percent body fat (the doctor told him anything less would seriously challenge his endurance) frame.

The humidity index on the seats of most of the women in the arena increased dramatically at the sight. Not only for what he'd done, the reason he was here, but now, how he looked made a lot of women want to give birth to his child at the nearest concession stand (for access to hot water). He was truly magnificent.

But the "aw shucks" forever humble Bob really wasn't conceited enough to absorb the moment for personal glory, as he was entirely focused and deep within the recesses of his fighting mind. Bonnie was halfway across the front of her seat, hands clenched in front of her chest, fully absorbing and sharing the moment with Bob as though she was his second layer of skin. Oh, how she wished it was now forty-eight minutes later. It would be all over and whatever was to happen would've happened and any and all questions answered. Either way, she was very anxious to get just get their lives back and have Bob resolve this last chapter for himself.

Jenny had finished a wonderfully executed rendition of the national anthem and now it was time to rumble. The ref called both fighters to center ring. If eyes could talk, the looks and stares between Corey and Bob would have filled volumes.

It was now time to answer the final question of who *really* was the best.

CHAPTER 47

Jerry was applying the last touches of Vaseline across Bob's eyebrows and around his cheekbones. In the meantime, Johnny was peppering him with last minute instructions.

"Remember what we worked on in the gym; keep circling to his left and work the body and arms the first couple rounds. Dirty fight or not the last time, this kid has lightning in his right hand and the tonnage to match. Do not, I repeat, do NOT leave yourself open to that right. We watched hours of films to realize he changed his style since last time and understand his body pattern before he was about to unload. Pay attention! Do not let him dictate the fight. Hurt him in the body and let him do the rest by exhausting himself trying to knock you into the ceiling."

Johnny put the back of his hand under Bob's chin and poured water into his mouth, which he swooshed around and spat into an open bucket. The audience was shouting its usual intelligent encouragement, "Kill him, make him pay, Bob," or, "Tear his ugly head of his shoulders," or, "Pound the cocksucker in the chest until he spits blood."

There also were the requisite signs people holding up as the cameras panned the crowd: *From Island Nation to the Garden, Make it Count*, and *Tear His Heart Out. After that cut off his Johnson and stuff it in his mouth to shut him up!* Nice, huh?

The last poster the cameras opted out and had to be careful in general with panning the crowd because they were out for blood and their choice of communicating it was a bit dicey to say the least. The next advice came from Jerry.

"Keep your head up, big boy. We've seen from the films that his second choice of destruction is a very strong and quick uppercut. If one slips through and your head is down, the better the chance is of opening up one of your eyebrows. One good slice would have blood pouring into your eyes. I'm pretty good at what I do, if I don't say so myself, but I'm no magician and can't work miracles if he opens up a two-inch wide or better gash."

Bob was breathing evenly. He had a way of sending a mild current of serene calm throughout his whole body before a fight. He never attended a yoga class or any other type of meditation training. This was something he developed by himself, for himself, and it worked well throughout his career.

Meanwhile, in Corey's corner, the genius was pounding his chest with his glove and making the "slit the throat" gesture again. Boy, if anything else, this guy put on a great show.

Bob was off his stool and started to pace back and forth. All of the insults, memories of the last fixed fight disgracing and hurting him and the more recent name-calling and extortion allegations rose to the surface in a bubble of ferocity, bringing a pinnacle of anger and hatred that made his nostrils flare and a low guttural sound vibrate from his throat.

As Johnny and Jerry settled back to their positions beside the ring, both could hear the sounds of an animal growling. Bob was now completely shut out from the outside world and from any further communication. Johnny realized anything else he might have wanted to say to his boxer would now be lost in a tornado of emotion. Bob felt the blood coursing through his veins while still remaining calm, feeling invincible, powerful, and taking deadly aim to his target in front of him. As he paced, his eyes never left Corey. It was like some animal posturing itself before a vicious and brutal attack. His body started to rev up, slowly increasing in power, ready to explode.

The bell rang and the fighters approached center ring. Neither wanted the traditional touching of the gloves. There would be no standing eight-count and no knockdown saved by the bell. You couldn't hear yourself think with the roar of the crowd urging the fuse be lit to get the battle underway.

Although working a full twelve rounds in the gym (against some bimbo journeyman), going all the way in a real fight would prove to be very exhausting for Corey. As he didn't get past the fourth round in his last fights because of finishing his work early, he came out of this first round as though he wanted to deliver the knockout blow get it over with. Big mistake.

As he threw a right haymaker, a left jab, another right, an uppercut, another left jab and then a second attempt at a right haymaker, Bob was "running the reeds," "dodging and jabbing approaching ducks," watching Corey's hands as though they were Louise's pawing at the ducks, all in his mind's eye. This left Corey's barrage one hundred percent useless, costing him some valuable energy. He didn't come within four inches of Bob where normally he would've had his opponent's knees buckling by now.

Throwing away hours of training and Johnny's last minute instructions a few moments ago, Bob waited for the last right hook to miss, exposing the left side of Corey's face. He cocked his torso in a one-quarter turn to leverage himself and plowed his right fist with all his weight behind it into the right side of Corey's face. Corey hit the ground and, as announcers love to say, "kissed the canvas," and Bob reveled even more when the opportunity existed in the fact that this was the first time in his professional career that Corey was knocked on his ass.

He remained on the canvas and got up at the count of eight, sporting a fractured orbital bone and heavy contusion under his left eyebrow. A little dancing and holding on to Bob brought the bell and the end of round one. Corey wandered back to his corner, looking a little lost for the most part, as his brain was still recovering from this massive detonation.

"What are you doing?" Johnny asked as Bob plopped down on his stool. "Just what the fuck are you doing? We spent hours watching film and even more time in the gym developing a strategy for this fight. You totally ignore me and go out there and act like you're in some sort of schoolyard fight. Work the body, for Christ's sake! This guy is tough, has a strong chin and thick head and can take a punch. His ego is stronger than any energy his own adrenaline can give him. He's dangerous, Bob. All he needs is one opening and he could put you on your ass for good."

Bob's hair was beginning to mat down on his head and the sweat was pouring.

"At least let me put the fucking hair in a ponytail, pull it away from your face and get some sort of ventilation going."

Bob only glanced up at him almost too calmly and said, "There's nothing wrong with my hair. I'm fine, Johnny, really."

Bob had it in pulled back so that it was long enough to wedge itself nicely around the back of his ear, looping below the earlobe and resting on his shoulders.

Johnny pleaded, "Please stick to our game plan. Spend the next few rounds softening him up and making him lose some of his steam. I don't know what type of work out and training you did on your own on the islands, but it seems that you've got enough power behind you to knock down a wall. Be patient. You'll have your chance. Just box for the next few rounds. No heroics and don't get reckless. Jesus fucking Christ!" Johnny is so excitable, isn't he?

So that was what exactly he did for the next three rounds. While Corey did manage to rock Bob with some really hard shots, Bob's body work provided a slow and agonizing demise for Corey's dexterity. He would return to his corner after each round feeling like a car had run over him.

Bill kept telling him to get Bob on the ropes, underneath him and to work his way up. Corey nodded, but was starting to lose his sharpness. The right side of his rib cage and kidneys were now a source of extreme pain. Bob had been pounding away and broke two of Corey's ribs in the process. Both of Corey's trainers were aware of this and thought the attention to the pain might wear off the next couple of rounds. What they didn't know was that cracked ribs don't "wear off." And "the next couple rounds" was going to prove to be a distance into deeper water that challenged Corey's endurance.

The bell of the fifth round rang and once again both fighters approached center ring. Bob's left eyebrow was starting to swell up from the few damaging blows that slipped through his defense (a few "ducks" proved smarter than they looked) . Bob continue to work the body and, while "still running the reeds", dodged most of Corey's attempts at connecting. At that point, statistics showed that Corey had connected with seventeen percent of his 273 punches. Bob's stat sheet looked a hell of a lot better with him connecting fifty-three percent of his 347 punches. It was at this point that Bob now started working the head and landing some crushing blows.

He would get Corey up against the ropes and start pounding away until Corey started to lean back and sit on the ropes. People were screaming, "Finish him! Kick the shit out of him and finish him off.!" It was truly frustrating to watch.

Instead, Bob would stop dead in his tracks, leaving Corey a complete mess, walk calmly back to the center of the ring and stand there waiting for Corey to join him. Corey would rather die, which he was quickly inviting, than not to challenge this insult and meet Bob at center ring again.

Again, this steady pummeling of the body left Corey's arms weak, making it more and more meaningless to try and throw a punch. This gave Bob complete carte blanche in landing any of his cornerstone punches and easily finishing Corey off just as the crowd was getting increasingly impatient for this to end.

Bob now had Corey in his own corner, smothering him with a flurry of heavily delivered pounding. Corey was now bleeding from his left ear, but the ref was hesitant about stopping the fight. Although there was no standing eight-count, the ref asked Corey on several occasions if he could go on. And of course Corey said yes, but if you asked him his middle name, his guess would have been as good as yours.

He was convinced he'd catch a second wind, hoping the enthusiasm would get him more points on the board should this torment go the full twelve rounds. Being delusional is not a good enough a word here. Just as Corey was starting to sink into a bloody mess, once again Bob would stop, back away, walk back the center ring and wait.

Corey's trainer was now rolling up a white towel, preparing to throw it in as Corey spied him through his good right eye (as his left was now completely shut) and motioned for him to put down the towel; he was going to continue.

"He's punishing him," Corey's trainer screamed above the crowd with panic in his voice. "He's setting him up and Corey's too big of an ego machine to concede defeat. He might as well drive a car off a cliff if he expects to walk out of the ring on both legs. If this goes on another round, the towel goes in."

And it did continue into the next round, much the same as the previous three, this time Bob breaking Corey's nose, splattering blood on his green satin boxer shorts and also tattooing Bob from the gush spewed from the impact.

One more time, Bob had Corey at the edge of unconsciousness. He backed up and walked back to center ring, waiting for Corey to join him once again.

This time Corey could not oblige him.

EPILOGUE

I had eighteen more fights after that night with Corey, twelve of which were title defenses, the first being a rematch with Corey. I won by decision, but, like the last fight, it was tough going. I had the good grace to win the other seventeen.

I was doing well as a boxer and stayed in the game until I was thirty four years old and a mild case of tinnitus forced an early retirement. I'd officially retired, with forty-five wins, two losses and one draw (the second loss was proven to have qualified as a forfeit, but nothing could be done about it now). Pretty close to Rocky's record, but not close enough.

It had taken Bonnie a few years of very skillful nagging (and I say this in the most affectionate sense) before I finally gave in and, in the late-eighties, hung up my gloves for good. Oh yeah, we did get married. Whadya expect? Our love and the experiences we shared over the years had turned each day into another coin in the bank of our devotion to each other. She means everything to me in so many different ways.

Over the years, boxing became increasingly popular, the marketing more skillful in promotion, which, along with the advent of pay-per-view cable TV, gleaned healthier purses for the fighters. Last two fights, I was making close to eleven to thirteen million a fight. I'd invested the money into a number of projects; real estate, securities, a few charitable foundations and portions of some very promising businesses. Most of them worked out okay, some of them didn't. That all goes with the turf, I guess.

I also became a boxing analyst for ESPN and serve on the boards of four corporations. Yeah, retiring from boxing was hard, especially the physicality of it, but I've managed the transition and am now doing some things meaningful and important to me (along with the skillful hand of Bonnie's confidence and advice).

We bought a second home in Vero Beach, Florida to enjoy the warmer weather as the bitter cold winters up north were starting to get to us, especially me. After years of being sledge hammered in the ring, the cold would make me stiffen up and quite uncomfortable. We still kept the home up north because you can't beat autumn in New England and Thanksgiving dinner with a fire roaring in the fireplace and football all day long. It's simply too intoxicating.

Bonnie continued to cultivate a successful practice after we left the Svenkia Islands. She (we, I guess; I gave her a real break on business loan with no interest or pay-down) owns three clinics with five psychologists attending to each, not to mention the cadre of clerical staff to maintain schedules and billing. We had two beautiful children, four years apart, Robby and Peter Perry.

As for the "charter members" of the now internationally renowned and storybook islands, all seemed to have gotten back to continuing on with their lives rather quickly. Natalia married a nearby neighborhood boy and had three beautiful children, two girls and a boy.

Brother Stefan caught the travel bug, backpacking across Europe in his teens. It was in Italy that his eyes settled in amazement on the art and architecture of Rome.

Inspiration gave way to attending art school in Venice where he now is a leading graphic artist, focusing primarily in building websites. At twenty-nine, he is still single and banging Italian models in his spare time (Irinia continues to wring her arthritic hands in the hope that he'll settle down and give her more grandchildren).

Sergei followed the natural progression of assuming what would be first the role of the governor of the islands during their societal development. The islands developed democratic ideology, held elections and eventually gave Sergei the honor of being the island nation's first president. Not bad, eh Sergei?

Dana Ruminski morphed from a journalist to a bestselling author. She had changed her mind and remained on the Svenkia Islands (her mom passed away not to soon after Dana settled down). Her trilogy of the rescue, development and creation of a new country won her acclaims and a nod from Oslo, coming close in the voting but not the winning contender for the Noble Prize in Literature. This, however, was countered by winning a Pulitzer Prize and a sweet movie deal for her work in chronicling the life and times of the people of the Svenkia Islands.

Lynne Albright also remained on the island, selling (or giving away) all her worldly possessions back in the States, making the landscape and horticulture of the islands her passion and life's work. She still marched about, barking orders at the age of eighty-four to the staff of her small company. She never did quite get Lord Parisellan into a tux and down the aisle, as he returned to his native England to retire in good grace with his memories of

Beatrice until his death in 1995. He did, however, lift the one hundred percent trade embargo for the islands five years after their official christening where they were actively trading now with their main export being wool and other textiles.

And Louise, ah, my dear, sweet Louise. She was chasing ducks for eight years until old age finally came a-knocking and took her away from me. Strangely enough, her BFF, my Emma, died not too shortly afterwards, even though she was firmly replanted thousands of mile away back in the states. Both held a special place in my heart and served as loveable and faithful companions.

This floated in my mind like a photo album on my way to visit my urologist, Dr. Bloom, for the results of a biopsy I had taken the week before. It all started about a month ago after a routine visit with our family doctor, Dr. Mandulla. For those guys over forty, you know the drill; probing around in your ears and nose with a light, chest x-rays, EKG, visual body scans for unwelcomed spots, drawing two or three vials of blood, and the grand finale, the "I don't enjoy this either" digital exam.

The chance of prostate issues increases for men after they pass the forty-year-old mark and should be checked each year. I guess this could be analogous to a woman having her breasts checked for lumps and other areas for irregular firmness, but this a decidedly different and less intrusive examination. The digital exam is where you have the undeniable pleasure laying on your side, bringing our knees up to your chest, holding your breath and hope like hell he finishes quickly without going into a tirade about last week's Giants game and their loss to the

Raiders. Nobody likes this, but it is a necessary part of the exam nonetheless.

About a week later, the results of my blood test came back to the office whereupon the nurse called me and explained that my PSA levels were a bit high and, just as a precautionary measure, it may be a good idea to just have this double checked with an urologist. OK.

Enter Dr. Bloom. Nice enough guy, very thorough, very professional and undoubtedly very dedicated to his work. We shared a mutual respect in that we selflessly dedicated our lives to the well-being of other; his currently, mine twenty four years ago on the islands. I visited his office, where more blood was taken and, instead of lying on the table and bringing my knees to my chest, I was bent over the gurney like some barmaid doing a patron a favor, finger inserted probably up to his wrist, and handed a few tissues after he was finished. As he was probing around inside, he took a little bit longer than I had been used to (and there was only so long I could hold my breath during this ordeal).

"The right side seems a little firm to me," he said. "This could be nothing, but this, along with your PSA results, makes me want to do a little further investigation." I've been through this dance before where further tests based on physician suspicion always came up clean.

This led to another blood sample for a Free PSA where if the results of which come back twenty-five percent or greater, it usually suggests non-cancerous benign prostate hyperplasia (BPH) and no further treatment is warranted. You just keep a tab on your PSA levels with check-ups every six months instead of once a year.

Anything under twenty five percent and closer to zero percent suggests a strong correlation of probability of prostate cancer.

Mine came in at twelve percent. OK, now I started to hear a small chorus of panic rise in the back of my brain.

"Mr. Perry, twelve percent leaves me a little more than concerned," Dr. Bloom explained. "I think this is enough information for me to recommend a biopsy of your prostate."

Now the alarm bells in my belfry were starting to chime even louder. I had the biopsy done the very next day. That was a week ago. At that time, an appointment was made a week later for what Pam, Dr. Bloom's nurse, termed "the talk." She also had told me that if the results came back and were negative, they would call me before with the results and "the talk" would not be necessary.

I received no such phone call and returned that next week. I walked into the office and the opaque sliding glass doors opened above the counter, where I was greeted by Pam. Now, Pam was the sort who had been doing her job for thirty plus years and, in addition to her medical expertise, worked magic in calming patients down and making a terrifying process palatable. She had her own bout with breast cancer, clearly reigned victoriously and wasn't shy in sharing the experience. This provided an incredible calming effect for me. I greeted my Florence Nightingale when she responded, "Oh, hello, Mr. Perry. The doctor will be with you in a moment," she said with a declining cadence in her voice with the word "moment" while not meeting my eyes.

Shit, I'm definitely am not getting a good vibe from

this at all!

I signed in and went to the waiting room, grabbing a magazine off the rack. Being the genius that I am, I left my glasses in the car and had all but managed to read the larger print, holding the magazine at more than arm's length. The results were looking at just the pictures processing none of it after Pam's melancholy greeting.

She finally opened up the door into the exam rooms and doctors' offices. "Come on in, Mr. Perry," As she directed me to the office of Dr. Bloom, she said, "He'll be with you shortly." She was looking at me. But then again, she wasn't looking at me… her eyes were blank windows to an empty rom. She turned and left the office.

As Dr. Bloom was a senior physician in this practice, he had a corner office overlooking the northern portion of Vero Beach's vast landscapes; lush with evergreens and palm trees of every kind. It was that time of day when the sun was casting the final rays of its honey glazed hue. Everything always looked so beautiful this time of day.

Sitting in one of two leather chairs in front of his mahogany desk, I had a clear view from the two corner windows of what I consider God's greatest work of nature. I watched as the breeze gently caressed the fronds of the palm trees, moving them to and fro as though fingers orchestrating a grand and silent symphony. The golden light on these graceful fingers from God seemed to remind a person to take time out and appreciate being alive.

Dr. Bloom entered the office, looking down into an open folder in his hand and almost by the manual, in a rote tone, said, "As you know, we took a biopsy last week to see whether or not there were any abnormalities within your prostate. The test results came back last Tuesday and I'm so sorry to tell you, Mr. Perry, but malignant cells were found."

"I have cancer?"

"Yes, I'm afraid so."

I felt every fiber of my being collapse like when you see those buildings demolished with everything imploding into a mass of crumbled debris into itself. Memories from school days flooded from the back of my mind and reminded me of when I was being sent to the principal's office and in big trouble. It was kind of weird, as it felt as though I had done something wrong and was being punished. Did I eat right? Yes, Bonnie saw to that. How about the occasional cigar? Naw, I would have got cancer in the mouth, right? The only other activity that would qualify as a vice was the few cocktails and beers I had during the week. Not exactly enough to get me going to AA. What could it be? What part of my life did I screw up?

My eyes looked toward the window again at the palm tree, whose fronds continued to conduct its orchestra that no one could hear but me.

My first thought was, *I will never get to see this again. How beautiful a sight, how wonderful a feeling, the day's come to an end and it's time to have dinner with the family. Tomorrow, I won't be able to do this. Tomorrow, I'll be gone, I'll be dead.*

I had explained to Bonnie that I had wanted to come alone. As much as I love her, and much to her objection that it ended up in very heated argument, this was something I was sure was routine and did not want her to miss a very important lecture she planned on attending. How wrong I was. I needed her now more than the air in my lungs. This is something we needed to share and comfort each other. Oh, how I wished she were there with me now. I couldn't imagine dying. Please, dear God, not now!

As he had probably done hundreds of times before, Dr. Bloom gave me time to process this information in my head by not speaking for a few moments. He knew a person needed to dust themselves off and get back on their feet unassisted after this bomb was denoted beneath them.

The silence was then precisely broken by him saying, "The greatest weapon you can have now is information. I'm going to give you some literature (pamphlets), but I'm also going to recommend a book that's helped many patients understand what's going on inside their bodies. The more you understand about this, the more courage you'll be astonished to find you have. You have very good chance of a complete cure, but it's you who has to decide what type of treatment you'll have."

"You mean, there's a chance that I can rid myself of cancer completely?"

"Yes. We were lucky enough to catch this at a very early stage and there is very good chance it can be completely eradicated from your body. You can live to be in your eighties."

Dr. Bloom held a great deal of credibility with me and I hung on to his every word. But I couldn't help but think, and have heard many times before, in a situation where the odds of survival were very small, encouraging words of hope nonetheless. Much the same as I did for my father when he was diagnosed with liver cancer. The only difference now was that I was on the receiving end; and a year and a half after he died. I began to feel bitter resentment toward life and how unjustifiable unfair it could be at times. Sound familiar?

"What we can do now is schedule surgery, and that can always be changed based on what you read and which course you decide you'd like to take if it is not surgery, but we need to schedule now in any case." He flipped open his schedule book, took a look and ran his fingers down the page and said, "We could do this, um, November 24th, Thanksgiving Day. You'll have to have your turkey a couple of days later," he offered lightheartedly.

"Dr. Bloom, that's three months from now!" I couldn't take another day knowing that I had cancer inside my body and what could happen in three months.

He assured me that prostate cancer is the slowest growing cancer of all of the different flavors of cancer. Three months was not going to change too much of what was already there. He explained to me that ninety-five percent of men who reach the age of ninety-five will have prostate cancer (like you would give a shit at ninety-five!). He said if you were to have cancer, prostate cancer would be the best choice. Best choice, my ass. Cancer is cancer and I wanted it out of my body!

The next day after a few meetings at work, and believe me it was the longest day at work I've ever experienced, I went to the bookstore to pick up a copy of *Prostate and Cancer* by Sheldon Marks. This book was so well-written and clear, it was kind of like a "Prostate Cancer for Dummies" book. And Dr. Bloom was right. The more I read and the more I understood about cancer, I can't say the less fearful I was, but the more comfortable I was and I felt empowered with the understanding I drew from Dr. Marks's book.

November 24th rolled around quicker than I would've liked. At 6AM., I was lying on a gurney, succumbing to the "twilight" drug they inject you with prior to the anesthesiologist doing her job. She first hooked me up to an epidermal drip that would help ease the pain of the major construction that was about to happen in my lower abdomen.

The room was dimly lit and I remember looking at the big round clock on the opposite wall. In only a matter of minutes, my life would change forever. I thoroughly scoured Dr. Marks's book at least five times and I knew the possible consequences of this operation. First, there was the issue of incontinence; the involuntary dripping of urine due to the absence of some supporting structure like the prostate to help your sphincter do its job. That part of it I could live with. It was the potential level of impotency that most concerned me. Dr. Bloom was a very cautious and pragmatic physician.

In voicing my concerns Bonnie, she had assured me that intercourse was only one facet of lovemaking for a woman. She explained to me that it was the affection, love, gentle caressing, holding and all the other things that went into the expression of love rather than the one act of intercourse. As a man, I was afraid these words didn't do anything to mitigate my dread. I enjoyed lovemaking, I enjoyed the anticipation of lovemaking and physically was exhilarated by the whole experience of sex.

Making love to someone we care deeply about is exponentially beautiful. I was about to give up an important part of myself to save my life. And the price was a burden that I would have to learn to cultivate in my own mind and do some readjustments to the emotional fabric that made up my self-expression, and yes, my own satisfaction. I felt as though I was going to a funeral for part of my body that was now dead.

I'd chosen the route of the radical prostatectomy as, quite simply, I wanted the damn cancer out of my body completely! No chance of anything left over that radiation missed or that cryotherapy failed to freeze to death; I wanted it completely gone. Hence, the price of the great possibility of losing my ability of attaining a pleasure every man enjoys.

There was this new procedure for the prostatectomy that is executed through laparoscopic surgery. Back in the day, the surgeon would make an incision from your belly button down to the base of your abdomen right above the penis. Then clamps each lip of the incision and spread you open making a double door entrance to the area of the operation.

This new procedure was performed using a machine called the Чудо лечения, or Miracle Cure in Russian, with four tarantula like arms bent at the elbow, each bending appendage about two feet in length. At the very tip of one arm, is a high resolution 3-D camera with the other three individually brandishing their own specialized surgical tool. It would make four tiny incisions, two at the top left and right sides and two similar incisions at the base of the abdomen. That would act as small portals into the area of operation where the after effect of scarring would be minimal, if not completely negligible.

This sci-fi spider would hover over you, its movements being manipulated by the surgeon working through a PC from another room!! I mean, the guy could be at home in his boxer shorts performing the operation from his den in Montana for God's sake! The whole idea just, as my kids would say, "blew me away."

These cameras at the end of spider boy's tentacles offered 200x magnification, whereas the surgeon only wearing goggles at 20x magnification due to the fact that he was hovering over the patient at a distance. Bottom line, the procedure was more precise, more thorough and minimized the damage to any nerve bundles that were left behind.

In order to be successful, the incision would have to be so precise as to disconnect the prostate from the rectal wall without damaging the outer rectal wall on which it rests. This was where the procedure got a little dicey. If the surgeon, wearing goggles, got too close to the rectal wall, and he did not have the magnification to be as thorough as he would have liked, he would not want to damage this delicate membrane. Doing so would mean having a permanent aperture portal in my lower abdomen and taking a crap through a tube without ever having a sit down again; and hey! No fear of running out of toilet paper!

Yes, the cancer could be "cured," but it would take the most precise movement of the blade to accomplish this. It was only through a joystick and trackball like devices on the computer console that would guide the steadiest and most directed cuts. This machine was my only salvation, for many reasons.

The nurse came in to raise the bars around the gurney with a pleasant smile and wheeled me into the operating room as I watched the ceiling pass above me. I was guided with expert hands until I saw the stadium lights above me. The attending nurse placed an oxygen tube in my nostrils, where I felt a fresh gush of air fill my lungs. The anesthesiologist came in and greeted me and started to insert tubes into the pre-inserted syringe taped to the top of my left hand.

She said that I would be asleep soon and I think I barely heard the word "soon" when I opened up my eyes again and I was back in my hospital room. I could feel the tension in my lower abdomen and spotted two tubes sprouting from either side. Both oozed a cranberry colored liquid to clear vinyl bags that were attached to either side of the bed. I gradually regained and focused my vision and looked at them, and then saw Bonnie, who undoubtedly had been at my bedside since they wheeled me in.

"So how is my prostate-less bad boy doing?"

I'm sure you think this is cruel, but you have to understand my wife's sense of humor. On paper, it is extremely cruel, but so cruel that it's funny, if you get my drift. This made me feel a little bit better. I mean, the woman's a genius.

"You're sure I still have the rest of my body parts?"

"You sure do, but there's a catheter running up the middle into your bladder, which means you can lie on the couch watching football and not miss a play without having to get up to pee. I kind of envy you."

She continued the rhythm of levity with, "Would that also mean I wouldn't have to get up and get you a beer?"

"You never did before, so what difference would it make?"

We both smiled.

My eyes sank a little lower with my expression, which Bonnie's antenna picked up immediately.

"I know this is trying for you, sweetie. Try to keep a positive attitude. I'm gonna take good care of you and you'll be back to normal before you know it."

"Yeah, normal, right. Like when we go out for dinner and after a few cocktails, can't wait to get home so we can rip each other's clothes off and make illicit love. Or, if in the middle of the night, inspiration strikes, you can strike back. Or, my favorite, when you bend over to pick up the laundry I sneak up behind you and clock in. Bonnie, don't you see? I'll never be the same."

"Bob, we talked about this. Life is full of adjustments and you'll adjust to this. I'll make sure that you'll be as happy and satisfied. I promise you this."

"Sure, thanks, honey. I know you will."

I wanted to believe this, but you know what, it still would not be the same. What was really making me nervous was the pathologist's pending report. This would be the tell all and end all as to whether the Russians had done their homework thoroughly enough and, if only being a partial man, at least being an alive man. I was only fifty years old and hadn't yet seen my grandchildren who were still just twinkles in the eyes of my sons. I wanted to spend the next thirty years with my wife, watch our children start their families, have them and their children over our house for Christmas (and then summarily have them leave at 7PM when we were done with them; perks of grandparents). Doesn't get much better than that!

Nurse Cratchit (her real name was Dolores, but I'm a big Jack Nicholson fan) reminded us that visiting hours were over and my lovely wife would have to leave my side. Frowning, she kissed me on the forehead, stroked my cheek and assured me she'd be there first thing in the morning.

As she was leaving, Dr. Bloom entered with a fresh-faced med student at his heels, obviously being mentored in postoperative rounds etiquette. After greeting me, Dr. B pulled over the covers on the right side to check out the four square swatches on my upper and lower abdomen and the two tubes draining a cranberry liquid into two bags on either side of the bed. "Cranberry" was a color he was pleased with in that this meant the bleeding was slowly starting to subside and the healing beginning.

"You look fabulous!"

Fabulous? I just opened my eyes after four hours of heavy sedation, had a good portion of the hardware from my lower abdomen expelled and he was telling me I looked like Mel Gibson? Yeah, doctor talk.

"Tomorrow you're going to have to get up on your feet and get the blood moving again. This is very important for the healing process."

"You can't be serious? I just feel like I had just been run over by an eighteen wheeler and you want me to get out of bed?"

"Well, it's getting late and you need to get some sleep. If you need me tomorrow, you can find me somewhere in the hallways making my rounds. Rest up. Tomorrow's gonna be a busy day for you."

As he left the room, I thought he might've gone insane, but before I had a chance to even resist the thought, my eyes grew heavy and I fell into a deep sleep.

The next morning I finally had some solid food in the form of toast and Jell-O. To me, this was a big treat as I hadn't really eaten anything solid in the last few days.

Nurse Cratchit came in all fired up to get me out of bed. I could swear the woman had a smirk on her face. First one leg and then the other leg over the bedside and instantly I felt dizzy. Her demeanor changed and she suddenly morphed into a soothing nurse telling me to take my time in a very calm and reassuring voice.

I made several attempts getting a little further and further each time until I was able to walk into the hallway, but not looking for Dr. Bloom. I already knew I looked fabulous! At that point, I was so proud of getting myself to the nearest water fountain. The pathology reports had come back after sampling the tissues that had been removed and all the margins were clear. In short, dear friends, the cancer was gone! It seemed the machine's magnification was sensitive enough to make clear, concise cuts with minimal damage, leaving a cavity that muscle and tissue would re-occupy over the years and my other plumbing was well intact.

And get this. During the procedure, the increased magnification revealed the right nerve bundles that were originally scheduled for deportation had enough clearance to also be preserved. This still did not guarantee full functionality, but was at least twice as good as having only one side left in place as was originally planned.

Visiting hours would be starting soon and I looked

forward to seeing my wife. A smile came across my face as I remembered our conversation from the other day, especially about the laundry room episodes. My brain filled with the image, which turned into my usual fantasy of how this would happen so spontaneously. Yeah, I know this makes me sound like a fourteen-year-old, but my wife does have an award-winning ass even if she's in the autumn of her years.

As she would be bending over picking up whatever it was, I would walk behind her and snuggle against her backside. As I was walking down the hall, I could visualize it now as she started to sway her hips ever so slightly. The more I become engrossed in this thought, the more I could feel my face grow flush. Well, at least I hadn't lost my libido.

As I was working my way through the imagery, I could feel life start to surge in my penis! The feeling was like somebody is turning on a bright light inside of you and you start to grow. Jesus God in heaven, I could feel my penis starting to get hard. I could feel the life traveling through as it became firmer and firmer, taking up slack on the catheter until I had a full, USA Grade-A, FDA-approved erection! My God! I can still make proper love to my wife and experience the exhilaration that I thought I'd lost forever. I felt whole again, as a man. This Russian made machine *was* a miracle!

The sexual mosaic of the laundry room in my mind was beginning to make the front of my hospital gown resemble a Bass Pro Shop tent. Normally I would look to do everything I could to hide it or to turn the other way or sit down or do whatever I could to avoid the embarrassment. But I continued walking (maybe teetering is a better word) as though I was carrying out the American flag during the opening ceremonies of the Olympics.

By this time, Nurse Cratchit came looking for me and found me, although very slowly and carefully, literally semi-strutting down the hallway.

With the corner of her lips curled in a smile, she asked, “And just what parade are you leading?” looking down at my protruding hospital gown.

“Would you look at that? Just look at that!” I said pointing to the front of my gown.

“Well, well, seems like an old friend has decided it isn’t time to leave,” she replied sheepishly.

I’m sure Dolores had seen her fair share of medical advances in her twenty seven years of nursing, mostly diagnostic (CAT scans, MRI, bone scans, etc.), but this was one of the very few times I bet she’d seen success in any new treatment technology and witnessed the benefit and joy it had on a human being firsthand only few days after being treated. Her lips quivered, but her eyes were bright, as though she couldn’t quite decide whether to laugh or cry. She chose the former and burst out laughing. “And it’s a beaut.”

The reality of the moment started to sink in and I could feel the embarrassment creep up my neck and into my flushing red cheeks. There were also three nurses at the floor station watching this whole exchange. With that, my penis decided the show was over and retreated gracefully back to its dressing room. Thank You and well done.

“This Miracle Cure machine! I have to see this machine, this thing that saved my life in more ways than one way. Where is it? Where can I see it?"

She put her hand inside my arm and slowly guided me down the hallway tethered to the rolling "cranberry juice" stand. We made a right down at the end, passing the rectangular windows on the left that looked like some type of lab until we reached the door at the end.

She stopped and said, "It's in there, stored before prepping for the next surgery." She unlocked the door for me, but still left it closed for me to open it up myself. She turned around and walked down the hallway to visit some of her other patients. "Don't forget to lock up by the inner door lock when you're done. You're not really supposed to be in there."

I opened the door, slowly letting the light from the hallway illuminate the dark room. There, against the center back wall, surrounded by consoles of dials and meters and every other electronic control you could think of, was this large spider-like robot. Its arms were perched in the air as though posturing for attack, yet appearing to be frozen in place.

The lights beaming in from the hallway were enough for me to navigate around, as I didn't want to turn on the lab's overhead light to attract attention. I stepped toward the machine in reverence, almost feeling as though I had to pause and genuflect in gratitude to give homage and thanks. There was a small desk lamp on a table beside Gargantuan that I turned on to get a better look.

I studied it up and down and looked around from every angle as much as my still fragile body and attached apparatus would allow. It had to be terribly complex to work so precisely in the manner that Dr. Bloom used it!

This whole thing was operated through a PC by the surgeon in another room. Yeah, I know I'm repeating myself, but I still couldn't get over the whole notion.

Although I knew I probably shouldn't have, for bacteria reasons or whatever, I started to run by hands along the side of one of the consoles hooked up to the beast as though caressing and padding a huge stallion after coming to my rescue. My hand slid along the side of the console until my fingers ran over the brass plate riveted to the lower right-hand corner, which was the final stamp of the manufacturer before shipping it off to the hospital.

I wondered who made something so incredibly powerful in its specialty. I marveled at who had the magical knowledge and genius to research, prototype and test safely to offer such a wonderful solution to a very invasive disease. Ever so gently, I bent down, making sure the tubes didn't slip out and read,

"Made in the Svenkia Islands"

My God, the Svenkia Islands!

"Someday we will return the favor, my friend."

Yes, Sergei.
Yes indeed.

www.ingramcontent.com/pod-product-compliance
Lightning Source LLC
Chambersburg PA
CBHW030821310726
48980CB00006B/581/J

* 9 7 8 0 6 1 5 6 1 6 5 2 0 *